FAMILY MATTERS

FAMILY MATTERS

Dolores Chernoski Moses

ISBN: 978-1-64871-683-6   (Paperback Edition)
ISBN: 978-1-64871-686-7   (Hardcover Edition)

Characters and events in this book are fictitious. Any similarity to real persons, living or dead, is coincidental and not intended by the author.

Book Ordering Information

Phone Number: 347-901-4929 or 347-901-4920
Email: info@globalsummithouse.com
Global Summit House
www.globalsummithouse.com

Printed in the United States of America

Contents

FAMILY MATTERS

Chapter One

B ARELY THREE weeks ago, it had begun: at dinner, his offhand synoptic re-creations of first one, then another, of the phone calls from corporate headquarters. It had been Blum or Lindquist mostly – rarely, Blanchard himself. Yet, within the past two weeks, as calls to his Los Angeles office had burgeoned, his domestic reprises had become ever more harried, detailed, and unfocused, delivered as they were with growing intensity and rising insistence across their dining room table nightly.

Alcon was certainly evidencing nervous concern over Barry's Chinese language program. Methodically initiated four years ago at Fort Horton, the program's pedagogic fundamentals and allied training procedures had been carefully developed in conjunction with high-level, skilled Navy Sinologists, based at the Presidio, the same group who continued to monitor it even now. Presumably, upon its final, convincing, standardized demonstration of superior workability and measurable results, the Pentagon was prepared to finalize its contract for it with Alcon.

Recent hints from the Beltway, however, soon enough evolved into outright, even pointed, questions, judging from Barry's evening replays. His oversight methodologies regarding the fifty or so linguists, psychologists, statisticians, and assorted technocrats involved in the Fort Horton project had come under particular scrutiny. Standards of accountability were probed, and following a decent interval of innocuous exchanges with headquarters – circumlocutions and generalized evaluations, mainly – gleaming from his tightlipped, difficult-to-read expositions, at the beginning of the week, what she had already more-than-anticipated for the past several weeks finally came to pass: The (inevitable) Letter had arrived.

No circumlocution here. Absent time-wasting grace notes or rhetorical flourishes, mordantly concise, Corporate Intelligence, bearing Blanchard's inimitable signature, recommended Barry's speedy return to the Washington scene, to Mother Beltway, for renewal, reassessment, and reorganization – whatever that would come to mean. Suggested travel timetables followed apace incoming letters – a few days later. Alex was almost sure that, for Barry, having turned 63 as he had on his last birthday, this flurry of activity likely presaged a corporate-conceived-and-planned early retirement. His Last Hurrah.

Mindful of the painful hiatuses in Barry's last night's maundering evaluation of recent events, during the conveniently leisurely getting-to-bed ritual, the contrapuntal music of truth had been forced back – well back – until it could no longer be detected at all. Instead, she listened to his spin of a fairly credible fictional interpretation of current developments – one they could both live with for the present. But, this once, Alex, the truth-teller, the straight-from-the-shoulder, no-holds-barred messenger of the God's or whomever or whatever, would not, could not, speak her version of the truth to and for Barry. Accurate as her insights might prove to be, they would have to wait for his own personal discovery of them, his private admission of their reality. She was not going to assume the burden of delivering such a message of cruelty.

THE left quarter of Serena's sculpturesque Afro-coiffed head appeared briefly margined, approximately five-and-a-half feet up into the frame of the doorway, the connecting door always kept open between their offices.

"Allie, how's that capital call letter coming? J. D.'s been asking for it all morning," she said, managing the efficiently incentivizing secretary ploy while still preserving the casual tone of unflappability she had become known for.

Alex redirected a squirting gaze toward the dim eye of her aging computer. "It's coming, it's coming..." she murmured.

Miss Blumenthal, her Latin teacher at Thompsonville Central, had periodically and proudly announced to her hand-picked cadre of third and fourth year Latinists that, after studying Latin with her – 'til the day of Death – they should be awakened in the middle of the Night – an ambiguous situation which Alex always found hard to imagine – they could nonetheless give the correct past perfect, 3rd person, singular, of *amare, dare* or *esse*, for example. Miss Blumenthal had not been boasting, merely emphasizing the supreme importance of discipline and good habits.

Alex wasn't so sure about the Latin anymore. But in spite of the legalisms, the technicalities, the (as Russell, her boss, called it) "Losing them in Sherwood Forest" techniques, so carefully honed over time, she was certain of her ability to craft the difficult, circumlocutory communications to investors that she was responsible for. She could sculpt them, replete with deft rationales almost beyond the wit of man, and certainly frequently beyond his endurance – Night or Day. Maybe, even as Miss Blumenthal had claimed, upon being wakened in the middle of the Night. Maybe. And why not? Why the hell not?

She'd had enough practice, God knows, allowing herself the indulgence of one of her own rueful, inner smiles. Why shouldn't she be as proud of these self-enclosed, Byzantine productions, which managed to turn just the right decorous, fiscally-responsible and suitably-impressed, dissecting, but hardly discerning gaze of investors? Surely, what she did was, in its way, as acrobatically deft as the cat burglar sidling from roof to parapet (Cary Grant immediately suggested himself), or as adroit as the long-experienced fingers of the safecracker at his trade, à la Jimmy Valentine, for instance. Why shouldn't she be proud! She was damned good at her job.

Rather than themselves recipients of fat sales proceeds or participants in other happy eventualities, of late, and increasingly, investors had dangled, wriggling, on the receiving end of bad news. Worse luck, Alex grimaced, bits of sharply hostile, threatening phone calls splaying and replaying themselves altogether and at once on the floor of her mind – multimillion-dollar "limited partners" sustaining half-million-dollar tax "hits' they had not anticipated.

In the investments the Company offered, investors enjoyed tax "write-offs" in the early years, while the Company used their money to rehabilitate newly-acquired Department of Housing and Urban Development ("HUD") projects. But, over time, many of these same government-subsidized properties fell once again into the decay and debility from which they had originally been rescued. Only, by this time-some eight, nine, ten years after the initial renovations had been made-no investor money remained to spend on fresh reconstruction. Naturally, with cash flow dwindling the properties, dependent now on the meager proceeds from often unsubsidized rentals only, too frequently developed the typical chronic systemic maladies prelude to sinking into slumhood-plumbing, heating, air conditioning, and elevators failures, peeling paint and rickety stair rails, broken bathroom fixtures and smashed windows. The old litany. Her annual real-estate property reports were rife with tiresome repetitions of these depressing exigencies.

To make matters worse, in the past few years, after the "other Party" had taken over – sometime in the late 80's – the Company had sustained several dramatic setbacks – one after another. Within a two-year period, it had lost more than a dozen multi-million dollar apartment complexes in a number of important metropolitan centers – Chicago, Houston, Detroit. Somehow, the boss, the big boss – had found himself – and the Company – *persona non grata* with key people at the Agency, as HUD was politely referred to in the office. HUD biggies had suddenly made massive cuts in Section 8 rental subsidies to these needy giants or stipulated that Agency help would not be forthcoming unless matched by new, unrealistically-large recapitalizations from original investor-owners. Hence, the capital calls.

The ultimate outcome was invariably the same: foreclosure. As Linden Gables or Elmhurst Arms failed to meet minimal HUD standards year after year, the Agency put them up for public auction. The amount of the "hit" for an individual investor the depended upon the size of his initial investment, plus the sum total of "losses" he had taken over the duration of his investment. The original investment money the Company had used to refurbish the failing property, which had been prorated back to him in the form of tax "write-offs," had now to be "recaptured" – recognized, and reported to the IRS as a capital gain. And taxes paid on this amount, accordingly.

Oh, it wasn't as bad as the 50% tax rate on income over $50,000 that had been exacted at the time of most initial investment. Not that bad. But, bad enough. Judging from the state of traumatized hysteria with which investors invariably greeted announcements of foreclosure – no matter how many ominous property reports had previously been lobbed over the transom at them predicting the funeral, bad enough, indeed!

Not surprisingly, however, though ingenious in argument and crafted with cunning, these capital calls were proving a dry hole: it was becoming depressingly clear that the affluent doctors, lawyers, and Indian chiefs out there, had no intention of providing ongoing funding to failing real estate ventures. Especially considering the dwindling tax write-offs the law now allowed. No, sir. Since 1991, these write-offs had been reduced to zero. Zilch. Nada. Cipher-insky. What did we take them for, anyway? they protested.

Sure, they had been willing and eager to claim losses, they conceded, early on. Why not? After all, wasn't that the way the investment was *supposed* to work ?: that's what their broker-dealers had told them. (And that's all their broker-dealers had told them, Alex ruefully reflected.) Having traveled this doleful road hundreds of times before, Alex consoled herself that millionaires cultivated unusually short memories and were especially prone to the "What have you done for me recently?" school of economics.

THE knife but both ways, however. Just a year-and-a-half ago, 60 employee-victims, mostly lower-level number-crunchers in the real-estate management section of their business, had been laid off. All on a single Friday afternoon, in April, just after tax season. All in two hours.

Just like that. No one had had a clue. It was wonderful... really... how they had managed to keep it so secret.

At three-thirty, Belinda, then Marj, the Sam had been quietly summoned to various offices... one to that of her own Department Supervisor, one to Personnel, one to the Payroll office. Executions had been evenly divided amongst appropriately assigned staff so that all terminations should be effected tidily by five o'clock, sharp. It was a neat ploy, beautifully realized.

After the first two or three stricken faces had emerged from behind closed doors, other coworkers began to get the idea, all right. Something unusual was afoot. Another three... then another, and the secret was out – everyone now waited for the holocaust to touch down into their cubicle. Like the finger of God pressing down on the Titanic,

Alex recited, hating herself immediately for belching up Sister Louisa's shabby cliché after all these years.

A great quietude had invaded the floor. That was what Alex most remembered about the day. A terrible stillness. The vast, beautifully appointed, freshly painted and carpeted fifth floor on Wilshire's fashionable West Side, every modern facility and convenience in evidence, enveloped by this dense hush –

Of course, there must have been speech. There had to have been. But, not that one could remember. Not really. Hardly anyone said anything to anyone else. Not even in whispers. Certainly, no one protested. No one complained. Not audibly. Only a few people trooped out to the elevator before their usual five o'clock quitting time. But most of them fussed about wordlessly, gathering their few personal belongings together into the brown paper sacks that had held their lunch. And they left, without good-bye's alone, or in small clusters, at their usual hour.

ALEX hit the Print button on the computer and pushed back her chair. She took the long route to the printer, stopping at her own 16th story, forever-sealed window, to stare down at the eight lanes of Mercedes', Lexuses, and Audi's crawling along Wilshire Boulevard in their preordained channels – the occasional battered lawn-maintenance truck of a Latino gardener, his bareheaded, sunburnt "helpers" sitting in the open back, betwixt mowers and rakes, the only evidence of flesh-and-blood humanity in the down-there silent procession of the affluent and important.

SHE'D have to follow him, of course. Eventually. Suddenly tired as someone who had been hauling luggage back and forth through O'Hare for hours on end, she allowed herself the comfort of a full, rich, audible, up-from-the-belly sigh. Yes, she'd go. Alcon would have hustled him off to D.C., giving him well-nigh *carte blanche* at selected motels and restaurants for the interim month or months he needed to find new suitable living-quarters for them, and she would be left to arrange for the move of household goods and get through all the tedious, meticulous details of terminating their lives in Los Angeles.

Nor had she yet broached the possibility of a move to Madi. She would have to, of course. While completing the last demanding remained last Spring, to a hectic, albeit systematic and meticulous, search for her first serious position. Crossing and recrossing the country for the five or so hard-won final interview, she had finally decided – despite the relative meagerness of salary and the relative high cost of living in the area – to accept a fairly mundane laboratory assistant position with Dr. Rosendfeld's group, based at Johns Hopkins, and presently conducting, in her estimate, perhaps the most rewarding cancer trials to date. Just last month, after a letter and telephone reminder to Murray, Barry's old Baltimore friend, and the Woodstons, their old neighbors from Delaware now living in a Baltimore suburb, Madi had boarded the plane at LAX, not knowing that it might well be her last trip to LA for several years. Yes, there was Madi to consider, Alex sighed – admiring, respecting, in truth, cherishing her somber, virginal, dedicated daughter – but, admitting to herself at the same moment, one who intimidated her by the sheer thrust of her unswerving, self-denying purpose.

One final all-encompassing glance at the street below, and she moved toward the printer. No, she had no love for this big overgrown playpen of millionaires and smooth-talking shysters, bobbed boobs and nose job, overpriced gourmet restaurants, and cocaine-flushed movie moguls. But, as someone she knew had once said, "You get used to hangin', if you hang long enough." And, she once again discovered that she had, apparently, hanged long enough.

"IT'S over its fit," Serena quipped. "It was refusing to do anything after I had it do the mail-merge this morning... For this last capital call..." she reminded.

"Yeah," Alex agreed mechanically, watching the succession of long white tongues extend themselves with measured dignity to their full length from out the silvered maw of the printer, and, with barely a muffled click, lay themselves serenely into its plastic bib.

"They've got their own personalities, that's for sure," Alex observed, tapping the printer. (Why *did* one feel one had to say something? Blah, blah, blah, would have done just as well.) So, feeling guilty, and make up for the possibly inadequate stroking, passing Serena's desk, Alex gave her a specially warm grin.

At her own work station, she squared off the corners of her copy and began composing her *pro forma*, cool, balanced, terribly informal, but Machiavellianly indirect note to J.D., using the regulation throw-away stick-um. It was a matter of some tact to bring his attention momentarily to the capital call letter he had just this morning insisted be ready for mailing by four o'clock.

Then she started across the no-man's land of half-a-mile of office expanse.

FORTUNATELY, of course, the Company would sell the condo and pay the movers. They always did that. She should feel grateful, she remonstrated.

Ghosts. Everywhere, ghosts. Ever since Lu had been taken away two years ago. Always unexpected... never a moment of warning. There, as she passed, his beautiful, downturned, aureoled head reflected from the back-lit tax manager's window. And she unprepared, with nothing to say. No greeting. No message. Stupidly blank. And then he was gone. Again.

Barry's slightly off-sides cousin Laura, who was into Yoga and who-knows-what-else, but always so kind, so really viscerally compassionate, had said, "There's something special about him, you know. He has an *aura*."

"An aura?" she had repeated politely at Aunt Jane's now regulation Christmas Eve party, a responsibility she had felt constrained to assume after Lottie's death. Alex swizzled the remaining ice-cubes in her glass, estimating whether she could decorously ask for a refill of bourbon and water in just his ten-minute interval. The point, of course, was to get through this festal celebration without having made any mark of any sort whatsoever – not to have spoken too loudly or too honestly, not to have been too hilarious, or, God Forbid, too provocative or challenging. The main point was to cast no shadow, leave no afterthought, produce no memory. To have achieved the compleat Invisible Man.

"He does have an aura," Laura whispered, repeating. "There's something *special* about him," she insisted.

Alex now caught her breath as she entered the Executive Salon. "Curse that aura. Curse it. Marking Lu... her dear, loved, first-born, so cruelly. Would he had been ordinary! Even dull. And lived out his threescore years and ten instead..."

JEANNIE, her pencil poking into the meticulous confection of her bouffant hairdo, giggled into the receiver. But, not too loudly. J.D. liked to have her appear available at all times and all places. And, of course, she was, she was, but, while she was typing copy from the transcriber, a purely mechanical operation, after all, it was as good a time as any for catching up her best buddy, Cindy, on the latest, and sharing the last horrific episode of her divorce proceedings from The Bastard. Why you couldn't even imagine things that... that lowlife, that creature... dream up to bargain about with her lawyer. He was, truly, inn-crre-dible.

Alex decided to wait the customary two minutes for Jeannie to interrupt her conversation and look up; then, with a few mumbled words, she'd slip the capital call copy into J.D.'s IN-box on Jeannie's desk and be on her way.

But even as she moved closer to the desk, Jeannie finally giving her a little acknowledging smirk without dropping a syllable of her narrative to Cindy, J.D.'s small, dapper self materialized in the doorway of his office, closely orbited by big Al, the Company comptroller. As J.D. inched to the left, or forward, Al moved with him as if attached by invisible strings. As usual, Al had successfully borne himself aloft on his own fancy and found himself in passionate, joyous verbal mid-flight regarding a possible oblique interpretation of the tax code that promised to yield astonishingly rewarding results for the business.

While J.D. did not appear to be listening to Al, neither did he seem to see Alex standing beside Jeannie's desk. But, she now considered herself, nevertheless, stuck. Now, she'd have to speak to him. Or something. Invent some innocuous non-speech before she could decently flee from the encounter, back to the safe-haven of her station. Irritated and guilty that she had never mastered her Dagwood Bumstead to J.D.'s Mr. Dithers, she fidgeted until he should initiate their perfunctory meeting.

But, as usual, this would happen – slowly. For a full minute while, through the open door of his office, she reperused the pre-Columbian and African masks that were plainly visible on the facing wall, reminding herself of the flags, swords, shields, and daggers impressively mounted on the other three inside walls, which she had observed on those rare incursions into the inner sanctum, the two men stood planted in the doorway, rapt in discourse as two saints prophesying a miracle to each other.

After a full clock-minutes, J.D., barely twitching in her direction, extended a short, besuited arm leftwards, and instructed his fingers to perform a small inscrutable gesture, as if the individual digits plucked tiny leaves or nuts or berries from off a nearby low-lying bush. Taking this as her cue, Alex quickly inserted the most recent capital call copy into his hand and, grinning widely, and she hoped casually, without further speech, walked briskly away and out the area.

"WELL, it's on its way, Serena. I just delivered the baby!"

"Good for you. I got the envelopes ready to go... Think we'll have it tomorrow?"

"Who knows with J.D.? It could be tomorrow... it could be two months from now... if some glitch develops in the get-along. I figure sending J.D. copy is like putting a note in a bottle and throwing it out to sea..." Alex gibed, companionably leaning against the wall next Serena's desk.

Serena harrumphed. "You shorely be jokin', woman..." she returned the serve, in mock imitation of Southern Black speech, and flashed Alex an insider grin. They both knew the parameters, of course.

For but a moment, she considered telling Serena about her possible leaving. About the imminence of her giving notice of job termination. But only for a moment. Until Barry returned from his Washington trip next week, time schedules remained uncertain. They might not know absolutely even after his return. Oh, there would be time, there would be time, she parroted uncomfortably.

"You know, he not so bad," Serena continued, still in self-imposed character, as she sorted stacks of mail on her desk. "Jeannie tell me he just come back from Bal-tee-more. Been with his Mom in the hospital all week – she be dyin' of cancer. 'Course she be an old lady, by now. Still, 'ccordin' to Jeannie, who oughta know, 'cause she balance his checkbook every month, he pickin' up thousands in hospital bills and all. He don' have to do that, you know! 'Parently, he got a brother. Just as successful, just as much of a muck-a-muck, don't be doin' *nothin'* for his Mom."

Their relationship, to use that antiseptic nomenclature, had already altered after Serena's bout with breast cancer last year. After her mastectomy, it had all become somehow different. Alex and Barry had visited her frequently at the hospital during her recovery... not for show, not even for decorum, but from some inner sense of its needing an army of combatants to stave off this particular scourge. They were part of that army. They had become unalterably, eternally, part of that army upon the terrifying onslaught of Lu's death. On their return from this unspeakable, obscenely-violating experience, there had been sympathy and sensitivity from Serena, but – still – no nexus. But, since Serena's own illness, an exchange of moccasins had quietly taken place.

"HMMM..." Alex picked up an investor letter from the pile and disinterestedly glanced at the return address.

"And besides that," Serena went on, now assuming her more recognizable California persona, "did you know that he has been providing his Mother with yearly Winter trips to Florida... best condos available... Boca Raton, and all that? Living expenses, entertainment, wardrobe, the works... for yeeears?" she testified. "I'd say that's... pretty damn good," she repeated judiciously. "Pretty damn good."

Alex caught Serena's glance. Briefly, she looked directly into her bottomless eyes, then turned away. From whence, this bearing of witness? The cancer? Momentarily, lost for what to say or think, ritualistically, Alex tapped the edge of Serena's desk twice with her fingertips, shrugged, and retreated into her own office.

SHE remembered Murray, Barry's old college roommate who hailed from Baltimore, telling them – two Thanksgiving dinners ago – that he'd looked up Joel Davidoff in his high school Yearbook after a previous LA visit with them when they'd stirred his memory and piqued his curiosity with satirical reports of Alex's boss' eccentricities. Sure enough, his hunch had been right – Joel Davidoff had been a Senior at Compton High when Barry was in Sophomore year there. A little well-placed sleuthing amongst some of his other old cronies at lunch, and he corroborated that the Joel Davidoff he had identified in the Yearbook, was, indeed, one and the same as the Joel Davidoff, son of Joachim Davidoff, once proud owner of Davidoff's Kosher Meats, largest kosher establishments of its kind in the City's waterfront district.

Now he barely remembered that his Mother had even traded at Davidoff's occasionally – when his Father's real estate business took him into the waterfront area. Because of proven quality and reasonable prices, Murray recalled at those times; Mother had habitually phoned in a large meat order for Dad to pick up at Davidoff's. Then, when Murray had mentioned it to Uncle Jack at their weekly lunch get-togethers, his Uncle had confirmed his recollection without hesitation with a big nostalgic grin.

The upshot of the whole business was, one afternoon, covering a Baltimore Redevelopment story, Murray had found himself in the area, and, with just a little help from the telephone directory, located the original Davidoff meat emporium. It was still there. Still doing business under the old name. Old Man Davidoff had apparently established an enviable reputation for reliable quality and an honest pound.

Murray had had his camera with him, of course, and sent a snapshot of the storefront on to them in LA – which Alex still kept – well buried, under a mass of office supply detritus – in her top desk drawer.

ALEX walked to the window. Looking into the street, unseeing, she was suddenly overwhelmed with the raw disconnect of all things... of the brute, irrational ongoingness of events... of the irrelevancy most well-intentioned efforts to architect existence into something supportable, let alone decent and fair, let alone coherent or meaningful or aesthetic, in any lasting sense.

Here she was two years away from retirement – agitating like an adolescent, steeped in childish *angst* about all those old sophomoric questions... the Purpose of Man... the Meaning of Life... the Existence of God. More particularly, the purpose of Alex and Barry, and Lu and Madi... the "meaning" of their lives... and the yearned-for possibility of their receiving, Lu now forever excepted, some measure of that purifying, transcendent vision which should shed grace on their mortality. Lift their otherwise puny existence into something more significant than random, individually-dispensable Darwinian data.

She made several brave attempts – had thrown her full-hearted, ingenious efforts, into one, then another, culturally-or-philosophically approved subtexts, variously commended by School, Society. Or the Accreted Wisdom of the Ages. Something like that. But, of late, the emptiness had grown more gnawingly persistent, more ominous.

A change of scene. That was it! The move which seemed still so useless and distasteful, might actually prove a blessing in disguise. It could pump fresh *elan vital* into their marriage, their remaining careers – albeit, brief – themselves, she speculated, not yet convinced.

"ALLIE, pick up Line3," Serena's voice intruded from her desk outside the door. "Hurry... it's Barry, and he says he has to board a flight in just a few minutes..."

"Alex?..." Barry's familiar tenor crackled at the other end of the line.

"Yes, Barry..."

"Listen, I'm coming in earlier than expected. I'll be on United's 11 o'clock flight into LA. You don't have to come down to the airport. I'll take the SuperShuttle to the Condo". He paused for a few seconds of silence. "I'll explain when I get home," he added. "There's been a change of plans, and I'll be leaving for Washington a couple of weeks sooner than we had thought."

Still silence. "I'll explain in more detail when we're together. In about five short hours, Alex." Another brief pause. "Got to go now, Alex. They're calling for boarding..."

"Barry... Barry...?" Alex inquired, whatever it was she was about to say still unformulated. She replaced the receiver to the steady hum of a dead connection.

SHE felt so tired. Weary to the bone. She could not understand why she always felt so tired anymore.

Chapter Two

H E STARED at the screen on his laptop computer. In the cabin of the Boeing 747, lights had been dimmed, and without moving his head to the right, or even cutting his eyes in that direction, he could sense that the perpetual motion of the wriggling, cranky, thoroughly unhappy toddler, traveling with his pretty, distraught, and near-copeless mother, had finally abated, and the child had settled down across the middle seat between them, and if not quite sound asleep, had beneficently succumbed to a quiescent, immobile state.

The year-and-a-half-old had squirmed all the way to Pittsburg, cry-babbling, interspersing complaints with attention-demanding squeals and cries. Barry could not help but compare him to Lu, who spoke 100 words or more before he was one-year-old, or Madi, too, who thought not so early a talker, had, like Lu, been able to make her needs known in some less primitive way, and both of whom seemed, in retrospect, to have been far more effective in their over-all communication, even at that young age. He could truthfully never remember either child yammering and carrying on for hours on end without apparent purpose.

Barry smiled at himself. He was getting to be an Old Man. Old Men always thought everything in process of decline from some former Golden Age of near-perfection, comprised approximately of those years encompassing their own youth and pre-50's maturity. Continuing to stare at his empty computer screen, wryly and irrelevantly perhaps, he recalled accompanying his Mother on Sodality Home Visits to 90-some-year-old Mrs. Gallagher. Resting on her afghan, the old woman's gnarled hands had always been entwined in her long, wooden-beaded rosary – upon each visit and through each involuntary nap, waking or asleep. Now uninstructed, the computer screen waited, staring back at him blankly. *His* rosary.

It was almost always bumpy over and just-after Pittsburgh, and tonight was no exception. While his glance automatically flicked up to the "Fasten Seat Belt" sign which had just been flashed on, Barry smiled again, remembering that Pittsburgh was "one of their towns."

FRESH out of his Doctorate Program at Wisconsin, he had put in five years of helping to set up and articulate a standardized testing program for the University at New Colony in Delaware. About this time, on a day like any other, he had been approached by Joel Hill, one of his many "outside" business contacts, associated with a Beltway consultant firm, Alcon, about a potential opening in Hill's firm. They were looking for a psychologically and statistically trained and experienced professional to head up a new Human Resources study and develop a potential contract program at Aberdeen. Credentials for the position, Joel argued, very like Barry's own. Almost tailor-made. If Barry landed the job, he would not only be enhancing his career base and future prospects, Joel contended, but could even continue living in his present home in New Colony, commuting the do-able distance across the Delaware line to Maryland daily. Why, it was a natural!

Though flattered by Joel's gratuitous recognition, Barry's first reaction was to dismiss the suggestion as needlessly risky – even foolhardy. But, after a week-and-a-half's reflection, the matter began to assume a different shape and dimension. His present position at the University, though secure at the moment, was something of a *cul de sac*, if not a dead-end, after all. The invariant, recurrent, predictable pedagogic and personal differences between himself and Nelson, Head of the University Testing Service, in which Nelson unfailingly carried the day, were frankly becoming something of a personal cliché. A bore, really. The upshot was that after applying for and being offered the new position by Alcon, he had succumbed finally to the augmented glamor of a corporate title – not to mention the sizable increase in salary and perks that went along with it.

He'd then put in several successful years at Aberdeen, but just about the time Lu was ready to enter the University, an opportunity for crafting and contracting yet another Human Resources program once again offered itself to Alcon – this time and for Life Assurance at their corporate headquarters in Pittsburgh. While the location and the requester were patently atypical of Alcon's more-usual operating orbits and Pentagon contacts, the Corporation was not about to squander this perhaps-maverick opportunity. After advising Barry of the situation, Alcon recommended him for the position: and, with mixed feelings, considerably assuaged by a substantial raise in salary, the family – minus Lu – were moved to Pittsburgh.

HE RESPONDED to the doorbell at their Foxglove Street home in suburban Pittsburgh. Standing at the door, luggage laundry bag resting against his jeaned leg, Lu flashed his Dad a typical Lu smile, at once droll and pixie-ish.

"Hi, Dad. Remember your Number One son?"

"Come on in, you lovable screwball." He pulled Lu's laundry bag into the hall and flung his arm around Number One's shoulder.

"Hey, great to see you," Barry said, a little breathless. "But... a little unexpected. Semester's over, I take it?"

"Yeah," Lu said, desultorily, distracted, focusing his attention on the arching cathedral ceiling, the curving hallway, the presentation of pewter and greenery arranged on discreetly placed shelves along the ascending two-story-high entryway walls.

"Hey, Dad, not bad... not bad at all," he soughed, avoiding, but approximating, the expected approving whistle.

"Yeah," Barry allowed. "It's pretty impressive, isn't it? Of course, it's all your Mother's doing... C'mon, let's go downstairs," he said, leading the way down the curving, wrought-iron balustrade staircase to the lower floor, here unconventionally compromising the "living" rooms of the house – living room, dining room, kitchen, den, half-bath, and utility-workroom. The stairway itself terminated in a tacked-away, diminutive, semicircular parquet alcove, invitingly private, in which, on the facing wall, Lu's framed sixth-grade, prize-winning batik now hung and below which Lu's old walnut spinet had been lovingly installed.

Wordlessly, Lu slipped onto the bench and let his fingers search out a series of ascending chords, then rendered the riveting theme from *2001* with full bravura, then several phrases of a Mozart sonata, and concluded with, for Barry, a heartrending bit of melody from "Für Elise," Lu's first piano recital piece. Lu rose from the bench and gave

Barry's shoulder a tight squeeze, and together they moved toward the kitchen.

THAT'S how Barry was always remembering Lu. With that hurt, that recognition, behind his eyeballs. Or was being retrospectively prescient? Hadn't he really been aware – always, of some kind of knowledge Lu had been burdened with, knowledge or insight he would have preferred to have been spared? Lu's averted gaze intended kindly to spare the observer....

TWO days later, while Barry was at work, Charlie McDougall had apparently showed up and, according to Alex, both young men had spent the afternoon looking through the Pittsburgh newspapers for possible gigs, following up with mostly unproductive phone calls. Charlie played drums in Lu's rock group. That evening, over broiled Hawaiian chicken, which Charlie volubly appreciated and consumed, he and Alex were told of Charlie's doting aunt, living conveniently close in nearby McKeesport, who had not only consented to board Charlie through the summer, but indefinitely, if need be. Doting indeed, Barry ruminated dourly.

Yet, incredibly, at the end of two weeks, Lu's group had been signed on as the back-up combo for a locally popular, fairly well-known lead singer, after he and Charlie had scurried to contact the three remaining stray members of their original group, and the combo had dutifully appeared – informal matched costumes and all – for competitive tryouts somewhere at a summer club in Northeast Pittsburgh. They had been awarded the job, Lu announced that evening with cheerful, almost blasé, aplomb. Fortunately, the three scapegraces that had materialized on their doorstep the evening before this feat, seemingly out of thin air, likewise, disappeared as readily, nightly, into what Barry could only imagine were a succession of cheap (probably sordid) motel rooms in the nearby area.

Frantic, friendly telephone calls from Moses Brown to Lu, with last minute time and equipment arrangements for particular supper clubs, restaurants, or nightclubs scheduled for that evening or weekend, along with fervent, disputatious exchanges about the order and arrangement of musical numbers, became the order of most days, according, again, to Alex. So, through July, then half of August, Alex and he became gravitationally aware of this frenetic activity. Lu, leaving regularly, early evenings, quietly letting himself in, early mornings. Passing Lu in the bathroom at dawn one morning, Barry felt himself being companionably patted on the back, while Lu sleepily remarked over his shoulder, "You know, Dad, Pittsburgh drivers! Whew! It's not a matter of *if*, but *when*, I'm going to get creamed some morning on my way back home. "With that, Lu had disappeared into the den-bedroom that had become his sleeping quarters for the season. Barry was left meandering over whether to call Lu back and be sternly demanding, laying down the law, or merely amused.

AS THE end of August approached, the air of tension between himself and Alex rose to a silent shriek. Neither could broach the excruciating subject. Not even to each other,

What provided the "proximate cause," Barry smirked at his sophomoric terminology, was The Joint. After a near cataclysmic eruption in Lu's late high school career, when such an object first fell out of about which, to this day, Barry felt perplexed and embarrassed p for he had actually flung his son against the wall in a fit of rage and despair – what had happened after that... is that... *nothing* had happened. All evidence, even covert evidence, of marijuana usage, had, of as usual, but, while school authorities callously continued to pester and embarrass Alex over Lu's truancies, his dress, and assorted additional trivialities, and Lu continued to be monitored and even frisked routinely in his high school corridors by suspecting and ambitious officials, no palpable evidence was ever found. But, it was an open secret anyway, an open secret: the problem had simply gone underground.

So, Barry knew. He had known all along. Lu exercised a degree of decorum about his usage, and nobody in the family talked about it.

BUT, come late August, once and again – especially on the occasion of Charlie's dropping in of an afternoon, Lu and Charlie had taken to sharing a joint in Lu's back den-bedroom.

As Barry came downstairs that evening, he was greeted by Alex's unspeaking drilling gaze. And he could smell it. The sweetness, the spiciness. With his sinuses, it was still one of the few odors that got to him...

That evening after supper and Charlie's leave-taking, the tension was almost more than Barry could bear.

"LU, YOU'VE always had the..." (he almost laughed at his own spinsterish fastidiousness) "...well, the *courtesy* to use The Stuff somewhere else. You know how I... outback... somewhere... and spare us the smell."

Lu looked back at him with hooded eyes. "Sure, Dad. Sure." Lu stole a covert glance at Alex across the table. "Sorry."

"But since we've brought up one serious topic, let me ask you about another – Lu, just what do you plan to do in September? Your Mother and I... while we're happy for your... your *job* (he could hardly choke out the word), we can't help but wonder if you're planning to attend college, come September."

Somehow, Barry was already sure of the answer. He waited for Lu raise his head and say the words.

"I don't think so, Pop."

A long, deadly quiet.

In the softest, most reasonable voice he could produce, Barry heard himself say, "You know, Lu, your Mother, and I... we've never... well, pushed you. Tried to make you do what didn't seem right for you.

We've always tried to let you be on your own person. But, for Christ's sake, Son, for once, be practical. What are you going to do without even an undergraduate degree?"

"Dad, the impresario who managed Buddy Holly... he auditioned us. Last week. He liked us. He's lined up gigs from the Catskills to LA... he's still working on it. But we'd have to sign a contract for at least a year.

"What?" Hearing himself spluttering, Barry could feel his anger rising, as much at himself as at Lu.

"What do you mean, *Contract*? What are you talking about?" Barry looked over at Alex, who had turned in her chair and was staring out the side window, her napkin twisting between her clutching fingers.

"Is that what you want to do with your Life?" he whooped.

Since the silence was eating away at the very fabric of their communication, in self-defense, and devoid of any better strategy, he had thundered, repeating, "Is that what you want to do with your Life!"

"But, if I never *try*, Dad if I *never even try...* I'll never know what I could have done," was barely audible.

Again, no one spoke. Like mourners, they sat around the dining room table, not looking at each other, hoping for some extraordinary, extraterrestrial healing grace.

AFTER five, ten, who knew how many minutes, Lu got up and headed toward his room. A few more endless minutes and Barry watched as Lu mounted the stairs to the front door.

"So long Bothies..." he called quietly from the front door, using the locution they had all laughed at when he was four years old.

"So long," Barry whispered to himself as the pilot announced their passage over Denver, the time, prevalent weather conditions, and time of arrival in LA. Once again, Barry caught his breath, the familiar congestion gathering in his chest, his eyes smarting.

"WELL, that's OK for you, maybe, but that's not how I plan to spend the rest of *my* Life!" she had trumpeted impertinently, flicking the legal-length log sheets of anthropometric data literally under his nose. That concluded another stimulating (scaring) episode of discussion (argument) that periodically gathered and burst through the Math Survey Room with gale force.

At regular intervals, these verbal confrontations served to reduce tensions between the "slaves" – Corinthians of Liberal Arts persuasion who did the grunt work for the Patterson Anthropometric Survey – and the "egg-heads" – Patterson Field-associated "statisticians," who, with the single exception of the Manager himself, were all just students like the Liberal Art majors – except that they were Math or Psychology majors, sometimes with a minor in Statistics, overseeing the other Corinthians' effort on a daily basis. Semiweekly, Dr. Augustus Powell, "Augie" as he was known familiarly amongst them in private conversation, but a moniker no one would have dared use in his actual presence, Ph.D. mathematician and statistician, touched down at the second-floor Corinthian installation in North hall, reviewed ongoing results, and concluded his day with a brief oversight meeting with the "eggheads."

"Well, whatever you plan to do or not to do with the rest of your Life, make sure you have these double-checked," he added unnecessarily, knowing that she would, of course, follow the usual procedure in having all statistical formulae based on the raw data from the log sheets rechecked – mean, median, sigma, etc. Yet, it would have been less than masterly for him to have simply allowed her "to have the last word."

She had stared back at him as if a small tree had just sprouted from his forehead.

NEXT year would be his Senior year as a double Mathematician-Psychology Major at Cornell, and he had felt lucky when his advisor had notified him that he had been one of the people awarded a summer "internship" job at Patterson Field, just outside Dayton, actually overseeing, or helping to oversee, a part of a vasty study being conducted by the Air Force, the Patterson Anthropometric Survey. The data, provided by the Air Force, were all kinds of macro and micro measurements of the human body – from skull circumference to finger length. Correlations of the data would be invaluable in many ways – everything from more precise placement of instrumentation on control panels of airplanes to more accurate manufacturing specs for airmen's gloves and oxygen masks.

After the first week of general orientation, Dr. Powell had assigned him to the Corinth College contingent; it took him about 40 minutes by bus every morning – from his room at the Dayton "Y" to his desk in North Hall on Corinth's campus.

Still unable to dismiss the last flurry from his thinking, he felt compelled presently to reenter the Mart Survey Room to check on the card sorter: it was always fouling up. His first sight was that of Alex Borys' desk, nearest the window. There she sat, pleased as Punch with herself. That was one of the troubles with these Liberal Arts majors; he reaffirmed: touchy as bugs, selfish as cats.

Nothing about her was real, really. Nobody *really* had hair that color – deep, deep auburn: wine-colored. Or, brown eyes, with that color hair. Huuuge, brown eyes. The expression on her face reminded him of one of his Mother's framed Art Deco posters, which Mom had posted in her own most private space – sewing room, vanity alcove, bathroom – that same short upper-lip: the perpetual half-startled glance of astonishment or, conversely, of profound melancholy. Now, her oversized shirts and khaki shorts were always suitably boxy and unrevealing, but the shapeliness of the long legs emerging were – again – astonishing, disconcerting, and she must have some awareness of this effect.

Unreal. That was Alex Borys altogether: she came at you from all angles. At once. She wasn't safe. Even her name, for God's sake: Alexandra... Sandy, Alex, Sandra, Andy, Allie... just to name a few of the variants: she was called each of these names... by someone. And, to top it off, that ridiculous last name – Borys – surely much more like someone's given name!

Alex looked up over her shoulder at Barry. Under her gaze, he felt almost as if he were not there.

"Everybody says Shakespeare Festival is wonderful," Barry speculated. "You're a Litnik! How about taking a Math troglodyte to see *Henvy V*? Might help civilize him."

"Are you asking me for a date? She countered levelly.

"Seems so."

"You buying the tickets?"

"Sure."

She opened her upper right-hand desk drawer, took out a brochure, opened it, and was soon running her finger down a list of performances on an inner page.

"Saturday, 203 Brook Hall, 7:30, for an 8 o'clock performance?"

"Sounds great... I'll be there. With tickets tucked away in my pocket."

He had never seen her smile before. He could feel himself wince slightly, involuntarily – both shocked and delighted.

"You're not so bad," she said under her breath, turning to the log sheets before her, and resuming her calculations. "Even though you *are* a terrible stuffed shirt."

"Neither are you... Crue-e-l Beauty..." he ventured, as he left the room, spiraling momentarily, recklessly into the rhetoric of what seemed to him the language of Shakespearean sonnets.

Her sardonic chortle followed him into the hall.

"So what do you think?" she sallied, during intermission. "Prudent, conscientious, just, unflinching, modest, humble, honest, religious, sympathetic to all classes of men, the Renaissance "ideal Prince"' – do you this that's a fair description?" she queried, reading archly from the printed programme.

"Yeah, and besides all that," he added, "it's a good play."

"It is, isn't it?" she said simply, spontaneously giving his upper arm a little squeeze. "Besides, I think they're doing a wonderful job with the acting... the production..."

When the lights dimmed for Act IV, she did not object to his cradling her hand in his.

"So, do you think I'm much like Katherine?" she could not help prodding as the left after the performance. "Demure, but clever? Simple, but wise?"

He did not answer immediately as they crossed the lawn between the silhouetted trees. In the background, scurrying prop men and a bustle of theatrical housekeeping, while he tried to shield the incandescent glow enveloping him. Protect it even from that cheerful badinage that served as the medium of their communication.

"No, you're not at all like Katherine," he forced himself to admit finally. "You're a much smarter, sexier, and tougher Old Girl altogether."

ALTHOUGH he never actually "gave up" his room at the "Y" in Dayton, by the end of the summer, he had been staying in Alex's room most weekday evenings, and almost every weekend. Periodically, he showed up in Dayton for a change of clothes and to pay the rent. While he and Alex kept up a superficial, impersonal formality at work, by the beginning of August, their relationship was no secret to either the slaves or eggheads amongst them.

HE NEVER remembered talking so much. Three-hour hamburger suppers at The Sulphur Spring Café, as often as they could afford them. Hour-long unplanned reminiscences in the midst of evening cleanup of work-related assignments, whispered exchanges during the walks in the College's lovely rustic forest acreage known as The Arbor. Talk of their past, their parents, their friends, their dreams for the future.

And the early, yet mystical, lovemaking. The wonder of it. The ravishment. "You're not at all like that *other* Barry – when you make love..." she had said, sitting up in bed, pulling the crushed sheet around her knees. "You are *not*," she reiterated with childlike plaintiveness. "You are quite simply wonderful."

He did not argue that she seemed to be liking that other Barry, even him, well enough, by now. God knows, he loved all the Alex's there were to love.

THEY were banking to land... right on time, Barry noted. He folded up his laptop and rechecked the contents of the envelope in his breast pocket so as to assure his baggage claim checks were all in order. On the intervening seat, the little guy had awakened and sat, eyes like peeled hard-boiled eggs, back propped against the seat, in a semi-stuporous, Buddha-like trance. Next to him, his girl-mother fidgeted about, nervously replacing items into a plastic satchel.

THEY had been circumspect. At the end of that summer, how he remembered her glorious wine-colored hair hiding half her face as he pushed it back to kiss her good-bye. Her wonderful soul-filled eyes – averted. They had decided that she would complete her last year at Corinth, and go on to earn a Master's – likely at Michigan or Iowa – and, concurrently, he would work toward his Ph.D. at Wisconsin. Of course, he would visit whenever possible – subject to the pressures of graduate study and the availability of cash.

Finally, without ever having discussed a full-fledged, coherent prospectus, he had assumed she would visit his parental home in Collingsfield come next Christmas. The few times the subject had been approached – indirectly, amorphously – she had neither approved nor rejected the idea. She had never mentioned a similar visit to the Borys' in Thompsonville.

WHAT would he tell her now? What could he say? Would they again be required to migrate – this time to Alexandria, Virginia – only to find themselves, in a year or less, in one of the country's most expensive cost-of-living areas, virtual strangers, and now, forced retirees?

Lindquist had been amorphous about his agenda of emendations for the Language Program. To effect these, supposedly whatever they might finally turn out to be, to assure Barry's ready oversight, Blanchard had deemed his resettlement in the Alexandria are "advisable," according to Lindquist. Lindquist had been equally vague concerning Barry's eventual and continued interface and management of the personnel at Fort Horton. As usual, Barry evaluated, it was assumed total commitment on one side; preservation of cool, judicious choice on the other. Hardly a fair balance.

AS HE trudged up the ramp from the airplane, patting his breast pocket once more, Barry was quite suddenly overwhelmed with a wave of fatigue, well-nigh unto nausea. He could scarcely ever remember feeling so tired.

Chapter Three

DEBARKING THE elevator on the second floor, Alex moved toward their condominium, involuntarily as heartbeat or pressure of blood against artery, just right and down the blue-carpeted, untenanted hallway: here a communal chapel hush prevailed, inviting discharge of that world-at-large just exited, the Freeway megacosm of potential drive-by shootings, swivel-hipped car weaving suicidally, murderously, through clotted traffic, the collapsed civilization of the homeless unequally camouflaged by the shrubbery and flowering plants expensively manicured along the City's arterial rims. Once more, she sought day's end and encapsulation in this noiseless haven of ostensible peace, beauty and refuge. Deftly, Alex opened both locks of Unit 2222 and entered.

As if magnetized, she crossed through the living room area toward the ceiling-to-floor glass patio door, pushed it aside, and stepped onto the postage-stamp-sized patio. This tiny appendage sat surrounded by an abutting hillside of seemingly uncontrollable growth – bushed and trees almost upon one, in which uncountable flocks of mourning doves, jays, sparrows, crows, and blackbirds, as well as other frequently glimpsed unidentified species of birds, made their home. Tonight, however, dusk had already deepened into something approaching evening, and all was still. Nonetheless, before turning to go on again, Alex breathed deeply, comforted in the knowledge that they indeed, were there.

Primitive, this, Alex, reflected: this reliable, instinctual joyous warmth upon homecoming. Even a homecoming such as this – to a small, furnished, rectangular space, enclosed anonymously in yet a longer rectangular stretch of space, one of thousands of boxes, contained in yet other thousands of larger wood, stucco, glass, and steel boxes comprising the City.

Moving forward the refrigerator, she had already traversed the two-or-three step proposition that by now had become ritualized into negative perfection. No, she would not choose to go to a nearby Pasadena coffee shop for dinner – too much trouble, and besides, she had just gotten *out* of the car! No, she would not prepare a whole TV dinner, either, with or without salad, for just herself, alone. As usual, popping two slices of whole wheat into the toaster, an open-faced tuna sandwich would do just fine. And a cup of instant, of course.

Tray before her on the coffee table, she removed her shoes and scanned known CNN, C-Span, A&E, History, Court, and Weather channels, settling finally upon CNN. Five minutes later, sports coverage up, Alex pressed down the Mute button.

NOW, these kinds of doings would never have been acceptable to Lottie Byrnes! Tuna fish snacks for dinner, indeed! Alex smiled as she recalled her mother-in-law's discomfiture in the face of the improvised makeshift. No, Lottie could not *sit*, literally could not *sit*, if there was one soiled teacup in the sink, one ashtray that gave evidence of having been used, one person in the room unattended as to food, drink, or proper attention, whatever that might be, given the occasion.

THE Byrnes' large, brick rancher sat on a sizable corner lot, taking advantage of its position by having its two major wings set well back at the juncture of the intersecting streets. Its walled expanse and high-placed windows, handsome and substantial, though unmemorable, were appropriately outlined with pleasingly varied, neatly trimmed shrubbery, redolent of an architectural drawing. Concessions had been made for the season, however: a beautiful holly tree on the larger street-side stood festooned with tiny white sparkling lights; a crimson door on this side of the house also bore an enormous wreath above it, tastefully electrified, while beribboned garland had been arranged above the tripartite front windows. As she and Barry moved toward a vestibule in the smaller, less-trafficked street side, Alex observed that the theme of wreaths and garlands had been consistently carried out upon this smaller wing also. While Alex had been too preoccupied with the anticipated parental meeting to be much aware of the streets they had just traveled, she had nevertheless absorbed an over-all, generalized impression of large, dignified, modern, and expensive dwellings, each attractively established in its own varied but conventional, setting. Much like what she and her father had often dubbed "Dentists' Row" in Thompsonville's newest, most recently fashionable Southside.

At the Greyhound Station, she and Barry had embraced and kissed, nerves and passion warring; moved toward Barry's father's Buick with but small, meaningless speech; entered the car, and drive the distance to the Byrnes' with no additional nervous, breathless questions from Alex, nor preparatory suggestions or preambles from Barry.

Neither had Barry disputed the issue with her a week ago when she had insisted that she should arrive *on* Christmas day itself, not, as he originally suggested, on Christmas Eve for the "big Christmas bash" his mother held annually for family, friends, and assorted neighbors. Never mind that she would be traveling most of Christmas Eve night and taking a bus from Philadelphia to Collingsfield in New Jersey early Christmas morning.

Personal acquaintanceship with Barry's parents would, in any case, have eventually become patently necessary, and besides, she had promised... but for one had preferred to sojourn alone through most of her early turbulent years at Corinth, this "introduction" had involuntarily taken on attributes of concession.

AFTER hanging up their coats in the outer coat closet and exiting the entrance hall into the half-football-field-sized family room, for, but a moment, Alex felt herself drawing in a long, tremulous breath before her expression was made to settle into the diffident, but, she hoped, amiable smile she was to wear for the rest of the afternoon and evening.

But, there were so many of them! She had not expected so many! Clusters of two's and three's – some seated, others standing beside chairs or sofas. A pair of elderly men in mid-conversation, leaning up against the mantel over the fireplace, simultaneously studying a log transmogrifying itself into ash below, the while half-resting their arms and matched, squat, companionable whiskey glasses in the holly-laden mantel shelf above.

Seconds later, from somewhere behind a grouping of armchairs in an area immediately adjacent to and appearing to open into a dining hall, a tall – very tall – burly man, remarkable in crimson blazer and Christmas plaid tie, advanced toward and upon them, arm and hand extended. His slightly beaked, large nose, horn-rimmed glasses glinting before a pair of large, sharp-blue round eyes, a boyish shock of sandy-red hair, all fit into the square, well-fleshed countenance which beamed welcoming geniality and general high animal spirits.

"Alexandra... Alex... Welcome... Welcome... And, Merry Christmas!" he boomed, shaking her hand, his hand just as quickly now under her elbow, pivoting her easily, presenting her thus to the room's Company-at-large. As she was being turned, for the first time since entering the room, she took note of Barry, standing beside this formidable figure. Barry, whom she knew to be six feet tall, looked willowy, frankly diminutive, his frame rendered somehow ambiguous in the intensity of the other man's ambience. Barry's blue-black, already graying hair, his thoughtful long-oval head, and face, with its deeply-lashed blue eyes, flickered into adolescent, stripling comeliness by comparison.

"Dad, this is Alex..." Barry's voice was heard to add redundantly.

Dr. Byrnes had already led them to a smallish woman sitting in one of the tweed armchairs on either side of the fireplace. More even than Barry, the set of the ling oval head, the attentive posture, radiated birdlike responsiveness, heedful advertence. Her electric-blue eyes were directly seen to contrast startlingly with her soft, snow-white aureole of hair – once probably more jet black even than Barry's – and intensified in their effect by the wool suit of identical color that she wore.

"Lottie, our guest – Barry's young friend, Alex."

Instantly, Lottie's hand reached out and cupped one of Alex's own in both of hers. "Delighted, my dear. Did you have a hard trip down? I couldn't believe Barry would let you travel on the *very* Day. But he insisted. He said you'd both agreed." She stood up suddenly, barely reaching the Doctor's shoulder.

"But, let's not just stand here. Charlie, find out what Alex and Barry would like to drink, and –" catching up a painfully slender, elderly Black maid by the elbow as she bore a laden tray past, "- Rose, this is Alex I've been telling you about. Barry's... friends."

Rose smiled genially, proffering a tray bearing jumbo stuffed mushrooms, while her other handheld out small plates and cocktail napkins. "They're dee-lee-cious! Doctor Charles always says they're the best they is... anywhere." She smiled up at the Doctor, reprising their oft-shared camaraderie.

"Alex, I'd like you to meet Barry's older brother, Ken. And – his fiancée," the Doctor resumed, propelling Alex past a visibly declining number of guests, as the desultorily noted that, at the door, Lottie was already accepting and returning affable good-bye's and hearty Merry Christmases from persons bundled in coats and scarves.

As they approached a sofa on the other side of the room, furthest distant from the dining room, a handsome, assured, sandy-haired male rose briskly, militarily to his feet. He could be seen to have abruptly terminated his dialogue with a languid, long-legged blonde at the other end of the divan, who now bent to place a champagne glass noiselessly on the coffee table before them.

Forward of each arm of the sofa stood matched Morris chairs, and nearing them, the Doctor lifted an additional light, brocaded side-chair from behind him, completing an informal circle of seats facing the couch. For an awkward second, Alex hesitated, then moved toward Ken's side of the sofa and took his extended hand.

"That's Ken, Barry big brother," the Doctor said. "And this is Alex, Ken, Barry's *new* friend."

"And Maggie..." Ken nodded toward the other end of the couch. "My fiancée." Glancing at the sylph-like apparition in the opposite corner, arrayed in form-defining, muted-aqua crepe, Alex nodded, scarcely crediting her with a name like "Maggie." Alex stood a bit taller in her best gray Pendleton suit.

"I was just filling Maggie in about the Urban Renewal project Len talked about the other day, Dad. Exciting stuff! From what I can tell, the Philly Democratic pols really mean to push for it. You just wait and see, Dad, after the next election..." He made a graceful little half-swing with his right arm as if pitching a ball into place.

The Doctor guffawed, looking across from Alex to Barry with a pleased, deprecating smile. "Haven't you got enough trouble with your own practice Ken...? You *looking* for more misery than you can handle...? Because that's what you're in for, mark my words, Son. Playing politics is a mean, rough business, not for amateurs."

"It's also the way to really get ahead, Dad. The way to get in and get things done! I don't mind telling you, I'm interested, *very* interested, in getting in on the ground floor with some of these new projects. And I don't flatter myself when I say the interest is *mutual*," he added levelly, earnestly.

Lottie interrupted to remind the Doctor that Jack Simpson was leaving. The Doctor excused himself momentarily.

"He hasn't gotten you a drink yet?" Lottie scolded. "For Heaven's Sake! Kenny, at least go fetch up a couple of glasses of champagne for Alex and Barry, Kenny, go... go..." Lottie shooed.

Lottie, in turn, scampered off to tend to final dinner preparations with Rose and Sidonia. But before the conversation could be redirected on a new tack, Ken reappeared bearing two champagne glasses of Cold Duck, with the Doctor immediately behind.

"I tell you, Dad, it's the wave of the future," Ken recouped without pause. "I've already broached the subject with Uncle Bart, and, far from minding, he's quite enthusiastic about the potential added business that would flow to the Firm from wide-scale Renewal activities – that is, if we could get our oar in time. Tax and fiduciary counseling, contracting... It'd be a bonanza for the Firm, great for the City, too – good for everyone, in fact."

The Doctor smiled globally, allowing a complacent glance to settle finally upon Alex. "As I've said, I've never been able to tell the boys a thing," he complained. "Not a thing. Now, I had advised Ken to apply to Medical School... follow in his old Dad's footsteps. Did he? Would he?" He pointed a long, strong index finger at Ken, nailing him with a grin. "You bet *not*! He wanted to practice Law instead." (It was becoming difficult for Alex to maintain eye-contact with the Doctor and an air of courteous interest in his evolving mock argument where, for purposes of his histrionic presentation, she had now been cast in the role of a hypothetical adversary.)

"Well, I guess it wasn't such a bad decision, after all," the Doctor countered his own prosecutorial accusation. "Ken's Uncle – my brother Bart... is a senior partner in an admittedly reputable law firm. Byrnes, Biggars, and Howe, you know. In Philadelphia." Abruptly, with mumbled excuse, Maggie lifted first herself, then her champagne of glass, and retreated in the direction of the kitchen.

"Now, Barry here comes along... and it's the same damned thing all over again... pardon my French. Only, this time it's worse even than Kenny. He comes up with the cockamamie idea he wants to be..." the Doctor snorted volubly, "a psychologist. He wants to study Social Psychology, whatever the Hell that is, with a minor in Statistic I tell you, for a simple country Doctor like himself, it's too much. Entirely too much."

While Alex tried to sort out the gravamen in the Doctor's charge: was he complaining of his sons' perverse willfulness or praising their independence of judgment, a flushed, rosy young man in his late teens suddenly catapulted through the vestibule doorway and halfway into the room. He carried a hockey stick in one hand, a puck in the other: his eyes focused on the clock above the mantel. "Am I late for dinner?" he breathed.

"So – *there* – is our best hope." Doctor Charles broadcast over his shoulder. "Little Stevie. Now, he *does* wish to pursue medical studies... to become a physician. Enrolled in the pre-Med course at Rochester for next year. Redeem the family honor. Right, Steve?

"Right, Dad, " Steve returned distractedly, letting his length fall into an easy chair close behind his Father's, quickly followed by a sweet, unassuming smile at Alex. "When do we eat?"

"Right now," Lottie said, appearing in the archway to the dining room.

"Please come in, everyone. Dinner is served."

THEY all took their seats, Alex again placed next to Ken, and directly across from Maggie, while Steve made up the rest of the party on their side of the table. Alex had expected something like the two Standard quatrains of conventional grace before the meal, nor was she unduly surprised at Doctor Charles' continuing solemn intonation of an *Our Father* at this holiday season, but when Lottie piped for a quavery *Hail Mary,* and the Doctor further persisted with a half-chanted recital of the *Apostle's Creed,* she could not refrain from a quick glance down the table at Barry – seated across from Stephen – his serious downturned face totally unrevealing – then shifted her full concentration on forcibly turning the irrepressible smile twitching at her mouth into something resembling a dour grimace of piety.

The smile leapt out, however, instantly counterfeit as a sharp, dry cough, when Lottie ceremonially lifted a tiny, silver bell at her right hand, rang it briefly, and Sidonia and Rose proceeded from the kitchen in formal procession, Sidonia bearing an enormous silver salver upon which sat a perfectly roasted turkey, and behind her, Rose, with another empty silver platter – both uniformed servers formally installing their offerings before the Doctor.

The Doctor's deft and anatomically accurate and aesthetic reduction of the holiday bird to white and dark, wing and joint, were approving lauded by almost everyone at the table, a procedure which Alex noted took at least another quarter of an hour. The Doctor finally loaded stuffing into yet awaiting covered silver receptacle, and Rose and Sidonia carried platter after platter around the table, offering each in turn to individual diners, before silently disappearing out the service door to the kitchen.

"We're certainly lucky to be together again this Holiday season," Lottie directed joyously to the table at large. And lucky to have a special guest this time, too," she added, singling Alex out and smiling. "But, I suppose our gain is your parents' loss, my dear. I'm sure they'll miss you at Christmas. Do you have brothers and sisters that'll be home this time of year, Alex?"

"No, I'm afraid I'm *It*, Mrs. Byrnes. Regretfully, I'm an *only* child," Alex explained.

"Please... *Lottie*... my dear... Lottie..." Mrs. Byrnes corrected.

"But my Dad comes from a big *Catholic* family, Lottie... eight of them," Alex added staunchly, unable to keep herself from highlighting this positive alignment with the Byrnes family. "So, he and Mom will be at Aunt Emily's for Christmas dinner with a small *army* of family members."

An imperceptible hiatus as everyone addressed their dinner. Munching stuffing replete with chestnuts and oysters, Alex allowed as everything could be said to approach perfection, decidedly gourmet quality, but nothing akin at Aunt Emily's equally proudly-prepared grated potato and bacon, sauerkraut-and-sausage stuffing, deliciously made to bifurcate the cavity of their traditional Borys holiday bird.

"AND what does your father *do*?" the Doctor inquired briskly from the head of the table.

Alex finished her mouthful before replying in a habitual defensive, generic way. "He's employed at North American Business Machines. The Company's home offices are located nearby... in Watkin's Cove."

"Yes, that Henson is one forward-looking, smart businessman," the Doctor resumed. "*Forbes* tracks his acquisition of the Company pretty impressively. By the time he retired in 1949, he'd brought the Company to world prominence, producing all kinds of business machines. Even built, or caused to have built, I should say, one of the first of these electronic computers. Why, even before the War, he approached a Harvard engineering professor, with an idea to build an electromechanical calculator. You've heard of the Mark I, haven't you, Barry?

"Excellent Company," the Doctor affirmed, as Lottie once again rang the little silver bell, and Sidonia and Rose began to repeat performance with freshly refurbished platters.

"Sure, Dad, but they've come a long way since then. They moved into first place with their ABM 701. Today, they dominate the punch-card business machine systems. You know, Alex – the kind we used in the Anthropometric Survey."

Alex nodded. "But the cutting edge is 'scaling down,'" Barry observed. "If the electronic digital computer circuits could be miniaturized, it would just make a world of difference... in the speed and efficiency of performance. They're working on it. And, you'll see, it'll happen. And it'll be revolutionary!" Barry remarked raptly.

"Hey, Barr... aren't you getting just a bit carried away? From what I can tell, it'll certainly be another useful computational tool – far more advanced than anything we have right now, but not, after all, the telephone, telegraph, and motor car all rolled into one," Ken remarked laughing, looking around consecutively at each of the persons at the table with an air at once sanguine, but sophisticated.

"I don't know, Ken," the Doctor corrected equitably. "They're already talking about automated liberal retrieval systems for hospitals... keeping track of patient records, medications, treatments ordered. I'd be interested in something like that!" Just suddenly, however, he looked back at Alex, "What does your father do at ABM?"

Alex inched the remainder of her mashed potatoes toward the edge of the plate. "To tell you the truth, Doctor, I don't really know. He's an accountant in Payroll. It's not this... this highly technical stuff, though... that Barry's always talking about." She smiled at the Doctor and then at Lottie. "You know, he's just an ordinary guy, really." Then added, "Well... to me... of course, he's *extraordinary*, because he's my Dad. But, he's not a Specialist," she concluded cheerfully, uncomfortable with her exposition.

"I'm sure he is," Lottie emphasized. "But speaking of extraordinary, we're anticipating some special events of our own in the near future. Has Barry told you that our Kenny and Maggie are to be married in late April?" Lottie inquired.

At this, Maggie pushed her plate slightly forward and reached for a cigarette. Lighting it, she drawled, "That is if all these tiresome arrangements can be got through. Frankly, the way thing's have been going... Mum's precious little help, I can tell you, Lottie. She fusses about everything, but almost nothing finally gets *decided*," she complained. "Fact is, all I'm *really* sure about... at this point, is that our travel arrangements are more or less in order... But we'd best *be* married by mid-April, Ken, "she repeated, staring across the table through a small cloud of smoke at her prospective spouse, "Else, I can't vouch for our reservation at the *pensione* in Florence."

Ken grinned back at Maggie. "I *mean* it, Ken!" Maggie insisted. "If we can't make Florence by early May... before the heat... the floods of tourists, none of our friends'll be there. Midsummer's for schoolteacher and student... exclusively."

For the first time that evening, Ken turned toward Alex. "As you can see, Maggie's got her heart set on Florence. For our honeymoon. She went to convent school there for two years... as a young teacher, and fell in love with the place.

"But even on honeymoon," Maggie continued, "one simply has to have someone to talk to, for Heaven's Sake. Of course, "She observed, stubbing out her cigarette in a tiny silver shell next to her plate, "whenever one goes – anywhere in Europe, for that matter, it does seem as if one *keeps* meeting the same two or three hundred persons over and over, everywhere. The others must all live in Trenton... or somewhere," she giggled drily, making them all beneficiaries of her drollery.

Maintaining a forbearant tone, Lottie interjected somewhat stiffly, "I assume your parents have already spoken to Archbishop Manning about the Cathedral... and the Warwick for the reception?"

"I suppose they have, Lottie... But Mother gets so excited about every infinitesimal detail... and there are so many of them..."

"I'm sure it will all go smoothly and be a beautiful... memorable affair," Lottie concluded, ringing the bell for dessert.

Sidonia came in bearing a mounded plum pudding, darkly fundamental, smugly ensconced in yet another gleaming silver bowl. Seriously attentive, the Doctor carefully poured a generous libation of brandy over the crouching, encrusted idol, touched a match to it, and stood back slightly, as it blazed into final glory, to the anticipated gasps and unspontaneous wonder of the gathered celebrants.

"One of England's happier contributions to Civilization, the Doctor proclaimed, using a slight Irish brogue to spice his dedication.

ALEX awoke to a jangle of color, a jumble of sound as video images of faces, objects, and words shot, twisted, and pursued each other relentlessly, insistently across the screen. "Another damned seven commercials," she rumbled to herself, sitting upright and reaching for the remote control. She turned down the volume but hesitated turning off her surrealistic companion.

She did not want to be alone with her memories.

Because after Barry and Steve had played and listened to the Ronald Colman records of *The Christmas Carol* – another family tradition, although the Doctor and Ken had stolen out of the family room after the appearance of Christmas Past to inspect the Doctor's new driver and special putter Lottie had given him for Christmas; after this, and two succeeding decades of colorful postcards from Aegean ("Just cruising in and around the islands, with an occasional swim in beautiful, azure waters") – yes, Ken had written "azure" – because Madi had asked what *azure* meant; and another from somewhere deep in the land of Stanley and Livingstone ("In densest Africa," it averred. "Our dependable jeep follows us faithfully on our exciting photographic safari... What wonderful fun!"). And from Machu Picchu, "These Incas must have been *tiny* people... the steps, incredibly narrow, hundreds and hundreds of them, and they running up and down them all day long..." And Australia, "down under," and the Danube ("Remember, Meeester Strauss, Barr...?"), and the U.S.S.R., and the Netherlands, and everywhere else... after all this, and a modest accumulation of perhaps something approaching a million – but, of course, who asked and who counted – it had become unambiguously clear that Ken and Maggie knew how to choose the good life, the correct life box. Steve, practicing Pediatrics, and wife Nancy, lived decorously in Collingsfield, close to the parents, and, while declining to enter into competition with Ken and Maggie as world travelers and established Main Liners, were themselves unquestionably well-and-permanently settled in their own niche, *à la* camper, boat, and van in inviolable secure suburban enclosure.

It would appear, and, a moment's thought confirmed that it had undoubtedly *always* appeared – although no one ostensibly noticed, and certainly, no one in the family ever commented, that Barry and Alex, on the other hand, seemed – well, such "hard luck" cases, always. So deserving, really, such pluggers; highly intelligent; imaginative even, and yet, and yet...

And that very evening while Alex waited for Barry to join her in the music alcove finally, for she was to occupy a guest room upstairs in this very house, and it seemed scarcely appropriate that Barry should join her private chat there – behind closed doors in his parents' house on the very day she had been first introduced to them – as the evening wore on, Lottie quite suddenly appeared, taking her place unobtrusively next to Alex on the piano bench.

Lottie allowed her waxen fingers to search out a few, sweet familiar chords of an Irish song.

"YOU mustn't think things are entirely the way they seem," Lottie mused aloud.

"You know that Charlie's father, Al Byrnes, really was considered to have 'made it' when he was awarded the construction contract for the Saxon and Trumbull buildings in downtown Philadelphia. Then – and for decades after – the two most valuable commercial properties in the City!

"Oh, he was not undeserving," she continued. "Even competent, by the standards of those days. And, passably honest, as things were reckoned the. But – up to his ears – with that Charlie, perhaps too harshly, like to call the 'the pols.'

"That's how all the successful Irish made it then! No other way! Networking, it's called today. No one else to look out for them, you know.

"Anyway, Al Byrnes did well. Built that mansion on the Main Line. But, still, he was always an *arriviste* – nasty word, that! A Catholic, too, of course. Like all of us Irish. But Al Byrnes never forgot, never forgave, all those many people who had tried to hobble him on his way up. You bet not!

"Always made sure his dues were paid up, though- downtown – personal *and* financial.

"So, you see, Charlie's brother Bart... and brother Fred and brother John... showed themselves cut from a more traditional Byrnes' pattern. They're businessmen, politicians, lawyers...

"Father Byrnes was nothing less than livid when Charlie wanted to go to Medical School, instead of putting in with brother Bart!

"Bless him," she chortled, "my Kenny's much more to the Old Man's liking if he could see him now than my Charlie ever was. My Kenny's smack in the middle of the Tradition," she'd reminisced, smiling ruthfully.

BUT whatever Lottie may have experienced privately, Alex recalled, in more than the decade before her untimely death, they had all been expected, cajoled, and, if necessary, gently humiliated into unflinching protocol in their worship of the household gods. Each perceived ritual acknowledge had been exacted with Levitical precision.

"TALK is cheap, Smilin' Damn Villain!" Alex repeated aloud to herself, without venom or conviction, here in this pleasant condominium on this forever mild California evening.

After Lottie's death, Doctor Charles had married a childhood friend, another now-established Main Line dowager, and the preservation of the Byrnes' Irish Catholic upward-thrusting heritage more or less, by default, to and upon Ken and Maggie.

And, most recently, since the Doctor's death a few years ago, the cutting edge of the whole issue had become blunted, even irrelevant. Seemingly, moribund. Or had it merely changed venue? Waiting to appear... suddenly... reliably, in each of them, from the permanently-imprinted mental and emotional circuitry they carried inside themselves?

AS ALEX stacked the few supper plates into the dishwasher and poured herself a substantial brandy, she reminded herself that it was already past midnight, and still no call from Barry. Suddenly transfixed, she stood upright, brandy glass in hand, willing the same intense, silent prayer upon the atmosphere that had been wrung from her uncountable times of late.

Nonsense, she reiterated soundlessly. Making her way toward the bedroom, the more pedestrian realization that the cell-and-tissue vitality of the Byrnes' values – the more submerged but equally hopeful Borys' dreams – should now persist in pristine synonymy or equally precise antimony for an incalculable half-life to come, notwithstanding, offered a modicum or ironic, shopworn comfort and a promise of bargain-basement immortality for herself as well as for Barry.

But what had happened to Alex and Barry... so busy, so loving, so passionate for self-discovery, so yearning for self-transcendence? Sleepwalkers – innocent and unwilling. Were they to become finally merely automatic spokesmen for a sepulchral past?

Chapter Four

ENTERING AND traversing the first of the succession of airport waiting areas, now, near midnight, thinly peopled by the usual assortment of drowsing, disheveled, anonymous occupants, Barry consciously, peremptorily, dismissed the hectoring impulse to call Alex from one of the freestanding phone carrels on his way to baggage claim. He did not wish her to stay awake, or even, to allow herself to doze only fitfully until she should hear his key in the lock – under the injunction of knowing the time of his arrival. This last leg of his journey, he estimated, might well stretch minimally to an hour, or more likely, an hour-and-a-half, depending on his luck in catching an unreserved SuperShuttle ride home.

Having, once more, hauled his luggage off the conveyer belt, presented claim checks to the door attendant, and stepped into the temperate miasma of a Los Angeles October night, he was not altogether unprepared for his by-now habitual onslaught of disorientation, followed by random anxiety, immediate upon his return to the City. Unreal always. The palm trees, improbable; the traffic shrewdly strategic, but continuing homicidal; the same trash-rich streets to be confronted shortly, displaying miles of dusty, tinny, jerrybuilt structures, neon-punctuated, filled him with a unique blend of personal witch's brew upon each homecoming. No matter: he was growing to expect it.

Luckily, in less than ten minutes, the young airport traffic coordinator was able to hail down a Pasadena-bound SuperShuttle carrying only two passengers and, the driver nodding consent, Barry quickly climbed into the empty third-row seats, grateful for his good luck.

Soon, swivel-hipping around buses, airport limos, and the occupied vans of local shuttle competitors, they swept down ramps into Sepulveda. The other two passengers, elderly who had promptly identified themselves to the driver as bound for Mount Washington, immediately resumed their ongoing dialogue.

"... I CAN'T imagine what Joel could have been thinking of when he decided to become a Sikh! Why he's such a... such a... mild, *peaceable* boy – you remember Joel – I've spoken of him often. He's the nephew who came out here to Berkeley for his Masters. Ginger's oldest boy. You remember Ginger, my niece in Philadelphia – practically the only niece I visit regularly, nowadays. She's such a sweet girl! Really, the nicest of my sister Bea's children."

"You should know, Clara, there must have been several *variant* Sikh sects. And who can possibly tell what brand of Sikh-ness... Sikhdom... what have you, they were peddling at Berkeley in the 60's!"

"Oh, I suppose you're right, Belle. I suppose. Still, they're said to be so proud of their warlike heritage. Terrible, really. I had no idea."

"Clara, surely you remember your Kipling..."

"No, I've never Kippled..." Clara tittered, pleased with herself.

BARRY smiled involuntarily, settling himself more deeply into his seat. Clara and Belle's conversation went on to comparisons of their recollections of the names of the five rivers giving Punjab its name. Establishment of the correct nomenclatures called for much precise recall, with many disagreements and corrections along the way, while Barry's attention had already begun to drift to observing and corroborating the familiar order of the exit signs along the Harbor Freeway. But, he had nonetheless concluded before divagating, you had to give the old girls their due. Still as sharp and lively as two sparrows. Courageous, too. All the ways to India and back!

"ALL the way to Pittsburgh, Barry? Alex's Mother had protested. "Why, Dad, and I will never get to see you and Alex. I know you have no real choice... it's your *job*, after all. But it's still not right – it's not *fair* – separating families that way. Companies just think they can to *anything* nowadays! Anything they choose."

"But... it's just a little farther than we are from Thompsonville right now, Ma," Alex was quick to point out. "We'll still get to see you just about as often as we do now."

"And how often is that, for Heaven's sakes? Once a year!" Velma had aimed and hit her target, while the opportunity presented itself.

Alex shrugged, Barry noting the suppressed angry flush beginning to rise above her controlled smile. He could hear her oft-repeated, painfully-charged observation to his in-laws on many previous occasions that each of their "Homes" was equidistant from the other, followed too often by her rueful reminder that she and Barry had made all but one of the annual visitations in the past decade. Instead, he watched her lapse into suffused, stony reserve.

Velma tossed her head barely, as she deftly assembled and began to baste patterned-pinned, paper pieces of a jacket she was crafting for Madi. His mother-in-law was a skillful, almost professional seamstress: wryly, Barry recalled, in their several years of marriage, Alex had declined even an occasional request to sew a button on his shirt.

Meanwhile, from his desk in the corner of the Borys' nondescript basement family room, John Borys lifted his glasses to rest atop his graying head, and allowed himself a long, affectionate, if quizzical, appraisal of the family scene before him.

"Well, Madi, dear, come here and let me see how this fits," Velma was instructing. "Take your sweater off, dear, else I can't get *any* idea of the thing."

"ONCE it's *out*, you know, it's difficult to get the toothpaste back *in* the tube," John Borys commented to the newspaper before him. "Yep, not only *difficult*," he corrected, "but I'd say, well-nigh *impossible*."

John Borys droll, economical, accountant-worthy summary of the situation, Barry recalled – on this no-occasion of more-than-a-year since his father-in-law's death – had passed almost unnoticed. Except that with a few rapid steps, Alex had gained father's chair and followed up with a quick, spontaneous hug to his shoulders, one that nonetheless gave no hint of concession on the former subject of her mother's censure.

THAT'S the way it went. Barry tossed his head slightly, giving up on the exit signs, and attempting to resume his eavesdropping on the ladies' conversation. He willed dismissal of the wave of profound, sad, world-weary irrelevance his father-in-law's death had evoked.

"Still, I thought *that* the most beautiful part of the country. The mountains... the villages, even... didn't you, Clara? So much nicer than some of those dirty, dusty, beggarly and congested southern provinces, for instance," Belle opined, adjusting her broad-brimmed, very-California-*joie-de-vivre*, in-your-face hat, "and the *smells...* my God, the smells," her face puckered in distaste.

NO QUESTION. Even though it may have been in a limited, uncomplex-granted-unsophisticated way, John Borys had always been a peacemaker. Blessed are the Peacemakers, for they shall be called the Children of God. Without warning, Barry felt a deep liquefying warmth rise through his chest.

Though it made him feel ancient – and he was not ancient – not yet, after all - he reassured himself, throughout his entire lie, he could barely remember a half-dozen persons as clean-run as old John. Seemingly, without ulterior motive, without a personal agenda ceaselessly being adjusted to an evolving situation – consciously or unconsciously – focused upon his own personal empowerment. Oh. You could call the others – survival of the fittest, the shrewdest, the most aggressive, the most inventive – but whatever name you gave them, whatever it was they did, hadn't much to do with caring overly for others.

Yet, it was all so damned complicated. He had thought about these matters – hours, months, and years. But he had never felt really comfortable, really convinced by any of the "conclusions" he had finally, if tentatively, arrived at. No matter how painfully honest or scrupulously fair he had tried to be, was still to be, in examining these absolutes, these rock-bottom fundamentals in his life, so as, hopefully, to inch toward some kind of credible, convincing closure about them, patterns of related ideas persisted in shifting upon each reexamination, and even the least readjustments of trivial terms, proliferated bewildering, maddening new arrangements in this unremitting game of philosophical Origami.

TAKE Andy, for example. Was he, in truth, the Shakespearean Machiavel of Alex's conception? That was hard for him to believe. That's not how working with Andy – or against him, even – had *felt* at the time. Then, how *had* it felt?

PAUL Hascomb was a formidable figure – all six-and-a-half feet of him, from his glistening bald rotunda of a skull to his size 13, black, wing-tipped shoes. He turned swiftly from the 18th floor Assurance Building window, overlooking one of Pittsburgh's three rivers, where he had presumably been observing the effects of last night's near-office-closing blizzard.

"Come in, Barry. Come in. Have a seat," he pointed to a tan leather chair stationed before the desk. "You and your wife comfortably settled into your motel suite by now? I trust it's satisfactory."

Barry smiled self-deprecatingly. "It's luxurious, Mr. Hascomb. More than satisfactory."

"Good. Good."

Mr. Hascomb's gaze settled on Barry for a long minute, then moved to a folder before him on the desk, which he opened quickly, unceremoniously, and, in the intervening silence, quietly riffled the first few of its pages. His oversized hand and wrist came to rest on one of the open sheets.

"I'll let Longstreth take care of all the Personnel details," he muttered, making some slight gesture with his free hand. "What I'm interested in... primarily, secondarily, and exclusively... is the efficiency... the productivity... of our total operation. And, as we've come to discover by now, the optimal way to achieve this goal is to make employees stakeholders in the enterprise. Compensation schedules, hiring, promoting, placing, even terminating, employees – all need to be reexamined from *their* strategic perspective. That's where you come in. as Human Resources Coordinator, you'll be closely tied into making all this happen."

Mr. Hascomb's eyes remained riveted on his own hand before him. "I don't mind telling you that the Insurance business is, if nothing else, a labor-intensive one. I also don't mind telling you that my predecessor of some two decades duration had a somewhat different view of how to go about achieving maximum productivity from a varied labor force – coding clerk to underwriter. I might even say – not only different but diametrically opposite to my own. But, to give the Devil his due, those were different times, with different solutions.

"Not to digress too widely," he emended, continuing, "we've certainly come a long way forward since then. He applied what was thought to be smart – even model – practice, in his day. Hired industrial engineers who generated the reorganization of most of our departments – altered everything from floor work arrangements to employee break schedules. But," he emphasized, "as you might well imagine, all generated from the top down." He fixed Barry in unsighted scrutiny. "All legislated by management... and, to be quite blunt, in daily operation, inclined to be not a little autocratic in tone.

"Well, it's an old story by now. After we've had time – couple of decades, in fact – to see how those methods worked themselves out. And, not to put too fine a point on it, we've had the benefit of the example and experience of such countries as Japan as well, where supervisory practice is geared to engendering maximum employee participation. Something we'd never even considered at that time.

"But – again, I digress. Under his Directorship, Personnel turn-over rose. Productivity leveled off. Assembly-line-like boredom and escalating employee absenteeism took their toll and factored into what turned out to be a disappointing final equation."

Mr. Hascomb rose, gravitating once more to the bank of windows behind his desk, but compromising with a stance half-turned toward Barry, half toward the window.

"I think you may be getting the idea by now," he persevered. "Not that I expect you set up the whole Program... I recognize your expertise is primarily a kind of oversight and overview of the whole plan. And that's exactly what I expect will be your *unique* contribution." He raised his hand, bowed slightly, and resumed his seat behind the desk.

"So... the first task on your agenda, as I see it, will be to get with Andy Calhoun, whom we're bringing up from Winston-Salem in the next few weeks – where. I should mention, he's had fair success in putting just such a program in place. But it's necessarily been a homegrown effort. Local stuff, even with Headquarters' approval and blessing. Your job will be to orient him to the Big Picture – the big, *theoretical* picture of a full-fledged Resources strategy. And it'll be *his* job then to interface with Personnel, and they, in turn, to bring on line all the various departments.

"So, to recapitulate, *your* job will be keeping everyone on track, including the Human Resources Manager. *And*, perhaps most important, taking charge of collecting, organizing, and analyzing the data generated from accountability studies and surveys, seeing what, if anything, you can make of it. To give us, ultimately, the *Big Answer* – overtime, of course, probably to be measured in years: 'Does the System Work? Is the Human Resources as currently envisioned – a viable, useable, worthwhile method of organizing our labor force?'"

Paul Hascomb looked over at him then – searchingly, seriously, without levity. "You think you're up to it?"

Barry was somewhat mindful of the scope, but not the full implications or responsibilities Mr. Hascomb's explanation and rhetoric portended for the job. He knew intuitively, and from the past experience, that these could not be known anyway, not until he himself had plunged into the pool and begun swimming, as it were. He had sat through many another initiating monologue, Human Resources methods notwithstanding, where he had assumed the composed role of the fresh-eyed novice-expert, and where a similar phoenix-like pep talk had been pitched at him. He responded now with a smile as guileless as he could manage and geared the tone of his voice somewhere between decent modesty and mature self-confidence. "I believe I can, Mr. Hascomb. You can certainly be assured of my *best* effort.

AFTER a few additional ceremonial niceties by way of protocol, he had finally been discharged into the care of the Personnel Manager Jim Longstreth, who would now undoubtedly begin sorting out the real grit and sweat of the task at hand.

"This Andy Calhoun," Barry spoke to Jim, as they strode toward the 10th floor Conference Room some three weeks later, Andy having "come on board" and been accorded a week for moving into his office and arranging an over-all situation and schedule to his own satisfaction before a general orientation meeting should be called. "You know him? Been with the Company a long time?"

At this juncture, Barry himself had formed no firm estimate of the man who, according to Hascomb, was to be his closest associate in this effort. Two days after Andy had occupied his office, Barry had stopped in briefly to introduce himself and establish some speaking contact. Andy had appeared preoccupied, and not particularly pleased at this mannerly interruption: at least, it was Andy's general busyness that

Barry told himself was the simple, ostensible reason for his fairly chilly equanimity and what might be considered laconic brusqueness. One thing, Barry jibed at himself; this was no robust glad-hander or superficial PR mouthpiece.

He could see that Calhoun's name had registered with Longstreth from the barely perceptible tightening around Jim's eyes, but Jim continued walking along for several minutes before acknowledging having heard the question.

"I guess it's natural you should ask," Jim finally responded; they turned into another corridor. "As a matter of fact, a couple of our managers have worked with him rather closely. Before they were transferred up here to Headquarters location. You *did* know they brought Andy Calhoun up from the Winston-Salem plant?"

"Yes – as Human Resources Manager," Barry added.

Reaching the Conference Room, Barry filled in, with a grin, "Just to keep things straight. My moniker is Human Resources *Coordinator*."

Jim opened the door to the Conference Room and waved Barry in. "Yes, by all means, we must keep things tidy and straight," Jim chuckled in the same spirit of camaraderie.

HE HAD considered he had done a prudent job in outlining the goals for the whole effort, indicating some of the immediate data that would be necessary in the short term, so as to establish an accurate baseline upon which to build, but without detailing the intimidating mass of information he knew would eventually be required. His presentation of methods and strategies for setting up employee problem-solving committees and garnering first-time employee feedback had been, in his own estimate, fairly deft – properly enthusiastic yet practically helpful.

They would have to commence by producing exhaustive wage and salary schedules – Max Petry's, their Wage and Salary Coordinator's, daunting task – and unavoidable. Then, Wage and Salary Coordinator Petry would be asked to set up the committees for real employee input, this translating into extensive meetings with Hank Schuler, Personnel Manager in charge of Hourlies and Ted Mansfield, Manager in charge of Salaried Employees, as well as many other Department Supervisors. Their mutual final product would amount to a fresh summary of educational levels, requisite skills – even personality qualities – necessary and desirable for each performances-level job or salaried position. Schedules for monitoring and tracking turnovers, absenteeism, worker autonomy, and a host of related matters would follow. But all in good time. Most importantly, he knew one had to allow time for the people to adjust to new relationships – both Managers and employees. The biggest enemy of quality of work-life programs in his experience had been impatience for quick, measurable results.

So, having done his half-hour *shtick*, he had gone on to introduce Andy to the group in a relaxed, assured, and, as he now recalled dourly, completely unsuspecting manner.

Before addressing the group, before he had spoken a single word, Andy had distributed a voluminous, if attractively packaged, prospectus of directives to each attendee for use in creating accountability guidelines for his specific area of assignment. After a brief explanation of this handout, he had asked for deadlines to be set by each Manager for submission of these guidelines, dates to be reported to his secretary by the end of the week. Following this business, he had finally begun his formal address to the troops, heavy with suggestions that sounded like cautionary injunctions: top management must set a role model and demand that subordinates also set role model and demand that subordinates also set role models; middle management involvement was crucial from the earliest stages on; just asking for occasional reports form supervisory personnel and considering this sufficient involvement was bound to result in failure; and finally, in no way, could the program be used simply as a surrogate for increasing productivity. He concluded with an announcement of an upcoming week-long Quality Circle Workshop under the entire Personnel Management staff as well as supervisors from a number of key Departments had been enrolled – the purpose of which was to broaden perspectives on various labor problems and identify and strengthen personal skills upon which the success of any such program would ultimately depend.

Upon termination of the talk, Barry's gaze swept across the faces and physiques of his newly acquired colleagues, and it was clear to him that, though the preacher had managed to sing a song of perfect humane orthodoxy – utilizing all the right words, he had totally botched the tune. The meeting over, to a man, the staff rose and chatted amongst themselves nervously, laughing rarely and overloud and avoiding any glance, let alone physical approach, to their demanding new mentor.

Except for himself. He had strolled up and engaged Andy in a studiously informal conversation, trying the while to glide him toward one of the clusters of conversing managers. But Andy, having a first made only a few distracted responses, ceased speaking altogether as he continued packing up his materials, and suddenly nodding to his secretary, exited the Conference Room abruptly.

Week after week, month after month, while standards and schedules of accountability were dutifully crafted and submitted, along with bulky reams of underlying data substantiating the claims forecast in these documents, relationship between the staff of the Personnel Department and the Human Resources Manager became visibly more constrained. By the end of Andy's first year, Barry remembered, whenever the Human Resources Manager entered the Conference Room, a kind of prison attentiveness stiffened all backs, casual chat stopped, and all levity was squelched. Contrast in staff attitude before and after Andy's entrance became so marked, in fact, that it bordered on a joke – a sick one, at that.

But to Barry, this was no laughing matter! While data was made to flow into and through his own computerized systems, he had tried, now and again, gently but unsuccessfully, to turn matters around. To suggest to Andy that they move more slowly. That quantification of especially difficult, complexly-evaluative subjective materials should be put to further and repeated staff and employee review for fresh input. Mostly, he tried to suggest smaller, less ambitious correlations: the effect, for example, of a particular employee training program on job attitude. The positive result of offering overtime to employees instead of bringing in extra hires. In other words, specific, affirmative measures that employees themselves had already enthusiastically proposed, and that might help start the ball rolling toward their broader participation in the over-all process.

After two or three years into the program, his own research had continued to reveal pitifully puny results, only the most hesitant advances toward the major espoused goals of the program. Frankly, insignificant.

In the quarterly meetings amongst Andy, Hascomb, and himself, Hascomb had remained tolerant, maintaining sanguine support, still charmed, it appeared, by Andy's ingenious explanations of methodology. Barry himself tried to avoid any candid admission that, for him, it was proving a disappointing effort.

BUT, as he had finally come to appreciate, as he had not appreciated in his greener years, crises generally heaved themselves at you from a place you were not watching, and at a time you did not expect. Certainly, from the beginning, Andy had found dealing with Felicia Whitcomb, at the least, uncomfortable. Felicia was a late fortyish, hardworking, surprisingly-attractive-but-nonetheless-unmarried blonde, thoroughly amicable and accommodating writer-editor of the Company Newsletter. Highly intelligent, even surreptitiously cultivated, this Radcliffe and Northwestern alumna had continued to pour her entire soul and self into her job. Why this was so was not readily discernible: for Barry, it remained one of those mysteries that one simply accepted.

But for Andy, the problem of Felicia rankled like a tiny pebble in the brain. Despite their innumerable meetings and painstakingly refinements of terms and methods, the excruciating and exhausting "discussions" on drafting guidelines, these two could not arrive at mutually satisfactory, conclusive, quantitative standards of accountability for Felicia's over-all Communications function. Not ones translatable into useable, statistical data.

Their impasse had, in fact, become something of a Department cliché – a persistent, mild embarrassment everyone pretended not to notice.

THE van climbed a precipitous two-lane road barely cut into the side of the mountain.

"You'd better let Belle off first," Clara was saying. "She lives at the very top of the mountain. There's a *cul de sac* right behind her house where you can turn the van around. Then you can let me off about halfway down the other side. My house doesn't even have a driveway!"

"I thought you ladies lived together," the driver remarked involuntarily.

"Heavens no," Belle quipped. "We're both much too independent for that!"

The driver made his turn in the *cul de sac*, Barry noting the rear wheels of the van only inches away from the cliff-like drop behind them. As the driver unloaded Belle's bags and carried them to her door,

Barry decided that picturesque as Mount Washington might be, it was not something he would wish to take as part of his daily commute.

The van resuming its descent, Barry could not help observing aloud to Clara, "Boy, this is *steep*. I don't mind telling you; I find it a bit scary..."

"Well, so do I!" Clara snorted. "When Belle drives us down every morning, I keep my eyes tight shut all the way."

A few minutes later, they deposited Clara and her luggage at her door and, amidst much cheerful fuss, said their good-bye's. Momentarily, Barry regretted the departure of his two animated, talkative fellow passengers. As the vehicle continued its descent, Barry reviewed the route from this locale to his own condominium with the driver once again.

WALKING into Jim's office, he was immediately aware of something out of joint. Jim set his pipe into its oft-admired Delft holder deliberately, and turned swivel chair all the way around, to face Barry full-front.

"Well, he's done it this time. The SOB really ripped it good!" From a five-year acquaintance with him, Barry knew that Jim never used profanity... not even in initiated or abbreviated form. So this was going to be something serious.

"Felicia, Andy, and I met this morning to go over her annual Performance Reviews with her. Both mine and his, I went first, he followed – as he is now ranking supervisor. You can imagine – I almost fell off my chair when he announced after a deal of high-level BS that he was recommending her for a six-months Probation! Then, right after the meeting, he didn't waste a minute running off and delivering both reviews to Hascomb!"

Barry sat silent for several minutes, watching Jim poke at the contents of his pipe bowl, preparatory to the subtle fuss of relighting it.

"Can't you do anything about it? Technically, you are still her *immediate* superior," Barry asked quietly.

"But he's *ranking* one. Of course, I'll do all I can. But you know Communications has always been a maverick. When Andy signed on, Felicia's function was shifted to his bailiwick, and most of the oversight has been his."

"Do what you can, Jim," Barry'd repeated.

"It's those damned Accountability guidelines. She's twisted every which way to get something definite down on paper..." Jim said, rising from his chair and starting to pace the width of the room. "It's ridiculous: she's won all kinds of awards for the Newsletter over the years!"

"Do what you can, Jim," Barry muttered again, letting himself out of the office. Steps away from Jim's door, Barry stopped and stood still in the empty hallways for more than a minute. He had been on his way to Felicia's area but now turned back toward his own office for a quiet think instead.

NEW methodologies notwithstanding, management protocol dictated that one never neglected to observe the Chain of Command in bringing attention to one's particular concerns. Thus, by the end of the following week, Jim had composed a well-crafted, decorous Memorandum to his immediate supervisor, Andrew Calhoun, Human Resources Manager, re: Felicia Whitcom, Communication Director, in which he summarized her nine-years' Performance ratings at this site, her present professional activities, and concluded with a projected assessment of the potential deleterious effect submission of a Probationary Notice to her Personnel dossier might well exert on her ongoing career with the Company. He, therefore, requested another meeting – Andy, Barry, and himself attending – at Andy's convenience, to be set up to reevaluate taking this significant step.

Before sending off this potentially incendiary communication, Jim had carried it to Barry's office and waited for him to read and respond to it. Barry had done more than that. Wordlessly, he had taken out his pen and footnoted the Memo with a few handwritten sentences of personal observation: he called attention to the employees' consistent positive reaction to the Newsletter and their broadly held estimate of its Editors' unfailing accuracy and even-handedness in presenting their issues.

Both Jim and Barry had signed.

Two biweekly Department meetings and a month of workdays passed: no response from Andy.

IN THE week following that interval, Jim crafted a short but courteous follow-up Memo to Andy, reminding him that they had yet to resolve the matter of the Probation Notice for Felicia's dossier. He allowed Barry the note, but this time Jim was the only signer.

A month later, Barry attended the regular quarterly meeting with Hascomb and Andy, where they reviewed current matters, but at which no mention was made of Felicia or her job situation. However, Hascomb had lingered until Andy left. Taking his cue from Hascomb, Barry also delayed his departure.

"BARRY, I'll be frank with you. I don't like this friction over that Whitcomb person. Get it cleared up. From what Andy has told me... *and* shown me, it's eating away at Personnel Department morale. You're the Coordinator. Talk to Jim. Tell him to drop that argument over the Probation, and get that woman to cooperate."

"Paul, it's not that simple. It's just about impossible to submit measurable accountability guidelines for something as subjective as changes in attitude or action as a response to reading a newspaper! I'm sure you can appreciate that."

"Figure something out. Polls. Something. I'm sure it's been done before. Has to have been."

"She's really tried, Paul. And she's good at her job."

"Trying is for children. Adults *succeed*."

NOW Jim became adamant and would not budge on the issue of Felicia's Probation. Neither Andy nor Jim brought up the subject in their joint meetings. At the end of the six months, Felicia's probationary period was extended for another six months. Three months hence, she was offered a Communication position at their Tampa, Florida location.

During the weeks in which Felicia's decision about Tampa was pending, Barry had been notified to touch base with Alcon at its home location in its Washington suburb. A meeting had been scheduled with Mr. Lindquist. It opened with Lindquist's enthusiastic review of a new Chinese Language Program being set up at Fort Horton, and only subsequently, tactfully, was Barry informed of Hascomb's decision: at this time, Andrew Calhoun was considered ready to assume complete responsibility for the Human Resources Program at Pittsburgh, Barry having, of course, "given the Program legs and taught it to walk." A liaison statistician would continue to visit the site periodically to aid in collecting relevant data. But, it was felt, no full-time Manager from Alcon was currently needed on this site. Mr. Lindquist noted in summary that, at any rate, most Assurance data could be crunched right here at Headquarters by their own experts. Barry would begin the Fort Horton assignment in six weeks.

ONE of the things Barry had always loved about Alex was her self-sufficiency. Like a wonderful precocious kid, really. She had just served up some difficult, delicious casserole for dinner, after a brain-draining day at work, and now she was reading and annotating Hofstadter, or somebody equally opaque, with the rigor of a graduate student preparing for an exam. This evening, however, abstemious as he usually preferred to be, he slipped into the kitchen after dinner and poured both of them a double-bourbon nightcap.

"Alex?"

Alex put down her book. He handed her one of the drinks and sat down in his favorite armchair, facing the sofa.

"What's the matter, Barry?"

"But I am, after all, a Psychologist. *Too*." He guffawed so loudly, spastically, a little of his bourbon dribbled onto his sneaker.

"But, tonight, bear with me. I *do* want to talk theory. OK?"

Alex continued to look at him.

"Now, Alex. I want to tell you, I *do* want to tell you... there is a difference, a difference in the *Progress* of understanding – and the *Exercise* of understanding at any given stage of development. See...

Progress in understanding depends on... creation of *new codes* by, well, empirical induction, refinements of abstraction and discrimination, new associations, bi-sociations. You remember all that stuff from Psych 201 from Corinth. Intellectual house-building. What I'm calling 'vertical' construction. Basically, how we think.

"But the *Exercise* of understanding, that's different. That means being sensitive enough to subsume particular events, you understand, *particular*, highly personal events, specific, individual events, under many codes at once, conscious, and unconscious. Not only codes of past experience, but codes that are inbuilt and unconscious – like dreams, for example; or codes that are just in the process of formation; or codes that are embedded and not readily available to our conscious perception; or codes that have become rigidified from conditioning and upon which we force our experience as on a Procrustean bed; even codes that eventuate from the very structure of the language and thought itself, et cetera, et cetera. So that, at any one time, maybe a given individual can verbalize that X is a particular variant of T; and he can verbalize that X is an instance of R, also; but he may simultaneously act on an insight that X is also an instance of G, which, however, he *can't* verbalize yet, and it may also occur to him as a kind quiet 'lights on' experience that X and Y also have something mysterious in common, but he doesn't quite 'get' it yet. You still with me?"

"I'm not sure, Barry. Keep going."

"So-o-o, hey, this is what's important, Al. So, the *Exercise* of understanding *means* that in this particular instance, we are acting on a multitude of relevant relational features which are instances of more general, universal relations, some of which we have previously conveniently abstracted and encoded, but some of which are unconscious, and some only half-perceived. The *Exercise* of understanding, in other words, is not just a clean-cut, total, verbally-expressible, 'vertical' matter."

"Barry..."

"You're being stubborn, Alex. You just don't *want* to understand. Giving a verbal explanation of something – like on an exam – in no way reveals the degree or scope of this more important and *comprehensive* understanding. In fact, there are persons who go on building Towers of Abstraction... Towers of Babel... indefinitely, but have a very thin 'connectedness' for their understanding of individual life experiences.

"We know this from personal experience and observation. How often have you heard someone say that while their Physics professor friend may have a thorough theoretical, or 'vertical' understanding, they'd just lief have their own mechanic fix their carburetor? Or a good, old reliable nanny take care of Junior, rather than some University-credentialed Child Psychologist? And they're right! They're Right, Alex. Because truly useable understanding isn't just 'vertical'... to be judged by 'absolute height.' What we're really seeking is that richness of connectedness underlying and inspiriting behavior – conscious or unconscious – allowing persons to act from a fullness of being. That's the real *Exercise* of understanding."

"Barry, it's beautiful. And impassioned. But haven't you stacked the deck? Are you telling me that Progress hasn't ultimately always depended on development of purely theoretical knowledge? Knowledge that is then applied over time in any number of practical ways? Because, if you are, I'm telling you, you're full of crap, darling."

"But I'm telling *you*, Alex, that until this kind of knowledge is achieved, becomes a part of our mother reflexes, our hands and feet, our viscera, and yeah... yeah," he semi-shouted, moving toward the kitchen and laying hands on the bottle of bourbon, "until the, it's pretty *thin* gruel."

Alex stood in the kitchen doorjamb.

"You know something, Barry? I don't know what we're talking about! And honestly, sometimes, sometimes, I wonder why you didn't major in Philosophy, rather than statistics. I even sometimes suspect you being... Oh, forget it..."

Barry returned to his chair, followed by Alex, who resumed her seat on the sofa. He placed his drink carefully on the carpet next to his feet.

"You can stop shouting now, Alex. I'm sitting right here, I know I might have left something out, that my explanation may suffer a little from lack of... well, coherence... but I'm serious. I'm serious." He took in a mouthful of bourbon. "That son-of-a-bitch was building Castles in the Air, and we're going to Los Angeles!"

"Oh, Barry..." Alex moaned.

They sat in silence for several minutes.

"Not 'we', Barry. I told you. I won't permit Madi to be taken out of her high school in her Senior Year."

"I know. I know. I agree. But, *eventually*, dear Madi's going on to College, and that Bastard is still responsible for our having to move."

"Why make excuses for him, then?" Alex stood up and strode toward the kitchen. There was considerable banging of cupboard doors. "Why do you always have to be such a Nice Guy! I *hate* Nice Guys. I've listened long enough to his sadistic game-playing with Felicia, his cute power-plays against you, and you and Jim. Calhoun's a brute a bully! Plain and simple. And that's that."

Barry met her at the kitchen door again, and they both walked back into the living room. "But that's what I'm telling you. He isn't. He's a kind of intellectual monster – a Dr. Mengele, A Frankenstein of Human Resources."

"nonsense."

"He's *so* smart, Alex, he has no idea what he's going, "Barry repeated, following her.

They both reseated themselves on the couch, next to each other. Each stared at the full stone wall before them, at the fireplace they had both so much admired in their Pittsburgh Foxglove Street house.

"You know, Alex. Before... like in College. Even at the University... even as late as first coming to Pittsburgh... you know, I always kind of thought I was running my own life. Oh, I didn't sit around thinking consciously, 'I am the Master of My Fate / I am the Captain of my Soul.' But I assume. It acted on it. I'm not so sure anymore. And it frightens me."

"And before Andrea left LU..." Alex murmured.

"Yeah... that, too..."

Alex stood up again, began turning off the lights.

"You know, Bar, maybe that's what the kids when they mean when they say "Keep the Faith, Baby.'"

"Yeah, maybe. But that's going to require something I don't know if I've got."

"What's that, Barry?"

"Courage. Simple, raw Courage."

THE van passed the Park at the foot of Mariana. It was a pretty spread of grass and trees with 1920's-vintage camp-style cabins in gaily painted colors with deep overhanging bungalow-style roofs and wrap-around porches set here and there amongst the trees – probably for storing lawn-tending and gardening equipment for City employees.

"It's straight up the hill. Just keep going right up, crest the hill, and, as you're just coming down the other side, you'll see it. Hayward Terrace. Two white stucco buildings with bright blue roofs, facing each other."

"OK, Mr. Byrnes... I'll be on the alert."

The driver swung into the correct parking area without hesitation and had Barry's luggage out of the van before Barry himself had climbed out. Barry paid and tipped and was putting away his wallet when the driver waved at him through the open window of the departing van.

SHE had left the hall light on in the condominium, but he decided to check the master bedroom before toting his luggage in from the living room.

The night light was on in the bedroom, Alex sound asleep, her face averted, her hands tucked firmly under his unused pillow. Several photo-albums were stacked neatly on his side of the bed, a half-dozen portrait-size studies of Lu, Madi, Lucille, John, and others, barely perceptible, fanned over the top.

Treading as lightly as possible, he left the master bedroom doorway, retrieved his overnighter from the living room floor, and tiptoed to the bedroom-study adjacent to the master bedroom. Soundlessly, he started undressing for bed.

AS HE snuggled under the quilt of the fairly uncomfortable twin-sized couch-bed, he felt the pressure of Jim's final handshake after lunch, the day he had come home early to pack for his trip to Washington.

At lunch, Jim had said, reluctantly, uncharacteristically embarrassed, "I should have been more up-front right from the beginning. You know, I am, usually. At the time, I don't know; I didn't think it was fair." His laugh was almost bitter.

"But, I knew Ted had worked hard to get a transfer to Pittsburgh – after coming head-to-head with Andy down at Winston-Salem. And just before you came, Bob Mitchell, whom we had down here on a trial basis – for him and us – as possible new OSHA Manager, was here when the news of Andy's transfer was first being considered. He had been on the brink of accepting the position with us – been here a couple of months already, had even by then interviewed a real estate agent, and had just arranged for his wife to visit for a final decision on a house, when, quite suddenly, he asked to be taken out of consideration and returned to his former position in Cleveland, if it was still open. It was, and he did, that was only days after he learned for certain that we were going to bring Andy Calhoun up from North Carolina. Of course, Bob himself never *said* anything, but, getting his dossier ready for return to Cleveland, I noticed that some six years previous, *he* had been located at Winston-Salem." Jim had unconsciously crumbled an end roll between his fingertips as he spoke.

"I finally asked him. He was cautious, said the move was turning out to pose complications for his family that he had not, at first, anticipated. But I knew, and he knew I knew, and we left it at that. I don't know if it would have made any difference to you... probably now."

"Hey, Jim, it's OK."

"Yeah. I guess it has to be," Jim had concluded dispiritedly.

After lunch, they had shook hands, and that was the last Barry had seen him.

HE TURNED his face to the wall, away from the single window, through which though which, though0 draped, the outside floodlights on the hillside penetrated. In the near distance followed the failing cadence of the plaintive night song of a mourning dice unconsciousness.

Chapter Five

O NLY SINCE Lu's death had the "best" family photo album become a permanent occupant of the lower of two drawers in Alex's fine Borys' hand-me-down mahogany night table next to their bed. Still, she refused to think of it there: like the brandy nightcaps, or the sleeping pills, she knew this had become a kind of crutch, a ready emotional gimmick whereby the tears could be made to flow, and the dreary return visit to the ideality of a highly reconstructed fictive past initiated spontaneously.

But even perusing the images in the album could not always serve as a successful mantra. Nor could entering into the pictured scenes be made an ever-made Alice's looking glass: mourning for Margaret frequently diverted along the way, too often of late replaced by hot rising pillars of anvil-headed anger.

She had opened now desultory to facing, rigid pages of snapshots taken by Carruthers, Jean Carruthers' husband. Jean, as Head of New Colony High School's English Department, had assumed responsibility for making the lengthy, heavily discussed, elaborate arrangements for Alex's farewell party, this terminal celebration having been held at the Carruthers' home with principal, three vice-principals, and the entire English Department attending. This intricately strategized fete had assumed suitably memorable proportions in the school's annual social calendar in the year of the Byrnes' move to Pittsburgh, Jean Carruthers generally touted as not only a wonderful friend and colleague but an incomparable hostess and gourmet cook. As Alex inspected the familiar faces in the pictures before her – of the 70 or more "shots," two of herself only, both in company with someone else – a complicated tangle of resentment, irony, pride, and confusion stirred reflexively. As she turned the pages, submerged as these images were in oceanic memory, not a single perceptible strand of rational thought managed to float into sunlit understanding.

SHE had felt so lucky, so "set up," passing through the gauntlet of application letters and interviews to win a teaching at New Colony's reputably excellent high school. It was all working out so well: Barry comfortably ensconced in the Testing department at the University downtown Lu well placed in a carefully chosen nursery school nearby. Those had been bright, halcyon days of career plans dedication and a promising coherent future.

Four years later, when she and Barry had decided to have a second child, and Barry was now employed by Alcon as a consultant at Aberdeen, she herself had resigned for the time being to tunes of glory and high praise for her as Chairman of the English Department in the new high school. Her glowing record of achievement with the Advanced Placement program, everyone assured her, had been daily recorded in her personnel file and only awaited future ready reference.

But despite all this, when Madi, in turn, had been enrolled in nursery school and Alex had reapplied for a renewal of her teaching position, present events failed to duplicate the past. Mr. Grimes, the new principal at New Colony, was kind enough and had agreed finally to take her on, but she felt immediately the absence of her old friend and principal, Dr. Schultz, with his Old-World enthusiasm and deep respect for learning. Mr. Grimes affable baritone sonorities fell colorless compared to the Doctor's droll Pennsylvania Dutch aphorisms and observations. And his generous, compassionate heart.

That first year back in the late '60s, the highlight of the day had soon become her 10th grade Advanced Placement class, unfortunately, the very last class before daily dismissal. Though there were "hippies" and "flakes" aplenty amongst this brood, they were still recognizably familiar, enthusiastic, teachable kids, the kind she'd always known and loved. But, her other classes, virtually all, remedial to average, had apparently embarked upon new kind of scholastic guerrilla warfare, with the teacher invariably cast as tormentor-mentor.

Why had it taken her so many months to recognize this state of affairs to begin to comprehend, if not to understand, the depth and inexorability of the students' seemingly inassuagable hostility?

FIFTH period was always something of a nightmare: one of those "split" classes: half a class before lunch, half after. These eleventh graders, although fairly bright, were always having to be cajoled, diverted, or reined in. Twice. Once before lunch, then again, after.

Yesterday, they had poured over Shelly's "Ode to the West Wind" and contributed for class consideration some tolerably thoughtful individual comments about the poem's intent: Today might mark two days of reprieve from their settled resentment: a record. The day was lovely: lacy upper branches of a towering beech in the schoolyard clearly visible through the open second-floor school windows. Distant traffic noises blended pleasingly with occasional vibrant bird calls in the nearer distance: and amidst this happy ambience they had read aloud Keats "Ode on a Grecian Urn," had struggled – not unhappily – toward something resembling the inner core of the poem, when, noticing they were now only five minutes before the lunch bell she called on Sylvia to read again the poem's final stanza before they should leave.

> *O Attic shape! Fair attitude1 with brede*
> > *Of marble men and maidens overwrought,*
> *With forest branches and the trodden weed;*
> > *Thou, silent form, dost tease us out of thought*
> *As doth eternity: Cold Pastoral!*
> > *When old age shall this generation waste,*
> *Thou shalt remain, in midst of other woe*
> > *Than ours, a friend to man, to whom thou say'st*
> *"Beauty is truth,..."*

A flying missive, an indistinguishable scrotum-like object flew inches before Alex's face and plopped moistly just aside her desk. The force of the impact opened the hastily twisted-shut baggie and a large, brown turd rolled to the center of the clear space at the front of the room.

For seconds, the class was transfixed in breath-held curiosity: then someone toward the back of the room snickered, another close to the window hooted, and the class conflagrated into screaming, derisive pandemonium. The bell sent a final electric charge the hysteria, as Alex stood back against the blackboard, silent, until individual students, pushing and shoving, catapulted past her desk and out the door.

HALF an hour was assigned for lunch. Of the actual twenty minutes remaining, after using the restroom and walking the three city block distance to the cafeteria, today, Alex chose to hide in a corner of the Faculty Lounge, cuddling a cup of coffee. She did not even try to sort out the complexities in the situation. She was simply trying to nerve herself to move toward her classroom at the sounding of the end-of-lunch bell and get through the day.

BUT there were to be no end-of-the-period jitters to contend with. By the time the janitor had removed the entire doorknob assembly of Room 206 – a key had first been broken off in the lock and then the lock stuffed with gummy plastic material – the period was mercifully at an end.

THE usually graceful even fastidious, Amy Pearson, allowed her petite self to drop unceremoniously into one of the shabby, vinyl-covered Faculty Lounge leatherette easy chairs. She smiled ruefully at her fellow English teachers, Jean Carruthers, betty Carson and Alex, all busily grading themes, ranged before her on the matching battered vinyl sofa. Now veteran pedagogues in these early '70's, they had all become more-or-less adept survivors in the daily student-teacher trench warfare of Vietnam protest, race riots, and drug addiction.

"So, what new and interesting are you doing in your Senior Advanced Placement class now, Alex?" Amy probed. As former long-standing head of their Department, now "bumped up" to Main Street as Chief Administrator of a new Humanities Curriculum, Amy nonetheless kept her hand in by retaining a few English classes at the High School. Her daily midmorning classes over, she often stayed to lunch with her former confreres, listening to their most pressing woes, meanwhile keeping tabs on a miscellany of curriculum matters that helped her assess the viability of the high school English program. Years ago, she had been stalwart in her recommendation of Alex for Chair of the English Department at the new high school, and Alex considered her not only an unimpeachable professional but a good and honest friend.

"well, it may be a strange idea... but we're rewriting Dmitri's trial scene from *The Brothers Karamazov*, and we're going to present it as a mini-drama in class as a kind of coup... climax... to our unit on the Novel. Then, we'll conclude with general class discussion as to the appropriateness of the prosecutors' final verdict. Everyone will be involved in some way." Alex looked 'round at her fellow teachers. "That'll take us nicely right up to the introduction to the Drama unit, too," she added.

"For Christ's sake," Betty remarked ruminatively, "For Christ's sake," she repeated under her breath, smiling. For more than a dozen years, Betty had maintained a proud record of traditionalism in her teaching of Nineteenth-Century English Literature, and such scapegrace carryings-on, though delightfully startling, left her unconvinced. Altogether, Betty's Junior year "solid" teaching of mainline English literature to all students, including and especially Advanced Placement, had been a matter beyond question for more than a decade.

"Whatever gave you *that* idea?" Jean asked tentatively after a considerable pause. She gathered up her themes into a buttery buff leather briefcase, as Christmas present from John, accompanied by a hummingbird-quick glance in Amy's direction, unnoticed by the others. "It's certainly," she considered, "well, it's certainly *unusual*, to say the least."

"I don't know," Alex admitted. "I'm always trying to discover a better way to teach this... this *structural* approach to genre... I've built the whole year's Senior program around it, as a matter of fact." She looked open-eyed at all her fellow instructors. "What I had hoped to achieve is something like a thoughtful, almost, you might say – organic – way of viewing the evolution of different literary forms. I wanted to avoid just handling students another poem or novel to read, discussing the work, and then filling in with biographical and historical data. Instead, I thought it would be a refreshing experiment to put the student in a more active position, that of the writer, as it were, seeing *his* narrative goals... and problems... and how he... given his historical context, of course, went about creating, constructing his work of art. How he actually came to craft it as he did," she hypothecated, speaking as much to herself as to her auditors. "In the novel unit, for example, we've studied the evolution of the long narrative, from the epic to the romance, to the

perplexing variety of modern forms, from the inside out, so to speak...
Anyway, recasting the trial from a narrative to a dramatic form was
meant to provide insight into both the benefits... and limitations... of
each method. Besides, it's just fun," Alex admitted, grinning.

"I don't know," Jean said. "Sounds to me..." she shrugged, looking
skeptical, but willing to forebearant. "Seriously," she added, looking
directly at Amy, "it seemed to leave out too much that's important. I
always conduct a thorough review of theme, characterization... all
the fundamental aspects of the novel in any study. I don't see how..."

THE north side of the Faculty Lounge, sharing a common wall
with the Cafeteria, suddenly shook with an explosive tremor. Everyone
in the room looked up, and momentarily, no one moved. In seconds,
however, Alex rushed to the door, Amy directly behind her.

On their left, down the hall, Mr. Grimes lurched from his office
across the corridor toward the Cafeteria double-door entryway
pursued by Sandy Zeilander's yells. With one outstretched arm, the
student president held open the door to the Principal's office while
with the other, she waved a packet of papers frantically in the air.

"You Mother-fucking Grimes, you bastard, you deceived us again,"
she shrieked. "Do you hear me? You tricked us into this meeting
blackmailed us out of our rights, and now you're trying to run away,"
she roared so that she could be heard throughout the whole first floor.
"You Mother-fuckin' bastard, you fuckin' coward," she gasped finally,
going limp, her body plopping heavily against the wall and slowly
slithering into a seated position on the floor.

By this time, Amy and Alex stood in the Cafeteria entryway;
Garbage cans, food, milk containers, metal pop cans, plates, and
silverware flew willy-nilly through the air. Somewhere toward the
center of the room, around the focal point of the hubbub, a tight band
of interlocked student bodies formed a human wall behind which an
unmistakable sound of flesh impacting flesh could be heard.

Suddenly, diminutive Mr. Blodgett, eldest member of their English
faculty, was leading each of them by an elbow firmly and not too
decorously, back toward the Faculty Lounge.

"What's the matter with you two ladies?" he said. "Don't use the
sense you were born with!" opening the door to the Lounge; he pushed

them inside. "Now, for God's sake, don't leave. For any reason," he said, slamming the door shut.

Dazed, they made their way back to the seats they had just vacated. Jean sat mesmerized and erect; Betty stared ahead with a sad, thoughtful expression. The room was full of teachers; most of them men, Alex noted automatically, involuntarily. Not one of them moved or looked as if he was about to move. Hardly anyone spoke.

Police sirens could now be heard approaching, then ceasing. A heavy rush of feet in the vicinity of the hall, Cafeteria, and back-court sanitation service area. Scuffling, a few shouts, and then, gradually, quiet.

The intercom buzzed, then crackled. The voice of Mr. Barnes, Second Assistant Principal, sounded: "We regret the disturbance we have all unfortunately just sustained. We are sorry to report further that outside agitators have just been apprehended in the building and on the grounds of our campus and have been taken into custody for further questioning by the New Colony Police. While such incidents are regrettable, rest assured that everything is now under control. Repeat: Everything is now under control.

"Students are advised to proceed with their normal schedule changing to Sixth-period class at the next bell. Each of the remaining two afternoon periods will be shortened by fifteen minutes, allowing for normal dismissal time at 2:45 p.m."

Another crackle, a shrill beep, and silence.

In hushed voices, everyone began talking at once.

HENRY Blodgett entered the Lounge, looked around, and strode directly toward the nodule of familiar English faculty.

"They just took Grimes off in an ambulance," he reported. "He caught a garbage can right on the side of the head... I guess they want to test for concussion. The police are saying that a group of student activist agitators from Wilmington... maybe, even further away than Wilmington, were sent up here to stir things up. They're going to try to establish whatever connection they can to students here... They feel the outsiders were called in deliberately, and that's the reason for the whole thing's getting out of hand." Mr. Blodgett stopped to wipe his bald forehead and head carefully with a clean folded handkerchief he had extracted from a back pocket. He appeared neither winded nor upset, but rather grim and businesslike in his while stance and demeanor.

He looked over at Amy, whom he had known and taught with for over two decades. "I'll tell you what, Amelia, if I weren't retiring at the end of this year, I'd agitate for the Union to put in for hazardous duty pay for teachers. I swear to God I would, "he said, pocketing his handkerchief and moving toward the alternate rear door of the Lounge without a backward glance.

ALEX caught Alex's eyes, raised an eyebrow, and smiled quizzically, wryly, "What do you think friend?" she said finally.

Alex shrugged, glancing up at the clock, in order to have somewhere to put her eyes.

"Well, I'll be frank," Amy said. "Henry is entirely right. After twenty years at this game, and I think I have some reason to believe I'm an apt game-player, I can barely make it through each day. I don't know how to describe it..."

Alex looked at Amy, who was staring down at her hands in her lap.

"I don't know how to express it... except that... it's like walking into a wall of hatred every day."

The bell rang loud, harsh, and inexorable. Inadequate as she felt her response to be, Alex could only give Amy's shoulder a soft, affectionate squeeze as she filed out of the Lounge to her sixth-period class.

UNBEKNOWNST to herself then as only a year preceding their move to Pittsburgh, now well into the '70s, Alex continued slugging it out with her first period English 12 Advanced Placement class each weekday morning at New Colony. She was still struggling to perfect a "structural" approach to the literature she taught and, she assured herself, her program was good and always getting better – solid with quality reading and writing, innovative in its presentations, and consistently exciting in its variety and originality of student participatory activities.

Of course, there were always changes. There would always be changes. Some things worked out better than others. More time was needed for some coverages; other materials were dumped entirely, and, always, at least a modicum of fresh materials was being introduced. For the past two years now, the class had embarked on a Black Literature mini-unit, usually directly following the Novel unit, toward the end of Spring term. This study had been initiated tentatively with four or five carefully chosen books by Black novelists but had now expanded to include Black poetry and even a modest brush with Black American history such as the Harlem Renaissance.

ALEX moved from the second of six five-person discussion groups: apparently in fair shape, this group had already decided unanimously on their representative spokesman to the terminal class discussion on *The Autobiography of Malcolm X* and were focusing individual and group reactions to the book into useful written questions, suitable for cogent participation in a final debate. Overseeing these small exchange units, Alex tried earnestly to adopt a "fly on the wall" presence, offering scant comment or question and only if matters seemed totally amiss.

Moving toward the rear of the room and the next circle, she could already hear Delia's strident tone and see her turgid bosom push forward into Wendy's space. Regrettably, Sam and Delia were the only two Black students that had qualified and then elected to be enrolled in Senior English Advanced Placement and regrettably, too, Alex had noticed they invariably moved as a set – Delia reminding Alex distressingly of Big Nurse in *One Flew Over the Cuckoo's Nest*, ever in the lead, followed by Samantha, wide-eyed, soft-spoken, and by far the more gifted English student, assuming unfailingly the role of mute satellite.

"There is *no* compromise," Delia proclaimed. "All the rest of that stuff you're talking about is Shit, Wendy. It's just *Shit!*"

"But how will ever be able to get together?" Wendy pleaded. "Look, I agree with you. We Whites committed an unpardonable sin in bringing your people here, enslaving them, and denying them most of their human rights. I agree. All reasonable people agree. But what can we do about it *now*? Are we going to hate and fight each other forever?"

Jack Perkins snickered and wrote something down on his clipboard. He looked up, about to speak, when Delia persisted.

"That's just what Malcolm X meant! And he wasn't buying any of it: all those mealy-mouthed solutions you liberals are proposing to solve our real problems. Bussing, quotas, huh," she snorted. "What we need is a New Deal. Our own space, our own schools, our own government."

Jack finally interrupted. "Hey, guys, this isn't getting us anywhere. We're not going to have anything to contribute to the discussion if we..."

"Screw your discussion! This is what *I* want to contribute. A genuine Black point of view." She drummed a long, graceful Black index finger against Jack's clipboard. "Go ahead, Whitney. Write that down. 'Our group's opinion is that Malcolm X's uncompromising attitude has been a revelation to Blacks everywhere. Malcolm X is the first of a new breed of Black Nationalists standing up for the separation of the races, toward the end of giving Blacks, at long last, the honest fair chance they deserve.'"

Jack's mouth tightened into a straight line as he sat unmoving, staring back at Delia.

"Why the hell aren't you writing that down?" Delia challenged. "Write it down, Jacky-boy!"

"Delia," Sam whispered, barely audible.

"Aren't we ever to be forgiven?" Wendy entreated at Delia's elbow.

"You bet *Not*," Delia shouted. "You've heard of the 'sins of the Father,' haven't you? Well, that's it! You just can't walk away from it. No way. No how."

"But *I*, personally, didn't do anything." Wendy insisted. "I cannot help what my great-great-grandparents might have done." Wendy's eyes appeared large and suspiciously moist at the rims.

"Where would this Black space be?" Don, who had not spoken a word throughout the interchange, asked in a quiet, reasonable voice. "Would it be another Liberia? Or, perhaps we could give up Puerto Rico to the Cause? Or, maybe we could convince New Mexico or Wyoming or Montana to cede over some of their land?" Don's unassuming words became progressively freighted with sarcasm as he went on.

"Cut the Crap, Donny," Delia barked.

"I'll not cut the Crap, and don't call me Donny! *Ever*," Don pronounced with starchy dignity, standing up.

Only then did Don glance back at Alex, standing behind Jack, then looked hard at Jack as if expecting him to join him in impromptu secession.

"I don't know about you, Jack," Don said, "but I've just about had enough of this." He gathered his books from under the seat, slid his jacket off the back of the chair, and started toward the door. Jack looked down at the floor but did not move.

Alex managed to precede Don to the door and block his passage. "Don," she said, unconsciously laying a hand on his arm. He pulled it back roughly. "Don. I'm sorry it's going so badly," she said. "I'd like to talk to you for a moment. Would you wait for me in my Office across the hall?"

Without replying, he left the room.

IN A masterful speech of equivocation and deferral, Alex hurriedly disbanded the remainder of the explosive nuclear bevy asking each of them to submit a single page of individual items for final discussion and promising to meet with them tomorrow to help decide on a group spokesman, or possibly two, if this was necessary – in the event of irreconcilable differences of opinion. She had managed to maintain ostensible equanimity, even in the face of Wendy's silent tears. She could not suppress the memory of only weeks ago, when Wendy, youngest daughter of the Head of the Physics Department at the University, had accompanied her parents on a final trip to Brown University to identify and reclaim her brother's body. He had been found hanging in the College Infirmary, victim of his own ultimate solution to delayed LSD reaction. Wendy, who had just last week also refused formal admittance to the coveted Honor Society, despite being Valedictorian of the Senior Class, in a long, impassioned letter to the School Board, which she had asked Alex to edit before she sent off, in her letter, she had argued that such literal recognitions as admittance into exclusive clubs for grades could in no way represent any meaningful differentiation of human worth or potential.

Departing from approved procedure, only ten minutes left remaining in the period, Alex advised the class she would now be leaving for a brief conference on her own Office across the hall, and instructed them to excuse themselves at the bell.

SHE stood with her back against the door, taking in the picture of Don Sperling on the edge of a chair, staring back at her with indecipherable neutrality. It occurred to her that she did not know what to say.

"Don," she began, wondering what she would hear next. "Don, I'm sorry about what just happened. I won't be so presumptuous as to apologize for Delia. She has her reasons, and I know you are smart enough and sensitive enough to know at least some of those reasons. I would just ask you to try work around them at this time, to try to salvage this thing...?" she hesitated on a rising note, questioningly.

Don continued staring at her, then lowered his eyes, indicating neither acquiescence nor surrender. "You know, Miz Brynes," he began judiciously, "I've enjoyed your class, even thought I got something out of it." Alex remembered all the other Sperlings she had taught: his sister Anne two years ago, his older brother the year before that. When Mrs. Sperling had appeared at graduation for Anne, leading a set of four-year-old Sperling twins, Alex had momentarily been transported into a lucid clairvoyant vision of herself, standing just here, in this very spot, a decade from now, still in the act of greeting Dr. And Mrs. Sperling at yet another graduation, this time for John and Jane, or whatever the babies' names were. She had almost gasped, recognizing herself so clearly.

"I've liked the class," Don continued. All the Sperling children could be trusted to display equanimity in difficult situations: it was their family hallmark. "I think you're a good teacher." He lowered his eye. "But the one thing I disrespect about you, Miz Byrnes, that I can't choke down, cannot accept, is your lack of pride." He stared into her face. "How can you take all the Crap from... from... anyone who wants to dish it out?" He stood up and picked up his books.

"Miz Brynes... every day... every day... you come in there..." he gestured generally toward the classroom across the hall, "and throw pearls before swine!"

Without being excused, he rushed out the Office door.

Holding to the back of a chair, stunned by the boy's monumental, universal impertinence, knowing nonetheless that she had been dealt a blow to some unseen part of her being, she allowed herself to stand there, holding onto the chair, until the bell finally sounded.

SO WHAT had it all been *about*? What had it all been *for*? Alex shut the album tenderly, in an attempt to protect it.

Just the next day, in the midst of a discussion that was already getting out of control, the intercom had cleared its throat into the growing lurid atmosphere of the classroom.

"Miz Byrnes, you are wanted on the telephone in the Main Office," disembodied woman's voice announced.

"Could you take the number, I'll call back directly after class," Alex had suggested promptly, assuming another importunate call from a worried or irate parent.

A pause. "Miz Byrnes, I'm afraid this is something of an emergency. Not a *medical* emergency," the voice advised hurriedly. Another pause. In a more diffident tone, "It's your son's high school... and they want you to call immediately."

Another pause. "Miz Byrnes, Mr. Barnes will be up there in a few minutes to take charge of the class." The intercom crackled into palpable silence.

A VICE-PRINCIPAL at Lu's high school informed her testily that Lu and his fiend Charlie had just been picked up and searched for possession of drugs, specifically marijuana. Although the school authorities had found no reefer-butt on either boy, their pulse rates and other physical symptoms observed and recorded by the school nurse had been abnormal and highly suspicious. The vice-principal declared that he personally was almost 100% certain the boys had just shared a joint and were making a last-minute attempt to get to their next class before opening bell when they had been waylaid. In any case, the vice-principal wanted to meet with Alex and her husband as soon a possible... perhaps first thing tomorrow?

ALEX patted the album cover and reached over to switch off the bedside light.

It hadn't served to bring the tears tonight. Not tonight.

Instead, she lay abandoned once more to that no-man's-land with which she was now so familiar. That no-man's land of muddle and inarticulate regret.

Chapter Six

O N THAT early Friday evening, at the anxious conclusion of his impromptu visit to Alexandria, as something of a personal payback to himself for the inconvenience, if not the ignominy, of this most recent "command performance" for Alcon, Barry had impulsively decided on a quick trip up the coast to see Madi, Marcy, and Vivvy. He had just push-buttoned Madi's Baltimore number and expectantly awaited her response.

In Baltimore, Vicky had already returned to the Lab for an evening check on her cultures, and Jean taken herself off in the company of Babs for a rare movie treat – the film, one of the much-discussed nominees for last year's Oscar. Her roommates having vacated the apartment, her own Lab notebook open before her for perusal and review, a stack of old, cherished Brandenburg Concertos already poised on the record feeder, Madi could not help but frown at the telephone as it began its insistent interruption. Momentarily, she considered ignoring it but finally reached over and lifted the receiver from its cradle.

"Madi dear, it's Dad. I'm calling from Washington."

"Dad?"

"I know – this must be something of a surprise. But I was called in last week for a kind of unscheduled meeting with Lindquist – about certain – difficulties – with the Language Program. At Horton. Anyway, we've cleared the business end;" a small clashing noise was followed by an indeterminate scuffling. "Sorry, dropped my damned rental car keys. Anyway, in the meantime, I've already arranged with Marcy to come up to Hughesville and take her and Vivvy out to dinner tomorrow evening." There was a brief pause. "Are you interested in coming along, Madi?"

In the ensuing lull, he filled in, "In any case, Madi, I was, of course, planning to call you right away, too, but – I wanted to set it up with

Marcy first, so I could strategize my trip up. Naturally, love you to join us. What'y'say?"

"I'm sorry, Dad, I just can't. I'm on duty at the Lab from seven to eleven tomorrow evening. We all take turns evenings and weekends. I usually go in for part of each weekend day, anyway."

She could hear his breath, a small clearing cough, a longish silence. "How about having lunch with your old Dad, then? There, in Baltimore. Tomorrow, sometime around noon – on my way up?"

A list of postponed weekends chores, from catching up on laundry to returning library books, scrolled through the back of Madi's mind, but she felt she owned Dad at least this insignificant consideration. Besides, she was fond of him and always enjoyed his company.

"Sure, Dad. Sure. I'd love to. When do you think you'll be getting in?"

More small papery noises; she could see his turning the pages of his discreet pocket notebook. "I don't guess it should take more than... an hour, say an hour-and-a-half, figuring on Saturday morning traffic, to do the forty miles. I've got good directions to Baltimore, but you'll have to fill me in on how to get to the University – or the Hospital – whichever."

Another pause. "Madi?"

"Yes, I'm here, Dad. I was just thinking. It might be easier for me to come downtown on the Metro and meet you at some known location like in front of the *Constellation* ... on Pier I." Her voice became more decisive. "Yes, I think that would be best... *and* simplest. Then, we can just walk over to Harborplace to eat. But... I'm not quite sure what exit you'd get off on," she puzzled. "I think 53. From I-95, of course... but I'm not really sure."

"Don't worry about it, dear. I'll find out."

"It's probably marked as the Inner harbor Exit, anyway. You've been to Inner Harbor before, haven't you, Dad?"

A pause, a truncated sigh. "Remember, we *all* went. Together. Our last trip. To Lu's... new facility."

Of course, she remembered. But, with her Dad's frequent trips to Washington, his several old friends settled in and around Baltimore, his ratcheting up and down the northeastern coast on business, she had simply assumed he had found his way, now and again, to this popular tourist attraction. She had meant nothing more than this.

Instead, she had blundered into the wall of his grief. Best now to step aside from it quickly.

"Ok, then, Pop. How 'bout high noon tomorrow, directly in front of the *Constellation*, on Pier I?"

He followed suit immediately. "Wonderful, darling. I'll be there... with bells on."

"Until then, Dad. So long for now."

"Until tomorrow."

LATE morning Saturday, seated alone on the subway bench, barely having concluded only the second of the descriptive nature interludes in *The Waves* – fascinated – no, much more than fascinated – enchanted, "The light touched something green in the window corner and made it a lump of emerald, a cave of pure green like stoneless fruit" forced her to look up, away from the corpus of the book, directing an unseeing gaze through a sightless window, relief from such enervating beauty. Seconds later, her fingers turned the page to the second of the series of soliloquies, but she was not ready yet to go on.

SHE hoped to discern those caves of silence, avoid those deep crevices of shimmering heartsoreness into which she so often and unwittingly plunged these days in conversation with her parents. "Everything became softly amorphous" in the hazy, roseate memory of Lu's packing her and her best across-the-street buddy, Jess, into the back seat of his weather-beaten, proudly-owned-and-driven Austin, along with his current girlfriend in the front seat of the car, and their driving off all of them, full-spirited and noisy, loaded-for-adventure, to Monmouth Recreation Park. He had not had his license very long, and Mom had given permission only after a lengthy catechism of interrogation and instruction. But Lu had been careful. Flamboyant as he may have been, she had realized even then that he was always very careful with her. And kind, too. For a big teenaged brother, he was unusually kind. They had half-sickened on cotton candy and roller coaster rides, hot dogs and carousels, popcorn and Frankenstein's Fun House, it had been great good fun!

So there was, turning now and disappearing, turning, reappearing, this bursting-with-life sweet, comic brother Lu, and the other Lu, for her, an awesome, unapproachable 70's Heathcliff, Led Zeppelin in orbit, Wuthering marijuana, kitchen-confrontation, and school expulsion. Daring and dangerous. She had always assumed this was the realer Lu of the pair, her big brother.

And, though scarcely anyone had paid any attention, she had made up her mind, even then: she had preferred her own clean, lucid, thoughtful world of personal impressions and small, important private victories. She had supposed, embedded in this undeniable preference, like a stone in real fruit, was an ultimate judgment of Lu. And Lu's life.

Lying under the apple tree in late April, she could drown in the ocean of blossom above. Or forgotten on this late evening and now damply exhausted, sweating under the fluorescent lights Dad had put up over the workshop table, thrill as the electric engine she had so painstakingly assembled over days, finally purred into action. At school, geometry proofs were derived and constructed, grammar built into a big, imposing architecture – how thinking worked, in fact, began to emerge from out the quotation of detail and built into a genuine passion, a secret delight behind the humdrum of classes and the tedium of homework. Far more important than the good grades, although she was happy for Mom and Dad, always so proud of the rewarding report cards, was this inner drama she had discovered for herself.

She remembered just before starting First Grade, in those last humid, endless days of August, one enormous evening typhoon of emotions blasting about the kitchen table as Lu had made a last futile attempt to have Mother and Dad withdraw his enrollment in North Star's newest, most modern Catholic Ecumenical High School. For this his last year Junior High, he wished to be allowed instead to remain at Oglethorpe junior in the company of his boyhood cronies. The storm had raged back and forth, shouting replaced by impassioned pleading, on both sides, accusations sliced down by recriminations, pain slashing pain.

Now, wide-awake, she had finally been forced to creep down the hall to the bathroom, past the kitchen.

Lu sat collapsed in a kitchen chair against the far wall, his head in his hands, in a terrifying posture of despair.

"You don't understand," he had keened. "You don't understand at all how it is... to be so lonely most of the time." He drew in a deep audible breath, lifting his head to stare at his parents, his eyes beseeching. "I am always *so* lonely."

MADI lifter her book ritualistically and repositioned it methodically, mechanically, on her lap. No, Lu's world as just too frightening. Thrilling but terrifying. She had always welcomed her aloneness. She had protected and valued it.

A WHIRL of events, each more incredible than the last, intruded and accosted. His summer job at the famous Ocean City Fun House, Mom and Dad reconciled to it finally – defensively cutting a much remarked upon feature article from the *New York Times* about this very place – surprised at its local repute, its growing tourist recognition, and, finally, stilled into troubled, acquiescent silence. The telephone call from an Ocean City jail a month later where Lu had been taken and held overnight: he had been arrested on a charge of battery after an altercation with a young adolescent vandal who could not be made to stop tearing up the expensively appointed scenery in the cavernous Dracula room where Lu held sway in the character of this famous miscreant. Oh, Lu, had been in the right, after all; Mom and Dad had ever been proud of him for his honest, clever legal self-defense before the local magistrate, terminating in the culprit's complete confession.

But it had been crises, always. Unplanned, regretted, shocking, and destructive as auto accidents.

Jess' Mom, Mrs. Wollaston, had made light of having Madi in for dinner that evening and putting her up for the night, as Mom had arranged before she and Dad had driven to the seaside resort hours away, the time of their return uncertain. Her Day Camp's *First* Award for Nature Study had been proudly displayed on the Wollaston's mantel over the cold summer fireplace, Mr. Wollaston periodically drawing kindly-meant forced attention to it throughout the evening's preoccupied game playing.

And the Band – the Spinnakers. Lu's whole High School effort, really, with classes largely unattended in favor of impromptu rehearsals and other necessary assorted behaviors deemed indispensable to the leader of one New Colony's most popular local teenage Rock groups.

And, finally, Andrea. Her parents such Pillars of the Community. One paternal uncle, a Rhodes Scholar. Another, an internationally known medical missionary in Taiwan. All so up-and-up, all so seemingly safe and secure, Mom and Dad had breathed a sigh of relief that Lu had finally been rescued whole upon that opposite shore, safely delivered from the violent episodic *Carmina Burana* intermezzo of late male maturation. Andrea had left in less than a year. Moved in with a young bachelor dentist with whom she had been training as a dental hygienist. Lu had confessed that Lloyd Jenison, D.D.S. had purchased for Andrea a swift, blood-red Ferrari and had further arranged for her to meet twice weekly with one of Wilmington's most reputable psychiatrists to cleanse her soul of her own atavistic female maturational problems, at, of course, suitably astronomical fees. And, not incidentally, aid her recuperation from marriage to Lu... a spin-off of accumulated family wounds, unhealed, it had been insightfully decided by the illicit pair.

Lu's failed marriage to Andrea had left Mom distracted, forgetful, and irascible for more than a year afterward. The same year Plumberry Junior had carried Second in the Junior High Quiz aired on local and regional television, she serving as Team Captain. They had lost by only two points to Murphysville, Plumberry's Math prodigy, currently attending weekend tutorial at Johns Hopkins, having dropped the ball in identifying Henry II's wife, Eleanor of Aquitaine – generally and maddening acknowledged a commonplace fact fully covered in their Advanced Placement Ninth Grade History class.

But, after that, Lu had begun to change.

Slowly. Then, dramatically. Radically.

In a dizzying succession of upscaled positions, he had quickly risen from middle-management to executive status in first one company, then another. Latterly, as part of the management cadre in various Health Care Services. With his Director Marcy's encouragement, at his last post, after much-excited discussion between them, he had prepared and submitted a wide-ranging Proposal to the State Board of Health for restructuring and improving the housing, schooling, and general maintenance of specific intellectually and physically handicapped groups whose institutionalized upkeep the State Board of Health was considering terminating in favor of experimentation with, hopefully, more adequate, less costly, alternative plans. Thus, a burgeoning, individualized, and highly successful health care facility under his directorship, operating in the vicinity of Hughesville, had been the ultimate happy outcome. As was his soon-to-follow, quiet but satisfying, marriage to Marcy.

WHEN she had entered that mint-green and cream hospital cubicle, Lu's startling blue eyes had flickered open beneath his swathed skull in minuscule interval of apparent sentience. He had reached out an arm, his hand grasping her to the elbow, his face transformed into fleeting radiance by an inimitable sweet and pleading smile. Then his eyes had shut.

Oh, God, she thought even now, even as she had then, I am in the middle of a Nightmare that is True, that is Real. And I will never recover from This. The Earth has forever shifted under my feet, and I will never be the same. I will never know Myself as I have been.

For a half-week of agony, Marcy, Mom, and Dad, and she had sat stone-cold and still upon the cheap vinyl-upholstered chairs ranged about the foot of his bed. His eyes never reopened as his pulse rocketed to Marathon rates, his blood pressure plummeted, and his lungs filled with the drowning effluvia of pneumonia. One late evening, breath stopped tentatively, then altogether, the virulent metastasis of proliferating brain cancer having finally rendered his body null, and impressed his spirit into perpetual quietus.

THE damp October wind freshened across the deep harbor inlet, scouring the broad piers bordered with colorful shops and walls: it lifted the skirts of Madi's coat, thrusting them, sail-like, against her face. Pushing them aside peremptorily, not slackening her gait, she could already catch sight of him outlined against the forward mast of the backgrounding ship. Not merely a trick of perspective, while he stood rigidly erect, he now appeared smaller, shorter than she had remembered him last, but, she noticed, smiling, still sporting one of his many hats, this one a jaunty bicycle cap of some figured material. As she drew nearer, he had just turned to look past the ship across the water of the bay.

She could feel his slight spring forward as, approaching from behind, she slipped her arm under his elbow.

"Did I startle you, Dad?" she teased companionably, smiling up into his mildly startled, grinning countenance.

"Well, not to worry. I love it. You can scare me anytime," he quipped on cue as they began walking toward the Harborplace.

In the Gallery, they chose a table overlooking the water, as quietly removed as it was possible to be in the ceaseless din and bustle of the restaurant.

After they had ordered, Barry looked over at his daughter, staring out at the harbor and saw what he had always seen – an astonishingly pure oval face that seemed never to age past an indeterminate late adolescent, the skin so clear and thin, it appeared translucent. As always, her strawberry blond hair was drawn back in a simple amber clasp, the over-all nunlike severity of the style softened by its rich color and the irretrievable wisps of curl around the hairline. Everything about Madi was lucid and clean-run, spare, and graceful. Though instantly embarrassed by the mawkishness of his own thoughts, he had already sustained that familiar catch in his breath and momentarily succumbed to that generalized elated gratitude he always felt upon seeing her after even the briefest absence.

"So... you're all settled in and liking the job well enough, I hope?" he opened circumstantially, his voice still suspiciously thick.

Madi smiled back at her Dad. "I was lucky. One of our Lab staff had just accepted another position – she had shared the apartment with my two present roomies, Vicky and Jean. After I'd been at the Lab for a week or so, they offered me the chance to move in with them. We each pay a third. We have a decent kitchen, two baths, even a small porch-patio. It's actually very nice."

The waitress placed their crab salad lunches before them, and Madi looked at the array of vegetables and fish appreciatively.

"Some time since I've had Maryland crab," she observed lightly, hoping to keep the remark strictly circumscribed to the present.

"Nothing comes close," Barry rejoin, also lightheartedly. "I'm glad the living arrangements worked out so well. That can be a headache. How's the job itself? The work satisfying?"

Madi considered for a moment, finished her forkful of salad."Well, Dad, I do mostly grunt-work. You know how it is. It's enormously complicated. Painstaking. Highly technical. Various subsections of tests and data collection actually overseen by persons who have become expert in just those particular phases of the experimentation. I'm just getting acquainted with it all. Aware of the overall strategy. You know. But, there's a good atmosphere in the place! Initially, I'm being moved around so as to get a feel for the overall approach. But I'm included in staff meetings and hear exchanges and can ask questions freely..."

"Sounds good... I take it, then, that you'll be more or less given a free choice of what aspect you'll work on eventually...?"

"Something like that. Yes, I think that's a fair guess. But, you know, oh, I know it's corny and kiddish, but it is so serious. So challenging." She stopped and looked level-eyed at her Father. "It's *real*, Dad, and important. It's what I want to be doing."

Concealing the rising burr in his voice, Barry returned her gaze. "That's what I want to hear. Like to hear. Of course, I'll let your Mother know, too. She'll be very pleased. You can imagine..." he trailed off.

"I really admire Dr. Rosenfeld, too, Dad," Madi volunteered enthusiastically. "What a workhouse he lives for the Lab and the eventual outcome of his work. Besides, "her voice lowered, "he's a sort of Mother Theresa of the scientific world, you know."

THEY finished lunch, and Barry, surreptitiously checking his watch, suggested a half-hour stroll along the Harbor esplanade before heading for his parked rental car. Fortunately, the sun had finally visibly entered upon the scene, and the winds had died down, making a brisk walk bracing without being punishing. A pleasant quarter hour's distance later, with but scant, desultory small talk and motley "catching up," Barry once again suggested they had best turn about and make their way back.

Five minutes into the return walk, he laughingly drew them both toward an available bench, removed his cap, and ran his hand over his still neatly combed hair.

"The Old Man must be just a mite out of shape," he allowed hands into her lap. "Let's just sit down for a minute."

Madi looked at him quizzically, then concernedly, folding her hands into her lap.

Barry continued to stare across the water. Without looking into her face, he reached over and took Madi's hand.

"Sometimes I miss this place," he said. "Well, not *this* place specifically, of course; we never *did* live in Baltimore. But, you know, the East Coast. Home."

He turned now and looked at Madi. "You know, Madi, maybe you have come Home. Finally, and at last."

"Well," he said, giving her hand a small squeeze and releasing it with another laugh. "I may as well out with it – not that it's such powerful big news, at that! The reason for this trip to the East this time is that Alcon is once again being 'reorganized'"; a chortle, something between a bark and a gasp, tore the sentence loose. "I can't go through all the bureaucratic... boring... details of this process, whatever it finally turns out to be. But, the upshot is, dear, I have a very strong sense... intuition... that the Fort Horton Language Program will be ditched... and if not ditched, carefully and promptly peeled away from its former Director."

Madi barely touched her Father's shoulder.

"I'm sorry, Dad. I know you've spent so much effort and imagination on that Program. That it's been important to you."

Barry could feel her sit sharply upright against the bench. "But, Dad, so what? For once, *so what*? It's not like Pittsburgh or New Colony. I know. You think I didn't know that we all didn't know? They *can't* kick you out this time, or jerk you around because you've reached retirement age now, haven't you? Can't you just walk away with your severance pay and use your pension, whatever Social Security you've got coming to you, and whatever investment dividends you and Mom have got to live on from now on?"

Barry watched as a couple pushing a stroller, a small boy leading an unwilling terrier on a leash, and black youth jazzing to a radio set full-blast passed in quick succession.

"Dad, it can't *really* matter, can it? Madi persisted.

For some reason, Barry found himself unable to answer.

"It doesn't really matter, does it, Dad? You and Mom will be all right, won't you?"

Barry hung a droll, wistful grin on his features, and forced himself to turn toward his daughter.

"Yes, Madi, financially, your Mother and I will probably be OK. You know your Mother's penchant for projecting incomes and predicting monthly and annual incomes... never thought an English major could be so mercenary! So much successfully mercenary that I am, in fact1 if she hasn't made it all possible, he's certainly made t all credible, at least, credible to *me*. I could never have thought anyone could actually retire. No, she's the business brains in the family, for sure."

Moments later, Mad patted the top of Barry's exposed right hand then rested hers on his.

"Well, then... What's the matter, Dad?"

He still could not answer her; he was finding swallowing difficult, for a brief second, he even found himself wishing himself away and out of this closely affectionate, supportive dialogue.

He would have been content to sit here for another ten minutes, alone, puzzle out what was happening inside him, but his promise to Marcy, Vivvy's extracted telephone promise that Pop-pop would accompany her to Hughesville's newly-refurbished Farm Animal Zoo before dinner hung albatross-like on his accumulated social and family reflexes, if not his conscience. Guiltily, he reminded himself that he had always loved Madi, too. Without ever having spoken a word about it to each other, for Alex and himself, she had embodied the pure essence of their love, as Lu had been its passion and its turmoil. He could not let himself behave badly now, in the face of her genuine concern.

"Remember that album... song, rather... whatever... 'Thick as a Brick'? That's me. Come here to see that everything's all right with you... to sheer you up, for Heaven's sake, and carrying on like this! I hope I haven't upset you. Forgive me," he concluded quietly.

"Nonsense, Dad. Can that forgiveness crap!" she emphasized roughly, uncharacteristically. "You and Mom will be all right, won't you? That's all I'm concerned about."

"We'll be OK, believe me," he said earnestly, seriously. "OK. I guess I'm just a little disconcerted at the suddenness of it all. The need to make plans. To move again. You know. Change comes hard to us oldsters," he added sententiously, hoping to be as convincing as possible.

They both rose and walked toward Harborplace. Nearing Charles Street, where each of them needed to proceed in opposite directions, Barry gave Madi a quick, intense hug followed by a dismissing chuck under the chin.

"You don't want to bum along with me and visit Marcy...?" he offered terminally.

"I can't, Dad. I really can't. I'm monitoring the mice in 203 this evening, and I must tend to a few things beforehand. Besides," she added cheerfully, but not without a discernible admonitory note, "Marcy doesn't want to keep seeing Lu's kid sister. She's got her own life to live, Dad."

HE WAS hardly aware he had stood there as she walked a full block north toward Pennsylvania Station. He became aware of himself only when, crossing at the next intersection, she suddenly and unexpectedly turned, and seeing him standing there, waved cheerily, before bulleting even more intently, inexorably, toward her destination.

HE DROVE in a merciful limbo of disattachment for a full quarter-hour, before reflexively snapping into his more usual persona, realizing that in barely another quarter-hour, he should be deeply engaged with his daughter-in-law and had best begin nerving himself for this next joyous effort.

VIVVY was a *wunderkind*, no mistake. Like her mother, raven-haired, blue-eyed, and petite, this perpetually mobile creature effervescent with *elan vital*, moved from farm animal enclosure to enclosure, with hummingbird swiftness and overflowing delight.

"Look, look, Pop-pop, look at that *sweet* little pony! O-ahhh," she crooned, "he's cuddling right up to his Mom..." Her small hand closed over a wire rectangle of fence at eye level, as she left mother and Pop-pop momentarily, transported fully into the baby Palomino before her.

"She's wonderful," Barry whispered. "Wonderful. I can't decide if she makes me feel young again... or *very* old," he added with ironic circumspection, shaking his head.

"Come on now, Pop-pop. None of that!" Marcy responded dutifully, in character, derogating the implications of his remark.

They attended at cow-pen, hog enclosure, rabbit warren, all delightful: but the baby lambs in the final corral were programmed to effect the ultimate heart-hit and score that indelible love-wound that guaranteed return, Barry reflected. While he and Marcy settled gratefully on one of the rare benches in the park near enough to keep watch, Vivvy had posted herself as close by the fence as she could manage, her hand thrust through, and deeply buried in a lamb's woolly pate, unmoving, lovingly united with her equally blissful bovid friend.

"SO..." BARRY reached over and laid his arm lightly across the back of the bench above Marcy's shoulder. "How goes it, daughter-in-law?"

Marcy shrugged lightly. "As you might expect." They sat silently for some minutes before she glanced up at her father-in-law. "Of course, *I* miss him. *We* miss him. You know, Vivvy was the apple of Lu's eye, though she was adopted daughter." Marcy's voice trembled imperceptibly. "He loved her, Barry. He really did. As much, maybe more, than if she had been his own natural daughter."

It was Barry's turn to shrug and clear his throat. "For God's sake, woman, the child is a marvel. How could anyone *not* love her?" Barry dismissed.

Again they sat quietly, without speaking, their attention ostensibly directed toward the child at the fence. Vivvy's head now rested just above her hand, all still and motionless in classic *tableau vivant.*

"I DON'T know how you are going to react to this, Barry," Marcy said finally. "But I've been seeing Jack LeClerc... my attorney... on a fairly steady basis. You know, after Lu... was gone... Jack was so... so *more* than helpful... he was compassionate, showing such genuine personal concern for *my* welfare..." she testified, suddenly struggling for breath. "And Viv's, too, of course."

"Sometime later, by general agreement amongst our own Board of Directors, an invitation was sent to him to serve on the Board. Every one of us felt his law expertise, his interest in having such a facility as ours well established and successful in the community, not to mention his impressive network of lifelong friends... often with important political connections, all these factors made him potentially invaluable to the Board... personally and professionally. *And*, he has been that!

"Anyway, in the course of all this, we've become quite close," she concluded.

Barry allowed himself to ruffle the hair at the back of Marcy's head. Lightly, reassuringly, he hoped.

"I think it's fine." He corrected, "I think it's *great*... provided, *you* think it's great."

"I didn't think I could ever..." Marcy broke off.

Barry shrugged.

"Marcy. God knows it's not easy. For any of us. But, we've got to go on." He cleared his throat. "You're a young woman, after all. Lu wouldn't have wanted you posted off to a nunnery. He would have wanted you and Vivvy to have as normal a life as possible."

After a pause, Marcy said, "I know, Pop-pop. I know." After another considerable pause, she rose deliberately and walked over toward her daughter. "Vivvy, dear," she whispered, encouraging the little girl to her feet. "I think we'd better get ready to go. It's almost closing time, and Pop-pop wants to treat us to dinner at MacTiffen's before he drives back to Washington."

AFTER dinner, they strolled on the covert 18ᵗʰ-century paths box and juniper around MacTiffen's before spontaneously turning their steps in the direction of Barry's parked rental car. Vivvy, having just caught a glimpse of a late firefly, was now in determined pursuit of this prize and ran ahead zigzagging into the field next to the parking lot.

Barry and Marcy stood at the driver's side of Barry's automobile.

"You know, Barry, about Jack... It's really not quite as idyllic as I may have led you to believe. He's waiting on a final divorce decree. It's been... an ugly... bitter and prolonged affair, I'm afraid."

"It's often hard to know who has the right of it," Barry said noncommittally.

"Yes, it's been difficult. Difficult and complicated. Even though Jack is, of course, very knowledgeable. There is that implacable personal dimension. Intimidating, actually."

"I wish I could be of some help..." Barry said.

"You are; you have been," Marcy assured him, trying to cheer herself and Barry. "Talking to you always makes me feel better."

NOW Vivvy was back at the car door with hands cupped.

"Look at this, Pop-pop," she created a tiny crevasse between her palms. "See him? See him?" she said exultantly.

"I sure do. Boy, he's a big one! Dazzling!" Vivvy giggled complacently, taking a last peek.

After farewells and before moving toward her own vehicle, as Barry made final adjustments to his own driver's seat, Marcy suddenly leaned down into his open window.

"Barry, I don't mean to be mysterious.... But sometime in the next month or so, I would really like to talk to you and Alex about a very serious matter. A *legal* matter, really. I don't want to write... it's too complicated. And, I'd rather not phone, either. Too impersonal and, again, too complicated. What are the chances of your and Alex's getting east in the next several months? For Christmas, maybe?"

"I think the chances are pretty good. But... I just can't ever be sure... it's hard to know exactly when..." Barry glanced at his daughter-in-law quizzically, surprised at the urgency of her last-minute request, yet unwilling to press her. Intuitively, he felt the subject must be serious, probably distasteful else she would not have postponed it until then. He was aware, too, that he had purposely avoided the topic of his own possible imminent retirement, on the grounds that it was still too uncertain, but knowing more truthfully that he had had enough of that subject for one day. So they had both been holding back, he reflected.

AS he swung out of the parking lot, he gave a final double salute on his horn, waving out the window in the general direction of the two figures, receding in the twilight.

He needed to clear his mind and concentrate on driving if he were to make Washington in time for a normal night's rest. He was scheduled for a final meeting with Lindquist at breakfast at the motel in the morning.

Chapter Seven

B ARRY HAD been fitfully half-aware several times through the dawning morning: he had been semiconscious of turning in bed, pushing back scrambled images of strangely disturbing dreams, repeatedly willing himself back into the fuller insensibility of slumber. He must have managed this recapture several times, for as he opened his eyes and let them rest on Alex's seated figure at the edge of the sofa-bed, he simultaneously registered the time on the wall clock above her as only minutes before 10 a.m.

Alex turned and smiled at him. In one of those spontaneous, loving gestures, always unexpected, always gratifying, she ran the back of her hand partially down his temple. "You couldn't have had much sleep. When did you get in?" she asked.

He sat up and reached for his cigarettes. "Probably about 3:00 a.m. before I bedded down... finally."

"Why didn't you wake me?" she inquired, sauntering toward the window and partially pulling apart the heavy drapes that had nevertheless let in so much unwanted light earlier.

"You were asleep," he said inconsequentially."It seemed a shame to wake you. Hey!" he suddenly remembered. "What are you doing home? You're hopelessly late for work."

Alex stood very close to his own seated figure. So close, he could detect the light perfume of her dusting powder in her nightclothes. A wave of that same unaccountable tenderness he felt moments before rose and slowly spread to his limbs.

Alex winked at him. "I lied. I called in sick. Of course, Serena knows what I'm up to. She got your call from the airport yesterday. But, I have over fifteen sick-days accumulated, and what the hell!" she raised her arm in a gesture of abandon, as if flinging away any lingering misgivings.

"Besides," she added more seriously, reseating herself at the foot of the bed and looking directly into Barry's face. "I need to talk to you. *We* need to talk. Don't we?" she probed.

"I suppose so," he agreed reluctantly, trying not to let the weariness of this inevitable raking over of the week's events figure too patently in his response.

FROM force of habit, they chose a familiar old booth in what was once the smoking section of their favorite breakfast coffee shop, The Pepper pot. Long ago, Alex had stopped speculating about the improbability of the restaurants, neo-New England name here in typical sunny California. As they slid into their seats, she blandly reflected that she and Barry had almost reached the point of not minding that the entire restaurant was now nonsmoking. But not quite. With the usual serious expression, Raoul hurried toward them now with menus; off-handedly, she considered this lucky turn also – Raoul, with his precise service and diffident manner, was much better suited to the mood of the morning than Sissy would have been. Sissy's personal dial was stuck at Full, and since she, like Raoul, was often assigned this station, Alex felt glad this particular morning to be spared so much come-hither genial volubility.

In minutes, they were addressing their quesadilla – done to a fare-thee-well as usual – and for the briefest of moments, Alex realized that she would miss this authentic Mexican cooking available only in California and a handful of contiguous southwestern states – before reminding herself ruefully that it was one of the few authentic things she had found here. In yet another moment, she caught herself in mid-turn, watching herself: surprised to note that she was already thinking of this place in the past tense, with a degree of what? – wistfulness, perhaps.

"SO, WHAT'S it to be?" Alex proposed, half-way through breakfast.

For a short interval, Barry continued chewing ruminatively, then glanced up at Alex. "You know what Nero Wolfe would say to interrupting a good meal with talk about business," he quipped, stalling for time.

Again, he looked over at Alex, who had not acknowledged his comment, but in turn, sat munching quietly, waiting for him to respond.

"Well," he buckled to his task, "Lindquist wants me in Washington by the end of October. He's already made reservations at a local hotel. He's also contacted the company's real estate department – I was there when he phoned – and arranged for them to get in touch with our Los Angeles contingent to send over a couple of local appraisers within the week. Naturally, Alcon will also manage the sale through a realty company they'll identify. We could even have a ballpark figure for what the company is prepared to offer for the condo before I've left."

"So fast... so fast?!" Alex demurred. "Why so *fast*?"

"C'mon now, Alex." It was Barry's turn to take exception. "You know from past experience; once the process is initiated, it's always *been* fast."

"But there are all kinds of considerations they haven't taken into... into consideration," Alex objected. "I have a responsible, well-paying job. I have to give decent notice. And... and, we're both almost at retirement age... not likely to be able to land other jobs very easily. If at all!" Alex pushed aside her unfinished plate.

"And all this will have serious consequences on the level of our Social Security retirement payments, too, especially if we earn significantly less in our two final years of employment – let alone be forced to apply for *early* retirement. Why it's... mind-boggling... monstrous, really..." Barry watched as Alex reflexively started to reach for a cigarette, then push her purse aside, as though it bodily contained the very stuff of these major painful readjustments.

"This whole thing throws a terrible wrench into all our well-thought-out plans for a smooth, fiscally sustainable transition into retirement," she concluded in a final attempt at rationality and dignity.

Barry reached across the table and laid his hand over Alex's small clenched left fist.

"Alex, how is it different from when you were forced on short notice to leave a promising teaching career at New Colony? Or, giving up your hard-won come-back job in Pittsburgh?" He shook his head morosely. "We're just older, that's all. It just *feels* worse."

"No, it's not that simple, Barry. I wonder you don't see *that* immediately! I wonder at you, really." He watched Alex struggle to contain her anger. "I think we'd better continue this conversation at home," she snapped. "I'll wait for you outside."

WHEN they had returned to the condo, Alex excused herself directly and headed toward the kitchen. For want of some physical objective, she allowed herself to fuss about for nearly a quarter of an hour preparing a small pot of coffee. She had known it would come to this all along, of course. None of it was really a surprise. So why was she responding so childishly, tempestuously now, to realities she had more than half-suspected for several weeks? It was as if she had stepped out of her own *persona* and assumed an alternate character, one who wished to show no circumspection in the face of difficult circumstances, one who wished instead to indulge in noise rage and sheer self-satisfying protest. But this barrage of slings and arrows – so unfair, so utterly crushing!

Alex stood at the counter and very slowly and deliberately poured out two cups of steaming coffee.

ALEX placed the two cups of coffee on the small plastic table between Barry's patio chair and her own and seated herself. They sat quietly, enjoying the cool air of mid-October, looking out over the dense network of interwoven bushes and shrubs on the hillside before them. In protest, an occasional jay squawked at some territorial incursion, giving screaming chase to an intruder. A hummingbird flittered briefly into view, sipped at their hanging bougainvillea, and whirred away.

BARRY, if... *if*... your job is going to be terminal; we shouldn't plan to buy in the near-Washington area. Because, that's *not* where we'll be living... We *can't*. Unless you're employed, we can't afford it."

Barry cradled his coffee cup in both hands. He squinted over its rim at the hillside.

"But you see, Alex," he said finally, "that's where Alcon is prepared... is authorized to move me." He looked at her. "No place *else*."

SHE was loath to enter into this arena, but, as she had known and feared, it was to be unavoidable. Of late, she had reviewed numerous scenarios of possible viable locales and life-styles for Barry and herself in retirement – feeling uncomfortably as if she were god-of-the-universe moving pieces about in some impersonal master puzzle.

Unacknowledged and most painful of all throughout this survey was the absence of any irresistible gravitational pull toward some home-place, of an undeniable yearning to bond with remains of family, or evidence of intrepid effort at recapturing something uniquely their own.

"WHY don't we go with our original *Plan A*?" she heard herself pronounce crisply, startled at the revelation on her own remark, heretofore wholly occult now so happily serendipitous.

"What?" Barry said, sounding disoriented, momentarily stupefied.

"Well, we never *called* it Plan A, Barry. You know." Such reprise was immeasurable poignant. Roughly, she fought back, "You know, when we were planning our retirement with Lu." She barely gave Barry an upward glance. "We talked about retiring somewhere in the Chesapeake Bay area, some little town – hopefully, inexpensive but picturesque, close to the water – maybe even Hughesville!" she interjected blithely, mischievously. "You were all ready to buy a small sailboat, explore all the delicious slips and coves in the bay, study local history, keep an extensive catalog of water birds!"

This time she allowed herself a good full look at Barry, who sagged in his plastic seat, appearing unwilling and unequal even to perfunctory comment.

"I say, let's explore Plan A," she heard a voice, more robust than she felt, and far more confident, repeat. "First of all, it does bring us more or less back to some kind of home territory... after all, we lived in New Colony for years... Lu grew up there... and Madi was born there. Hughesville would be close enough to Madi, for instance, that we could run down and visit within an hour, and we'd be practically next door to Marcia and Vivian... Even within striking distance of your Philadelphia relatives for an occasional brief – I said, *brief* Barry – reunion, " she reminded, attempting drollery. "More important, Hughesville – or someplace like it – is a more or less rural community, where housing should be more affordable, traffic more manageable, services cheaper – where altogether the cost of living on a retirement income can be managed with a degree of dignity.

Barry sat stone still.

"I say, let's go with it," she rallied.

Barry rose, walked to the patio railing, and searched the overarching sky as if Alex were not there. He spoke to the air. "Alex. Alex," he crooned. "Look, Allie, I'm just not up to it. Now. Maybe later. I'm really more bushed than I thought. I'm for a nap," he said reasonably.

She watched him walk down the hall toward the study. "This schedule is really getting to me," he equivocated in a voice, decorous but dismissive. "Later, Allie, later..." she could hear him murmur, as he shut the door.

SHE sat on the patio for at least another ten minutes, half angry, half sympathetic to Barry's reaction, and Barry himself. Successively, she inspected her own responses to going for a walk, preparing a difficult casserole requiring long assembly and cooking times, and, finally, reading another hundred pages of Kierkegaard's *Postscript* – all, in their way, meritorious uses of a free afternoon: all, finally, to overwhelming to be mounted. Yet, to salvage something of the afternoon from total loss, she compelled herself, at last, to frump down to the master bathroom and begin gathering the soiled accumulated laundry from out the hamper, preparatory to scampering through the numerous cycles of hall trips required to monitor and adjust the automatic washer and dryer without interfering with someone else's scheduled turn.

She had assembled and spot-checked a load of laundry and stood at the condo door, stale bundle in arms, condo keys in pocket, when the telephone rang, for the duration of two rings, she stood still, waiting to hear Barry stir and then respond to the portable phone he kept next his bed wherever he slept. Absolute quiet. At the third ring, she deposited the armload into a chair and rushed into the kitchen to pick up the wall phone before he automatic message machine kicked in after the fourth ring.

"MRS. Byrnes..." a clear male voice sounded.

"This is she..."

(A well-modulated balance of business acumen and amiability.) "Mrs. Byrnes, I'm Lance Humphries with Westdale Realtors. We've just been notified by Alcon, here in L.A., that your condominium will be placed into listing with our firm shortly. We'd like to have a couple of independent appraisals on file before we initiate our sales effort, and

I wonder if it would be convenient... if I had... (he read articulately) Don Webster... come in some time toward the end of the week to make an appraisal?"

"I won't be free for the rest of the week," Alex responded more hastily than she would have wished. She adjusted pace and tone. "Perhaps, though, my husband, Barry, Barry Byrnes... might be available. Listen, (informally) why don't you give me your number, and I'll have him call you when he gets in..." she suggested.

(Affably) "Certainly." (With just perceptible ominous overtones.) "We are, as you might imagine, Mrs. Byrnes, trying to *expedite* Alcon's... plans... for the sale of your home, and (a chuckle) I had hoped, in fact, that we might even schedule another appraiser (another pause, another chuckle)... (read again) Larry Montavo... if he's available tomorrow... to drop by your condo. Of course, we'll make any necessary adjustment to accommodate your schedule..." he trailed off.

(She smiled, willing the electronic media to pick up on her strongly projected affability.) "Of course. Well, I'm sure we can arrange something mutually convenient. Could I have a number where Barry can reach you?" she inquired brightly. Scrabbling to the kitchen tumbler that held a miscellany of pencils, pens, spent rubber bands and small tools, she took down a succession of phone number, pager numbers, faxes, home phones, open-house alternative numbers, E-Mail, and even an 800 after-hours answering service that might have put the sale of their condo into what Alex could only imagine to be regional if not international significance.

AS SHE turned the corner from the laundry room into their own hall, Alex could already see Mr. Villanueva, her across-the-hall neighbor, with an even tinier, behatted woman just behind him, standing at the door of 2222. Almost each time she had used the laundry room in the past decade, Aurelio Villanueva had just been emptying the washing machine, or taking his clothes out of the dryer, or waiting for her to clear a load from one of the two machines. He was always ingratiating and self-effacing, but he had become an inevitable, annoying adjunct to doing the family wash.

One afternoon, and then upon a half-dozen other thwarted evenings, out of frustration and raw curiosity, Alex had peeked at the contents of his dryer load, trying to determine how one man could generate so much wash. Besides the usual underwear, socks, sheets, and towels, she found Villanueva laundering blankets, drapes, rugs, wall hangings, slipcovers, what-have-you, seemingly in endless succession. As she exited the elevator or covered the distance from elevator to condominium, she could frequently detect his surreptitious whisking toward the laundry room as early as six-thirty. Returning from the laundry room after yet another of their encounters, Alex had often observed to Barry, desultorily and ruefully, that this superlatively clean human being... possibly the most hygienically-acceptable male in the Los Angeles basin... should not be being wasted in conscientious mid-40's bachelorhood and dedicated nursing in the vast County/USC Medical Center. He should be a *padrone*, at least, responsible for a brood of babies, or alternatively, setting standards for Public Health in the County of Los Angeles. That, and his established status as a legitimate "Legal" from the Philippines, was all Alex had learned of Aurelio Villanueva after a near-decade-and-a-half of being his neighbor.

Now, out of politeness, she would not slacken her approach, nor exhibit undue surprise as she approached the pair.

"MRS. Byearnes..." Aurelio actually wrung his hands. "Mrs. Byearnes, I am *so* sorry!"

He touched the elbow of the lady aside him. "Mrs. Byearnes, this is my mother... from Manila. We were on our way to the garage... to go to the airport; Mother is to visit my sister in New York City," he said, indicating the two regular-sized suitcases next to the diminutive elderly woman, "...when Mama remembered she had left her coat on the back of a dining room chair. We hurried back. I let us in... (he struck his forehead an apologetic, histrionic blow)... we come into the hall, when (another blow) I remember I left keys... condo, car, all... on the buff*ette*. The buff*ette*," he moaned. "Oah! Such a stupid blunder!"

"Please, come in," Alex said, unlocking the door. She motioned them toward the two Danish chairs in the free foyer-like area close to the entrance.

"I have the name of a locksmith somewhere..." she said, hurrying to riffle through her kitchen phone file. We had to have the locks changed a couple of years ago," she continued over her shoulder.

"As I recall, this man was reliable... and inexpensive." She found the appropriate card, reentered the living room, and handed it to Aurelio. "You're welcome to use the phone in the kitchen."

As Aurelio made his call, Alex seated herself in a chair adjacent to Mrs. Villanueva's. She smiled at Aurelio's mother and nodded her head pleasantly, not sure that Mrs. Villanueva spoke any English. The call was taking longer than she might have expected.

"Do you speak English, Mrs. Villanueva?" Alex asked finally as lightly and casually as she could manage, prepared to go in any direction with her response.

"A leetle... leetle beet Anglish..." the woman smiled back, looking into Alex's face with equanimity.

"You're on your way to New York... that's a big adventure... trip," Alex emended, over-enthusiastic, aware of clumsy compensation for her own discomfort with these stiff inconsequentialities.

"My daughter," Mrs. Villanueva smiled – fully and unselfconsciously – "my daughter is Head Nurse, Mt. Sinai Hospital, New York. I go for visit..." Her eyebrows lifted in arch, girlish amusement. "I go for wedding in one... two... week maybe." She indicated the matter of some indecision by rotating a palm from side to side. "Aurelio come," she nodded toward the kitchen. "Everyones come... big, *big* wedding."

"Well, that's wonderful," Alex said.

"You havf childrens?" Mrs. Villanueva asked politely, in her turn.

"Yes. I have a daughter. She lives in Baltimore." It was too painful and inappropriate to speak about Lu. It was also painful not to speak of him.

"Only *one* childrens?" Mrs. Villanueva sympathized."Tsk, tsk. I havf *four* childrens," she added proudly, holding up four fingers of her left hand. "Four."

Alex smiled.

"I come to live America. Maybe, Aurelio. Maybe, Veronica." She laughed. "I *think* Veronica," she shrugged philosophically. "Womans... they know..." she shrugged again, taking Alex into her confidence. "I *be* Americann Citizen."

"Wonderful."

AURELIO came in from the kitchen. He said that Crown Lock was on its way and would arrive within half an hour. "We go down to Lobby now, Mama, so we can let the locksmith-man in, when he come." Aurelio lifted his mother into standing position gently by the elbow.

"You're welcome to wait here. I could make some coffee," Alex suggested, as earnestly as she could.

Mrs. Villanueva looked up at her son. Aurelio's lips were pursued, and he was moving his head vigorously from side to side. "No, no, Mrs. Byearns... you have been most kind. Most"... he rolled his eyes. "Most *nice*..."

He opened the door and began lifting his mother's suitcases.

"You havf granchildrens...?" Mrs. Villanueva persisted, cocking her head and inquiring amiably, seeming unwilling to leave.

"Come, Mama, come," Aurelio said, hurrying down the hall before her.

"Gudby, gudby," Mrs. Villanueva chanted, following well behind Aurelio. "I have *seven*," she added, holding up both hands, and laughing irrepressibly, scampering after Aurelio. "Gudby, gudby, *nice* lady."

AFTER she had listened for ten minutes to the running water and muffled movements in the "guest" bathroom across the hall from the den-bedroom, Alex rose from the couch and went into the kitchen to pour two bourbons-and-water for herself and Barry.

When she returned to the living room bearing two frosty tumblers, Barry was seated in one of the Morris chairs, propped as erect as a mannequin, both feet planted flat on the rug, a hand resting on each knee. Combed, tucked-in, and stiff, he glared into space.

Barry accepted the glass without turning his head, without changing his posture or looking up at Alex. "It's not a good idea for me to take naps in the daytime," he reproached. "It throws off my whole rhythm."

Alex sat down on the couch opposite him.

"I'M COMING with you... when you eve at the end of the month, or whenever," she said. "I'll put in a memorandum tomorrow... that I'll be taking my vacation at... whatever date you specify, you'll have to leave. It will give me a chance to be with you for a while in Alexandria, and for us to visit Madi and Marcia on the intervening weekend. Then, depending on how things work out, I might stay behind in Hughesville and look around for rentals in the Chesapeake Bay area. When I get back from that trip with you to the east, I'll put in notice of my termination." She sat quietly for some time, waiting for him to respond, but he continued enveloped in his trancelike state. "But, you'll have to give me a definite date for your leaving for Alexandria," she prompted finally.

After a pause of several minutes, Barry stirred. "How long a duration will you be proposing to them before your termination?" he asked.

"Well, since the Company is willing to put you up in a motel for at least a month or so, let's say, till the beginning of the new year?" Alex walked into the kitchen to fetch more ice. She came back with a bowl of cubes with which she replenished each of their glasses.

"How 'bout the end of the year, then? I could be packed and ready to go by then. The Company will have made some offer on the condo too, surely, and we'll have made arrangements for moving our goods... somewhere. I admit it's a bit free-form – we'd have to keep in touch and revise our plans as we went along, but, under the circumstances, I think it's unavoidable."

But, Alex, you said that buying in Alexandria is out of the question. What if the Company *doesn't* terminate me early? What if they play along with me for another year and a half until regular sixty-five retirement date?" Barry took a sip at his bourbon and shook his head. "That would be the best thing, really, all 'round. Financially, it certainly would."

Alex looked skeptical but continued sensibly. "Well, we'll live with that, of course. Even if we did purchase, let's say – inexpensively – in Hughesville – or environs – you'd have to continue living in Alexandria as modestly as possible, I guess and visit on weekends, or whenever possible." Alex strategized. "Look, Barry, I'm trying to make the best of a damn uncomfortable situation. Who the hell would have predicted this – this twist of circumstance – at the very end of a long already uncomfortable enough career with the Company?"

"I know you are, Alex. I know. I'm sorry."

BARRY stood up and walked to the patio door. "The birds are starting their evening activity period," he observed to himself. "They always get active just before sunset. *So* predictable," he remarked sadly to himself, then smiled. Without turning around, he inquired, "What'll you do about a job, Alex, while I'm busily covering the bases for Alcon in the nation's capital?"

"Well, I'll have to get something, of course. It's imperative that we both keep our income levels as high as possible, until legitimate retirement age – sixty-five – as it has a direct bearing on our final Social Security status. In Hughesville, or wherever, I could always apply for substitute teaching, I suppose."

"God, Woman, how could you even think of facing that scene again? I just hate to think of your having to do it!" Barry turned half-shuddering.

"Well, if it's unavoidable, it's unavoidable. Maybe, I can cadge a library job somewhere in one of those little communities..." she prognosticated more cheerfully.

They were both silent for another several minutes.

"I THOUGHT we were moving... deliberately... intelligently... with our initial plans for retirement," Barry argued to some unseen auditor in charge of adjudicating the case.

"We were," Alex defended.

They both paused, wishing to avoid animadverting to Lu's death as their first major derailment, both having a long ago, individually and together, tacitly agreed upon the inadmissibility of ever treating anything to do with Lu as cause for regret or remorse: it was each of them, sacrilegious. Mercifully, time filled over the developing hiatus.

"But, we *had* counted on an orderly retreat," Alex insisted. "Was that such an unreasonable expectation?"

"Yeah, all this..." Barry said, still staring out the door, and indicating a welter load of exigencies to the same judicious auditor, "All this – assure the hell throws a wrench into the 'best-laid plans.' It sure does," he snorted, turning 'round and facing Alex, his face rippling with vexation.

FOR some time now, Alex and Barry, while consumed with caring concern for one another, had found it more and more difficult to be simple and spontaneous in each other's company. They had together, evolved into a kind of corporation founded for the preservation of themselves. How this long-standing loving responsibility had come to exist as something of a barrier between them, not readily disregarded, obstructing their child-lovers meeting in open field of play, joy, and self-discovery, had itself become just another cruel, perplexing mystery that had been dealt them lately.

Clumsily, hesitatingly, they now approached each other – much as awkward adolescents, testing reality,

Almost intimidated, they embraced, discerning immediately the tidal rise of that familiar, yet fresh and ancient passion, within themselves. For a quarter of an hour, they stood so in place, lost in holy, intimate union.

BUT, complex, needful and aging adults as they necessarily and finally must know themselves to be, the hour being evening, space and time itself squared off into latitude and longitude, not to mention passing minutes and hours, the chart required filling for the day with workmanlike accuracy and circumspect discretion.

"HEY, Alex, dinner?
"Yes, dinner, Barry."

"I LOVE you, Barry," Alex whispered. "I love you. And we're going to make it."

"I love you, too, Alex. And... at least, we'll go out... with dignity," Barry countered. He kissed Alex's temple with infinite tenderness at the very nexus to the starlit center of her brain. "Because, Alex, none of us is ever going to make it... *finally...* expect... *all* the way out."

ALEX'S laugh was mordant, as he once more considered this sometimes impossible man she had married, the durability of their decades-long friendship, and the indistinguishability of their ageless tenderness.

Chapter Eight

WHEN MARCIA parked behind the white stucco Hughesville Health Center Services facility on this gold and crimson apotheosis of autumnal days, it was already well past nine. As was her custom upon arrival, except under the most pressing emergency circumstances, she walked the tree-shaded, bricked-in backcourt, provided with picnic tables and a mammoth stone grill Lu had had specially designed and built by Abel MacTaggert, the local, retired stonemason, who stayed on to become general handyman and Marcia's reliable guiding mentor for all things uncategorizable arising in the management of the Center.

Briskly she circled the left of the building to the front lobby, at this time of year, enclosed from waist-high wall to lobby roof with pull-up glass windows, readily replaced in milder weather with built-in alternative screening. She glimpsed now through these windows the inviting chintz-covered sofas, easy chairs, and variegated lobby tables, behind the healthy and becoming scrim of green potted foliage she had taken care to cultivate. Altogether, attractive, and appealing, she adjudged, for the more than five hundredth time, unashamedly pleased with the Center, herself, and Lu, whose sustaining vision and architectural acumen, she reminded herself complacently had made it all possible.

Opening the heavy brass-trimmed lobby double door, she nodded companionably to Lu's portrait, once again acknowledging her partnership with her crinkle-eyed, mischievously amused former husband and business partner, now fittingly and perpetually ensconced over the center's imposing stone fireplace.

A scant two hours later, she had completed all the required phone calls to various interfacing state agencies and servicing vendors.

the more personal inquiries to physicians and parents; checked menus and schedules for the week, and methodically studied the client files for those patients whose cases were scheduled for in-depth review for this week's Center Board Luncheon Conference meeting. Together, these tasks compromised her usual Monday morning regimen.

It was now time to take a turn through the Center's large central classroom, noting carefully but unobstrusively, the current activities of various clients, their individual progress, or lack of it, in the miscellany of verbal and motor skills presently being taught, monitored and recorded by her hard-working staff.

SCARCELY a quarter of an hour later, Marcia stood in the doorway of one of the smaller individual instruction rooms opening along the east wall of the main classroom. She listened as Gloria read aloud to Marie from a large text propped on a wooden cookbook stand, a clothespin holding open its ages on either side – one of Marie's common-sense inventions for securing the text within easy reading distance for her cerebral palsy student who could not hold a book up to eye level for more than a few minutes. Eight-year-old Gloria did appear to be doing remarkably well, Marcia observed, unable meantime to keep her own eyes off Marie's beaming, responsive face, nor suppress a reflexive smile, as Gloria vocalized each new, unfamiliar word correctly.

Nor could Marcia helped being specially interested in Gloria's adjustment to and progress at the Center, "Glory Be" being one of its most recent "clients," and something of an exception to the Center's more usual severely mentally, as well as physically, handicapped clientele. She recalled that Gloria had been lucky enough to have had an assigned home-teacher in the past year after the private school where she had been allowed to attend kindergarten and first grade regretfully informed her parents that their staff no longer could reasonably accommodate Gloria's growing physical size yet undiminished physical debility. But the scarcity and overloaded schedules of available instructor, the location of Gloria's home within easy access to the Center, and the Center's demonstrated availability of reliable transportation, had all militated the State Social Service Agency's decision finally last summer that henceforward, Gloria's education would be assumed by and at the Center. The child's skeptical parents had been assured repeatedly that the Center's more adequate program of daily instruction and exercise, overseen by a fully professional staff, could only mean overall improvement for their daughter. At the time, they were hardly convinced, and only in past weeks had Gloria's mother, standing like Marcia herself now stood in a doorway of her daughter's classroom, allowed herself a first tentative smile, then a pleased grin, as she attended to her child's reading recitation to Marie.

Thus, it had come to be, Marcia reviewed happily, that after an initial period of dejection, Gloria herself had been unable to resist warming toward Marie, the Center's irrepressible clinical psychologist and Gloria's present instructor – a real "natural teacher," in Marcia's opinion. Over weeks, under Marie's insightful tutelage, the girl's attention span had lengthened perceptibly, and her academic progress resumed measurably encouraging speed. Even her persistent, bedeviling habit of reading certain words backward, such as "was" for "saw," had significantly diminished and had all but been eradicated.

As Marcia stood in the doorway, her knowledge that Gloria's cerebral palsy still made it impossible for the girl to hold a book, or turn its pages, or manage the control of a pencil or crayon, were once again confirmed. Yet, the child's burgeoning reading skills had vitalized her overall effort and general demeanor to such an extent that her countenance now glowed, and her intellectual achievement appeared to be bounding forward. The Center, of course, continued working on the mastery of these concomitant, enabling fine motor skills; finger-painting was added to Gloria's school agenda, and she was provided with outside coloring books and cigar-sized crayons and chalk toward the goal of developing at least minimal digital mastery of these materials.

AT A natural break in their reading, Marie glanced at the wall clock and smiled fatefully. "Time for Jonesey to put you through your paces," she reminded.

At that moment, Jonesey, the Center's therapist, in Marcia's estimate comparable to Marie in her vocational giftedness, appeared in the doorway behind Marcia.

"OK, Glory-Be, you ready for your daily Olympics?" Gloria's forehead furrowed in premonitory distaste, but she attempted a purposely radiant smile as she unstrapped from her chair.

FOLLOWING at a decent interval, stopping for an informal word with both clients and instruction along the way, Marcia trailed Jonesey and Gloria to the Therapy Room. From a previous review of Gloria's chart, Marcia had already noted that the child was kept on a regimen of five different exercises for back, neck, ankles, toes, and legs daily: a Herculean chore, no doubt, concluding with what Jonesey had come to label "Gallop and Tort," and what amounted to fifty painful exertions for achieving reciprocal motion of the limbs.

By the time Marcia appeared, Jonesey had already removed Gloria's braces and strapped her into the appropriate apparatus. She first brought one of Gloria's feet up to her buttocks and then guided it down straight, then pushed the other foot up. After about twenty of these repetitions, Marcia, recalling that this excruciating procedure might well go on for almost an hour, slipped away to check with the cook on the Conference lunch menu.

Returning close to the fiftieth try, Marcia grimaced as Jonesey, damp with perspiration, fell back into a plastic chair in the corner of the Therapy Room, and permitted her own long legs to jut out before her. Almost desultorily, merely chattering companionably, Jonesey quipped, "OK, Glory-Be, you do it yourself now," knowing, of course, that Gloria has as yet managed this exercise alone.

Slowly, as Marcia and Jonesey looked on, Gloria lifted and bent her left knee and began to slide her left heel forward. Slowly, she lifted it until it stopped only two inches above its starting point.

Jonesey stiffened and sat upright in her chair. Now, Gloria brought the leg down. As the left foot descended, the right foot started up in a true reciprocal motion.

Jonesey let out what could only be called a rebel yell, despite her New Hampshire origins. A full cycle completed, Jonesey ran up and enveloped Gloria in an overwhelming embrace. From somewhere under Jonesey's uniform and sweater, Gloria panted, "I did it, Jonesey. I did it. All by *myself.*"

Jonesey, still hugging Gloria in a smothering grip, hopped about shouting, "She did it. She did it. God, she did it!"

INTUITIVELY, divining something of the significance of this latest achievement, Marcia merely gazed at the scene – strangely moved – not personally entering into the action. When she finally turned to leave, she discovered Jack LeClerc standing behind her in the doorway. Immediately, she discerned that his features had lost their usual sharp and satisfying clarity: instead, a clouded indistinctness hovered about his eyes. She knew at once that he too had perceived, simultaneously with herself, this small, if unchronicled, miracle.

In another few minutes, he slipped his arm companionably through her own, and they walked slowly toward the Conference Room together.

LUNCH was a simple affair of hot dogs and baked beans, soon gotten through. Marcia then initiated the Conference agenda with reports from each "house," the unique and individualizing facet of Center-oriented care. Fifteen such reconverted and adapted dwellings, scattered in various locales along the picturesque shores of the upper inlet of the Bay, had been purchased and fitted out by Lu originally, using grant funds, his dream of true "quality of life" deinstitutionalized living for the handicapped.

Housing three clients each, and maintained by staff through three distinct shifts a day, these "homes" were the base from which clients were daily delivered by van for the more disciplined, formal activities at the Center itself where appropriate therapies, mastery of gradated skills, and social interaction made up the clients' planned daytime activities. The single staff member who manned each shift in the home fulfilled the duties requisite to his particular period: thus, the "day" person drove clients to the Center, cleaned and put their home to rights, initiated preparations for dinner, and picked clients up for their return home at about four o'clock. The "evening" shift person served and cleaned up after dinner, set up entertainment and activities for the evening, and was responsible for toileting and showering clients before they were bedded down for the night. The "night" person generally assisted with the latter procedures, there being some overlap in shifts, completed whatever untended chores were still left to be done as indicated in the notes of the preceding two shift-personnel, and was then in charge of toileting, showering and dressing clients in the morning, as well as serving them breakfast, before their departure for the Center.

Reports from the homes proceeded routinely, with only infrequent, desultory staff recommendations for adjustments in specific menu items or other household supplies needful to individual houses, until it was Vicky's turn, Vicky serving as this month's "day" staffer in Home 14, located at charming Partridge Point. Marcia observed that Vicky had chosen a seat at the farther end of the Conference table and was now hesitating, looking about her, obviously reluctant to begin.

Marcia had already studied Hannah's medical report on the client's – Greta Hygher's – emergency visit to the Hughesville Clinic last Sunday night, Hannah being the "night" personnel assigned to Home 14 this month, but she had not as yet been free to meet with either woman personally to cull from her a more detailed explanation of this somewhat bizarre incident. Marcia was also not unmindful that, without being so advised by herself, Vicky had taken care that Hannah, the "night" staffer, should be sitting in on this meeting, along with where the "day" person usually served as the general spokesman for each location. As Vicky now focused upon Hannah, sitting two seats down the table fixing her in an unabashed stare, evidently wishing to defer to her in whatever should follow, Hannah declined the offer peremptorily with a sharp shake of her head and a small off-putting hand gesture.

"Client Greta Hygher," Vicky began, turning a copy of the medical report between her fingers, ad-libbing as she went along, "was taken to Hughesville Emergency at approximately 11:52 p.m. Sunday evening, after Hannah Pierson, doing routine night check, discovered the client lying on her side in bed, moaning – and in some distress. Upon further checking and subsequent toileting of the client, Hannah further discovered her to be bleeding – noticeably, but not profusely, from both vagina and rectum. She put Greta back to bed and went to check her meds: Greta's menstrual chart was found to be negative for this date, so Hannah proceeded to contact our "free" staffer of the evening – Louise, Louise Crandall – to sit the house while she – that is, Hannah – drove Greta down to the Clinic." Vicky's eyes widened, perplexed, as if she were hearing her dramatic reportage for the first time, unable herself to fathom its significance. 'No police report was made at this time.'

"I don't remember being called," Marcia interrupted almost demurely, nearly inaudibly, not wishing to detract from Vicky's presentation.

"We called you, Miz Byrnes, but we couldn't get through," Hannah murmured in turn. One of the few times she had permitted herself to leave home without either beeper or car phone, Marcia recalled this would have been just about the time Jack was delivering her at her own door from a private Sunday presentation of *Annie* in Wilmington, a recent production reprised exclusively for media and social service personnel, as wind-up and thank-you for their participation in a local TV fundraising marathon for muscular dystrophy.

"Never mind," Marcia dismissed even more quietly. "What were the Doctor's findings in Emergency?"

"Well," Vicky now turned and nodded at Hannah.

"Mi Byrnes, the doctor said there appeared to be – abrasions – to vagina and rectum," Hannah replied in a remarkably clear, undaunted voice. She looked around the table, visibly raising her eyebrows. "Enough so that the doctor ordered a Clinic gynecologist to monitor the patient on a regular basis for the next month, or until they are satisfied that all is – normal.

But Miz Byrnes," Hannah footnoted after hesitating another few indeterminate seconds, "our check of the client's records shows that she has had weekend visiting privileges with her family twice a month for... for the past six months. Greta's father brought her back to the home at approximately..." she checked her notes again, "8:03 p.m. on Sunday night."

"And what was her condition then?" Marcia inquired.

"She seemed fine. Just fine. Happy as a clam," Hannah stated. "Nothing out of the ordinary."

"How did the client react to the Emergency examination?" Marcia pursued, changing venue.

"Nothing. Calm as a cucumber. Happy for the extra attention, even" Hannah shrugged.

"And – since then?" Marcia persisted coolly, hoping to fend off another of Hannah's clichés.

"The same."

"And the bleeding?"

"Appears to have stopped. Completely. But the doctor set up an appointment with the gynecologist – a Dr. Mathews- for later in the week during regular Clinic office hours. For Friday at 11:00, I believe." She glanced at her notes. "Yes. For this Friday. At 11:00 a.m.."

"I see," Marcia said. Then added. "She seems – normal – then, at this time?"

"Yeah," Hannah said, philosophically, circumspectly. "In spite of everything."

MARCIA frowned. "Ginny, make sure to prepare a follow-up copy of the Emergency medical report to be sent to the Hygher family, along with the other requisite informational forms from the Clinic. We'll need an explanatory transmittal letter indicating suggested medical procedures for the immediate future, too. We'll probably have to get their signed consent for any ongoing arrangements, in any case. In the meantime, I'll call the Hygher's and explain, as best I can... about Friday's examination.

"Jack, could you get in touch with the Board of Health's Legal Department and confirm our reporting responsibilities and time frames?"

Hurriedly penciling notes on her clipboard, Marcia added, "I'll have to notify the Developmental Deficiency Agency immediately and see that Miss Ayers at Medicare is also on board with what's going on." She lifted her head formally, politely including her entire staff in an open sweeping glance, actually a visual contact become blindly involuted, rendering them all anonymous. Barely aware of her own rising intolerance at their presence, she rapped out finally, "And, yes, we'd better notify the Police right away, too."

Putting aside her notes, Marcia turned again to Ginny. "See me in my office sometime later today. I'd like us to review the Hygher communication before it goes out to the family." She spoke to the Center's nurse sitting at the other end of the table. Like Marcia's,

Ginny's countenance remained devoid of affect, settled into stony, uncommunicative gravity.

MARCIA heard almost nothing of the 15th "house's" report, which thankfully appeared to be entirely uneventful. Annoyed and perplexed, she could nonetheless not avoid being shaken out of her ominous preoccupation with the Hygher case by Jonesey's resent strident, ebullient proclamation.

"You won't believe this!" Jonesey near-shouted, tumbling out all the details of Glory-Be's not inconsiderable wonder of the morning, consistently cheered on by Marie, who concluded the Conference session, converting her own obbligato of Glory-Be's advances in reading into her own final ringing solo.

"The Child Guidance Clinic's been quoting I.Q. scores of 75 to 90 on Gloria's psychometric tests," Marie scoffed. "That's just the problem all of us face," she exhorted fellow staffers, enveloping them in one warm, inclusive glance. "What with severe limitations in life experiences *and* debilitating motor disabilities, how can they *tell* what our clients are capable of? How can they begin to guess with such... *such* assurance?" she demanded indignantly. "I say Glory-Be's I.Q. is probably somewhere nearer to a 120 to 140 range if we could only enrich and broaden her life experience to something like normal!"

CONFERENCE business was finally over: Marcia watched her staff file out, individually enlivened, some even inspired, by Marie's missionary zeal, some small part of which each of them, she knew, more or less, shared with her and which had originally dictated their own choice of employment. They trooped out lightly, visibly refreshed, eager once more to take up their daily tasks of mostly unnoted and unrewarded drudgery.

"BUSY? ... May I come in?" Jack inquired, poking his head into Marcia's open doorway.

Marcia smiled and indicated an easy chair in front of the desk.

"Had a little business with Ginny checking on forms for the Board of Health. I did call Saunders... but he wasn't in. His secretary will have him call my office in about an hour when he's expected back."

Jack had seated himself and now extended an arm across Marcia's desk, laying his hand across her free right one. They looked at each other for several seconds.

"I'm now a free man, Marcia," Jack said. "The final divorce decree came through this morning. I didn't call because I knew I'd be seeing you this afternoon."

They both say unmoving. Another several seconds of silence, before Jack removed his hand, clasping both of his between his knees.

"So..." he exclaimed finally, abruptly. "So... that's that!"

Marcia sat back in her chair, still holding Jack in her line of vision. "Jack," she spoke quietly, "nothing's changed. Nothing needs to go any faster... or slower... or change in any way. Not unless we *both* want it to."

"Claire didn't contest putting the house up for sale immediately," he went on. "What would either of us do with a four-bedroom, four-bath house, now...?!" he snorted. "Anyway, she doesn't want to live in beautiful, historic downtown Hughesville any longer... that's for sure, especially since her promotion to Supervisor in Obstetrics at Memorial. Oh well, she's got herself a nice apartment... somewhere in Claymont, I think.:" Jack shook his head. "Of course, we were going to fill *all* those bedrooms..." he trailed off idly, his voice catching.

"I don't think what you're doing is a good idea, Jack," Marcia observed evenly.

"Of course, the alimony payments are substantial... she's managed to tie up at least a third of my income. Chalk one up for Claire!" he grumped, staring ahead. "Barely five years... barely five... *not* a very good track record, I'd say."

Remembering her own divorce after even a shorter period, barely four years it had been, Vivvy not even three, the heartsoreness, guilt and grief of separation, Marcia could hardly force herself to verbalize words of conventional sympathy

"I'm sorry, Jack," she murmured at last, the best she could do.

THEY sat for another several seconds, unspeaking`lng. Jack rose finally and made his way toward the door. As he moved away, he half-turned only, avoiding Marcia's glance, Marcia's presence. "I'll call you tomorrow, Marcia. Tomorrow."

SHE answered Ginny's call, agreeing to meet with her in fifteen minutes. Replacing the receiver, she rose, walked to the windows behind her desk, and stared out at the vivid autumn scene before her: blazing maples and golden beech, birds silhouetted so high up, so high, in the glowing red sky, they were indistinguishable, each from each. Mere black, feathery outstretched V's. Idea of Birds, really, she remarked to herself just audibly, enjoying the shape of the sounds. Lu had always said this was his favorite time of year. Deservedly so, she yearned, aching for his close corporeal presence once again.

THERE was a tap at the door: Ginny quietly entered Marcia's office and placed her folder of materials on the desk. "Shall we get started on Greta's case, then?" she inquired, by way of introduction, seating herself in the chair Jack had vacated barely a quarter of an hour ago.

"WELL, it's working out all right with Blum. I'm supposedly helping him adapt the basic Fort Horton language program to fit specs laid down by two other interested services... the Air Force and the CIA, no less! Can you imagine?" Barry shook the cardboard out of his best California-Mexican sport shirt, fresh from the laundry. "You know, he's a damned smart kid, even though he's got an MBA from Harvard! Maybe because he was an Honors Linguistics major first – before the MBA. He says that even after he finally shifted over to business – his dad laid down the law sometime in his junior year: 'either choose a major that's going to lead to a job after graduation... or quit... Now!' he still managed to retain a heavy emphasis on international relations..." Barry chortled, slipping into his shirt. "Yeah, that's probably it. Oh, hell," he admitted, "I don't' know what's really *It*. Johnny's just a decent, sweet-natured kid... rare nowadays... like a kid brother to me... I'd say Alcon's lucky to have found someone like him."

"And so are you. Lucky, that is. To be working with someone as personable as he is." Alex patted her short 20's bob into cloche-like obedience, noting the loss of intensity in the color of her still abundant auburn hair before turning from the vanity. "Nothing really accounts for why people turn out the way they do," she added more seriously. "Why is Madi so good... I often ask myself. What did we do to make her that way?" Alex continued sorting and straightening stacks of undergarments into two suitcases. She stopped and stared at the wall. "I often feel we were *blessed* by Madi. We *certainly* didn't do anything to deserve her!"

"Nor Lu either... with all his problems, early on."

"Nor Lu either," Alex affirmed quietly, firmly.

"Anyway," Barry said, sitting down in one of the hotel bedroom's two available easy chairs in order to pull on his shoes. "Despite all Alcon's hustle and protocol... you know, marching me around the offices to all current contract managers... crap, Alex... pure crap... I can't even remember their names now... and it's not because I'm pushing Alzheimer's, either," he snorted defensively, companionably, "despite all this standard corporate tomfoolery, 'the floating research staff,' the 'pool secretaries,' 'the Internet guru advisers,'" he allowed himself an extravagant Shakespearean sweep of his arm, "despite all this BS, I know... and the know... I'm about to craft a proposal that'll sell computer installations to a South African mining syndicate, nor the POentagon's newest fighter planes to Kuwait. C'mon..." He tied both laces and looked up toward the window through two luminous blue eyes, into which Alex saw the short poignant as he was at the edge of his chair, arms slightly extended at either side, he appeared to her momentarily transfixed, even prophetic.

"So... I've become the understudy for this... this boy. This brilliant boy!" Barry guffawed. "And, I don't even mind." He laughed out loud. "In fact, I *like* it!"

Alex lowered her head, humbled, moved. While Alcon had crafted and scheduled Barry's dwindling months with the Company, for the past week, she had managed to be self-directed and responsible – the dependable helpmeet, the self-sufficient wife – planning an exhausting, it satisfying, day-trip to the National Gallery on Tuesday; reading; whiling away a long forenoon in a local fashionable shopping mall Wednesday; reading; and, Thursday, succumbing finally to the muscular ethos of the day, forcing herself to use the Exercise Room and Pool at the hotel. Not until this very morning, knowing the weekend and Marcia and Vivian, and everything else, were imminent, feeling out of bondage at last, exhilarated, but nonetheless somewhat intimidated by the anticipated reunion ahead, had she allowed herself to begin packing for the trip t Hughesville.

Now, before she could stop herself, the words were out of her mouth.

"Do you mean it?" she asked. "Are you really beginning to feel... OK... about it... about everything?"

NEITHER of them, in truth, wished to review the meaning of the growing lucid equation of past months: Barry's career and his age, his lifetime contribution, as conventional society accounted it in its conventional wisdom, now at an obvious point of termination. How could the situational equation be otherwise? In the nature of things, why should it be otherwise? Discounting the sticky flak of purely personal emotional hurt; born of years of inattention – lack of primal recognition for one's humanity – the powerlessness to effect ever any meaningful impression upon that great, controlling, anonymous presence of the Corporation, sitting in mammoth stone inscrutability over the landscape, revered and sacrificed to, as per visceral conditioning from the dominant culture, to the rhythm of "getting ahead," responding libidinally to the competitive challenge to prove oneself worthy – reduced not to irrelevancy, equation or no equation; those over-rehearsed, somehow-always-damp amateur importunate deliveries of the past, stained with the ludicrous. "Altogether," he heard himself testify to himself, "Altogether, a snare and delusion."

"No," Alex said judiciously. "No, that's not fair. You did what you had to do... given the circumstances... To survive. To save yourself. To save us. To nurture your children, to protect their future, and altogether make life possible... tolerable... for all of us. To you, *family matters*... has *always* mattered."

ON SATURDAY morning, having tramped through grass damp with dew, they climbed into the Company-leased Lexus. For a quarter of an hour, they traveled the impersonal, traffic-clogged Beltway before entering into I-95's more open roadway, where even modern road-building technology had not managed to obliterate the evolving gold of maturing trees, the sweep, promise, and raw beauty of the satisfying contours of the land itself.

"IT'LL be nice to be together again," Alex ruminated. "Although, after all this... time... and everything, it *is* a bit..."

"Hey, Alex, did you bring along the binoculars?" Barry interrupted. "It's duck migrating season, and there is nowhere, but nowhere... more wonderful for bird-watching the northern migrations than the Chesapeake bayslips and backwaters. I hope you remembered to pack them?"

"I did, Barry. I did."

"Wonderful," he exclaimed, his whole body relaxing into the automobile's graceful bank around a wide curve of the highway.

Feeling perceptible lighter, he experienced a sharp thrill of renewal for driving, seeing, just being in the midst of it all.

"I hope so. Because... we'll... I'll have to make the most of a fairly short time."

"Not if we move to Hughesville permanently," Alex proffered in a hushed voice, after a full pause.

"Oh, well..." Barry said, keeping the road in view and controlling the car, not aware that the innocence of his expression, the youthfulness of his spontaneous smile could so gladden Alex's still hopeful heart.

Coda One: Marcy

ALL HER life, she had been brought up to serve. It was so much a part of her rearing; in fact, she could hardly bring herself to resent it, even now as an adult. Father had always taken a severe, punctilious attitude toward household arrangements, demanding in his quiet, inflexible Pennsylvania Butch way that everything be scrubbed, well-ordered, and company-presentable at all times. Mother, working the switchboard at a suburban Baltimore hospital, the job she held until after her divorce, putting in eight to ten hours days, never questioned Dad's additional implicit household regulations. Showered, combed, and freshly-groomed, mother and three daughters awaited his daily evening arrival from his job as accountant for a small downtown Baltimore export-import business, with a home-cooked, "hot" supper on the table, countenances scoured free of any unseemly anxiety, and all but "lined up" for his inspection and approval.

Marcia, being the eldest, had been Mom's chief lieutenant – for as long as she could remember – early on, admitting to herself, having been cast in the supervisory role of directing – (that is, bullying and cajoling) – her younger sisters into preparations for dinner, dusting and "straightening" the house, "washing up" before supper, and, time permitting, even having Ellen and Jane initiate a pres-supper attack on their required homework assignments.

So it had gone for more than thirteen years.

Until mother had "caught" father on the phone to her own oldest and dearest friend, Elsie, bookkeeper at City Hospital, where Elsie and mother lunched together daily. He was overheard arranging what he came finally, with dignity, to admit had been his several-nights-a-week tryst since almost his first days of marriage to mother.

It had all been a ridiculous coincidence, really! Mother would never have come to have used the telephone so late in the evening, well after eleven, had Max not suddenly and terrifyingly gone into spasms, and all of them screaming at her to call the vets' emergency service in spite of the hour. Shocked, mother had stood mesmerized, unable to pull herself away from eavesdropping for the next ten minutes to what she was discovering to be a surprisingly breathy, romantic dialogue between father and Elsie – so heartbreakingly unlike anything she had ever experienced in her own relationship with him. While Marcia watched mother's face metamorphose from a russet ball of quivering tremors to a grayed-out specter washed over by tears, her parent stood horrified and fascinated, thrilled and appalled.

When mother had finally replaced the receiver and staggered to father's bedroom, throwing open the door and shuffling in, he neither hastened to terminate his call to Elsie nor sped up his adieus to his long-time paramour. Instead, he brought the telephone call to a graceful conclusion, rose from the bed, drew out one of the three suitcases from under it, and commented magisterially to mother, "So – *now* you know."

Nor did father ever explain or apologize later. Rather, throughout the balance of that week, he moved daily, methodically into Elsie's house.

While Mother cried unceasingly for six months, Marcia and her sisters, obeying a court order, visited father every weekend on a court-mandated schedule, fulfilling at "Auntie Elsie's" much the same functions they performed in their natal home – Elsie assuming – and getting from each of them, the same unquestioning perfection of regimen in their servitude, prompted by a sweeter, more defensible "Suthn" accent only. Father and Elsie went on to remodel Elsie's house, adding a wing with two extra bedrooms, a sun porch, and a patio, dined out regularly and graciously without the girls, or dined indecently, in the girls' company and with their reliable attendance – father and Elsie flattering and catering to each other in provocative latter-day sunset affection, the girls looking on, bemused and silent, but, fearful of making any rebellious move that might compromise their mother's economically dependent position Throughout her high school years, Marcia persisted in her established dominion over her younger sisters, making sure each one consistently appeared on the Honor Roll, arming each with a worthwhile and realistic academic plan for the immediate future, carefully crafted after hours of personal and group discussions, while she, valedictorian of her Senior Class, recipient of a scholarship to the University of Maryland, focused on a projected MBA in Public Health Administration. In retrospect, she considered she had lived at least three of her nine lives before ever having reached voting age.

As SHE rose again from her desk, a sudden tidal wave of heartsickness almost flung Marcia to the floor. No, not until Lu had she permitted herself to experience childhood. What a fresh wind he had been! What a resurrection! In his inimitable, quiet, sweet, and compassionate way... how efficient, how original, how talented, and how wise.

When he first took the second-in-command managerial post at Cerebral Palsy, she had held off forming close ties, even friendship, for months, inspecting herself regularly in the manner of a skeptical quarantine customs officer, expecting to discover that she, in some way as yet unbeknownst herself, had been infected with that peculiar adult virus, similar to dad's Venus-itch in his latter-day pubescence. Undeniable, narcissistic, and, ultimately, evil. If so, she'd prefer to suffer, but she'd *kill* it. She'd already sustained one devastating failure with Ned. And now there was Vivvy to care about.

But Lu, so seriously conscientious and competent at his job – day to day – so demanding of himself, even more than she, who served as Director of the facility. Courageous. Original. Deftly, after she had taken on the initiative for establishing comparable facilities at several new locations, he assumed the Directorship at the original Baltimore center and was soon collaborating with her toward improving operations in the more distant and rural sectors of the state.

It had been nothing like father's syndrome; it had turned out. For more than two years, Marcia and Lu did their site-work together, laboring hard; advising each other frequently and correcting one another's apparent vulnerabilities or myopic decisions – anything but romantic. Foxhole buddies, rather! Sex had not arisen as an issue.

Vivvy had come to anticipate Lu's visits to their home as enthusiastically as Marcia had. The child snuggled up to him to be read to before bedtime, without ever being instructed to do so, or without being corrected when she did. She included him in the bear hug ceremony before sleep. Lu accepted it all as he did everything. Calmly, appreciatively, lovingly. Without dropping a syllable, as Vivvy patted his face, he went on reading about Squirrel and Duck and Spot in their fascinating peregrinations through Wonder Forest.

WHEN had it happened, then she reflected?

When had it not?!

"My love," she whispered against the large mullioned and sectioned window that served as a backgrounding wall behind her solitary desk. "My unbelievable, beautiful and blessed, lost, lost love!"

Chapter Nine

M ID-AFTERNOON FRIDAY, Marcia awaited Alex and Barry's arrival, expected close upon dinnertime. She had come back from a late and harried lunch and began immediately to clear away the last work items remaining, which, disposed of, would free her to leave the Center, at last, retrieve Vivvy after-school nursery supervision, and arrive home in time to put herself, the house, and the *hor d'oeuvres* in order. She began by phoning John to pick up and deliver a list of food and drug items she considered needful at various houses for the weekend, confirmed that the local plumber had made the scheduled house call at House 7 and the bathroom sink was now draining properly and was just about to call Abel to arrange for a last Autumn grass-cutting at all three of the Chestnut Hollow houses, when, under her reach, the desk phone trembled, then burst into a harsh, discordant jangle.

"Miz Byrnes, this is Doctor Mathews at the Clinic."

"Yes, Doctor. I've been waiting for y our call..."

"I completed a full pelvic examination on your client... Greta... Greta Hygher... this morning. You'll recall, of course, that she was referred to us from Emergency as of... last Sunday, I believe."

"Yes, yes..."

"Oh, Miz Byrnes, I should also mention that I have now received all the Agency reporting forms from your nurse... Virginia Schweitzer... and I'll have them to you by the beginning of next week. Do you want me to send out copies to any other state agencies while I'm at it?"

"No, that'll be fine. We'll forward photographic copies to the requisite agencies ourselves," Marcia commented, feeling herself becoming tensely impatient over these bureaucratic niceties, but managing to maintain a superficial unstrained receptivity nonetheless.

"... Miz Byrnes, our examination confirmed the patient was suffering from vaginal inflammation that appears chronic in nature. Additionally, the vaginal-hymeneal wall, as well as the anal orifice, showed evidence of recent abrasion – now almost entirely ameliorated.

"Miz Byrnes...?" the Doctor pursued after yet another pause.

"Yes, yes, I'm here, Doctor."

An irrecoverably lengthy interval prevailed before Marcia heard herself ask: "Is it your opinion, then, Doctor, that the patient has... that her medical problems are... the result of a sexual... encounter...?"

"That would ordinarily be the most logical explanation, of course. Were it not that she – Greta – I assume, does not *have*, isn't involved *with*... ongoing sexual relations. And, I take it, her behavior *is* otherwise monitored consistently, so that she wouldn't be doing *herself* an injury...?"

Marcia immediately regretted the suspiration of breath audibly carried over the line even before her own modulated reply, "There's almost no question of *that*, Doctor, I'm almost certain. We have quarter-hour bed-checks throughout the night," Marcia affirmed. "No... I..."

"*If* the origin of the problem is some sort of sexual... 'penetration' ... it would appear to be happening on a fairly regular basis, I'm afraid, Miz Byrnes. Hence, the chronic vaginitis. In any case," the Doctor said in a vigorous change of pace, "we were too late, on this occasion, Friday, to be able to obtain any meaningful scrapings or sample specimens from either vaginal or anal cavities. Much too long after the event, you understand."

Almost before the Doctor had completed her sentence, Marcia interrupted reflexively. "In any case, Doctor Mathews, we can't take such samples without the express written permission of her parents who, despite the patient's age, act as guardians."

The Doctor was silent for several seconds, in turn.

"Do you recommend such a procedure, Doctor? Should we attempt to get such authorization?" Marcia asked finally.

The Doctor's voice was measured, circumspect. "Miz Byrnes, it has been my experience that... at least in the cases of juvenile sexual molestation I have been... regrettably... involved with, these... (Marcia could feel the Doctor choosing her words discretely, picking up one, discarding it, choosing now another, in this testy game of medical Scrabble-speech), "these *incidents* have a tendency to reoccur."

A ponderous silence flowed into the space between them and stuck there for several seconds.

"What do you plan to do, Miz Byrnes?" the Doctor inquired at length.

"I don't know, Doctor Mathews. I don't know... the Hyghers will receive a copy of your report, of course. We'll see, then, what they might wish to do..." Marcia extrapolated, her objectively sounding hollow and unconvincing even to herself.

Another silence.

"All right," the Doctor returned briskly. "I'll send these on then, and wait for further instructions from you, later...

"Oh, Miz Byrnes," the Doctor reminded, "you *are* aware, aren't you, that we have scheduled appointments for Greta on each succeeding Friday, for the balance of the month...?"

"Yes, Doctor. Yes. Of course. She'll be there. Thank you."

Marcia swiveled in her chair, fronting the twilight nuances in the facing, living landscape: long, irregular reaching shadow hands scooping up important patches of lawn from under the oldest trees; scintillating glints of light caught still in small leaf-colonies, struggling, independent, not to be extinguished; inexorably there, here, numinous shiftings of light and shadow, restricting the patterned message of her beloved home, her place, her and their round of earth. She drew the vision in with breath, yearning into reality almost, some at least partial communion with these exquisite natural presences before her – with her, but yet not her own, touchably near, but forever heartrendingly, out there.

DUTIFULLY, Marcia turned back to the desk, lifted the receiver from its cradle, and dialed the Hyghers' home phone number. Six interminable rings cum static later, Mrs. Abigail Hygher's vaulting unmistakably adenoidal voice, crackled into a brief canned message to leave a brief canned message. Marcia put down the receiver carefully and opened Greta Hygher's client folder, which sat before her. Fifteen minutes elapsing, a reprise of the same scenario.

From the rarely consulted filing portion of her desk, Marcia now ferreted out a compendious Xeroxed directory, once painstakingly complied upon her own behest by her office manager, and quickly located Mr. Lazarus Hygher's office phone number. She dialed, and eight rings later, the phone was answered by a crisp, if preoccupied, voice, only slightly annoyed.

"Lazarus Securities," it said. "Mr. Hygher's office."

Identifying herself promptly and being informed in turn that she was speaking to Mr. Hygher's private secretary, Marcia asked to be put through to Mr. Hygher, if possible, as the call concerned his daughter, Greta, and a medical question that had just arisen regarding her care – but in no case to be considered an emergency. Marcia was next informed that the Hyghers were expected to be away for the entire succeeding week, one of more than a dozen boat-owning participants in the harbor yacht Club's week-long tour of a number of picturesque and historic sites along the lower Bay, the fleet having commented journey just this very morning from their own Baltimore dock.

"But you must understand," Angela Wheaton exculpated, "Mr. Hygher made sure to check out the Club's boating schedule very carefully before having me call in their reservation. He wanted to be absolutely sure he… they… would be back in plenty of time to pick Greta up for her twice-a-month visit home." Angela's passionate vindication, failing to dislodge the expected responsive comment from Marcia, she went on, "Mr. Hygher is always *so* careful… *so* thoughtful about Greta! Always. A wonderful man, really, *and* a wonderful father."

Marcia spoke at last. "Well, as I said, miss Wheaton, while I would preferred to speak to the Hyghers about this matter sooner rather than later, it in no way poses any *immediate* problem. I guess I can discuss the matter with them when they pick Greta up at the end of the month.

"If necessary, Miz Byrnes, I can call the Club and… "Miss Wheaton suggested.

"No. No. That won't be necessary. I neither wish to alarm the Hyghers nor disrupt their trip. It can wait." For a moment, the thought that perhaps her nonchalance was not so well-advised, that perhaps she should press the matter forward at this time, flickered across Marcia's consciousness. "No," she repeated aloud instead, answering her own qualms. "In fact, Miss Wheaton, perhaps it would be best if I spoke to the Hyghers myself, *in person...* when they stop at the Center in a few weeks. Yes, I believe that would be best." (She had wished to avoid actually asking Miss Wheaton *not* to mention the matter to the Hyghers: requesting explicit that Miss Wheaton share a strategy with her for dealing with the Hyghers, whatever the circumstances, struck Marcia as complicitous, unseemly, possibly even censurable. Yet, this developing, professionally ambiguous situation was beginning to corrode measurably some impregnable center of righteous confidence she ordinarily and implicitly drew upon.)

"Whatever you think best, Miz Byrnes. I won't mention it to Mr. Hyghers... should he call. You understand I don't expect him to... but..."

"Yes, of course. I *will* be speaking to the Hyghers, then, come the end of the month, Miss Wheaton. Thank you... And, *do* have pleasant weekend yourself."

"Thank you; I shall try, Miz Byrnes. You, too, of course," Angele Wheaton appended politely.

As Marcia replaced the receiver, exasperated, and mildly depressed, she noted that it was now nearly four o'clock, and she had yet to make reservations at the Shore House for dinner that evening before she was free to leave the Center to reclaim Vivvy and drive home.

SHE had almost forgotten how much fun Alex and Barry could be! Together again, they enjoyed a delightful dinner t the Shore House, tastefully prepared and graciously served. Between courses and conversation, they oversaw the maneuvers of the flat iron-ore barges, the oil tankers, the few elegantly appointed schooners, and yachts bellow, queuing up now along the concrete canal embankments, waiting their turn – for Marcia, the entire scene infused with irresistible impressionistic reverie. She felt she could take in the ambience, as it were, as much through her fingertips as her eyes, the pictures before her rendered more palpable still, as it was glimpsed through enveloping tangible dusk and deepening roseate fog.

Suddenly, impetuously, waving her long-handled spoon above her head for emphasis, momentarily neglecting her pears grenadine, Alex let out what Marcia could only describe as a ladylike whoop. "I love it. I know it's silly... but I *do* so love it. Watching them, I always feel

I'm starting out on a long and adventurous journey! I imagine myself going somewhere... somewhere marvelous!" Barry and Marcia smiled back at Alex indulgently, empathetically. "Silly, silly," Alex footnoted with her next breath. "The reality is, I *hate* traveling anywhere. Mostly. Mostly, it's all quotidian bag and baggage, mountains of painstaking, mind-deadening detail. And *boring*."

"You've got to excuse Alex, Marcy," Barry emended wryly, catching Marcy in a sidelong glance. "I think we've moved once too often for Alex."

"Anyway... it's awfully good to see you two," Marcia responded, her voice furry. "Awfully good."

"Hey," Barry reminded, "we promised ourselves a turn down at the Canal wall, didn't we? It comes with the territory," he reminded jauntily, palming the bill, "and I intend to make my claim. Ladies? ..." he encouraged, helping Alex slide her chair away from the table.

"Barry," Alex said, "sometimes you are so... so *atavistic*... Ladies, indeed! Ladies! Honestly, Barry." Marcia heard herself laughing aloud.

"Why, *atavistic*, Alex?! As usual, you exaggerate, my love. Why not just *old-fashioned*?"

"Mom has a real flair for language, that's why," Marcia giggled as they made their way through the restaurant toward the door, Marcia positioning herself between Barry and Alex, now linking arms with each of them on either side.

THAT first evening had gone so quickly, Marcia remembered Barry had stopped to chat with the owner of the yacht who, garbed in regulation navy blazer and white flannels, walked the embankment above his immaculate craft, anxiously monitoring its every movement through the lock. Barry could hardly contain his enthusiastic awe for this man's unimaginable journey to Rio and points south, and all the way home, fairly overflowed with excited, incredulous speculation about all the potential unforeseen hazards and thrills in such a voyage. And then, having reached home, before her very eyes, Alex and Barry nearly deflated visibly, suddenly aware of their own accumulated fatigue, begging off for the remainder of the evening. Marcia could only agree to let them take themselves off summarily to their motel room. Her hand-formed plan of introducing any sensitive topic, so intimidating to herself still, would have to wait until the next day.

AS SHE had expected, late Saturday afternoon, Barry readily agreed to cook the steaks on Lu's almost brand-new0 gas grill, conveniently secured at the foot of the deck stairs for the evening. The day had fortunately remained unusually warm; not until Marcia and Alex had begun to clear the two large trestle tables well after dinner had they found it necessary to flick on one of the space heaters located at either end of the deck. It had been a successful, but early evening – as she planned; all the guests had departed by eight. Her sister Jane had left first, having to drive mother and herself back to Timonium. Marcia, Alex, Barry, and Vivvy had then walked their neighbors, Elaine and Hugh, across Marcia's acre-wide lawn to the Ruskin's property line, Hugh plying Barry nonstop with expert details of fishing strategies he planned to put to good use in tomorrow's fishing expedition to prentice Point with his two best buddies.

Having returned from walking the Ruskin's home, desultorily, she and Alex had then continued clearing the tables, carrying half-a-dozen trays of glasses and dishes into the kitchen, until the detritus at the sink became in turn so unmanageably dense, Marcia quietly shifted to rinsing and stacking plates and silverware into the oversized dishwasher. For both women, clearing away had fallen into a relaxed, humdrum, mindless back-and-forth, until Marcia, lifting her head from knee level at the dishwasher, stood riveted by Alex's stance, leaning against the den doorjamb as she was, dishcloth poised in midair. Wordlessly, Marcia walked to the den entrance and inserted herself in the space remaining next to Alex.

SNUGGLED up against Barry's left thigh, her whole upper torso fairly welded under the arm resting across her shoulder, Vivvy momentarily wriggled into a more erect posture so as better to study Barry's face. "But I don't understand, Pop-pop. Why does Heidi have to go back to Frankfurt with Aunt Dete? Heidi doesn't want to leave Grandfather... he loves her best of all! Better than her friend Clara ever could. Better than Grandmother Sesemann, even. Why doesn't he *stop* it?"

Thus challenged, mentally scrabbling to assemble significant plot complications from a faltering memory of this years-unrevisited story, Barry stared down at his adopted grandchild with a blank expression. Effortfully, he recalled the old man's disaffection and alienation, his eventual Christian redemption, but felt unequal still to crafting an explanation reasonable enough to be convincing to a seven-year-old child.

"Hey, Vivvy – darling – you told me you knew the *whole* story. You told me your mom has read the whole book to you three times over already! So... you're not playing fair with old Pop-pop. It's *your* turn to tell *me* the answer!" Barry protested, laughing.

Even so, he was surprised to feel Vivvy shift inches away from him, fixing her eyes on the space between two pink feet peeking from under her nightdress, and settling into a concentrated muse. Still smiling, Barry looked up at the women in the doorway for some sign of their endorsement in this evolving, perplexing scenario, but, fixated on Vivvy as they were, they appeared as rapt as his granddaughter.

"The answer *is*," Vivvy proclaimed, "I *don't know*... Because... it's *mister-e-us*," she added cryptically, at last.

Barry placed a bookmark into the book he had been reading and slid it quietly onto the coffee table before him. He was willing to accept her answer, as is, without further comment or explanation.

"... Like my Daddy who died," Vivvy went on. "That was mister-e-us, too."

Barry's breath caught as he glanced down at the coffee table.

"Because everybody loved him, too. And when I asked Mommy why *God* didn't stop it, she said she didn't know, and it was mis-ter-e-us."

At that, both women hurried into the room, both talking at once, Barry hearing neither of them. Marcia planted herself firmly before her daughter.

"OK, young lady, it's just about time for bed," she said. Glancing at the wall clock above the sofa, she added more sternly, "In fact, it's well past time..."

But Vivvy was not to be diverted so easily. She slid off the couch and taking Barry's hand, gently tugged him into a standing position. "Pop-pop, I want to show you a picture of Daddy that Mommy just had made for our piano. Come on, Pop-pop," she said, leading Barry out of the room toward the front of the house.

Marcia made no attempt to stop her daughter this time: instead, mutely, she and Alex file behind the pair to the foyer, through the double glass doors of the living room, and thence into the room itself. They were led to a child-battered spinet that had once been Lu's and Madi's bane and blessing. Standing before this still graceful instrument, they looked back at Lu seated at it, glancing over his shoulder, through a simple gold frame, a typically droll grin piquing their curiosity and giving a twist to their unexpungeable affection for him, as it had done, always.

"That's my Daddy who died," Vivvy announced proudly. "Isn't he *handsome*?" she added archly. "You're *his* Daddy, of course, Pop-pop," she completed justly, historically. No one spoke.

"We have a whole album full of pictures... of your *son*... Pop-pop. You could look at them if you want to..." Vivvy suggested enthusiastically.

"Not tonight, Vivvy dear," Marcia intercepted, leading the covey away from the piano and out of the room.

MARCIA, Alex, and Barry trekked upstairs behind Vivvy, and after a quarter hour's ritual of adjusting lights and kissing veteran teddies, monkeys and giraffes, not to mention a tired chartreuse snake that hung in two unequal halves, Vivvy was finally ensconced under her quilt.

The trio at the door, Vivvy sat up in bed, startling herself and her would-be escapees. "Will you be here tomorrow, Pop-pop?" she pleaded.

"You *betcha*," Barry confirmed.

A delighted giggle, and Vivvy's voice. "I'll show you my secret hiding place in the forest. It's at the end of our yard. Almost nobody knows about it! It has a swing and everything!"

"Wonderful," Barry agreed.

"Mom-mom is going to be here for the whole week. Looking at houses for her and Pop-pop to move into," Marcia added brightly. But, for whatever reason – the transfer of information suddenly too ambiguous in its implications, or too complicated, or too extensive,

Vivvy abruptly rolled to her side, gave her favorite teddy a last kiss, and murmured, "Goodnight, Pop-pop. G'night, everybody."

"See you tomorrow, Pop-pop," Vivvy's voice from under muffled bedcovers barely audible followed them as they moved toward the stairs.

MARCIA and Alex "finished up" in the kitchen, Marcia insisting that Alex let her complete the ultimate necessary maintenance on chairs and tabletops, while her mother-in-law joined Barry in the den to catch the conclusion of a *Mystery*! She had missed at an earlier viewing. It was proving an interminable, if substantial, evening, Marcia reflected, glad finally to have some time alone. Half hour later, the television having been stilled, Marcia carried a tray of three Irish coffees into the den.

HAVING served her father-in-law's favorite after-dinner liquid refreshment, Marcia allows herself to settle into the wing chair opposite the sofa.

"It makes it a bit rough, I guess..." she began without prelude. "But I've always encouraged Vivvy to be open... natural... in her references to Lu. You know... no painful circumlocutions... no embarrassing euphemisms... no indefensible mythologies..."

"Absolutely!" Alex remarked in full voice, bluntly.

"The way Lu would have it..." Barry murmured a moment later.

"And I think it will be so good for Vivvy to have both of you living close by... I'm really looking forward to that!" Marcia stood and walked over to a large roll-top desk in a corner of the room. Quickly, she pushed back the top and retrieved a thick folder of clippings and brochures from the desktop. "In fact, Alex – I hope you don't mind – but I've collected some brochures of recent local real estate ventures – condos and the like – ads from the Sunday papers – Sunday's are best for this purpose – *and*," holding up two or three business cards, "even two or three cards of Hughesville's most popular, reputable, Realtors – this, thanks to Jack, who's retained as attorney by at least two of them... That should give you something to start with on Monday..." Marcia remarked, carrying the folder over to Alex.

"Well, I'm certainly grateful..." Alex said, beginning to leaf through the printed materials, turning some over, laying others aside. Barry looked on meanwhile, having thus far successfully maintained what he hoped presented itself as an alert, pleasant, yet noncommittal expression, but now becoming half aware that his body tautened in the encroaching mental struggle against this inexorable tide of events. Flowing, as it seemed to be, all in one unalterable direction.

"Who is this Foley...?" Alex piped up. "She seems t be mentioned everywhere... in this area..."

"Oh, she's *good*," Marcia said. "They're all three good... but I think Jack's recommendation was for Rapp... Elmo Rapp... a little more conservative, perhaps, but *very* reliable, non-high pressure, allowing you plenty of breathing... thinking time..."

"Alex," Barry finally interrupted, his comment targeted at her right shoulder and barely audible in the rest of the room. "Alex, I thought this trip was to be *exploratory*..." Alex looked up at him with a quizzical expression. "We were going to give ourselves time to, you know, look around, get the feel of the place..." Barry turned now to Marcia. "It's all *still* undecided, you understand."

With head bent, obscuring a clear view of her face, for several silent seconds, Alex continued shuffling through the materials in her lap, until Marcia nodded, stood, and began collecting cups.

"Marcia," Barry said, "you *had* mentioned, my last trip up, you had some legal matters you wanted to discuss with us..."

Caught off guard, in turn, Marcia knew immediately that she would be utterly unequal tonight to disclosing the heart of the matter she had so long carried with her, to share with Alex and Barry at this moment the more than physical determination of an action, rather the inviolable commitment of herself and them, each individually, to a sacrosanct ethical position. With such far-reaching, even intimidating, responsibilities, and consequences inherent for the future. No, this could not be the time. Everything at odds; everything out of joint. Worst of all, in the wake of some incipient ferment between her in-laws.

FROM a drawer in the same roll-top desk, Marcia now extracted several voluminous documents, which she distributed between Alex and Barry. One document, they discovered, established Vivvy's formal adoption by Lu; another confirmed Vivvy as the recipient of an initial trust investment of $10,000, plus the accumulated dividends to be earned in the near decade-and-a-half interim period, upon reaching her majority; the pair having exchanged and perused these two legal records, their demurral to mounting a close inspection of the thick bundle of the Will was mutual and instantaneous, evident in their quietly laying it aside unread between them on the sofa.

After having distributed the legal papers, Marcia had busied herself in the kitchen for a full quarter of an hour; she now reentered the den quietly and reseated herself in the wing chair.

"It all seems perfectly in order..." Barry began.

"You spoke to us about the major provisions of the Will... at the time," Alex reminded, unable to disguise a hint of befuddlement in her tone.

"It was the Trust document; I wanted you specially to see. That $10,000 actually represented the down payment on our *first* house... generously provided by you, you'll remember..." Marcia recounted.

Barry and Alex maintained an alert, vacant attention.

"Well, that's *it*!" Marcia said.

"What's *it*?" Barry chuckled.

"Well, that money is technically yours and Alex's... really... with Lu gone. But it was his idea to do something like that with it... *and*... so... I *did*. Anyway, I wanted everything open and above board between us... If you had felt otherwise..."

Barry now gathered up the three documents and carried them to the desk. On his way back to his seat, he stopped before Marcia, pulled her gently to her feet, and gave her a warm hug. Standing together, he whispered at her, "You know, you are some *crazy* lady... Don't ever give it a second thought!"

"Imagine that..." Alex said, bemused. "Imagine even thinking of *that*..." she repeated to herself with just a touch of incredulous annoyance.

"Pop-pop," Marcy volunteered affectionately, taking heart at their spontaneous approval of her action, "I know there are all kinds of things we could use you for at the Center if we could only get you up here, all to ourselves. I've been wanting, for instance... to make an exhaustive comparative financial study for the State Board of Health of our kind of personal, quality-type case, as opposed to warehousing clients in large, impersonal institutions. And... I know for a fact that Jack's brother is up to his ears in personnel problems with his employees, who are objecting to *everything*, as this merger with ACC goes through... anything you could do by way of Human Resources would be a godsend! And... the University is looking for qualified, experienced statisticians. With your background at that institution... Well, you get my drift, Barry. There's just lots of opportunity here. I *know* it."

Barry gave his daughter-in-law another hug and said nothing.

ALTOGETHER, watching Barry steer the pitch-dark country road toward the motel, Alex admitted she was vexed. Hadn't he agreed, implicitly, with their course of action? Hadn't he even indicated a certain happy reconciliation to their mutual plan? Once again, he had cast her in the role of a moral bully. But she would be damned if she was going to keep him up bickering over these twists and turns on the eve of his solo reverie amongst the eel and bay grasses, ducks, and Canada geese, planned with near-religious piety for the morrow. She would not be forced to play the Savanarola to his spiritual Sunday, Infidel Intruder to his Quest of the Holy Grail.

AS MARCIA threw the bolt on the massive oak front door, in the light of the vestibule lamp, she could discern the now bare limbs of the dogwood tree Lu had planted in their front lawn the first weeks of their move, now mere six feet of skeletal memory of a once blushing pink-and-white Spring presence. Planted in her mid-heart and brain, pit and root, her own most secret wish once more pushed aside, once more necessarily delayed, once more unconsidered, likely and tragically, never to bloom into living fruition.

Coda 2: Barry

WATERMAN'S, HERE. Bumping over gravel, tires crunching and spewing stones, striking against car doors. Parking lot deserted. To be expected. Smell of docks coming up sharp, saline, and life-giving, as loving sex. Better even than expected.

Ernie said he'd leave the dinghy in the small craft shed. Up the sloping shed dockway. Fingers stinging, just a little, just enough to feel alive, brushing across the loose, weather-beaten, peeling shed boards, loosening. Building's side all rosy in the rising sun, greening shutters above, missing boards. A beautiful place, such warm flooding in the chest. To be expected.

Standing here at the end of the walkway, out there, out there, is why I came. Hello, beauty! Hello, lovely love! You're utterly still now, aren't you? I hear your answer. I hear it!

Handfuls of waves, gathering and releasing – mysterious, random little bursts. Not to be comprehended. Not to be taken in easily. Everywhere, gulping, swallowing sounds of calm gray-green water.

I love you, heard sounds, repeating. Go ahead, surprise me... beguile me: I want to be your loving fool!

But I am not shamed. There, from out that clinging envelope of mist, a perfect crimson sun, God damn it! Emerging now yellow gold, squeezing itself from out the amniotic gray-blue envelope. Live birth, afterbirth falling away.

You're beautiful, Sun! Keep on trying. You'll make it. You and me... we'll make it!

It's just where he said it would be. Stow photographer's bag. Yeah, notebook edge and pencil under the leather, Roger Tory Peterson sitting atop, all in order in the sack. Canvas-covered foam-rubber cushion underneath the prow. Oar pins in sockets. Slow, underhand strokes, into the shallow green-gold shelf, past dock pilings, now a dolphin, into still shallow open bay. Some fool already out there. Way out. Purple apparition, underlined triangle-mounted rectangle, maybe a mile and a half off.

In and out. Like breathing. Better. Ebony-tipped wings of snow-white goose, snow goose, *Chen Caerulessens*, at the end of his arms. None aloft. No wine-bottled beauties houcking to him from above.

Now a bit out. Look about. Sun coming up. Wake of a motor launch, cradling dinghy, back and forth.

Back to shoreline. Now barely dinghy-wide inlet, hiding beneath cutting edge bay grasses, stiff on bamboo-dry stalks. Then, feather boas of cushiony kiln-brick painted reed. Slush of single fingers into soft leather gloves. Here.

No trees... marsh... marsh as far as you can see... boat needs pulling through to... perhaps... Here. Packed slit. Pretty solid.

Marsh and water. Water and marsh. Sit still. Staring. Quiet. Wide and narrow sweep. Narrow and wide. Still. Hush. Wait.

A boy, waiting. Well, not a boy, really. A man... very young man. So hopeful so passionate. Are young men always so passionate and hopeful? Foolish. Sighing. Somewhere. Moving to deflect the sound.

WHAT is this? My God, after ten, already? What's happened? Had he bee...? Grasses parting. On stilt black unsure legs, white as angel wing, backward S-neck, and head, drawn exquisitely into black-tipped yellow beak, planted in marsh-mud, yellow eye focused, unfocused... nowhere and eternity. Lucky. Lucky and beautiful. *Casmeridius albus*, a voice recited.

Far enough away, but slow, s-l-o-w... now the bag, now the notebook. The date, place, habitat, weather, time, all noted, stub of pencil back in place. Beak in water, churning insects with bill, stock-still stopping, head erect. Up. Off, sail-wide wing cover bottle

Body, sapling-long black legs dragging behind, beneath, inverted-S neck, filling with flight, growing taut. Straightening.

Through reed grass. Derelict boat left to decay, hand-held rudder tied to bare dead stick of tree. Quiet. Pair of Canada geese, one dark amber gold stately breast forward, white coverted black rump of partner backgrounded against it, blackhead poised and gleaning the ground opposite. Tableau. Foraging sedge seed and grasses. *Branta Canadensis*.

UP TO forest's edge. Another cove around bend. Dock stretching toward brown, sun-porched cottage, almost out of view. Coming back, early settling mist, fog rising, long, slender unexpected slip of marsh, incising parallel to water's-edge short grassy margin, white masses of breath-seizing white, white-white down-cushioned forms, now separated into slim-necked single beings, flock of snow geese, brooding, breathing upon the waters.

STAND. Still. Old Army boots sinking slowly in ooze. Beneath... No matter... Still. Still. Whole and holy.

NOW, why does a man need to come out here to think? The voice asked. And well it should. Those middle years filled to brimming with concerned details, wasn't it right? To be a loving father and husband. Adequate, if unmemorable provider, general well-wisher to humanity at large? That's the ticket; Doctor Charles would have said. That's the ticket!

And, what ticket was that, pray? What ticket? Pray, indeed!

At its best, it was good, like a warm loaf of bread in hand. Or a cuddling egg fetched just from the nest. But boy-Shaman had what? ... evaporated, diffused, disappeared... under a muffling load of 'considerations'... considerations... evaluations... analyses and adjustments. Intellect made possible the science of living, but then... then...

AND now all were there... around, above, shoulder-side, eye-level, and above... fluttering, imperative, prescient, heralding cross... dazzling, black-tipped, sacrament of the Holy Ghost enveloping, absorbing. Filling the sky with grace, ... Amazing Grace...

GRASPING the oars, Barry Byrnes recited to himself that even Barry Byrnes could occasionally get the message. His eyes shifting to his oars, across the bay and back, the freshly painted dinghy sparkling beneath him, he knew he would wait. He would see. He would do nothing. He would be still. And listen. For he meant to find Barry Byrnes again.

Chapter Ten

O N THE following Saturday morning, with considerably mixed feelings, Marcia waved good-bye to Alex and Barry, keeping their rented Lexus in view while it made its final turning onto the Old Mill Road toward Hughesville, and thence toward the local I-95 entrance for Washington.

She regretted that Jack had been unable to join them for dinner the preceding weekend, and had had to be away in Baltimore for the whole ensuing week. It was a missed opportunity for him to have met her former in-laws and become acquainted with them, which, despite her mild trepidation regarding this meeting, she would have finally welcomed.

Late the previous Wednesday evening, Vivvy, having already been tucked into bed, Marcia was neither surprised nor displeased when the den phone rang, and Jack was on the line.

"Marcia. How are you?" Formula dispensed with, his voice immediately took on some urgency. "Marcia, can you arrange for us to have dinner together Saturday evening? You know, make certain Jean can baby-sit... and all that. Negotiations should be finalized by Saturday afternoon, and I would be back home by early evening," A brief pause. "I've really missed you," his voice flat and somehow dispirited, she thought.

"Sure, Jack. Certainly." After a bit, "You don't sound too good. Have the proceedings been... tiring...?"

A guffaw, tinged with unmistakable bitterness. "Even with Arnold's representing us, it's been an unequal contest all the way, I can tell you. You know, Battle of the Titans, or something akin! Allied General's legal talent is nothing if sharp, sophisticated, competent *and* determined. Certainly, determined," laughter congesting under his breath. "Brother Armand, of course, tried to hold up on the price, and, for once in his life, the pompous bastard even tried to get Allied to make some specific commitments, *in writing*, about retention of employees, pensions, and so forth. Nothing doing! Turned out to be pretty much of a Mexican stand-off! Those Allied guys can recognize a potential concession a mile away. They're not about to give anything up freely. Their ostensible position, of course, is that they still have to firm idea of how they will utilize our business... ultimately."

Marcia had never inquired deeply into the LeClerc Company. When she and Lu had first used LeClerc, Hughes, and Lebrand's, reputedly the most prestigious law firm in town, she had in the course of things met Jacques LeClerc, a personable, surprisingly diffident, decorous, Victorian younger son of the LeClerc family. She had come to perceive this data of him and know of his position in the community, casually, effortlessly – as anyone might who had lived in Hughesville for any length of time. The LeClerc Works had once been, she had been told on a number of occasions, the largest single industry in town, employing at least half of the townspeople, and the family had over decades come to enjoy that particular inerodable esteem and status granted a small town's most prominent family. But she had never thought much about it or them. The LeClerc phenomenon had not mattered to her, or Lu, or their life in Hughesville. Marcia and Lu variegated imported professionals now serving in Hughesville's new hospital, Veterans' facilities, or other assorted growing enterprises.

"Four generations..." Jack's sigh carried across the line. "'Course, it's a far cry from when Great-great Grandfather had LeClerc's rolling their own sheet iron on site. That went, and in Grandfather's time, they were already dipping black plates... mostly imported. It's all changed now, of course. LeClerc's has tinplate delivered in huge ninety-sheet boxes. I'm not even quite sure how many body blanks the factory stamps out regularly now... now how many processing techniques we're still capable of sustaining..."

"Well," she laughed. "All *I* know is that LeCLerc's manufactures tin cans... for soups, and fish, and things," she footnoted brightly, feeling somewhat stupid.

"Yeah... It's been a decent living, OK..." his delivery sardonic. A longish pause.

"Could you meet me at the Carriage House for drinks first?" Jack hesitated. "It would be nice to have some time alone... just the two of us..."

This time she was responsible for the hiatus. In the year and a half, she and Jack had begun to see each other regularly, and then seriously, she had always been very clear about – when it *had* come to that finally, on the remarkably few – actually rare – irresistibly sexual occasions between them, they should never spend the night together here, at her home. About that, she had remained adamant. Vivvy would never be subjected to one, let alone a succession of mother's "boyfriends." The thought was frankly repugnant to her, totally inadmissible.

So, it had come to be the Carriage House – Jack's remodeled second-floor apartment, over what was once the carriage house, now garage, a handsome building set well behind the LeClerc Main House and fitted out with central air conditioning, electric heat, sauna steam – as charming as Winterthur's Carriage House farther up the road, if on a reduced scale, comfortable as toast and efficient as a microchip.

"You know I don't like driving onto the property," Marcia protested. "Your mother always recognizes my Saturn or one of the Center's vans, I gather from the scuttlebutt around town. It's so... so *obvious*. And, not a little embarrassing, I might add." Her tone admittedly querulous, she was directly discomfited by her on callowness.

"I thought... I thought it might not matter to you by this time... that is, what *they* thought..." She flushed upon his confirming her own estimate of herself, yet thinking him unfair.

"OK. I don't. Not really. Let's say, seven, then. On Saturday."

"Marcia," he murmured. "I... I'm so looking forward to seeing you Saturday," ceremonial, but importunate.

"I'll be there," in command again, Marcia quipped.

"Jack..." He was not there. "Jack..."

"Goodnight, Marcia... Saturday."

"Goodnight, Jack."

THE LeClerc property sat above an inlet of the bay, half concealed on a quarter-mile high bluff above it, the circumscribed cove glimpsed from the house through now a patterned screen of amber maples and purple-hued dogwood, pale buff beech and wine-colored red oak, and a close, rich panoply of evergreens. Whenever Marcia's Saturn had climbed the winding road on her way to Jack's approaching, the passing, the LeClerc Main House on the right, she could not restrain herself from gazing, for as many seconds as safe driving permitted, upon the original centrally-placed symmetrical Georgian brick mansion, replete with five dormers and crowned with a widow's walk, the focal edifice of the whole superstructure; then, steering the automobile past a long sweep of serpentine brick wall, lined with boxwood, leading toward the rear of the grounds, quickly catching a sideways glance at the connecting wings, stretching right and left of Main House, joining two perfect diminutive replicas of the mansion to itself on either side. Each time, she unfailingly recalled Jack's account of Main House now being occupied by Armand and his wife Blanche; the children's bedrooms and servants' quarters having been settled into the left-wing, and mother Amanda established in dignified and autonomous privacy for what she reminded everyone periodically would be the remainder of her mortal life into the right. A comely, gracious prospect altogether, Marcia invariably concluded, just as an indistinguishably tiny smirk of proprietary complacence momentarily dominated her smiling countenance.

AFTER turning the Saturn to face the arched Palladian garage window with door beneath and shutting off the motor, Marcia quickly scooped up her coat from the adjacent front seat. Of course, all this was what Claire had envisioned as her own marital ambience for the future. Claire, not quite a Hughesville native, but near enough from Boar's Head Point, had earned a *summa cum laude* degree and R.N. from the University and its hospital, and then returned to serve in the newly endowed Hughesville Hospital upon its opening nearly a decade ago. She had come to meet Jack then, his father, following unsuccessful by-pass surgery, having lingered for many months in the Coronary Ward under Claire's nursing supervision. Of course, Marcia had never probed into the details of the matter with Jack, since she had simply and intuitively known that, had it been possible, Armand would certainly have been Claire's first choice, everything else considered. But, climbing the curving right-hand brick steps to Jack's apartment, Marcia admitted that that was hardly an original or generous thought, in light of Jack's unquestioned knightly submission to his Lancelot-like life script, probably handed him from earliest childhood, wherein, he, arguably the more brilliant, the more courageous and even more imaginative of the two brothers, she surmised, should forever consent to be cast in the role of second-best.

Marcia lifted the weighty and heavily polished brass knocker on the gleaming carved oak door and let it drop into place... once, twice. For a minute, she stood with her back toward it before, through the high arched window above, she could see on the facing bricks, the reflection of the hallway light having just been turned on, heard footsteps and then turned to face Jack himself, who quickly and silently drew her inside.

Once inside the entresol, without uttering a word, Jack slipped his arm under her coat, his hand sliding across her back, walked her into the living room, where, again wordlessly, he drew off her coat, flung it gently onto one of the white armchairs, and enfolded her intently, inexorably, into a siege of prolonged, searching, passionate kisses. Overwhelmed, as was he, she fell instantly, irresistibly, along with him, into a lotus-well of drugged, amnesiac, and rapturous embraces. It was some minutes before he assumed a more erect posture and half-led, half-carried her toward one of the facing love-seats, where, somewhat dazed, they seated themselves individually, stiffly, almost decorously.

It was some minutes before she unclasped her hands and looked at Jack fully and directly.

"Jack..." an inappropriate titter. "For Heaven's sake, what's the matter?"

He allowed his head to rest on the back of the sofa, smiled, and looked at her with unabashed tenderness. "Nothing. Nothing's the matter." His left hand reached over and squeezed both of hers, clasped together once more. "I just love you. Is that all right?"

"Well, of course. And, I too..."

One long kiss more, as if to reassure himself, and Jack rose, moved to the serving island between living and dining room, uncorked the bottle of wine that had been cooling in the ice bucket, and poured out two drinks.

"AS FOR that, I guess it's all backing up... how was your visit with your in-laws?" he diverted, handing her a wine goblet.

"Oh, that came off splendidly! You know, Vivvy just adores Barry." They both sipped quietly. "But it was a productive trip for Alex, too. She found a small, reasonably priced old house at Lighthouse Point that she thinks will be just right for them. That they can afford to buy... and maintain on their retirement income."

"Great..." Jack rose to refresh their glasses.

"You think it's going to be 'uncomfortable,' with the here?"

"Not a bit of it!" Marcia flashed back. "But now that you bring it up, Jack, why *should* it be?"

He shrugged. "Well, I guess it depends on where you think *we're* going?"

"To dinner," facetiously, before she could restrain herself.

Reseated, he spoke toward the center of the room; his eyes focused indefinitely before him. "Those evenings after negotiations... left lots of time for me... alone, in my hotel room. Plenty of time to think. You know, for Claire once there was no possibility of children, or should I say, practically no possibility, the marriage somehow lost its... well, its point, I suppose. She found she wasn't that interested in me... solely for myself. And, I guess I have to admit that I became aware that I could not be interested in the sort of person she was turning out to be... to have been all along... if I could only have seen it in time."

"Are you saying that she was more interested in being part of the LeClerc *family* than in being Mrs. *Jack* LeClerc?"

"Not exactly. Not exactly." Jack walked over to a side window and leaned his forehead against its darkening pane. "You know, nothing is ever exactly as simple as we might wish it to be. Anyway," unconsciously shaking himself and starting back toward the sofa. "There was no sustaining passion in our marriage... appetite, yes, but no passion..." He laughed self-consciously. "I'm afraid I'm real Romantic. I believe that sex without this kind of passion becomes... well, in the long haul, athletic, arduous." He snorted. "Effortful and alien to the spirit."

"Some people call that kind of passion *love*..." Marcia interdicted in a level voice from her end of the couch.

"Well, love is something else again... bigger, more encompassing," Jack mused, "...harder to achieve."

"Achieve, Jack? *Achieve*? For Heaven's sake, one doesn't have to *achieve* love, does one?"

Sitting next to Marcia, he turned to look into her face. "Yes, I think you do, Marcia."

A pause. He carried their glasses to the counter and set them.

"ANYWAY, Marcia, to get back to our original question. Where are we *headed*? What do you *want*?"

Agitated, restless, Marcia rose in turn, and arbitrarily sat down in one of the farther-positioned armchairs. She looked back at Jack. "A *good* life. A *real* family. Love and meaningful work."

"You say a *real* family. But suppose you and I were unable to have children, as Claire and I discovered to our chagrin and mutual astonishment... wouldn't I just turn out to be an appendage to the "family" you already have? You know, Marcia, the real reproductive problem was identified as *mine*, primarily, not Claire's?"

"Oooh... sometime..." reseating herself. "You've made it all sound so mechanical. So... so... dynastic... even."

"I don't mean to sound any particular way, Marcia. I'm just trying to be honest, and to face the possibilities of grave problems for us in the future... Christ, Marcia," he pleaded finally, his voice edging toward stridency, "would you *not* want me to bring to bear what I have learned from one heart-wrenching, useless decade of my life? How many more decades do you think I have to squander?" He heard her gasp. "I'm sorry, I guess I'm getting maudlin. I'm sorry."

"Yes, you *are*. And I want... I want a friend and companion, a father for Vivvy, not just a *stud*, for God's sake!'

"You say that now... but..."

"*But* be damned!: Marcia planted herself directly in front of him. "Besides, there is no possibility of our *not* being able to have children if it comes to that..."

"I know, Marcia, there are newer techniques..."

"I'm not talking about newer techniques..."

She had Jack's attention and suddenly felt unequal to the task. "Jack, right now, right this instant, there is a substantial sperm specimen being held for me in a sperm bank in Baltimore. Ready to be implanted on two or more ova contributed from myself... *in vitro*... whenever I choose."

They looked at each other for a full minute: Jack was first to lower his eyes.

"Why haven't you told me this before, Marcia?"

She shrugged, diverting her own gaze, a wave of mild nausea gathering somewhere in her depths.

"I don't know." She threw up her hands. "I honestly don't know. I've been thinking about it, OK? About what to do about it."

"You haven't spoken to Alex and Barry about it, either?"

"No."

Once more, disturbed, Marcia began to pace around the room. "I don't know. I don't know."

Stationed behind one of the armchairs, "At first, at first, there was no question in my mind. Of course, when the people at the sperm bank first got in touch with me... afterwards... by mail... I was just going to contribute the... the material, if they needed or wanted it. After all, they'd taken an extensive history on Lu, et cetera, et cetera, and he was, in their over-all estimate, an excellent candidate." Choking on her laugh, "This is *all* so painful, somehow.

"But, for some reason, I just didn't do *anything*. I couldn't seem to do anything. I just let it ride. I even half forgot about it.

"And, then, one day, it occurred to me that I could still have another child, Lu's child, if I *wanted* to. It shocked me. One part of my Mind, my very soul, said to me, 'Oh, Marcia, what a beautiful, immortal idea,' but another said, 'Marcia, you are some kind of ghoul. Stop. Stop. Before you do something irreparably *evil*." Face in her hands, "Let the poor man *die*," she whispered.

After a long silence, Jack's voice, "And, where are you now?"

"I don't know."

ONCE more, Jack rose, refilled their glasses, and placed both goblets on the coffee table before the love-seat.

"First of all, I want to tell you quite plainly, that if this... this plan of having another baby were to be pursued, *and if you and I were married*, I have absolutely no objection to using Lu's sperm as it may well be necessary to use someone's sperm and why, in God's name, should I object to Lu's over some stranger's?

"But, *never* before Alex and Barry were told, and fully agreed to it." Another long silence.

"And, I think *that* is highly unlikely."

SILENCE again. "But, I haven't emptied myself of all this yet," Jack breathed. "How could you wish to bring a child into the world already missing a father? Why would you wish to do such a... I'm sorry, Marcia... selfish... foolish thing?"

"It's done all the time..." Marcia half shrieked. "There are single mothers and gays, and God only knows who all having babies... all the time. The times have changed, Jack! They've changed. Only old duffers like yourself..." Maddeningly, she found she was weeping.

"I repeat, Marcia. Why would you want to do such a self-serving, selfish thing?"

"Well, for God's sake, Jack, Vivvy has no father! Should I dispose of her!?"

"I won't insult either of us by answering that! When a child is unfortunate enough to have lost a parent... whatever the reason... of course, of course, we do the best we can with nurturing..."

"Jack, you have just been divorced yourself. How can you be so... so self-righteous..."

Marcia turned her head away from Jack and leaned it against the sofa. She allowed herself a full weep, quiet, undramatic, a puckered, red-eye, nose-running child bawl, as she had not allowed to happen since the months immediately following Lu's death.

JACK slid his arm under Marcia's torso, turning her head toward him. He kissed her tenderly, consolingly, as one kisses a child who has suffered. She placed her hands on either side of his face, and drawing him close, kissed him to relieve all the grieving compassion of their mutual kind. So, both sat, tears sleeting across their cheeks, heartbroken, happy, united, and concerned.

ON SOME intuitive, reflexive cue, they both stood and walked toward the next room, Jack's bedroom.

MARCIA awoke to Jack's stroking her cheek. She looked up into his well-modeled, almost waxen face, and felt drunk, disoriented. Without raising her body, she turned and reached for the alarm clock; she knew he kept on that side of the bed. Ten-thirty.

"I'd best get dressed, Jack. Even on weekends, Jean has a twelve o'clock curfew."

Carefully, methodically, in reverence to normalcy, Marcia began putting on her clothing. Jack sat up in bed, watched her dress, but made no move to get up himself.

"We never finished our conversation, Marcia." Soberly, "At the risk of boring you, I will just repeat that I love you. I want you to be part of my life."

Marcia pushed her foot into a shoe. "Is that a proposal, Jack?"

"It's whatever you want it to be, Marcia. But, certainly, at least a proposal." He rose now and swung on his bathrobe.

"You really would not object to using... if it *were* necessary?"

"I said I wouldn't."

"That's one of the most generous things I've ever..." she shook her head.

"But why, Jack? Not why about... but why do you love *me*?"

He sat on the edge of the bed. "When I worked with you over all those legal details... right after... Claire and I were already deep into our division of property... and everything else." A rueful laugh, "And the contrast to you... your attitude... was an agony to me, a revelation. Your inconsolable grief, your caring, Vivvy's loving trauma... I knew no one; no one had ever loved me like that. Never and I was sure no one ever would."

"Jack, I don't know that to say... or do. I don't know. But, you have helped me wish to... to be alive... again." Marcia walked out of the room, Jack following. She reclaimed her coat from the armchair and began to put it on. "I have to go."

Jack walked her to the door. "Don't be afraid, Marcia. I have enough certainty for both of us. Let's say, we're both old caregivers, and as unlikely a match as that may appear to be, it may also turn out to be a marriage made in heaven."

"Two middle-aged caregivers! Counselor, you make me feel at least a million years old," Marcia smiled sadly.

At the door, "But don't forget, you owe me a dinner. Imagine sending a guest home..."

A lingering for-real, no-nonsense kiss, and shaking her upraised arm over her head as she descended the stairs, "You are a piece of work, Jack... A unique..."

"I'LL phone you tomorrow, midmorning," he called after her.
"Whatever you say, counselor."

JACK had lit the stairwell down to the car, and breathing in the damp and chilling night air, the yearning to retrieve her steps and rush back toward the warm haven she'd just abandoned was barely endurable.

Chapter Eleven

T HE INTERVENING week had passed quickly and uneventfully: Marcia had scheduled this two o'clock Friday meeting with Ginny for review of med-logs preparatory to Monday's routine conference, both noting upon check-over of Greta's folder, that, as of this client's last medical examination, Dr. Mathews had more or less "signed off" on her, indicating that current weekly visits would now be discontinued, one quarterly checkup only scheduled a few months hence. Concluding their update of Greta's folder, Ginny aimed a searching, quizzical look at Marcia: Marcia merely smiled back, albeit with a resigned, fateful air, unwilling to tip the precarious balance in this situation with any premonitory opinions.

Directly after lunch was cleared away, Marcia had received her weekly call from Alex in Los Angeles. In a breezy, offhand manner, Alex announced she had just handed in an official letter of resignation to her immediate supervisor, effective as of the end of the year. She went on to inform Marcia that Westdale's had been put in charge of selling their condominium and were already holding open-house every Sunday. Non-stop, she recounted how she had consulted three major national firms for moving cost estimates and, one already having been completed, she was forwarding the information to Alcon today. After this impromptu, helter-skelter summary of recent events, Marcia ventured onto a more sensitive topic with her mother-in-law.

"And what position is Alcon taking on moving your household to Lighthouse Point, rather than to Alexandria...?"

A few seconds and Alex's voice, grim, humorless crackled across the wire. "We're still negotiating about that. Barry has managed to smooth over some of the difficulties..." she added. "After all, the company is aware he's only a year away from retirement... that should make a difference, especially since we are prepared to make some sacrifices, too.

"We'll see, we'll see," Alex speculated. "It's all up in the air still."

"Are you excited?" Marcia asked lightheartedly, wishing to move away from this troubled aspect of the subject.

"Or, sad, maybe?" she added.

A discernible pause. "Oh, I don't give a damn about the job!" Alex protested. "Nor even about Los Angeles, for that matter. Take away the symphony and the museums, and what've you got?... Beverly Hill, the homeless, on-location shooting, and assorted crimes. No, no..." her voice faded. "I think I'm scared."

"Scared? You, Alex? For, Heaven's sake, why? It's your reward after hard labor."

"That's just it." An audible intake of breath. "I'm scared because what I have always told myself I wanted to do and thought I could do, I now have to *prove*, to myself at least, I *can* do."

"And what's that?" Marcia asked, genuinely nonplused, never ever having recalled Alex revealing any impelling career goal.

"Well, making it as a freelancer, at least. Doing something worthwhile and individual with my writing."

"Of course," Marcia assented, suddenly connected into the now obviously predictable coherence of this goal.

"Or, of course *not*," Alex mocked.

Marcia was stilled, at a loss for what to say. Of a sudden confronting senior anxiety, indistinguishable from adolescent anomie, in retrospect, Barry's fits and starts of the evening of the cookout flashing across her mind, there seemed nothing to say.

Yet, she had so much to do, and the call had gone on now for nearly a half-hour; she needed to bring to as gracious a close as possible.

Alex's call terminated, still bewildered by her mother-in-law's unsuspected doubts, Marcia nonetheless put this matter aside, immediately turning to the phone, locating John, and proceeding with explicit instructions for last-minute weekend deliveries to one or two of the houses.

JUST as the pre-four-o'clock bustle of rounding up clients for their afternoon return to individual homes had started, a very erect and decorous appearing Ginny escorted Mr. and Mrs. Hygher into Marcia's office. Vacuously, she mumbled a few introductory phrases while graciously indicating two gold armchairs in a semicircle before Marcia's desk. Their guests seated, she found herself an unobtrusive armchair out of the Hyghers' line of vision, and seating herself, placed the thick folder she was carrying (undoubtedly Greta's Marcia surmised), carefully, sacramentally in her lap.

Mr. Hyghers took more than a few minutes with a solicitous business of painstakingly adjusting his wife's coat at the back of her chair. But Marcia assessed correctly who was to be in charge of the meeting when Mr. Hygher made a small but deliberate realignment of his seat from the curved facing companionship of the nearer armchair to a position directly in front and only inches away from her desk. For barely a few seconds Marcia considered initiating the interview by handing both Mr. and Mrs. Hygher Dr. Mathews' formal written medical report and going from there (too impersonal, she decided); then letting Ginny introduce the whole matter on her authoritative role as medical liaison (too cowardly, by far, she admitted); and now unconscious of the deep breath she took while reaching across her desk to shake their hands, she refocused herself as best she could toward making a quest, serious beginning.

"Let us, first off," a clam, flat delivery, "assure you that Greta is mentally and physically in good health. But, we regret having to report that she did sustain an *unusual*, a troubling incident a few weeks ago."

Rapt stillness.

Marcia now began a methodical reprise of the client's behavior that had prompted Hannah to take Greta to the Emergency Room several Sundays previous; the result of Dr. Mathews' initial and subsequent examinations, but ultimately inconclusive findings; ongoing physical examinations since; and Greta's present normal unremarkable physical condition. Throughout hew measured recital, neither of the Hyghers spoke a word... they neither asked a question, nor made a comment, nor registered any protest. They just sat there until she had finished. As there was now nothing more for her to say, Marcia merely signified to Ginny to give each of Hyghers a copy of Dr. Mathews' completed medical report.

The Hyghers sat for at least another full five minutes looking over these medical forms, again neither of them saying a word, although Mr. Hygher's face flushed crimson once, and blanched at another time. Having concluded their perusal, Mrs. Hyghers inched her chair closer to her husband's, almost directly behind his, fell into a grown of catatonic, pleading stare at the back of his head, her eyes enormous, orbs upturned, recalling for Marcia nothing so much as the face of one of the grieving women at the foot of the Cross in some famous Renaissance portrayal of the Crucifixion.

"For God's sake, Miz Byrnes, with all this... this... Why didn't you get in touch with us immediately?" As imagined speech from the oracle at Delphi, the voice had begun softly, in almost tremulous whisper, but ended in a pitching burst of rage.

Stunned also, momentarily unable to avoid echoing the speaker's horror, "Under the circumstances..." Marcia stuttered.

"What circumstances... what circumstances?! Lazarus Hygher erupted.

In an voice geared toward reintroducing rationality into the exchange: "Mr. Hygher, please remember that when we took Greta to Emergency, we could only conjecture about her real symptoms, let alone their cause. We actually had no firm, definite findings, or diagnosis, until we heard from Dr. Mathews at the end of the week."

"That is when you should have immediately - *immediately* - gotten in touch with us," he slammed back.

"I did try," Marcia said halfheartedly. "I called your home... and then your office. Miss Wheaton informed me that you had just taken off for a long cruise in the company of your yacht mates... a kind of fleet... or regatta?"

"It was no damned *regatta!*"

"... But even so, it was an obvious, carefully planned activity... you were not readily available... and ... meanwhile, Greta was under close medical supervision, no emergency of any sort existed, so that... And I knew I would be seeing you shortly.

"What kind of operation are you running here, Miz Byrnes?" Mt Hyger hissed coldly, worse than his explosions.

"You have every right to be concerned, of course..." her tone faltering.

"Concerned, *concerned!*" he glared at her incredulously. "Miz Byrnes, are you *insane*? Do you realize that Abby and I have spent more care, more time, more money, more raw worry over this child than all of our other children put together?

And I mean that quite literally! For a heartbreaking decade and a half, we struggled with her care at home, one after another live-in nurse, caretaker, companion pulling away from the wrenching responsibilities of caring for Gretty. As she got older, bigger... it just became too much! We placed her in one supposedly excellent facility after another. We were almost at our wit's end! When we found the Center here, we had already spent months – months! – visiting different private facilities, sanatoriums, what have you... Well, I needn't tell you... how ecstatic, how impressed we were with the Center before we decided to place our Greta here."

"Mr. Hygher, I just want to assure you that we have *never, never* had a male nurse or monitor in that house... not even in emergencies. And... and... painful as it maybe this, this incident followed immediately upon Greta's being returned from a home visit."

Mr. Hygher sprang from his chair and shouted across the desk at Marcia. "That *does* it, Miz Byrnes. That just about does it! Are you implying...?"

"I'm not implying anything. But simple honesty... and fundamental fairness dictate that we look at the *facts* of the case."

"Facts. Facts. Miz Byrnes, I want Greta's things packed up right now. Right this instant! She's going home. And *staying* home."

Ginny had left the room and returned with Hannah and Greta, both of whom stood in the doorway, looking dismayed. Mr. Hygher turned and half-pushed the whole group toward the door. Just out the room, he turned back. "But you'll be hearing from our lawyers, Miz Byrnes. You can be sure of that. And I'll tell you right now; you better start collecting specimens from your entire male house personnel... if not the whole staff! Come on, Abby... for Christ's sake."

As he piloted the convey of daughter and wife, nurse, and house monitor through the Center's large activity room, Marcia bestirred herself and hurried after them. Hannah was already loading Greta into the van wheelchair when Marcia tried once again as calmly as possible: "Mr. Hygher, Dr. Mathews said that there was no way of collecting any possible specimen, as none existed... it was too far after the event, you see... if there was an event."

Mr. Hygher turned. "Well, what about the doctor in Emergency?"

"I believe, he, too, found it difficult, or..."

"Miz Byrnes, his difficulties have just begun. He will be hearing from our lawyers, too," Hygher pronounced, pulling one of the van doors shut, as Hannah slammed the other into place.

With a melodramatic mini-splurge of gravel, the van turned into the main road, taking a right at the intersection and heading toward Partridge Point. Marcia glanced at Ginny, standing on what had been the other side of the vehicle. Without looking at each other, hunched against the suddenly sleeting rain, the women ran toward the warmth and shelter of the Center.

ALTHOUGH Jack had never acted as counsel to the LeClerc family and brother to its present director, Armand, his involvement with company affairs, though held always at what he was scrupulous to keep at suitable business and psychic arms-length, was inescapable. Like his tactful but cool relationship with his mother, and decorous, even punctilious association with his sister-in-law-Blanche, for Jack, family membership supportable by himself required continual vigilance, monitoring, and course correction. Strictly in a legal sense, did he consider himself an *amicus familiae.*

Armand had told him that he and a select management staff had scheduled a meeting for ten o'clock this Friday morning with core union leadership in the third-floor Industrial Relations Conference Room. He had asked Jack to meet him there about noon to accompany him to their mother's home after the meeting, essentially to serve as back-up, Armand said, should there be any need to clarify legal terminology or explain obscure terms to their parent in the documents she was about to sign. Jack, more than suspected that his older brother also found it distasteful to face their mother in these terminal stages of arranging for the sale of the family business.

Nels, an "old-timer" known to Jack for decades, had been posted as *pro-tem* security guard at the foot of the staircase leading to friendly greetings, he waved Jack past at eleven forty-five.

From the Conference Room door, Jack managed a quick, but unseen glimpse, at the Union side of the table: he knew them all. In the center, the District Director of the parent union, National Consolidated Containers United, Don Bartosh; on his right, recording secretary Gary Letzger; and on his left, the president and vice-president of the Local Union, Jamie McClintock and Paul Doran. At the foot of the table, his back to the door was, Jack conjectured, Union counsel, whom he did not recognize, with but slightly individual variation for age and appearance, the Union men looked unvaryingly grim, desolate and unconvinced. Paul Doran, the oldest of the men perhaps, a big, burly man, barely contained in his chair, breathing heavily, looked utterly dismayed.

Their own Company counselor, Stewart Carleton, in his usual reasonable, well-modulated baritone, seemed to be summarizing some matters under discussion as Jack claimed a seat in the small lobby outside the Conference Room, extracting a pack of cigarettes from his breast pocket. As he lit up, he heard his brother's voice interrupt: "I don't know what all this last-minute clutching is about," he was saying in a bland, confident, start-athlete, "One of the boys" delivery. "Nothing new here. Nothing new at all. No surprises," His tone became more sedate. "For a decade now, the business has shown every classic sign of trouble. We've barely weathered downturns in the economy. Since my father's last years, the business has been only marginally profitable. The plant getting older all the time, needing modernization, admittedly, with no money with which to do it, and precious little borrowing potential, either. We've reduced production. We've had periodic layoffs."

"But, we had a kind of gentleman's agreement with your father... with previous management," Paul's voice broke in, husky and imperative, "that they were committed to modernization. That they were dedicated to keeping the plant competitive..."

There was a momentary silence.

"Forget it, Paul," came the voice of Don Bartosh of the parent union. "The cord is cut. From what Mr. LeClerc is saying, it's a done deal. No opportunity for last-minute measures..." There was some scraping of chair legs, some shuffling of paper when Don's voice resumed. "But I do think we have a right to know where we stand. Since the successor plant is purchasing during the term of our labor agreement, will they stand by its terms, or will they enter into an extension agreement...?"

Carleton. Self- possessed, unruffled. "Such a legal ruling only holds in the case where there has *not* been any substantial change in the employing industry... if the basic operation remains intact."

Armand's voice interjected again, not without edge. "And what I've been trying to get across to you men is that Allied General, as part of their purchasing stipulations, want to retain the freedom to further evaluate how they will ultimately use the facility. They insist on it as part of the contract."

"Can't this be negotiated?" Jamie McClintock, president of the Local. "I think you owe us that much, Mr. LeClerc," he said in dead-earnest reproach.

Jack could not see his brother's face, but he well-imagined his thoughts. They had circled this point for hours with Allied General's counsel, to no avail. Nor was Armand about to lose a sale over it, Jack felt certain.

"There are very strict legal guidelines governing the judgment that the employing industry has remained substantially the same," Carleton's voice persisted, explaining. "It includes, amongst other matters, continuity of the same business operation, use of the same plant, maintenance of the same jobs under the same working conditions, same supervisory staff, same machinery and equipment, same method, same products... The successor company is not willing nor able at this time to give such assurances..."

Jack stubbed out his cigarette, stood up soundlessly, and planted himself, parallel to and against the wall next to the door, unseen: he was unable to restrain his raw, natural curiosity.

Again, he could see only the union side of the table. The man just sat there. Nobody seemed to know what to do next. Jack watched them fight a massive of disbelief.

"... but there are still unresolved issues relative to unequal overtime pay, the security of the pension plan, layoff schedules," Doran roused himself in a last bullish effort.

Softly, Carleton. "These matters will have to be reintroduced to new management," he said. "At this time, the situation is unresolved... fluid... We can make no promises..."

"Christ, this is like Pearl Harbor," Gary Letzger barked. "What're we going to tell the men?"

"Well, they had *some* idea I was coming," Bartosh said fiercely, picking up the papers in front of him and standing up. "Five, ten years ago," he insisted cruelly. "I guess they knew when you finally milk the damned thing dry; you sell it to the highest bidder."

Jack barely managed to be standing by the big wall of paned windows looking out at the buff, rolling, peaceful, fall-away meadow dropping to the bay on that side of the plant. He had never cared about the business, one way or the other. But for the first time in his life, he felt something akin to an overwhelming scourge of sorrow, under whose crack he bowed defenseless.

THE room emptied of men – first the union people, and then, one after the other, Zach Blaine, LeClerc's Personnel Manager; Dick Stilton, Industrial Relations Coordinator; Carleton, shrugging on a London Fog raincoat, all left silently, hurrying out of the Conference Room and heading toward the stairs. Jack continued standing by the window, in a corner of the lobby, watching them. Armand himself finally emerged, carrying a light cashmere topcoat over his arm, his cap already on. Outside the Conference Room door, his brother stopped, turned a full half-circle for better surveillance of the room. Spotting Jack, he began pulling on his coat.

"What'y' doing hiding there in her corner, Jack?"

Without waiting for an answer, he, too, began walking toward the staircase, Jack catching up. In mid-fight, "... you know those negotiations ended in Baltimore. Allied General wasn't going to promise anything before they finally bought the business, lock, stock, and tin can." They were almost at the exit door. "And, though I'd like to think that it's a pretty sure thing by now... anything can happen... and, at any time." They were out the door and walking toward Armand's Lincoln Town Car parked in a reserved space conveniently close to the exit, just steps away from the plant. They got into the car. "Christ, that's all we need," Armand grumbled. "That's all we need is for them to find we're up to our dorks in labor problems." Intuitively, he turned the ignition key and drove the car smoothly, expertly out of the parking lot onto the picturesque arbored back road that led to Bay View Drive, edging the upper bluff, upon whose apex were ensconced Main House and its several outlying structures.

Jack looked over at his brother, heavier than he had been, but still handsome, with his rugged Dick Tracy profile, assured, sanguine as a full-grown elk, and just as ready for battle. At just over 50, what would he do with all the brute energy for another quarter of a century? Was there enough deep sea fishing, sailing, hunting, and regional power politicking to fuel off the seemingly inexhaustible carnal vigor of the man, Jack speculated.

Armand flashed a belligerent look in Jack's direction. "Look, Jacques," (he always called Jack by his formal, given name when he was on attack), "I don't want to hear any of your sanctimonious crap about what the company owes the men. You've kept the business conveniently at arm's length... all of your life... while, I might add, still reaping the benefits of the LeClerc name and prestige for your own adopted law firm. It hasn't hurt a bit; I bet... has it now?

"You're entirely right, Armand." Jack had been over this ground so many times... he knew just what was going to be said, how it was going to be said, and how he would feel after it had been said. Games people play, he almost muttered aloud, lending himself instead to his predestined role in a by-now habitual spirit of despondency. "But, as you know, I confronted Dad with all that before going to Hamilton... and before Yale Law School."

"Yeah, yeah... I know. 'Cut me off without a cent, Dad. Just get me my fishing license first.'" Armand turned the car sharply onto Bay View Drive, and they began to climb steeply, circuitously along the crest. "Christ, Jack, give me a break! What if *I* had taken that same tack?"

"I respect the LeClerc heritage, Armand. More than you have probably ever imagined. And I respect what you did, what you were able to do, especially under difficult circumstances." As he finished speaking, Jack gazed over brother's shoulder at a gray-green field, cut through with a stand of autumnal honey-colored oak and amber maple, falling to the still, sunlit bay below. "But I also knew myself. If you wish, you can just leave it at this: I didn't have the right stuff."

"No one's trying to wrench an apology out of you, Jack. I'm just asking you to be as reasonable with me as I am with you."

THEY waited in the library for mother to finish lunching with old Judge and Mrs. Lebrand, amongst Amanda's oldest friends, now steadily but irregularly entertaining each other at social functions primarily during daylight hours, before she finally joined her sons, and inquiring about their having had lunch, ordered up a tray of sandwiches and coffee immediately. Soon enough, however, they hunkered down to the mind-stunning, meticulous job of reviewing the various preliminary sales documents. Toward four o'clock, Armand's attention and patience both wearing thin, he unwisely, in Jack's estimate, let drop a casual observation that there was a possibility that "labor complications" at the LeClerc Works might ultimately undo any potential sale. Amanda sat back stunned at this remark, as Jack gamely hastened to explain that the position, usually approved by the courts, well after-sale was effected, was that a successor employer was liable for any unfair labor practices of the predecessor. But Jacks, attempt to ameliorate the LeClerc position, only drove Amanda well past her limit.

"What *is* all this, Jack?" she demanded, turning to Armand. "Jack, I don't understand *one* thing you've said. I never *do*! I never *have*! I will just have to have Hugh go over these *details* with me. And... and explain about this other... untenable situation." (Hugh Lebrand, his associate, her personal lawyer, and nephew to old Judge Lebrand, was Armand's age, correct, generally acknowledged a substantial professional, about whom no one, not even his personal secretary, could offer more evaluation than that he was impeccable in attendance at social and community functions, with a "perfectly lovely" wife and children, about whom no one could remember anything unseemly either, as indeed no one could recall much of anything about him at all. Having practiced with him for a decade and a half, Jack himself had few salient personal impressions of his colleague, except for a few individualized half-notions that added up to nothing at all. Yet Hugh Lebrand, Jack had become aware, had managed over time to inspire a granite confidence and unextinguished admiration in most of the dowagers of Hughesville. Indeed, managing their affairs made up the bulk of his not inconsiderable practice.)

"What do *you* think, Armand?" Amanda pleaded, her tone hovering between tears and girlish sexual entreaty.

"Ithinkyoushoulddoexactlywhatyouthinkbest,mother," Armand responded with manly courtesy, frowning to show his disapprobation at all such vulnerability, yet understanding its inescapable source. Slipping his mother's cashmere shawl about her shoulders, he led her now to the oaken double door of the library with minuet delicacy and grace, managing thereby to bring about the penultimate, if informal, conclusion to this afternoon of exhausting family business.

FOR whatever reasons, none of which he was willing to explore when Armand accompanied Mother out the library, Jack sprang toward the French doors that led directly into the garden and made his own timely escape. He loped toward the garage, and finding Mr. Nichols, Amanda's chauffeur cum general handyman, inside, polishing the car, he requested a ride back to the plant so as to reclaim his own vehicle. As usual, Nichols was both prompt and obliging, and under the circumstances, even tolerable company. At the parking lot and into his own car finally, instead of at once returning to the vicinity of Main House, Jack drove to his law office downtown, ferreted out some unfinished documents from his desk, then headed out of Shore House in what was now a fine misting rain. He seated himself at the very end of the bar, away from the other few innocuous chatting customers, ordered and downed two double scotched within less than half an hour, but finally succumbed to common sense and presented himself for dinner in the main dining room. The light supper he ordered perfunctorily remained largely uneaten. On the way out the entresol of Shore House, the antique grandfather's clock, almost buried under a stand of corn stalks and rubicund pumpkin, showed minutes past eleven o'clock. Jack dutifully swathed himself in his discriminatingly chosen outer garment and left the restaurant to face the elements.

HE WOULD not have checked the answering machine that evening, nor notice the signal of an incoming message, had it not been that he automatically proceeded to his study desk to deposit the documents that had remained unexamined throughout the evening. Annoyed now at seeing the blinking light, more than half-anticipating some corollary suggestion or brisk adjuration from his brother regarding this afternoon's family interview, Jack could not refrain from an involuntary curse under his breath, as he dutifully punched the message button.

In a shaken, but highly controlled voice, Marcia's measured contralto. "Jack, it's now... oh, about ten, I guess. You're apparently not home yet... of course," a giggle meant to register inconsequential but ending in something suspiciously like a sob. A deep breath. "Jack, the Hyghers stopped to pick Greta up this afternoon for her monthly visit... Of course, I had to review..." Another pause, as if she were examining how she came to choose this particular inappropriate locution. "I had o *tell* them, Jack. About recent events." Another deep breath and full ten seconds. "They took her home... *Permanently*. They're going to sue." This time she didn't try to suppress a full-blown groan. "Could I talk to you about this? Soon? But... on second thought, you'd better not call tonight. It'll be too late. Just recently, if Vivvy happens to be waked t night, by the telephone, or whatever, she can't seem to get back to sleep... for hours." Another pause. "If you could, would you call at about midday tomorrow? I'll have Jen come over for a few hours at lunchtime. Maybe, we can go out... and this over." Another long pause. "Oh, Jack, I am *so* sorry to bother you... I'm sorry, really... Goodnight, Jack."

His hand was already reaching for the telephone before he became fully alert again to the injunction in Marcia's message, stopping him in mid-action. Instead, he allowed himself to drop into his desk chair, pushed the message button once more, and listened.

This time, he did not so much hear the words as the rhythm of importunity, indeed pleading; the music of anguish which bore the individual words, the message, like so much whirling flotsam on a tide of pain.

"Poor, dear Marcia," he whispered. "You poor, dear sap," he repeated.

He sat dumped in his chair, irresolute and miserable... about Marcia... about himself... about the state of the world in general, until another quarter-hour later, he abruptly placed himself under his own charge and sensibly put himself to bed.

Coda Three: Jack

A WAKENING TO a gray, indiscriminate wash of November dawn next morning, Jack felt a familiar emptiness, those pliant, plastic, hypothetical parts of his body – lungs, heart, liver, and spleen, and the more nether abdominal appurtenances, assumed in place. They would stay obedient, reliably there, as he gazed through the window of the back bedroom at the gray-green undulations of a landscape as barren and lonely as his heart. Alice, no less hypothetically, could not prevent her fall through a fissure in that imperfect universe, so he stood now, forever thirteen, riveted and staring, across that desolate soccer field behind his room at Rhodes School. Though held erect then by successive layers of school duties, ancient interlinear codes as clinging as batting, infused with ubiquitous varnish, dust, and the stentorian sounds of high virtues regularly proclaimed, his self had known intuitively how to gather himself together for yet another daily effort at creating himself.

Nor had he ever been homesick. That was a luxury for boys who had loved and been loved in their homes. He had never suffered such a loss.

He was simply devoid, hollow. From repetitive childhood enactments of rejection, from a flamboyant mother cossetting and flirting with a charming elder brother, a father whose virile sorties at fairness invariably terminated in bewilderment, for how could any red-blooded, rightly-constructed male, child or adult, neither ride a horse competently nor catch a fish with decent aplomb, whatever other academic honors were offered periodically, a pulling form of compensation, all things considered.

THUS, early on, Jack had learned to generate and occupy his own space. Like Frankenstein, he was his own creation, this time, without benefit of doctor. Never mind mother, father, Armand, and latterly,

Claire and Lebrand, he had created his own religion of compassionate rationality as the only alternative tolerable world in which he could live. There was enough to do, more than enough, God knows, forever watchful to understand more fully, forever at pains to make those necessary adjustments in his own attitudes and behavior, to fill more than one existence. But- one selfish prerogative he had insisted on – everything under an undeniable protective shield of impenetrable personal privacy.

This morning, mechanically – punishing, cleansing – he forced himself to shower thoroughly and methodically as always, shave, dress casually but painstakingly, made up his bed into drum-like tightness, set his apartment to rights, and set off a turn about the grounds...

ARBITRARILY, he descended the left curving steps of the Carriage House, sauntering toward the serpentine brick wall hugged by aromatic box. He followed the structure's regular undulations toward the low brick wall that outlined the crest of the bluff, holding Main House placidly saucered in its leafy concave summit. The bay – beautiful, wide, and peaceful – stretched away from these proprietary civilized claims – itself. Out of time, Jack allowed himself an unmeasured morning communion.

REGENERATED, he ordered himself to walk the wide, well-tended lawn across the back of the property, facing the bay, his mother's wing in full morning sunshine – fresh, strong, declarative. The east side of Armand's Main House bathed in sunlight, vast trees shading its west side, its main entrance shadowed mysteriously. The children's wing hesitant in chiaroscuro, waiting for discovery by the sun.

THERE was no one about. No one anywhere. Jack stood in the grass beholding Main House... its slate-roofed symmetrical perfection... its promise of what? ... eternal continuity... inexpungible destiny. Yet through the filtering mist and discriminating sunlight, *no one was there.*

It *was* beautiful. Pyramid on the Chesapeake. It was intuitively, intellectual reassuring. *Here is the church, here is the steeple, here are the doors, and here are the people.*

But no one was there. No one had ever been for him. There had never been anyone there!

The idea appalled him, took such hold, it drove him around the side of the children's wing, up the Carriage House steps, and directly into his study.

IT WAS still too early to call Marcia. Marcia and Vivvy would be up and about by now, but Marcia would not likely have had time to make arrangements with Jean about lunchtime babysitting.

HE SAT as his desk, desultorily opened a folder of documents for review. Counselor, indeed! The law which at first had seemed to promise such a codification of that compassionate rationalism he so espoused developed instead skills of feint and counter-feint worthy of a fencing master; logic-chopping, double-speak, and obfuscation enough to bewilder a Talmudic scholar; compromises making Chamberlain appear a mere novice. Games-master is what he had become. Umpire and advisor in a tight, rough, no-holds-barred struggle for money and position.

HOW had Marcia come to find herself in this contentious arena? He was not absolutely certain that something might not have happened to Greta at the Center; one needed always to allow for any possibility, however distasteful, but his common sense, and mostly, the presumed chronology of events as they had occurred, seemed to argue against it. Why, for example, had the symptoms first emerged shortly after Greta's return from a home visit?

On the other hand, one had to be careful in precipitously assuming her nearest family were somehow responsible. One really knew nothing of the operations of the Hyghers' household, or, indeed, the specific schedule of events on the preceding contiguous days in Baltimore.

Of one thing he *was* certain: Marcia was as concerned to find out the truth in this matter, as were the Hyghers. Not a bit less. But it would be a messy, painstakingly, prolonged, and hurtful business. For everyone.

What could Marcia do but, with care and alacrity, respond to all legitimate requests upon her Agency...? Of course, he would be there to advise and oversee. But what he would have much preferred was to remove this burden from her entirely. He could see no way to do that.

HE HAD considered, but there was no use considering. He was once again reaching out from his own protected space to be, fully be, with another human being. All his reasoned compassion was as dust blown across a road. He did not fully understand why, although, of course, he had his reasons. Hadn't he had good reasons with Claire, too? Any self-respecting counselor perforce always had good reasons.

DEEPLY braced for more of the same, even now, he knew the futility in his situation, for he was powerless to stop himself. Apparently, something in him continued wanting to live and love, as fully, as romantically, as fulfillingly as any God's endless parade of feckless, urgent beings.

JACK reached for the telephone, conscientiously having noted it was now almost noon.

Chapter Twelve

T HE MONDAY morning after Barry and Alex had left, Vivvy did not slide into the less tousled side of the king-size bed before seven as she did every other morning to snuggle her mother's smooth, satiny warmth emanating cozily from under the purple and pink chintz quilts and mounded bedcover. Marcia opened her eyes and lay still in bed. Strips of pale gray light inserted themselves across both front windowsills beneath the dusky rose shades. She sat up and looked at the face of the digital clock on her bed-table. Eight-ten. A twist of panic, as she fingered the alarm mechanism and found it turned off. Slipping out of bed and rushing toward Vivvy's room, she could not remember when she had last acted so irresponsible.

Vivvy's powder blue sheet and lace coverlet were balled under her right ear; she, half uncovered, lay quietly, deeply asleep. Marcy slipped to the opposite side of the bed and automatically placed her hand on her daughter's forehead. Warm. Very warm. Only after her hand had rested there for a full clock minute, did Vivvy's eyelids flutter, and a fleck of blue-green appear and then disappear.

"Hi, Mommy," she said. In a bit, "I don't feel so good."

"I'll be right back, honey," reassuringly, as she hurried back to her own bathroom to fetch the child ear-thermometer.

Vivvy still lying prone, and still, Marcia noted, as she gently inserted the thermometer.

"Now, you've gone and done it," cheerfully. "You've got yourself a 101 degrees! And it's still only morning."

Now in full control, Marcia went to the hall phone and dialed the Center. She left a message for Ginny with the receptionist Angie that she would not be in this morning, or perhaps, the day. She would call Ginny again later.

Returning to Vivvy's room, her daughter again slumbering fitfully, Marcia whispered to her to rest and went off to shower and dress before calling Helen Trumbull, their pediatrician. They would try to fit them in at about 10:30, the nurse-reception said: and, please, under the circumstances, use the other – the contagion – waiting room.

Getting the rag-doll-armed-and-legged Vivvy dressed and, later, coated was a trying, time-consuming operation.

NO SURPRISE: it was one of the ubiquitous flus, with a not inconsiderable threat of ear infection to follow. Marcia remained home, doling out antibiotics, juices, broths, and sympathy for two full days, interspersed with reading sections of Vivvy's favorite stories. But late Tuesday, her second afternoon away from the job, she faced domestic reality and her parallel responsibility to the Center. She worked through all the troublesome arrangements for the very expensive adult babysitting service she used on just such occasions to come in for the rest of the week. They agreed to send her Mrs. Galliard again; she was free, gratefully – a buxom, copeful widow Lu and she had always called upon for truly "serious" baby-sitting. It was Mrs. Galliard who stayed with Vivvy when Marcia and Lu had made their weekend jaunt to New York for their first anniversary. Mrs. Galliard did not "do" windows, but she took reasonably good care of the house, cooked palatable meals from raw materials, and consistently exhibited rare common sense in the kind of prosaic, bedeviling decisions that spring up in any ordinary day with children.

Vivvy had always liked coming to the Center and had done so occasionally after school upon some special day of a medical or dental appointment, ballet lesson, or other out-of-the-ordinary event. In the summer months following first grade, she had, in fact, insisted on spending at least one day a week at the Center, rather than at her old nursery school. Marcia had allowed it, at first only reluctantly, but she became aware that the staff seemed to enjoy her daughter's visits: they smiled at each other as Vivvy went skipping amongst the many wheelchairs and prone matted figures of the severely handicapped with total ease and aplomb, their gnarled bodies and sometimes comic twisted expression that many adults found insupportably repulsive, accepted as easily and naturally as a playground full of rowdy second-graders. Indeed, Vivvy had managed to make friends, good friends with several of the clients. They could be seen smiling moist, appreciative smiles as she handed them their favorite doll or squatted next to their chairs for a spell of chat. Though most were incapable of more than a few words of coherent speech, they shook their heads at her and touched her shoulder, or arm, her hand or face, repeatedly, as she gabbled at them happily. She gave one a brisk ride around the Activity Room, joked with another, and fetched him a chocolate-chip cookie from the kitchen. Patently, they had become an indistinguishable part of her host of accepted friends.

This Thursday afternoon, Vivvy having been fever-free for 12 hours, Mrs. Galliard called the Center to ask if she could drop her off for perhaps an hour while she herself tended to getting in some necessary groceries for dinner and the next day: Marcia could at the same time provide her with required funding. By the by, Mrs. Galliard observed, it would also serve to get Vivvy out of the house for a spell, as she was becoming just a "wee bit stir-crazy" *à la* Galliard.

And so it was that Vivvy came first to be acquainted with Glory-Be.

EVEN so, that afternoon, Vivvy was not her more usual sprightly self. She had first stopped in her mother's office briefly, desultorily strolled out into the Activity Room and greeted one or two of her old friends, and then stood at the doors of the individual peripheral classrooms taking in the "tutorials," before reaching what turned out to be Gloria's individual classroom. Marie was seen turning pager for her pupil, strapped in a chair, as she read about some King John *not* being a good man. He was apparently called *Jack*, like the Jack Mommy, and she knew, who was asking Father Christmas for a pocket knife or candy, or chocolates, or oranges or nuts, or what-you-have for the holidays, but, most particularly, he wanted a big, red India rubber ball. And when she came to the end of the reading,

> *And oh, Father Christmas*
> *My blessings on you fall*
> *for bringing him*
> *a big, red,*
> *india-rubber*
> *ball!*

she half rose in her chair, shouting out the words like a real actress on TV or the movies. Vivvy couldn't help joining in the laughter with Marie and the girl afterwards, as bent in half, they laughed, and laughed, until they sort of looked as if they were going to cry.

Vivvy stepped out of the doorway and into the tiny room itself.

"Hi, Vivvy," Marie said. "I didn't see you standing there. Have you been there long? Gloria and I were just reading," Marie unclasped pages from a clothespin holder and shut the book, back to front.

Turning toward Vivvy, Marie said, "Gloria, this is Vivian, Vivian Byrnes. She's Miz Byrnes' daughter. And Vivvy, this is my student, Gloria O'Neill. Glory-Be, we sometimes call her."

"That's a fun poem. I enjoyed hearing you read it," Vivvy chuckled.

"It is, isn't it?"Glory-Be giggled in turn. It's one of *my* favorites."

"You know what I want for *my* Christmas?" the ebony-haired, just like her own, her eyes, greener, larger maybe, persisted. Vivvy admired her lovely plaid tartan dress which covered Gloria to her knew, but still left her legs visible, stiff in two steel brackets sticking out in front of her, like separate twin swords.

"Do you know what I'm expecting any day now, *any* day, for *my* best Christmas present?"

"Gloria, our lesson is over," Marie interrupted. "I think your mother will be here soon."

"What?" Vivvy asked, fascinated, and curious.

"Dr. Joe measured me for crutched on my last visits. And, they're going to be in any day now!"

As Marie gathered up materials, she observed to Vivvy, offhandedly, "Glory-Be's been out there at the lobby door every morning... when the mail truck gets in." Marie walked over to Glory-Be, put her arm around the girl's shoulder, and spoke quietly.

"But, remember, Glory-Be, the doctor said you'd have to go slow. That it might even be a couple of months before you developed the coordination... the *balance*... to try a few steps alone with them."

"I know, I know," Glory-Be conceded. "But isn't it *exciting*, Vivvy?!"

"I think it's *wonderful!*" Vivvy exclaimed. "I think I'd like to have a pair for myself."

RETURNING to the Byrnes' house with Vivvy, Mrs. Galliard could scarcely get the child settled for an hour's TV rest while she made up a meatloaf and scrubbed up the baked potatoes for the Byrnes' dinner. When Marcia arrived home, Vivvy rushed into the kitchen, interrupting her mother's review of Friday's schedule with Mrs. Galliard, distracting and insisting she was now well enough to go to the Center mid-afternoon tomorrow and "read" with Glory-Be. She had already laid out her volume of *Heidi*. She had told Gloria she would try to come, and Marie said I was all right, too. Vivvy generated such a tumult over this unprecedented procedure that Marcia felt compelled finally to phone Marie and confirm a time for the girls to meet for a prearranged snack and a "read" after Marie's more formal instruction.

"I'll get Vivvy home tomorrow, then, Mrs. Galliard," Marcia said, resignedly. "I'll have the lasagna ready for your dinner, as planned," Mrs. Galliard twinkled. "The table set and all." Mrs. Galliard bustled into her coat, drew on her galoshes, adding nothing more to these adventitious arrangements before actually standing at the Byrnes' front door.

"Don't you worry, Miz Byrnes," seriously. "That child is put together rightly, as good as God could wish. Don't you worry yourself a bit," a sparkling, young-girl grin creased her fair face, adding an impish cast to her aging features. "God Bless her..." Mrs. Galliard added, "she's a real dear..." She flung open the door and trooped lightly through the rising slush toward her van parked in the drive.

TWICE in the week, Vivvy insisted that Marcia inform the school bus driver to drop her off at the Center, rather than at nursery school, at the end of the school day. After comparable demands and at least one stormy evening confrontation in the following week, Vivvy came home on a Wednesday afternoon with a fully articulated, disconcerting plan for a visit to the O'Neill, Gloria's family, on the coming Saturday afternoon. Apparently, Gloria had promised to make all necessary arrangements with her family, and phone Vivvy with the details on Thursday. Now, Vivvy insisted, she would finally get to meet Gloria's big and middle sisters, her baby brother, and especially her wonderful bog, Scott, a perfect paragon of a favorite author, the redoubtable Sir Walter himself.

Reflexively, Marcia countered with protestations, but when Mrs. O'Neill called Thursday evening and, speaking with Marcia herself, throughout the call Mrs. O'Neill broadcasting a kind of irresistible charm, and intelligence, sparkling with lightning-quick Gaelic wit, and formally invited Vivvy to lunch with them at the Crabbe Shack, to be followed by an afternoon with the O'Neill girls, who had already lined up a corking-good home movie and planned several other interesting activities, there was no other course for Marcia but to accept graciously. But not without simultaneous misgivings about her own reactions in this ostensibly simple matter.

Notwithstanding, on Friday, Marcia suddenly succumbed to an urge to have lunch "out," and, having confirmed Gloria's home address from the child's file folder, drove the exquisite autumnal distance to Hughesville's nearest adjacent village, Inglewood Pines, toward the address listed for the O'Neill homestead.

The O'Neill house sat at the end of the cul-de-sac CampionRoad, a comfortable Victorian spread, only feet away from a natural sandy beach on an inlet of the Bay: not unlike Main House, its central structure festooned into several outlying wings. The house itself, she could not help but notice, was pristine with gleaming white enamel paint and satisfying blue-gray shutters, a vision of Louisa May Alcott respectability. It was pleasantly nestled amongst two braceletting groves of ancient beech, chestnut, and sycamores, and situated as it was at the apex of the curve on Campion, Marcia's Saturn was neatly guided past the O'Neill's and back into the main road toward her present destination. Heading toward the Center, she glimpsed her own image in the rearview mirror. "Just what seems to be your problem, lady?" she indicated, frowning.

But instinct dies hard, Marcia acknowledged to herself upon her return, harder even than the abrasiveness of an energetic self-scolding. After their review of Monday's Med-Logs, her question to Ginny about the O'Neill's was flung out casually, almost accidentally. Miz Schweitzer had worked with her supervisor long enough, however, not to register immediately the sharp edge in Marcia's voice. She was far too wise and well-bred, on the other hand, to reveal the least sign of surprise, let alone, obloquy at her supervisor's disingenuous curiosity.

"Mr. O'Neill... I believe he's CEO for the Wilmington branch of some big Hartford insurance company. I don't know which. Very respectable, from what I understand... very substantial." Ginny, who had always maintained a perdurable secrecy about her own personal life, added soberly, "He's an Episcopalian, you know, like me. We Episcopalians don't have such an easy time of it in this mostly fundamentalist area. Of course, it's not as bad as being a Catholic... but almost," chuckling. "Almost."

'Quite a presence in our church, in fact," she continued. "Deacon... for years now. And, Mrs. O'Neill is no slouch, either. Very involved with lots of good causes. Specially those having to do with Cerebral Palsy, which should come as no surprise to you, of course."

Ginny stood up, reaching out and scooping in the outspread client file folders before her on the desk. "I'm just a little surprised that you haven't heard more about the O'Neill's before now."

Marcia shrugged.

ONE mid-month evening, Vivvy having just finished a homework science project, Marcia sitting across from her daughter at the kitchen table, inspecting "the books," Marcia gradually became aware that her daughter was, for seconds at a time, fixing her in a thoughtful, almost faraway gaze. After each such brown study, Vivvy had finally redirected her eyes elsewhere, reluctantly, busying herself alternately with gathering up and sorting materials she had just used for her school work.

"Anything on your mind, Vivvy?" without raising her head or looking at her daughter.

Several seconds. A deep, trembly sign from the other side of the table, Vivvy stood up and carried a box of crayons, some paints and alcohol pencils, pulled out a lower drawer of the kitchen cabinet, and stacked in her supplies. She turned, walked toward the table, and took a chair now next to her mother's.

"I've been thinking, Mommy. I've been trying to figure out something..."

Marcia went on studying figures blindly.

"I was going to ask you if Gloria could come to *our* house for a visit." She sighed another profound sigh, up from the diaphragm. "But, I don't know why," she half-squealed. "I don't know why, but I just thought... So, anyway, yesterday, when Gloria was still in therapy, I went over and talked to Marie." Vivvy brushed her hand across a nonexistent spot on the table, once, twice. "I asked her. Whether she thought if it wasn't a nice idea. After all," Vivvy's voice rose in urgent supplication. "After all, *Gloria* shouldn't always be the one who is doing nice things for me, and I never doing anything back. That's not fair, and it isn't even *polite*, for Heaven's sake," Vivvy burst out, breathless.

Marcia ran the back of her hand across her daughter's flushed cheek.

"But Marie said Gloria couldn't do that. That her house was fitted out with all kinds of gadgets and straps and bars that Gloria needed, all the time, that she *had to have*... just, just, you know, so's she could... *do* anything.

Marcia watched Vivvy's cheeks get larger, pinker, her eyes beginning to glisten suspiciously.

"Even if I invited her sisters and Scott, they can't bring over all that *stuff*..." she near-shouted. "They just can't!"

Vivvy stood up, then sat down, plunking her face into her hands, elbows riveted on the table. "It's just so... so *frus-ter-ra-ting*!"

Ashamed at having to suppress a smile, Marcia took the opportunity to hide her mixed emotions by rising from her chair and going over to give Vivvy a warm hug. After the briefest of hiatuses, "Marie is probably right, Vivvy, dear... She probably is..."

Vivvy again jumped from the chair and stood next to her parent. "I know, Mommy, I *know*. But how am I going to solve my problem?" she challenged.

It was now time for Marcia t find some busy, irrelevant fussing to take up time. She began clearing her end of the table.

Circumspectly, even cautiously. "Now, Vivvy, you know I don't usually like to interfere. But, maybe, this is one time... well, maybe, I could just find a time... sometime, to bring the subject up with Mrs. O'Neill, and let her know how you feel." Vivvy was shaking her head "no" halfway through her mother's suggestion.

"No, Mommy, *I* should do it. Gloria is *my* friend, not yours." Staunchly.

"I know, honey, but these are *very, very...* unusual circumstances."
(Vivvy unconvinced.) "After all, Vivvy, what you want Gloria to know
is how much you enjoy her as a friend. How much you value her
friendship." Mommy looked hard at Vivvy. "Am I right?"

"Sure, Mommy," Vivvy echoed skeptically.

Vivvy looked at her mother and then down at the table. "I guess
you could talk to Mrs. O'Neill..."

"She might even have something to suggest... something none of
us has even thought of... yet. She might even agree that Gloria could
visit – with some planning."

As she left the kitchen, Vivvy patted her mother's arm, outstretched
across the table. Once more, struggling against an irrepressible laugh
and a catch in her throat, Marcia barely responded to Vivvy's fleeting
glance, as the child marched stalwartly out of the kitchen and toward
the staircase.

"You're a good lady, Mom. You *mean* right. You really *do*. But, I
need more time to think about it, anyways," Vivvy declared, leaving
the room.

"Come, kiss me goodnight in a little bit, Mom," Vivvy called,
halfway up the stairs.

FROM the time Greta had been hustled from the Center, a steady
stream of communications and demands had flowed from the
Hyghers' lawyers and state and federal agencies interfacing with the
Center, Ginny and Jack helped Marcia respond to this official assault,
at the same time, steadying her inner poise against the onslaught.
The very last communication from the Hyghers indicated they were
about to investigate yet another possible source for viable DNA. At this,
Marcia's imagination set off in all directions in an effort to puzzle out
what they could possibly have in mind. Still, these days, an unrelieved
melancholy permanently shadowed her usual satisfaction with her
work at the Center. That the Hyghers continued to believe her facility,
and, indeed, herself, responsible for some undefined, unspeakable,
obscene violation of their daughter, daily abode with her, and she
grieved, that long after the incident had either been explained or laid
to rest inconclusively, it would remain palpably with her. For Marcia,
this soiling, troublesome accident would always represent a mature,

more bitter initiation to the fuller range of her professional experience in social services.

IT WAS Tuesday morning of Thanksgiving week, Glory-Be just this one forenoon having consented not to wait in the lobby for the mail delivery truck when Jonesey came into Marie's cubicle bearing a long cardboard package.

"The scissors, Marie, the scissors. Hurry," she urged, "I think *this* is *it*!" Strapped into her reading chair, Gloria twisted her body to a knife-edge, literally hanging over the side.

Jonesey lifted the crutches out of the box carefully.

"Aren't the *beautiful*," Gloria whispered, awed.

Reverently, Marie, Jonesey, and Gloria stared at the crutches. They were not the kind that fit under the armpit, as Jonesey had already taken pains to explain to them during recent therapy sessions. Instead, they rose to the elbow, with a four-inch leather cuff for the forearm. As Jonesey had further explicated, their construction would necessitate placing more weight on the legs and would not have the added disadvantages of overdeveloping Gloria's shoulder and upper arms.

"Please, *pu-leeze* let me try them!" Gloria wriggled, almost falling out of the chair. Marie and Jonesey finally released her from the straps, together slipping her hands through the cuffs to the grips.

"Not too fast, Glory... not too fast. Just get used to the feel..." Jonesey cautioned.

"I want to stand with them. I *want* to stand with them. Now."

Jonesey shot a glance at Marie and lifted Gloria to a standing position. After a few minutes, Jonesey cautioned, "OK, Glory-Be... now sit down again. Then stand up again. Until you get the feel. Until you get your balance. Like the doctor said."

But Gloria would not be deterred. She repeated this routine, perhaps six, seven times before Jonesey gently removed the crutches. "We'll try some more during therapy session, later on. It's enough for now."

Flushed, Gloria surrendered, looking as if she were about to weep.

THIS being a non-routine holiday week, Marcia had given Vivvy permission to stop at the Center after school on Tuesday and Wednesday before Thanksgiving, instead of holding her to her usual visiting days. It had just begun to snow ever so lightly when Vivvy descended the sleeted, slippery steps of the school bus, ran into the warm, cozy Center lobby, and arrowed directly toward Jonesey's therapy area, where she knew Gloria would be just finishing her daily session. She wanted to tell her about a new idea that had just come to her for bringing Cleo, her new kitten, to the Center on her next visit.

She tore into the therapy room, immediately catching sight of Gloria motioning to Jonesey, who fitted her friend's arms into a pair of crutched. Gloria stood up beaming and, shaking her head at Jonesey, who involuntarily reached out to steady her, Gloria came toward Vivvy. Glory-Be was all-over bright pink, her lower lip caught firmly between her teeth, "One, two, three..." Vivvy counted heartbeats, rooted in place. By the time it was "Six-seven-eight," Gloria had waxed ashen, and Viccy could see pearls of perspiration spring like dew on her forehead.

Now Jonesey stepped forward and put her arms firmly around Gloria's chest, carrying her patient back to her chair bodily.

Tears dropped unnoticed down Jonesey's rubicund cheeks, while Gloria and Vivvy hugged one another, rapturous smiles rain-bowing each of their faces.

"Did you *see*?" Gloria gasped at Vivvy. "Did you see me *walk*? All by *myself*?" Vivvy stood at Gloria's chair, hugging her dear friend hard, harder.

Repeatedly, she and Gloria and Jonesey looked at each other, registering each other's disbelief, exchanging quick, ecstatic, grateful smiles.

When Marcia called for Vivvy to drive home, she found Jonesey, Gloria, and Vivvy sitting together, babbling – incoherent, laughing and crying by turns – out of control, not to be reached.

Jonesey was the first to stand. "Gloria can *walk*, Miz Byrnes. Her new crutches came in today, and she can *walk*." Jonesey announced in an even, solemn voice.

"And now I can go *anywheres*," Gloria whooped. "I'll be as free as... as a bird... as *anything*."

AFTER Center closing the day before Thanksgiving, Jack drove Marcia, Vivvy, and himself to Marcia's for an impromptu supper before they were to meet again the following midmorning to make the trip to Marcia's mother's Timonium home for Thanksgiving dinner. Despite his general high spirits in anticipation of the holiday break from routine, Jack gradually uncomfortably aware of an uncommon silence in the car. Almost at Marcia's – a mere ten-minute ride from the Center- neither Marcia nor Vivvy had mumbled more than a half-dozen monosyllables to him and each other throughout the entire trip.

"Everything OK at the Center, Marcia?" Jack inquired jovially. I take it everything's right on schedule for that vaunted Thanksgiving feasts at each of the houses..." Expansively, turning into their final road home.

Marcia hitched her coat over her knees in a small, deprecating gesture. "Oh, that's all been taken care of. I *do* feel just a bit guilty now visiting round on the day itself, though..."

"C'mon now, Marcy, this once... you can take a break..." He remembered his own mild surprise and gratification when she had proffered him the invitation to her mother's for the traditional holiday feast. Some two weeks earlier, Marcia had asked if he would come, and he had, of course, agreed with alacrity, but without exhibiting any other telling or embarrassing sign either in expression or demeanor, and neither he nor she had indulged in even a single anxious circumlocution about the coming event at any time later.

"And, Miss Winsome, what about you...?" Jack flung back at Vivvy, spying in his rearview mirror her tumbled image in the backseat corner of his Pontiac.

Vivvy shrugged. Then sat up straighter. "What's 'winsome?" she parroted, not listening for an answer. She sighed. "I guess I'm just exhausted, Jack. We've been having so much going on at the Center these last two days." Another sigh. "Did Mommy tell you that Gloria's crutches came and that she tried them out, and she can walk, and *everything...*"

Jack turned into Marcia's driveway. "Well, I haven't seen your mother for a few days now. So, no, she hasn't had a chance to, Vivvy. Hey, though, that's spectacular news!" Having shut off the engine, free to turn to face Vivvy directly, Jack gave Marcia's shoulder a simultaneous small tap of approbation. "Great news!"

"Yeah, it is," Vivvy said, with unmistakable letdown.

They emptied the car, switched on the garage lights for the night, piled into the den, Marcia, and Vivvy meandering finally into the kitchen.

A QUARTER of an hour later, Jack, watching the Lehrer report on the den television, heard only distantly Marcia's shouted information from the kitchen that dinner would be ready in half an hour. He felt deeply, complacently comfortable, listening to the interviews on television, half-reading the front-page articles in the Hughesville *Record*, the momentarily unsettling notice of Vivvy's peculiar flat response to her friend's latest remarkable achievement already shuttled into forgetfulness.

"I WANT to do it, Mommy." Click of drawers shutting, random scrapings of cooking utensils.

"Cleo is *my* responsibility, too, Mommy. You always get to feed her!"

Hush. Awakening presentiment. "Be *careful*, Vivvy..." Shuffled steps, more brusque banging of drawers. "No, Vivvy." More brightly, but insistently. "Use the can opener we usually use... That one's too dangerous..." Muffled movements.

"I can *do* it, Mommy. I *can*!"

A considerable pause. A grunt.

"Oh, Mom, Mommy..." a smothered squeal. "Oh... oh... it's bleeding right into Cleo's dinner..."

"Vivvy... Oh, Vivvy, I *told* you... oh, Vivvy..."

Jack bounded into the kitchen, saw Vivvy standing next to the counter, eyes upturned, looking nevertheless annoyed, put out by the unpredictable, treacherous turn of events, thumb resting in a small pool at the edge of the flat counter, sliced deeply, twice across its base, vermillion blood spurting out periodically, over tin can, cat food, and hand, etching its way down Vivvy's inner arm.

Automatically, pulling open the drawer he knew held clean dishtowels, Jack flipped out the uppermost, and twisted it around Vivvy's thumb, tying its end into a tight, tourniqueted knot.

"Marcia, this is going to require stitches." Jack said. "It looks like a pretty nasty cut. Get Vivvy's coat. I'll take her to Emergency right now."

"Oh, Vivvy," Marcia keened, as she dug out their coats from the hall closet. "Oh, Vivvy, darling... Jack, I'm coming, too, of course. Oh, Vivvy... I told you..."

MUFFLED, disgruntled, they drove toward Emergency through a sleeting light snow and along slippery roads becoming treacherous with ice stick, which put Jack immediately in touch with a seventh sense, the muscle and visceral know-how of how and when to brake, how to manipulate the wheel to avoid the ultimate nasty surprise of sliding helplessly into a side ditch when least expecting it.

Once at the hospital, Vivvy seemed to come alive again, more so than she had been throughout the evening. Having filled out the requisite insurance forms, Marcia watched as the attending nurse marched Vivvy away into an Emergency cubicle, all the while, the nurse, though maintaining a cheerful equanimity, studiously ignoring her daughter's spate of questions about her "wound." Within minutes afterwards, Vivvy was shown into the Doctor and a scarce half-hour after that, having been released, patched, and "as good as new," according to Doctor Lyons, sat almost triumphantly between Jack and Marcia on the front seat of Jack's Pontiac.

On their trip home, Vivvy began recalling the whole medical procedure ecstatically, and in detail. She had insisted on watching as the young intern had threaded and stitched the significant slashes in her thumb with confident expertise. Now she enlarged upon every nuance of this process: how he had caught up the cleansed edges of the cut with a cuticle-thin needle, how he had tied off each stitch deftly afterwards, how finally he had bandaged the entire area, making sure to do so in such a way as to allow her almost total natural movement of her thumb. Interleaved between these fastidiously observed particulars ran exultant commentary on their unique and interesting aspects, Vivvy insisting indeed that this had been one of the most "fascinating" experiences of "her whole, entire life."

Sitting on Vivvy's other side, Marcia barely stirred throughout this recital."That may be, Vivvy honey," she demurred at last, "but I hope you have no plans for any repetitions... for a long, long time... if *ever*..." Jack glanced across Vivvy at Marcia, whose voice had become fatalistic, weary. He admitted to himself that the whole episode had left him enervated, as well: only Vivvy sat up – alert, fully attentive, and carefree.

"Well, you know, Mommy, I didn't *plan* this, of course. That would be just too silly! But... but I may not have been paying enough attention... Maybe, *that* did have something to do with it..."

No one spoke.

"Maybe, I've been a little discouraged about Glory... and *that* was on my mind..."

"But everything has been going so well... We've had such blessings... this very week. What were you discouraged *bout*, Vivvy dear?"

"Well, about Glory..."

They waited: no one chose to speak. They heard Vivvy take in a giant breath.

"I know, I know, she's done so *wonderful*. With the crutches and all. But...it doesn't seem *fair*, Mom... Jack." Jack felt a warm suffusion in his chest at her intuitive inclusion of him.

Vivvy dug one mittened hand into the other. "It doesn't seem fair that everything is so *hard* for her... and that it always will be... Things that you and Jack and me... well, we just *do*, without thinking... and..." Vivvy's breath escaped again, tremulous. "It just doesn't seem *fair*, that's all."

They were at Marcia's. Jack parked the car, but no one moved.

Jack spoke up finally, knowing they would all be held hostage, each feeling no entry into the house possible, before some mutual effort at resolution were at least attempted.

"Vivvy... maybe it *isn't* fair," Jack observed pensively.

Silence.

"*Fair* is something human beings have dreamed of and dreamed up, Vivvy. Do you understand me?"

"I don't think so."

"After a long, long time – millions of years of history – thoughtful, good people have come to believe that fairness is something we all ought to strive for. 'Course, we're a long way from achieving it, most of the time! But it is a thought, an 'ideal' we call it, Vivvy. It's something *we people* believe in... believe is right." After a very long pause, he added. "It isn't something that just happens. For example, Nature isn't *fair,"* he added, hopeless of being understood. "Nature definitely gives the advantage to some, over others."

"But, God is supposed to be in charge of... of... Everything, isn't He? And wouldn't He be *super-fair*? ... He's better than we are, isn't He? ... So why shouldn't he be fairer than we could ever be?"

No one spoke. Marcia looked crushed into her winter clothing, irretrievable, unavailable. Suddenly amused at his position, at himself, yet struggling with a magnificent, overwhelming weariness, Jack could hear the voice of one of his favorite law professors, saturnine and twinkling, backgrounding his own words, "You've taken on impossible defense here, Counselor..." Vivvy alone sat upright, staring intently through the ice crystals, inexorably laying down their interlocking, blinding and beautiful patterns over the windshield.

"I know what you're going to tell me," Vivvy exclaimed in clear, if resigned tones, at last. "You're going to tell me it's all... *mis-ter-e-us*." Again, no one spoke. "Aren't you? Aren't you going to tell me it's *mis-ter-e-us*?"

"Well, in a very real way, Vivvy, it *may* be. *We* can't know about *Everything*. So, maybe, we can only know what is *fair* for *us*... between *us*..." Even to himself, this sounded like fancy equivocation. Yet, it was his serious, adult best, no devious double talk to fool a kid at all.

"That's all right, Jack," Vivvy assured him, patting him on his coat sleeve. "That's all right."

Marcia opened the car door.

BY THE time Marcia had reheated her mother's crab-cakes and the baked potatoes, managed to dress the salad and set the table, Vivvy was asleep on the den couch, her head pressed against Jack's arm. Jack himself looked half-sleep, mummified into some soporific state, staring into the darkness, television off, newspapers at his feet.

His hand alone seemed a living extension of his self, resting lightly atop Vivvy's head, in a beatific, encompassing, and comforting gesture of secular benediction. Seeing both of them there together, her child asleep, her own adult male lover lost in thought, she herself fell into inarticulate silence. Without speaking to either of them, she returned to the kitchen, sat down in a chair, and surrendered herself to a full quarter-hour reverie. She thought how immensely grateful she was to

Jack, to Barry, to Lu; but she rebelled at last at her pedestrian, practical and always so ordinary role, never, ever, permitting herself to soar, somehow always folding laundry, heating dinners, and filling out forms on time. "Is this something I have done to myself?" she asked without conviction, simultaneously rejecting such melodramatic, adolescent soul-searching to be at base self-serving, superficial. "I do what needs to be done," she said aloud finally, it not proudly, at least with an indomitable sense of self-respect intact.

They bundled Vivvy into bed at last, and returning to the kitchen, made a decent, half-hour mechanical pretense of eating dinner. Jack stacked the dishwasher; Marcia put the kitchen to rights before they allowed themselves that final marginal liberty of a brief collapse in the den.

Jack was gratified to see Marcia carrying in two steaming Irish coffees on a tray.

"BEEN someday," his eyebrows lifted, his shoulders sagged.

"And tomorrow's another..." she warned, looking over at him under her lashes.

They sat quietly, sipping their coffees for several minutes. Uncharacteristically, Marcia rose quickly and, returning from the kitchen with the brandy, gave each cup a substantial additional dollop.

They continued just sitting.

Jack reached across the couch now and cupped Marcia's right hand in his. He pulled her toward him, and, very gently, tentatively, brushed his lips against hers. Almost immediately, the kisses became passionate, searching, before Jack, responding to something he himself did not understand, forced himself to sit up, separate. He focused his gaze upon Marcia, looking at her, with a glance just slightly askew, even vaguely comic. His voice issued funereally serious.

"Marcia. Marcia, darling." He stared directly into her eyes. "Marcia, we need to get married."

Marcia lifted her cup again. Sipped slowly. Looked down into it.

Finally, "Why, Jack? Why?"

"Because this isn't good enough..." His arm and hand made a circuitous, random gesture. "It's *cheating*." He looked at her with judicial gravity. "We care about each other. I care very much about you, I care about Vivvy, certainly as much as I care about myself... or anyone else I know. You... you, at least, care about me very much, too... It's just cowardice not to make a... a *stand*, Marcia. A stand. A commitment to each other.

He looked over at Marcia who was regarding him tenderly, a half-smile playing at the corners of her mouth. She finally lowered her eyes, her smile slowly vanishing.

"I've thought a lot about it, Marcia," Jack hurried on. "For my part, an elopement would just suit... something quick and quiet. After all, we're not exactly youngsters, nor is this our first time. Who needs all that flimflam..."

"I'd have to have Vivvy there, at least. It wouldn't have any reality for her, otherwise. And that would probably mean my mother, too... "Marcia adjusted in barely a whisper, in spite of herself.

"OK. But that, or something like that, would be all... We could actually be married by the New Year... by the time Alex and Barry moved to Lighthouse Point." In his excitement, Jack had stood up again, taken hold of Marcia's hand.

And, again, Marcia looked upon his dear, comely, compassionate countenance. Still... still...

"Jack. I don' know. I *do* love you. But it's... different... somehow." She shook her head. "I guess I'm just not ready for this, Jack. Not yet... anyway..."

Jack sat down again. Wordlessly, they inhabited space next to each other for a considerable time. Finally, Marcia touched the back of Jack's head hesitantly with the tips of her fingers.

"Jack... Jack... Are you angry with me, Jack?" she could scarcely be heard.

"Of course, I'm not angry. Disappointed..." He, in turn, shook his head. "And I'm not about to make ultimatums either, Marcia. But consider, we'll have thrown away something good... viable... ling... Sure, we can just go on seeing each other indefinitely, letting the relationship settle into... I don't know what, exactly. But I know it'll have nowhere to go. Nowhere to grow." Again, he shook his head, this time more violently. "I just think it's a big mistake. For both of us..."

WHEN Jack left a quarter of an hour later, he felt unfocussed, as if he might be ill the next day. Similarly, finding she was involuntarily shaking her head from side to side periodically, Marcia could yet not dislodge some spidery dark pall clutching at her mind.

AT THE door, briefly, Marcia and Jack joined hands, but no kiss followed.

MARCIA shut the door gently but quickly, wishing to block out any further view of Jack's leavetaking.

Chapter Thirteen

ABBY HYGHER'S principal gift to her husband Lazarus this last Christmas had been a new high-powered snowblower. Most Baltimorian homeowners continued to dismiss such a purchase as gratuitous, winters here predictably soggy, rainy, and raw, hardly boasting two inches of snow during even the heaviest snowfalls. But Abby had by now used up most of her more imaginative ideas for Russ' gifts – the cashmere sportcoats, the new set of golf clubs, the depth indicator for their trawler last Christmas...

LAZARUS stood leaning against the handle of his snow shovel, head raised momentarily, sampling wind gusts, sniffing the air. He figured it was somewhere around 20 miles per hour, temperature rising: well above freezing now in mid-afternoon, maybe even into low 40's. Not like last night's '20s, triggering the unusual more than four inches that had begun at twilight, just in time for a potentially lethal New Year's Eve. No, it was decidedly milder, brighter, the sun struggling to push out from behind a bank of mottled clouds.

From the sidewalk in front of the house, half-cleared, he stopped to watch Hiram striding down the double driveway in head-lowered concentration, snow feathering out from either flank like mounting wings. Together they had carefully read – and argued – over operating instructions before he suggested Hi take first crack at using the snowblower. Senior or not, Hiram loved a new machine, and Russ knew his brother would get a kick out of running it.

NEAR finished by now, Russ could see Abby's shadowy form behind the front curtains, bending from the wais to switch on their prized Tiffany lamp, the drapes now slowly shutting the dimly lit scene from street view.

BOTH brother Hi and Russ considered themselves latter-day apostates from a respectable century-old Pennsylvania Dutch plain heritage – something they rarely talked about – yet there were some things bred in the bone. Neither of them was much of a toper, for instance, though Russ' bar was substantially, if not exclusively, stocked, the best frequently and liberally poured out for his guests. But this was, after all, a special occasion. New Year's Day. And they'd done a heavy job of work in the cold. Russ handed Hi a mulled cider hot toddy concocted to a turn, in his humble opinion. They sat in the dim study, illuminated by two widely separated small green-shaded reading lamps only, each bother scarcely visible to the other, each deeply settled in one of a pair of matching wing chairs.

"I TAKE it that Rachel's better now. Well over," Russ cleared his throat, "whatever it was… ailing her…"

Russ saw Hiram's shoulder lift and drop. "As much as can be expected… You know, Russ, there's no getting *over* what's ailing her… Nor me, neither. Or thinking about it, much as you can."

"Yeah. I guess you're right." Russ took a long pull at his toddy. "Something like that… so serious… I'll be damned if I can put that Greta business out of *my* mind!"

"HOW is she?" Hi asked after a considerable silence.

"Well, I think she's fine. Now. After all that… We've arranged for her to go back to Elmhurst, you know. You remember that's where she was before…"

"Yes, I remember."

Of course he would, Russ reminded himself. He and Rachel were almost as close to the child as Abigail and himself were. How many times had they stepped into the breach when medical, or other emergencies had arisen with one or another of their other three children – spending long days and longer evenings – bathing, feeding, entertaining Great? They'd agree to motor in from their small town in Anne Arundel County, with never a complaint or excuse, if they could manage it all. Besides Estelle, their only child, Rachel and Hi had probably spent at least as much time with Greta, especially before – finally and in spite of all their best efforts – she had had to be placed in a facility for the handicapped. No, of that he was certain: Hi loved Greta like his own. Forever affixed in Russ' lifetime book of memories, were page after page of precious recollections of his brother's tender ministrations to his maimed, beloved girl-child.

"Still, I hate to see them get away with it." Russ slapped his fist into the palm of his other hand. "But Ingersoll's says it's hopeless... They can't get a good enough sample from the coat..."

"What *sample*...?" From the other end of the rooms, Hi's voice was barely audible.

"I thought I'd told you all this. I swear, this had got my brains so scrambles... I thought I'd told you, Hi," Russ repeated, perplexed.

"Maybe not. I've had so much on my mind lately... Well, we've been working cheek-by-jowl with this Ingersoll Lab, located just outside Baltimore, here. You've heard of them? They've done DNA work-ups for a number of famous legal cases recently...?" Hi sat silent. "Anyway, I've spent a small fortune on lawyers' fees and this lab... Ingersoll's... only to be told, well, it's *hopeless*."

"Hopeless...?"

"Well, as good as... Of course, we can't know when it happened... specifically. And... it may have happened several times before... and... and not been noticed. But you remember the night Leah and Arthur were here for their fifth? ... You remember. You and Rachel were here, too. For their anniversary party. It was *that* night that some night attendant at the Center picked up a problem with Greta... after we'd taken her back there that evening. It was a Sunday night. The attendant took her to Emergency, finally... up there to some Hughesville hospital. To check her out.

"But after we'd finally been told... and there's probably a lawsuit in that... after we'd finally been *told* and got Gretty out of there..." Russ heard a noise resembling a sob, a stab of fright at his sudden shortness of breath, bringing him up sharply into anxious self-awareness.

"... And... and... we began to *think*... Well, Abby went through all Gretty's clothes... Everything – nightgowns, under-things, everything – but they'd all been laundered already. Then, *Abby thought of the coat*."

"The coat...?"

"Yes, the coat. That was Abby's brilliant idea! The coat Greta wore that night. It was a long shot, of course. But we examined it, and, sure enough, there *were* telltale stains on the back lining..."

"Amazing..."

"Yeah, we thought so." Russ stood up and walked to the French doors on the other side of the study. "It *was* an amazing idea... but... even so, as it turned out, not amazing enough." Russ stood gazing out the doors. "No, Ingersoll's say they just can't get a good enough, useable sample from the coat."

Russ turned, looked at his brother across the darkened room. "So... I guess that closes the book on this whole ugly business, even though..."

HIRAM left his chair and walked slowly toward Russ. He took a position a few feet away from his younger brother, at the other end of the French doors.

"Try to put it out of your mind, Russ, or you'll eat yourself alive."

Russ stared at Hi. That's not what he wanted to hear. For a moment, angry confusion peaking, he stared at Hi, but then, even in this half-dark, glimpsing the pleading expression in his brother's eyes, he recalled himself.

RUSS reached across the space between them, and grasped Hi's shoulder. "I know you've had your share, Hi. I know. Forgive me."

They each stood for another minute before Russ turned and returned to his chair.

Still standing in place, Hi said, "Best put it out of your mind, Russ. And, please, I'm going to ask you and Abby *not* to discuss this incident with Rachel. It'll just upset her..."

Russ looked up at his brother. He could not see his expression from this distance.

"I haven't mentioned it, although I had thought I'd told *you*. I don't think Abby has either. That was our lawyer's advice. We know how sensitive Rachel... well, we know." After a minute, "Hi, what happened on that last trip to California?"

Hi shook his head, then slowly resumed his seat.

"WHAT happened...? What happened...?" Russ could barely hear Hi's voice, which trailed off, weary...

"You realize this is the *fourth* boyfriend Estelle's run off with, starting when she was twelve years old in junior high school... Of course, you know about all *that*..." It was quiet for so long, Russ thought his brother had finished talking for that afternoon.

"We've been chasing that kid around the country for ten years. *More* than ten years," came through the dark between them.

Russ was just about to suggest they join the women, as it was getting near supper time when his brother's voice went on. "This last time... this last time... Well, this last time, we had a devil of a time tracking her down... in the first place. Even with the help of a private detective and police cooperation out there in the Valley. Seems that particular religious sect's been moving periodically, for safety and security reasons, I guess, now's relocated in this tiny village in San Fernando Valley... But even after we'd found them, finally, we had to bunk in town for days... before their 'leader' had evaluated our visit... us... decided whether or not we could see them... her." He paused again. "Do you realize she has two babies now... two little boys...?"

Russ said nothing. He was not sure what his brother wanted to hear.

"So... what came of it all? In the end?" Russ asked neutrally.

"Nothing. Nothing came of it." Hi sighed deeply. "She absolutely refused to leave the compound. If anything, she seemed to hate us... especially me... even more bitterly than before. She wouldn't hear of our adopting either of the boys. That infuriated her!" he placed his face into his hands. "And she made such... such, unbelievable, guess accusations... against me..." Hiram lifted his head, appearing to have sustained a blow, struggling against some unacceptable idea. Then, for just a moment, Russ thought Hi might speak... something important... something conclusive. But, after staring into the dusk for several seconds, Hi simply shook his head, disentangling himself from some unctuous, spidery nightmare.

"I can only tell you that Rachel became so upset at these accusations... she became... physically ill. There. And then for months afterwards... at home. She's even talked of leaving me... when she's talked at all..."

THE injustice of it all struck Russ like a two-by-four thrust into his midriff. His brother had always been nothing if not exemplary... in every way. Vice-president of a small but prosperous bank, responsible for so many boating wharfs and fishing vessels remaining operative, undefunct, when loans were needed, under the sorriest circumstances, secured only by Hi's personal faith and judgment; deacon of his church; for years, a quiet, reliable, Council member doing good in his community. Why had such a destiny been allowed to befall him?

"Why, Hiram, why...?" Russ whispered, feeling somehow embarrassed by asking the question.

The voice was flat. "Because that's the way things work."

"What...?"

"And that's why I'm advising you to drop this madness... now. It's *over*. It's done with! You can't change anything. You'll just make everything *worse*." Hiram stood up; he was almost shouting, though his voice could barely again be heard. "Do you hear me? ... You'll just make everything *worse*."

God, he thought, how this poor guy has suffered! More than I had ever imagined. My own brother. My big, capable, always-there-for-me brother. Hiram, the best.

THOUGH the feelings in his chest could hardly settle down, though he felt still torn, helpless for his baby Greta, he stood at the rim of that other abyss... his brother's Gethsemane, his snake pit. What could he do but slip his arm about Hi's shoulder, leading him from their occasional afternoon tryst into the duller perhaps, but more reliable after all, more-to-be-trusted normalcy – the everyday lives they had carefully constructed for themselves over their lifetimes.

"They've been struggling with that Virginia ham all day... we'd better not disappoint them! You'd best make a fuss over the whole damned dinner!" Russ dug his thumb into his brother's side

"Yeah..." Hi murmured as Russ, and he walked toward the study door.

AT THE door, Hi stopped abruptly and turned toward his brother. Instantly, Russ could not turn aside from his brother's incendiary gaze.

"Russ... Russ..."

"Hi...?"

"Nothing. Nothing, Russ." Russ could feel Hi stagger against his elbow.

THEY walked side by side into the living room; Russ settled Hi onto the couch, turned on the television, and put the channel selector into his brother's hand. Hi taken care of, Russ searched out the woman in the kitchen, his wife found giving last-minute energetic and detailed instructions to Ruby on how to baste and serve the ham. He listened for a minute before reconnoitering Rachel. He spied her standing against a kitchen counter, carefully and correctly dressed in her usual discriminating manner, a faraway, introspective despair in her eyes, out of place here certainly, redolent more of the illustrations from his Pennsylvania Dutch junior high school texts of Scott's *Lady of the Lake*. Russ suppressed a feeling of uncomfortable disorientation, confusion at this whole dismal afternoon.

"We're ready for dinner... whenever you ladies are ready to serve...!" he boomed heartily, despite his ennui.

"Soon... soon..." Abby quipped, scarcely stopping in her instructions to Ruby.

Rachel turned her statuesque figure in his direction – he had always been aware of her more-than-average height – especially since Hi was a smallish, compact man – but now she appeared imposing, Medea-like, unpleasantly, threateningly ominous. Separate from this homely, commonplace scene, an enemy in their camp.

He was not prepared for her to fix him with that level, appraising gaze. A slow smile wound about her ivory features. Then settled into a dour grimace upon her carved stone lips. The bottom of his heart dropped out, and, as never before, he longed for the evening to be over, the cocoon of his own home wound about him – warm familiar, ordinary – resistant to all attack.

JACK had not mentioned marriage to Marcia since that evening of Vivvy's pre-Thanksgiving emergency. There had been intimate personal evenings between them, as well as more casual ones, but their meetings were now merely successive, no inherent growth toward some implicit shared goal. His own words of that evening replayed themselves each other indefinitely, letting the relationship settle into... nowhere to go, nowhere to grow."

By the grace of God, and perhaps, too, because of some obscure instinct of social deftness they both possessed, their situation avoided those gritty patches of awkwardness or mawkish compensatory effusion that might have occurred between them. Quite simply, they continued to enjoy each other's company and looked forward to their time together.

He puzzled now at today's letter from Hyghers' attorneys: circumlocutorily, it informed him of "the disappointing incapacity of the Ingersoll Laboratory" to produce the viable DNA sample the Lab "had originally expected would be forthcoming from the Hygher family's recent submission of a potential evidentiary sample." Perusing the rest of the letter, not without relief and a rising sardonic satisfaction, he again reached and re-read its satisfying concluding paragraph:

"Thus, considering these less than fortuitous recent clinical outcomes, the basis of the Hygher claim in our recent projected suit against Hughesville Center will not require updating and revision. Upon completion of such review and emendation, our firm will be in timely contact with you and your client regarding any and all future proposed actions."

"Good on us..." Jack murmured under his breath, glancing at his watch and smiling. Three-ten. Even having taken a late lunch, Marcia should be back at the Center by now. Though he noticed she had been CC'ed on this letter. Their legal respite needed to be shared. Such an unanticipated reprieve! He reached for the telephone.

"DID the letter from Simpson, Crane at al.?" he asked Marcia without preamble.

"Just... It was here with the afternoon mail when I got back from lunch..." On his end, he heard slippery, paper sounds as she must have reread what was before her. "Good, I guess. Yes?"

"Yes! At least for now. They haven't got anything to go on... They're fairly stymied..."

A long intake of breath. "Oh, God, I hope so, Jack. I *pray* so..."

"This calls for a celebration. How long since we drove into Brandywine country and ate at the Logan Inn?"

"So fancy..." she giggled. "So-o-o expensive. So wonderful!"

"You're worth it! We're worth it! How about Saturday evening at about seven? We'd have to leave here by six, though..."

"Sounds good to me..." A pause. "Counselor..."

"Yes..."

"I'm so... grateful..." Another pause. "See you Saturday." A click.

"Don't be grateful, my sweet," he said. "Don't be grateful. Just *love* me," he whispered at the blank receiver.

SHORTLY after her return from the Thanksgiving visit with Barry, Alex had prepared her pro-forma letter of resignation, delivering a copy to J.D., of course, but more importantly, to Big Lew – Al Lewis, CFO and her immediate supervisor, who would be, after all, in charge of finding her replacement. Now, only a week before the movers were scheduled to appear at the condominium next Friday; Big Lew had finally hired one of the handful of applicants he had interviewed for the position and had just apprised Alex of her replacement's anticipated appearance at the workplace on the following Monday.

Big Lew had sauntered down to their area a few minutes before, divulged this long-awaited news with bland nonchalance, and hustled off again to catch one of his endless telephone conference calls.

"Wow! A whole week!" Alex quipped at Serena, who merely smirked in return.

"Yeah, it really makes one feel indispensable. Important," Alex said, leaning against Serena's desk. Serena did not answer. Alex had told Serena about her resignation before she had composed the requisite letter to J.D. and Big Lew. Serena had said she was sorry but had avoided any warmer show of affection. In fact, Alex had observed over past weeks, a king of withdrawal or retreat in Serena, as if she were reclaiming herself from this terminating relationship. When Alex had noticed, more frequently than she would have wished, she blocked the small, sharp irrepressible twinge of hurt that always followed it.

Returning to her desk, Alex eyed the two empty cartons she had staked on the closer to her chair. She opened the top left drawer of her desk and desultorily began removing pencils and pens, rulers, notebooks – banding them, and placing them next to the box. Half-hour later, she had sorted through the lower-left file drawer, disposing of at least half its contents – the half-hopeful to-do's or to-read's of a decade. The wastebaskets stuffed to overflowing glanced back at her accusingly. Setting the remaining file folders into some precarious order at the bottom of the carton, Alex got on with her desolate task.

At the back of the top right-hand desk drawer, she peeled out from against a rear drawer divider, an old, curled-up snapshot, one sent to Barry by his old friend Murray some years ago, of Davidoff's Kosher Meats in Baltimore. Extracting it, she had torn away an edge and holding it up for closer inspection; she saw all its colors had neutralized to gray, and tiny brown spots as of acid appeared across its bottom half. She stared at the photo for several pensive seconds. Then, hesitatingly, she dropped it onto the top of the heap in the wastebasket.

As she started on her lower right drawer, she reflected that the good-bye party they had thrown for her last Wednesday had been decent enough. But even as she hugged and bid sentimental adieus to a half-dozen of her closest colleagues, vowing to write promptly and then regularly, there was a tacit acknowledgment amongst them that this was it, this would be all. Mincing religionist and social climber that she might have been, Jeanne Carruthers had "stayed in touch" for fifteen years. Upon Alex's occasional revisits to New Colony, Amy Pearson, Betty Carson, Henry Blodgett had roused themselves, called each other, and arranged a cocktail get-together in her honor at their favorite local pub for a decade after she'd left. But they were the latter-day Europeans of America: still impelled by some nostalgic sense of continuity in order to fully realize their own identities. In this western contingent of freewheeling swingers, it would be different. "Out of sight, out of mind." No one cast a shadow in the noonday brilliance of sunny southern California. *Die Frau ohne Schaaten*. You said it, baby!

At five-thirty, Alex moved past Serena's desk toward the elevator with her first box of take-aways. She was glad that Serena was not there.

She puzzled why she had come back up for the second box since she could just as well have taken it home Monday evening. On her way out his time, Serena, now at her desk, regarded Alex pleasantly but noncommittally, letting her eyes finally drop to the box in Alex's arms. "I see you're all packed up." She smiled. "Have a nice weekend, Alex," she murmured and turned to her computer.

"You too, Serena."

On that final Friday, the movers had come in – inspected, marked, and labeled each piece of furniture. There was nothing in the entire condominium that had not been tagged with possessing an identifiable scratch, stain, broken edge, soil discoloration, or other recognizable flaw. Walking through the piled wreckage of their furnishings, Alex was unaware she sidled from piece to piece in fair imitation of a junkyard dog.

After the corpus of their Pasadena condominium had finally been removed, Alex pushed open the patio door and walked toward the balcony railing. "Goodbye, you wonders," she sighed. "I've loved you. You've been a blessing and a joy to me and Barry." She walked directly up to the railing, addressing the individual bushes, trees, the steep slope basined in the twilit, still lucent sky. "Good-bye, good-bye," she prayed, pulling the door closed on her avian friends.

On her way out of the condominium, she caught a glimpse of Aurelio Villenueva's door, still hung with the miniature, ingenious replica of a wreath he always put up at Christmas. She looked at her watch. It was already five, time enough for him to have returned from the USC Medical Center, only a mile or so away, and judging from his established laundering habits. She tapped at the door. There was no response. She knocked more assertively. No answer.

Too late to escape Eunice Jefferson, acting condominium president, however, who appeared around the corner of the hall, relieved Alex of the thick packet of CCR's, and could not restrain herself from sauntering through the open door of the condominium. "This is a nice one," she allowed, having strolled through the kitchen and living area. "But you are having the rugs redone, aren't you?" she observed. "And the whole place repainted, of course?"

AFTER a night in a nearby Pasadena motel, a pickup by SuperShuttle, and the usual tedious, anxious preliminaries of air travel at the airport, she established herself in the window seat of her carrier. She hated air travel and always took the aisle seat when she flew with Barry. But this time, she would make an exception; for her, an agonizing decision. No other passengers had been assigned to this triad of seats, and this time, for the first time in over a decade, she was flying a one-way ticket.

AT LAST, as the plane finally taxied down the runway, Alex stiffened against the pulsing rush of escalating power humming under her torso. The man-made bird lifted itself heavily from the earth, one wing dipping, then another. With apparent assurance in reaching its ultimate destination, it lifted itself into an acrid sunlit ambience.

ALEX forced herself first to peek out the window at the beautiful, seemingly pristine bay below. Now, she turned her body to look fully out the window. Skirting a wall of craggy cliffs, surf foaming beneath, a great wrench of pity twisted somewhere in her chest. Such a beautiful land! Such a beautiful country!

HER orisons stilled, Alex moved her bag to the floor under the aisle seat. She drew out her book from her carry-on satchel. Over her shoulder, she murmured, "So long, LA---so long." She smiled. A slight tremor, a minuscule readjustment in posture, she quietly, eagerly resolved to reach out, this instant, toward that more authentic, more than *papier-mâché* Adventure land, to the land east Eden---where a reunion with a more enduring, fundamental self awaited.

Chapter Fourteen

"**W**E'RE PREPARED to keep you on half-salary for the balance of months remaining until you reach age 65 ... retaining you in the capacity of off-site consultant. That way, the status of your pension will hardly be affected ... need only minor readjustment. And ... and everything else would also stay in place ... as-is." Sitting across from Lindquist, Barry's consciousness registered the man's general impressive height, his relaxed self-possession, his understated, careful turn-out in deceptively casual, expensively coordinated clothes. They registered ... but only far away, nearly imperceptible, seen from the wrong end of his life scope. Instead, sparkling shards, breaking, and bouncing ... fragmentary images flying from out his own out-of-control memory reel. That trip back to Washington from Pittsburgh. It had been Lindquist then, too.

Then, Lindquist had been enthusiastic in his summary of the Fort Horton Language Program. "The position of a full-time manager from Alcon, you understand, now that Mr. Calhoun is in place, has necessarily been marginalized. Whatever consultation may be required, can be accomplished ... Of course, we've got you to thank for giving the program legs ... and teaching it to walk ..." Silly metaphor, silly ... and not a little demeaning.

"So, what do you think of it?" Lindquist rose, snapping Barry's attention into groove. About what, Barry stared. About what, for Christ's sake? He realized his ambient smile must appear vacant, moronic, as he struggled to catch the string of mislaid continuity.

"That will also make it possible for you to join your wife by ... well, as early as February, even. No long separations ... no gruesome commuting to... where is it?... Seacrest Point ...?" A benevolent expression invaded Lindquist's regular features. "And, of course, the Company will take care of the move ... since it was initiated and contracted for during your full-time term of service ..." Lindquist permitted himself a searching look into Barry's face. "We thought you'd be *par-ti-cular-ly* pleased about that," he laughed.

Yes, you ingrate you. "You will be taking over the supervisions of the Fort Horton Program in ... in barely six weeks!' Alex's beautiful face stared back at him, puzzled. He was telling her something important ... "But the *exercise* of understanding, Alex, that's different. That means being sensitive enough to subsume particular events, *particular*, highly personal events under many codes at once, conscious, or unconscious." Got that, Alex? Ho, ho. That's rich, Alex. Have –you-got-that?

"Of course, we hardly anticipate that john Blum will be having to get in touch with you ... absent some unforeseen emergency. Naturally, we appreciate how swiftly you've been able to bring him online, but at this point ..." Lindquist reseated himself at his desk, leaning over it companionably to face Barry. "Right now, he seems fully up to the job ... wouldn't you agree?"

"He's a bright lad. A quick study," Barry heard himself say equitably.

"Yes. We expect great things from him ..." Yes, yes, yes, Now, John, now that you've oriented yourself to the Big Picture ... the *big theoretical* picture, John, John-boy ... you must become adept at the Chain of Command, and other assorted corporate legerdemain. Got that, John? Or, it'll be Tampa for you, buddy. Or Winston-Salem. Or, better still, the Tower of Babel ... now that'll tax your vaunted linguistics skills, won't it? Come on, John, laugh. That was funny. Genuinely funny.

Lindquist rose again and walked toward his eighth-floor window. He gazed through the glass. That's right, Nelson. And you, too, Hascomb. And now, you Lindquist. You guys, you executive visionaries, you just need to see farther than the rest of us. Eighth, ninth, twenty-seventh, ninety-ninth floor windows ... they go with the job ... "So," Lindquist was saying. "So, everything seems in order." With arm extended, he walked toward Barry.

Barry rose and manfully grasped Lindquist's outstretched hand.

IN THE remaining hour before lunch, Barry sat at his desk, Idly, he touched the picture of Lu a quarter-inch to the right. He turned the digits on his perpetual calendar to today's date. He placed two pencil stubs into the Pittsburgh Steelers cup next to the coffee mug warmer. Then, he sat back in his chair and let his eyes hang upon the empty flat-painted drywall before him.

Dimly, he heard Isabel preparing to leave for lunch. He heard desk drawers' slam and ratcheting creaks from the desk chair. Distantly, he heard a return, clicking of computer keys, followed by the nasal whine of the printer.

Finally, his eyes began to smart. He blinked over dry eyeballs, wincing slightly. He watched his own arm reach across the desk toward the telephone; his fingers punch the too-many buttons of Alex's LA office number.

A familiar voice---Serena's---spoke briskly; quickly, she put him through to Alex.

"AMERICAN HOUSING. Investor Communications Department. Alex Byrnes speaking." He let Alex's deep contralto sink into his space.

A pause. "Alex Byrnes speaking. How may I help you?" the voice sharper, thin edge of impatience.

"Alex, I've just been in with Lindquist."

"Barry ...?"

"Yeah. Seems I'm about to be put out to pasture even sooner than I expected. By February. On a consultant basis ... with half-salary until 65. Everything else ... pension, benefits, et cetera, remain the same." Across the line, he heard a heavy, tremulous expulsion of breath.

"And the move ...?"

"That'll be covered ..."

Several tongue clicks, followed by a deep, but steadier, sigh.

"I guess we'll have to cash in some of our bonds until my Social Security payments are established." More firmly. "With the Social Security payments regularized and the investment dividends ... we'll have to start them flowing in as income instead of reinvesting ... and, and your half-salary, I think we'll be all right ... We'll have righted ourselves a quarter of a year." To herself, "I think we'll be all right."

"Well, you've always been a reliable bursar ..." His levity sounded flat and unconvincing.

"Barry ... Barry, are you all right? You ... you literally sound so far away ... unreachable.

"Yeah ... I'm all right. Also ... far away ... and unreachable."

"It's not all that bad, Barry," Alex's voice announced robustly.

"We'll be together almost immediately. And, no commuting. What a reprieve! We can get started on our *real life*. And, by keeping you on, even pro-forma, until 65, you'll be qualifying for a much more advantageous level of ongoing Social Security payments later on."

A long hiatus as he ingested her strenuous enthusiasm.

"Barry?" Alex's voice again. This time, a little breathless.

"Barry, it'll be all right. You'll see. Barry ...?

"Barry, I'll call you at the motel later. Ok?"

"Sure ..."

"And, Barry ... I love you." (Barry straightened his shoulders. Alex rarely maundered in this way. She *must* be worried.)

"I'm all right, Alex. Really."

Another pause.

"I'll call later, Barry." Then, mock-heroically. "Hang in there, kid."

"Yeah."

Barry replaced the receiver into its cradle.

JACK had not seen Armand over the New Years' holiday. For some reason best known to himself, Armand had finally accepted Uncle Jason's invitation to spend Christmas week and New Years Day with the Tuthills in New York City, an invitation that had been extended to his only living sister, Amanda, and her family, for lo! this past decade. Of course, Armand had perfunctorily mentioned the visit to Jack sometime before Christmas, invited him to join them, and, just as perfunctorily, Jack had found a ready excuse not to go along.

So, Amanda, Blanche, Armand, and the children had taken off for the city directly after Christmas Day. And Jack could only surmise that Uncle Jason---bluff, rotund, successful and very rich---would provide rejuvenating company for his brother. uncle might easily mash down in his sanguine progress down life's way, as there was no denying his possession of testosterone levels exclusive only to the most triumphant of males. But neither could one deny his general ever-present good humor, his family loyalty, his lavish and generous lifestyle. Beyond question, the Tuthill chicken empire, initiated modestly after World War II in Uncle Jason's native South, had now winged its way across the nation, evolving into a succession of breathtaking industries and entities, truly phenomenal, ballistically casting off golden eggs in all directions.

Sitting in his office this midmorning Wednesday after New Years, reperusing the happy missive from Simpson, Crane, et al., Jack was not only mildly surprised but even slightly annoyed to hear his brother's voice at the other end of his telephone line. Armand began with his usual ritual rhetoric re health and sundries, but, as usual, too, in seconds, got down to the real business of his call.

"Do you have any idea what's going on around town?" he asked.

Jack reflected momentarily on past weeks. There had been an article at the bottom of page one of the Hughesville *Record*---oh, perhaps a week or so ago, about workers' meetings at various churches and social clubs around town to discuss possible effects of the sale or eventual shutdown of the LeClerc Works. Then, last week, he recalled, there had been another piece on the Op-Ed page---strictly neutral in tone, superlatively nonpartisan, the paper adroitly having declined to take "sides"---about the growing "movement," the paper had dubbed it, of community interest. The article had reprised recent meetings at a local Baptist church and at a United Church of Christ meeting house. Jack had read the paper's commentary with piqued curiosity, but not without a mixture of contempt and fatalism. Contempt for the ongoing business negotiations with Allied General now in progress; and dubious contempt at their progressing to ultimate fruition. And fatalism---as to any possible eventual beneficent outcomes for anyone---anyone at all.

Under the circumstances, it had been easier to turn his attention to the Hyghers, Marcy, and the problems currently developing for the continuing successful operation of the Center.

"Now that you mention it ... I do recall a few articles on the anticipated sale of ..." Armand cut him short.

"The day after we got back from Uncle Jason's Carleton stopped by at the house. Do you understand? *At the house.* Do you know what that means? Carleton almost never stops at the house."

Jack permitted himself a responsive murmur.

"But, damn, if some kind of clutch isn't developing. There's some accursed collusion here, calling itself---get this---the Hughesville Ecumenical coalition, according to Carleton ... Catholics, protestants, even a rabbi ... wherever they managed to dig him up in this redneck backwoods. And, they're discussing the possibility of raising community funds to help buy out LeClerc's! On an ESOP! Employee Stock Ownership Plan ... Are you there3, for Christ's Sake?"

"I'm here." Jack straightened his pant leg, pulling the crease to knows. But it might not be a bad idea."

A whole half-minute. "Are you serious, Jack? Or is this your final revenge ... on the whole family?"

Thinking he could not forgive Armand, once again, for his wholly predictable reflexive response, Jack explained patiently, "From what I understand, Armand, there *are* substantial advantages to you ... as the seller ... tax-wise ... in divesting yourself of Company stock in this manner. Or, even better, to agree to Allied General's initiating such a divestiture, upon their acquisition..."

Armand was quiet for a whole minute. "I'll talk to Carleton ..." he finally acceded.

"Carleton won't do," Jack footnoted quietly, after another pause.

"What?" Armand growled. "What'y' mean?"

"What I mean, not to put too fine a point on it, is that he doesn't know enough about this matter. Just as I don't know enough. You're going to need to get specific, expert, highly technical advice. You'd need to work at it. At finding the right people and the right resources."

Again, silence,

"At the very least, you'd need additional legal counsel ... amongst other things."

"What's wrong with you ... and Carleton?" Armand bawled. "What's wrong with using my own people?" he repeated.

"It's a big, complex, sophisticated world, Armand. We're just not enough. We're just not knowledgeable enough."

HE COULD hear Armand snuffle as he manipulated the receiver. "I'll call you tomorrow, or later in the week ... Hear me? ... I'll be getting in touch with you as soon as I've talked to Carleton and got this whole thing figured out."

"Sure, Armand, you do that ... I'll be here," Jack said mildly to the dismissive click of Armand's receiver. "I'll be here," he grimaced, "after you've figured it all out," he added, sure his brother would have been impervious to the gentle irony in his tone.

Chapter Fifteen

W HEN JACK had adjusted the double blinds at his office window, quickly scanned the page of appointments and meetings for the day---depressingly scant---and tracked Suzanne as she installed the morning hottle of coffee on his discreetly placed desk warmer, he sighed and allowed himself to open the fresh Thursday weekly edition of the Hughesville *Record*. This week, Charlie Price had something more than a high school basketball victory or a citywide sewage problem for a headline. WASHINGTON REVISITS HUGHESVILLE, the headline read. With professional aplomb, the lead article, page one, formally detailed tomorrow evening's appearance at a local Presbyterian social facility of their local Congressman, in company with Irving Meyers, of the Institute of Policy Studies, who would be addressing a community group concerning possible area economic consequences of a LeClerc shutdown.

Hardly knowing what he had in mind, Jack hunched on his coat and headed for his car, telling Suzanne as he exited that he'd be back in an hour or so, offering nothing more by way of explanation or excuse.

He swept through the large central Activity Room where house personnel were gathering up detritus from the patients' last afternoon snack, some already carting in wheelchairs and other paraphernalia in preparation for their clients' daily return to home base. He swung around to the individual tutorial rooms, one of which held Gloria strapped into her elevated work chair, as usual, facing Vivvy across a raised worktable, each manipulating jumbo-sized crayons in oversized coloring books. After only a momentary started glance, they each sang out to him.

"Hi, Uncle Jack," together. Then, "Come on in ... Look, look," Vivvy said, holding up Gloria's coloring book. "Look what Gloria's done. She colored *all* in the lines. And, look, look how neat! Neater than mine!"

"Wonderful, wonderful," Jack murmured, forcing himself to glance over at the held-up page, as if evaluating Gloria's effort, "Vivvy, dear, have you seen your mother?"

"Before. When I came in ..." Vivvy said, having already returned to working on her picture. "Sometimes she's in the kitchen or in the courtyard in the afternoon...."

Vivvy peered over at Gloria's page. "Oooh, I never thought of that ... getting purple by putting the red right over the blue ... That's clever," Vivvy giggled. "You know you're clever, Glory-Be?" Vivvy rapped out, in perfect imitation of schoolteacherish encouragement. Gloria laughed without lifting her eyes from the picture or loosening her tortured hold on the crayon.

When he finally tracked Marcy down in the kitchen, finishing instructions to Cook for tomorrow's lunch menu, he waited patiently in the doorway, then followed her as she made her way back to her office.

Jack thrust the newspaper at her, pointing to the lead article.

She settled herself at her desk and began perusing the article. Jack took an armchair in front of the desk. In a few minutes, she put down the paper, a quizzical expression on her face.

"Well, I guess the situation is heating up. By the way ... how is the sale of LeClerc's coming along?" she asked, Jack suspecting more out of politeness than any genuine interest. She was already reaching for a stack of meds on her desk.

"I don't know ..." Marcy looked up, questioning. "I can tell you this kind of publicity isn't going to do it any good."

"I suppose," she shrugged.

"Marcy," Jack said, "I'd like to go to that meeting. The damn trouble is ... I'd be recognized immediately."

Marcy shrugged again, opening the top med file.

"Marcy, has there been much interest ... any talk ... around the Center about LeClerc's? You know ... husbands, brothers, sons ... working at the plant?"

"Not that I've been aware of ... You know we're heavy with single mothers, and assorted unmarried's ... You know that!'

"Well, I was wondering if anyone from the Center was going over to that meeting tomorrow. Of course, I'd still be recognized, but I'd achieve at least a degree of anonymity if I went as part of a small group. From the Center."

Again, Marcy studied him curiously.

"I'll see what I can do, Jack."

"You'll come, too, won't you?" Jack asked.

"Well, I can hardly drum up a party and *not* go myself!"

"We'll sit in the back ... Well out of sight ..."

"Maybe you can don a fake mustache and beard," Marcy snapped impatiently, reaching for the next file folder.

THE group from the Center---seven of them altogether---took folding chairs along the back wall of the Presbyterian Community Room, located in the Church basement, home of Head Start daily and Sunday School classes on the Sabbath.

A makeshift dais had been erected at the other end of the room and, although Jack could hardly make out most of the figures seated there, he immediately recognized Gary Letzger, the recording secretary of the local union, second chair to the lectern, and Jamie McClintock and Paul Doran, president and vice-president of the Local at the other end of the line of seats, to the left.

He looked around the hall, which was full---perhaps two hundred people. There was no crepe paper decor, no attempt at tricking out the facility or furbishing it in any way for the coming event. The air---stuffy and dank---rose and misted around the hospital-type ceiling light fixtures in foggy, ominous, Brownian globules.

After a fulminating ten-minute introduction by Jim Daniels, their local Congressman, detailing Meyer's background as historian economist, former professor at State, and all-around humanitarian,

Meyers stepped to the lectern and, in a remarkably quiet, undramatic voice, began a statement, grave if not solemn.

"The time has come," he said, "when business in America must stop operating as if in a moral vacuum, pretending there is no human dimension to economic action."

Disattaching the microphone and holding it in his hand, he bent forward toward his audience: "The purpose of community life is to serve all of us ... the *common* good. Economic decisions with wide-raging consequences cannot be left to the arbitrary judgment of a few privileged individuals, but are the responsibility and concern of every one of us---the wider, broader `community affected by these judgments."

After this initial statement only, a standing ovation.

Meyers went on to describe a possible strategy for the local "Save Our Community" campaign. Private investors were not interested in keeping the mill open, and the federal government would be slow, if effective at all, in helping out. The putative Buyer, and current owners, as recently as the week before Christmas, after intensive meetings with union leadership, had been reported adamant in their unwillingness to commit themselves regarding the immediate or future disposition of the LeClerc facility. Thus, it was becoming increasingly clear that should LeClerc employees and the community wish to preserve this industry as part of their own viable local economy, they and the community, led by the religious leaders of the area who had already shown themselves willing to dedicate themselves to this project, would have to raise the money themselves. And with this capitalization, to acquire stock in the LeClerc enterprise.

But, he warned, this was not going to be some fly-by-night matter: they would have to dedicate themselves to this end with the fervor and endurance of civil rights activists in the recent "Mississippi Summer."

At this, the whole hall rose in one thunderous approbation. On the podium, all were standing also. Jack could just glimpse Paul Doran drawing a fist across his gnarled features in an attempt to wipe his eyes, as he shouted some heartfelt exhortation at the speaker. Jack found himself shaking his head.

After the meeting, making their way toward Marcy's car, neither Marcy nor Jack had much to say. Though Marcy's destiny certainly did not depend on LeClerc's evolving fate, and Jack's, only peripherally so, they both experienced a degree of physical letdown, a mild depression, after the towering high spirits and imperative forward thrust of the foregoing assembly.

As she drove out of the parking lot, Marcy's disembodied voice mused, "Can they *do* that?"

"Can they do *what*?" Jack echoed.

"Can they structure one of these ESOPs around combined community *and* worker ownership? Could such an arrangement be made to be satisfactory for all concerned?" Marcy shifted gears. "I mean, it seems to me, that worker input, worker self-government, if you will, is really what it's all about. What they're striving for a base... is wanting to get hold of their own work-lives. How much input would workers actually have with that kind of arrangement, even if it ever came to pass...? And, of course, that's a great big *IF*, surely."

"I can't see it, either..." Jack agreed. "Even if it could be made to happen, as you say. There are different ways of structuring ESOPs, of course, but, with the little I know about them, not this way, not usually. At least, this has got to be difficult to put together, at best."

Marcy drove on. Ignorance, complexity, and muddle surrounding the whole topic further added to their mutual pervasive se3nse of helplessness. Marcy pulled into her driveway behind Jack's parked car, then, bethinking herself, backed the car out again and parked it aside of his, the vehicle's right wheels barely fitting the remaining concrete pad. For a moment, they both sat in place, neither seeming to have the will to move.

After another considerable silence, Marcy turned slightly toward Jack. "You know, Jack, Barry worked in Human Resources for years. That's been his career. He's come to know all sorts of, well, corporate big-shots, if you will, whose chief stock in trade is all this... this corporate high-level empire building. Often, in conversation, he'll come up knowing the oddest people... at least they're odd to me, here in little old Hughesville. Cabinet members, leading defense lawyers, bankers, even assorted lawbreakers..." She sighed. "I just thought I'd mention it. You might keep him in mind... as a possible resource person. He may be able to recommend someone who can help, with a matter like the ESOPs... even if he couldn't himself. If it ever comes to that... that is..."

"That's an idea," Jack acknowledged politely, forgetting the suggestion before he had finished speaking.

Marcy nodded, not holding Jack's apparent implicit judgment of Barry against him. After all, Jack hardly knew the man.

"Jack, I'm not going to invite you in tonight. I'm tired, frankly. You must be, too."

"A little, No, I'd just as soon get home, too."

As she walked toward her side entrance, and Jack proceeded to his car, he called after her. "Don't forget Saturday," he reminded. "I'll be here at six."

"Looking forward to seeing Logan Inn again," Marcy shouted back at him, waving as he pulled out of the driveway.

ON THE Monday following, Jack was surprised that here, already four o'clock, nearing the end of the business day, he had not heard from Armand, sat at his desk mulling the idea over for ten minutes, then dismissed it. Close upon three o'clock, Suzanne put through a call from his brother.

"I've been awfully busy," Armand began. "I just thought I'd let you know. I'll be out of town for a couple of weeks... meeting with Allied General's counsel and other financial people for final valuation of corporate stock... I know we've already had a preliminary valuation of corporate stock... I know we've already had a preliminary valuation, but Allied's asking for another independent appraisal. They've set up all kinds of meetings and appointments. You understand, Jack, our own company's accountants, and attorneys are irrelevant here... I assume this is Allied's last, serious pass at this whole issue before making a final offer."

"Of course..." Jack said. "You think they *will* finally come up with that closing offer...?"

Jack was surprised at the lengthy, tangible silence before his brother's moderated reply. "I *think* so, Armand said. "I *hope* so."

MOMENTARILY, Jack felt disoriented by his brother's apparent or assumed lack of certainty. Reflexively, he strove to structure a response that would show adequate interest, even sympathy, but yet sufficiently supple to be instantly flipped, if necessary, into protective, ironic drollery.

"After that," Armand's voice, "after that ... Blanche and I are taking a couple of weeks at Palm Beach. She's really not been herself, lately. Mother's coming down with Belle Lebrand for that last week, too ... They'll stay at The Breakers, as usual..."

"Sounds good," Jack dissimulated, covering up his own surprise and chagrin at being so thoroughly and effectively snubbed at what he sensed would likely become a fresh alignment of family forces.

"OK, Pal. You keep Nichols honest while we're gone, hear?" Suddenly recognizably his old self, blunt and plainspoken, Armand guffawed loudly at his own joke. "We'll be back in early March, glowing with deep suntans, ready to close in on the deal ..."

"Have a good one ..." Jack offered lamely. "I'll keep the home fires burning ..."

ARMAND'S absence cleared Jack's business calendar considerably, soon compounded by Marcy's month-long unavailability upon Alex's move to the Byrnes' Lighthouse Point cottage shortly after the first week of January. By mid-January, almost every shortly after the first week of January. By mid-January, almost every phone call to Marcy ended with some exhilarating plan for her Joining Alex on a Saturday afternoon to help arrange dishes in her cupboards or help unpack and organize linen closets on a Sunday morning. In two whole weeks, Jack had managed to meet Marcy for lunch only twice, and now, almost at the end of the month, and after so many weeks of unpacking at the cottage, he hoped to set up a dinner date at the Shore House with Marcy for this Saturday.

"Oh, I can't, Jack. I really can't. I promised to drive Alex into Wilmington tomorrow morning ... for some last-minute shopping ... you know ... and, then, Barry is coming in mid-afternoon. For good, Jack! Moving in ... Isn't it exciting? Vivvy is just thrilled to have inherited two live, wonderful grandparents ... right here, practically in her own backyard!" Marcy tittered girlishly.

"I'm beginning to miss you too ..." Jack muttered.

"But, Jack, wait. Alex has made a huge casserole of moussaka ... for Barry ... he loves Middle-Eastern. I'm sure she would love you to come to dinner with us. Oh, I'm just sure of it! And, it'd give you a chance to get acquainted with Barry. Shall I ask her ... and get right back to you?" Marcy was breathless.

"I don't know," Jack demurred, feeling like an intruder.

"Oh, Jack, say yes. Say, you'll come."

Before he could agree or disagree, she rung off, saying she'd call him back within the hour. Ten minutes later, she called back and, after going over the exact route to Alex's and Barry's cottage, reminded him to be there by four-thirty, for cocktails and cheese, before dinner.

As Jack drove home to his Carriage House apartment, feeling enervated and adolescent in his anticipation of tomorrow's meeting, he remained dismayed at how a still bereaved widow, with a child from a former marriage that had terminated in divorce, and two more-than- middle-aged retirees, not much younger than his own aging mother, parents of the deceased second husband, who himself remained an enigma both admired and feared, hovering over his relationship with Marcy---how this constellation of persons should have become the vibrant heart of his most real-world, holding between them the hopeful promise or baleful failure of his own return to life. "Family of Man," he snorted to himself, vaguely recalling the message of many of Fromm's avidly read books, failing utterly in his attempt at a protective, rationalizing cover, trusting his faith well-grounded, but knowing any pretended disbelief to be an unconvincing sham.

THOSE first few weeks ... those first few weeks ... there had been no escape from the oppression of clutter. Their boxed goods, the accumulated baggage of a lifetime, piled into every corner of the small living room, dining room, and kitchen, spilling onto the back porch stoop, meandering into the cellar ... There had been no help for it but unmitigated, head-down labor; drudgery that began with waking and stretched to near-collapse in early evening. On more than one occasion, as Alex had stood in the midst of the inescapable chaos about her, she had vowed that if ever, ever, she ... they ... should have to move again, she should pile all her earthly possessions into one indiscriminate heap in the middle of the backyard and set a match to it. The pledge so fervent, so deeply felt, that even now, she feared ever encountering a repetition of this situation, as she might well feel compelled to act upon it.

Still, all things end ... she ruefully observed to herself this bright Monday morning. With Marcy's frequent and buoyant intervention, her help and morale lift, something commodious and pleasant, something viably habitable ... less than gleaming domestic order beauty, and perfection, certainly ... had emerged from the chrysalis of cluttered cardboard. Not a shimmering butterfly, but something likable, livable, with the lineaments of Barry's and her life together reflected in the carefully arranged bookcases; the healthy, blooming plants; the piano and Barry's voluminous music collection.

The sun glinted off the kitchen tile around the sink this brilliant morning and spun ingenious Byzantine geometry on the wall above the cuckoo clock. Alex decided to slip on her coat and have a walkabout the house.

She stood at the back door looking down the long, narrow lot of their cottage, the land sweeping away toward the many bluffs overlooking one of the almost numberless coves along the bay. She walked toward the front entrance, the while appraising their tiny cottage, a white saltbox clapboard, more than a century old, with its bright green shutters and matching roof, its window boxes, its enormous beech spreading dappled sunshine and sun-filled shade across a minuscule front lawn. Desultorily, she wandered to the right-side flower border, which caught the first rays of morning sun, and peered down into the beds. Her heart raced to see a row of inch-long green hyacinth shoots poking through the decorative gravel!

And so it had been then, in their very first home at New Colony. Their first home, never mind that it was just another cheese box, Levittown construction. All their care had gone toward disguising or alleviating the disheartening jerrybuilt near-shoddiness of their mass-produced but affectionate home, never mind again the rust stains punctuating each nail hole in the carport, reminiscent of the misbehaving mascara on an overworked burlesque beauty queen. But the plantings, set in by the first short-term owners, were something they could be unashamedly proud of. Carefully selected, varied, and well-tended, they individualized their replicated home and were a source of unabashed pride to herself and Barry.

As she had glanced out that other kitchen window, she had seen Lu's wooden orange-and-blue kiddy cart abandoned just behind the privet hedge, the cart's front wheel jammed well into the bush itself. She had slipped on her coat then too, and scurried, looking over the front lawn and across the street as she approached the further side of the house. Toward the back of the side border, Lu stood transfixed, his scarcely two-and-a-half feet of snow-suited aplomb staring fixedly at the earth. As she came up aside him, he pointed excitedly to two or three emerging hyacinths below.

A moment of spontaneous mutual delight, before Alex stooped and cupped one of the hyacinth blossoms between her thumb and index finger. "Flower," she articulated, drawing in her breath. "Lu, 'flower,'" finally, she added in a whisper, "Pretty, very pretty," catching Lu in an upward glance, and smiling. He studied her face for what seemed a long minute, then glanced back down at the head of the hyacinth. First perplexed, then fascinated, at long last, he too smiled and looked up into her eyes. "Pretty," he repeated.

Alex now straightened herself and marched the length of the backyard briskly, until she stood looking over the bluff into the bay. After a short time, she turned and made for the ample, enclosed back porch. She mounted the short flight of steps and stood at the windowed kitchen door. For no reason that she would ever know, she placed her forehead against the pane of glass and closed her eyes. Gratefully, she encompassed the house in a wordless, prayerful blessing.

WHEN Jack arrived at the Lighthouse Point cottage shortly before 4:30, he sounded the front doorbell and was hailed into the house unceremoniously by a duet of hearty female voices somewhere from the interior. He found his way through a modest living room, a dining room, where the table was already set for dinner, into a kitchen. Marcy stood at a table, "Brie, Emmenthaler, and Stilton, how's that?" she announced complacently, arranging cheeses on an oversized wooden cheese board, while Alex bent over an open oven door, peering and occasionally poking at a large casserole.

"Hi," Marcy greeted Jack belatedly, reaching for a plastic bag of crab fingers next to the cheeses. "Go fetch Barry, will you ..." she ordered companionably, spreading the crab fingers into a large festive bowl. "In the garage ..."

Dismissed, Jack wandered out the back door toward the garage. The retracting door was up, and standing in the light of the entrance, Jack could barely make out Barry's tall, slightly stooped frame in the dim interior. After a few minutes, he saw that totally concentrated; Barry was feeding line through the leads of fishing rod. Jack hesitated to interrupt and was glad that, several seconds elapsing, bass voice finally emerged from the dimness.

"Guess I'll finally have some time to put this collection to good use. Don't you think?" Jack watched Barry replace the rod into a wooden holder and pull out a tackle box standing next to it. Barry opened the metal box and stirred the contents of a few dividers with his index finger. "You fish, Jack?"

Jack hesitated. "Not much, lately. I did as a kid," he footnoted.

"Yeah."

"I think the ladies would like us in for drinks," Jack reminded.

"Yeah," Barry said, making his slow way toward the light of the garage door.

EVEN after two martinis and a delicious, cheerful dinner, kept at high tide of conviviality by the women's unflagging conversation and Vivvy and her friend Debby's irrepressible high jinks, Jack felt he was not "getting to know" Barry any better than he had before, and there seemed scarce hope he ever would. When the women began to clear the table, and Vivvy and Debby skipped off to the upstairs guest room to catch their favorite series television show, Jack reluctantly followed the older man into the living room.

He watched Barry seat himself next to a front window, while he abstractedly claimed a facing armchair. Without staring, Jack was irritably aware of Barry's slow, methodical packing of a pipe from a carved rosewood humidor next to him on an end table. Leafing through the newspaper from the coffee table, Jack continued studying Barry as he lit up, puffed, and exhaled smoke against the filmy living room curtains.

At last, Jack heard himself near challenge, "Well, Barry, and what do you think of Employee Stock Ownership Plans... ESOPs?" For a full minute, Barry went on puffing, before turning a quizzical glance at Jack. He did not speak for another minute.

"That's a pretty tall older, Jack." More puffing. "What makes you ask? I should think that's not exactly in your line of business.

"I don't know if you've been following the local scene here ... in Hughesville. But, my brother is seriously negotiating to sell the family business ... LeClerc Works ... tin cans, tubing, et cetera. The locals are all up in arms. Meetings, and such. There's some talk of the workers and community trying to buy the business through an ESOP arrangement ... Do you think that's a good way to go?" Jack inquired, hearing his voice disconcertingly skeptical.

Barry tamped the tobacco in the pipe bowl. "Now, you understand I'm no expert ... If your brother's really serious about doing something like that, he'd need expert guidance as to actual schedules and procedures. But if you're asking me about ESOOPs in general ..." Barry shrugged, "or, more to the point, what I think of ESOPs in general..."

Barry sat up straighter in his armchair. "Well, ESOPs are a popular idea nowadays ... with conservatives *and* liberals. There's some reason for it, too. Right now, a very small percentage of the populace----let's say, five percent----own most of the corporate stock in the country. What happens in that, with this kind of closed-loop ownership, more and more wealth is being generated for those in ownership positions, while the poor get further and further away from any equity position. So, in that sense, ESOPs can be said to be a step toward equalizing and redistributing wealth more equitably."

Jack remained silent.

"It's worker-capitalism if you like," Barry mulled." From what I understand, employee-owned corporations are best set up so that shares are indirectly owned through a trust. The company deposits a block of stock as collateral for a loan with the trust. Over time, the company repays this loan from its current operating income ... but this repayment money does not have to be reported for tax purposes. That's what makes the plan so popular with owners! And as this loan is repaid, each employee's account is credited with so and so many shares, but the employee does not receive the value of the shares he owns until he leaves or retires. That way, the employee-ownership of the company is protected. Keeping the shares from being eventually bought up by managers or even outsiders."

"Seems like a move toward greater democracy ... greater worker autonomy ..." Jack admitted tentatively, not having anticipated a response of such ranging generality, feeling somewhat annoyed and out of his depth.

"Well, hold on ... It's not *that* simple." Barry tapped his pipe bowl over a capacious ceramic ashtray. "You see, this is *my* hang-up. ESOPs aren't really democratic, either. Not most of them, anyway. It's worker capitalism. Votes are attached to shares, and, naturally, there are widely varying numbers of shares held by various employees, depending on different pay rates, different longevity on the job, et cetera, et cetera. Like regular capitalism, voting rights in this setup are rights attached to *property*: they belong to you because you own the stock. Voting arrangements are made on the basis of this ownership, not on your work contribution. In others, as I've said, they are basically *property* rights, and not my idea of workplace democracy."

"Still, it seems a better idea ... better than the present arrangement ..." Jack countered.

"Maybe. Maybe. Depends on your point of view. Call me a purist. But the employment contract as it is now understood turns the capitalist corporation into an organ of governance over workers. Yet, workers have in no way agreed that the employer should represent them. In fact, you can damn well bet, most employees hold quite the opposite view. ESOPs don't change this: they don't disallow the effects of this fundamental employer-employment governance contract would obtain only when workers were member-owners. Where their control would be personal and attach to them as workers because they were fulfilling a *specific function*: their work product. Such personal rights are not transferable; they can't be bought or sold. They cannot be inherited. You'll observe that selling, transferring, and inheriting is what inheres in *property* rights---but not *personal* rights. So ... in a truly democratic company, control would be tied down to the person fulfilling a certain function----working. With me so far?" Barry questioned, looking a bit flown, but also discomfited.

"You see," Barry went on "we're always being told that the *public* sphere---government—is the sole and only arena where *personal* rights, as I defined them, apply. You have the right to voice your opinion ... to vote for the candidate of your choice. But everything else, we're told incessantly, everything else should be governed on the basis of private *property* rights. Any time anyone raises his voice seriously about *democratizing* the workplace, as I have described it, a whole chorus of voices scream Nationalization. Communism. State Socialism. But that's just nonsense! A democratic firm might just as easily be privately owned as not; it need to be government-owned. Membership rights in a democratic firm would carry inherent personal rights—one man, one vote. Upon leaving or retirement, the worker would be *paid out* his capital ownership from his ESOP shares, of course, but give up his membership rights—voting, et cetera— because he was no longer working."

"Jack guffawed uncomfortably, wondering how they had arrived at this juncture from his original dry and seemingly technical query. Neither man spoke. Barry withdrew into puffing on his pipe and staring through the curtains.

"I guess you got more than you bargained for ... eh?" Barry asked ruefully, finally, without looking at Jack. "I guess I'm still reacting, maybe overreacting, to the general idea that ESOPs are some kind of economic and political panacea, to hear the politicians tell it. Obviously, I don't think they are. Maybe they're a *good* idea, a step in the right direction ... but there's a hell of a long way to go after that ..."

"Oh, I don't know ... It's ... it's interesting ... It's a start ..." Jack said, ambiguously.

"Well, you've got to excuse an old man who's worked in Human Resources all his life and has heard all of the theories ..." Barry laughed. "Most of them, *just* that ... theories ..."

"Barry looked at Jack fully. "This ESOP ... is it your brother's idea?"

"I don't know."

"You don't know ...?"

"'It's what the ... the workers in the community ... are talking about ... hoping to propose to management. Marcy said you were knowledgeable, and I thought I might get a few pointers, in case ..."

Barry shook his head. "Listen, ESOP procedure is no sometime thing. I don't mean to be abrupt with you, Jack, but usually, in a company such as your brother's, where I assume he owns 100% of the stock, the typical scenario is that the seller wishes to retire but still protect the jobs of loyal company employees. The company is typically a modest affair, with good middle management, but no big-time CEO-type personnel at the top. The present owner comes to the decision that it would be to everyone's best advantage if he'd sell the company to a friendly buyer who would upgrade the facility and provide the kind of professional management it needs.

"So, anxious to take advantage of the tax-deferred rollout to companies who sell their stock to this ESOP. The buyer then establishes his own ESOP and acquires the seller's remaining stock.

Finally, both ESOPs are merged into the buyer's ESOP. Because of his tax savings, the seller may even be able to share his advantage in the form of a reduced price to the new buyer. But, I needn't tell you, such a procedure is long, arduous—fraught with technical difficulties—and invariably the result of a determined effort on the part of the seller. Is your brother committed to such a course of action?"

"No, he's not," Jack answered firmly. "I don't know if he ever will be. He may even be violently opposed." Jack frowned. "I guess I was on a fishing expedition ... talking about fishing ... the kind I do nowadays," he admitted self-deprecatingly. "Maybe even being presumptuous. I was frankly trying to ground myself—however superficially---in the subject, so that I might not be completely blank should the matter arise later. Should be community situation really heat up and some alternative course of action to my brother's current one be indicated."

"Are you official counsel to LeClerc Works?"

"No, not hardly, But, I am, in some hard-to-define, middling sort of way ... hard to describe ... largely familial ..." Barry was looking at him steadily, and Jack smiled back as honestly as he could.

"Sometimes, I can talk to him ..."

Barry's eyebrows lifted, but at exactly this moment, Alex, followed by Marcy, entered the living room and threw themselves into the remaining two armchairs, bringing a momentary halt to the men's conversation.

"Thank Goodness for dishwashers ..." Marcy sighed.

"That, and the air conditioning ... despite the century-old charm ... was what decided the matter ..." Alex testified. "Oh, and the extra bathroom."

"Yes, let's not forget the extra bathroom," Marcy echoed, laughing.

Marcy glanced at her watch. " But I should be about hustling Vivvy off ... I promised to get Debby home at a decent hour."

Without having actually spoken to the men, both women rose and headed toward the staircase.

A GOOD five minutes later, the sound of television from the upper story still drifting down uninterrupted, Barry took up the abandoned thread of their talk. It was now his turn to be precipitive.

"Do you like reading ... studying philosophy ...?"

Jack scowled. "I'll have to admit having been a Philosophy major in my undergraduate years. Before law school."

"You sound like you're owning up to a misspent youth ..." Barry observed dryly.

Jack shrugged, adding nothing further to Barry's assessment.

"Well, just a final observation on this other matter. Not really philosophic. Yet it puts me in mind of Hegel. You know the thesis-antithesis thing...." Barry stood up and walked toward the wall of bookcases opposite the living room windows. He puttered about the shelves for a time until he seemed to locate something he was looking for. But he did not remove any book from its place ... just stood there, inspecting the backs of the ranged volumes.

"You know, the originator of the ESOP idea, the first to propose it, was a banking lawyer. A guy named Louis Kelso. In one of his books, he describes ESOPs as the "antithesis of workplace democracy. "I think he even had some idea that they would wean workers off unions ultimately. In fact, unions have been standoffish about ESOPs in general. But in the event of a hostile takeover, union members have come to realize that ESOPs are better than nothing, that you may as well take stock as nothing, that you may as well take stock as nothing at all.

"Kelso's idea was to spread the capitalism, not the democracy. Believe it or not, Senator Russell Long loved Kelso's idea. He saw it as an extension of his father's 'spread the wealth' efforts, and it was he who spearheaded the Employee Retirement Income Security Act in 1974 ... popularly known as ERISA ... making employer contributions to an ESOP trust deductible from taxable corporate income. Still, you've got to remember that less than 10% of current ESOPs have the democratic attribute of one man-one vote. Most of them, in fact, are controlled by management and lenders. The average ESOP has less than 20% employee ownership.

"Anyway, I find it fascinating to speculate how such two diametrically opposite views found a single expression in the idea of ESOPs. It might not be strictly Hegelian, but it is reminiscent of his general description of the thesis-antithesis-synthesis movement of historical change. What d' ya think?"

"It's certainly no stranger than that two latter-day schools of Hegelian thought should be at each throats! Left-wing Marxists insisting on the revolutionary triumph of the working classes, and right-wingers championing the state-over-all, culminating in something compatible to Nazi philosophy," Jack rebounded.

"Touché ... touché. Complicated and fascinating, isn't it? But, you know, Hitler appealed primarily to the petit bourgeoisie, they were his firmest backers. And he was constantly talking up worker's rights and benefits."

"For Germans ..." Jack quipped brusquely, his words heavy with bitterness. "For that supposed ideal, he was willing to enslave the rest of the world ..."

Now the woman reappeared, Marcy in winter coat and scarf, the two children also dressed for leave-taking. Without pausing, Vivvy ran into the living room toward Barry, stretching out her arms for a quick parting hug. Barry swiftly bent down, lifted her up, and kissed her on both cheeks. "Don't forget, Pop-Pop. You're coming on Wednesday afternoon. And I'll introduce you to Glory-Be." Vivvy hugged Barry again and, having been joggled, briefly but gently, was slowly lowered to the floor. "You'll just *love* her!"

"I'll be there, Viv. Don't worry ..."

"Bye, Jack," Vivvy called as the trio exited the front door, Alex trailing behind.

Jack waited a decent interval before initiating his own parting ritual. Although politely making protestations of conventional regrets, neither Alex nor Barry pressed him to stay on longer. So Jack was somewhat surprised when Barry, jacketed, accompanied him out the front door, and walked silently beside him until they reached his car.

"Well, thanks for a pleasant afternoon ... and your help ..." standing at the car door, Jack tendered appreciatively, albeit self-consciously. He felt even more oddly formal, taking Barry's out-stretched hand in a firm clasp before entering the car. Seated in the vehicle, at last, Barry still planted aside it; Jack felt compelled to lower the window in acknowledgment of Barry's continued presence.

"I'm sorry I came on a little like an express train this afternoon," Barry's muffled bass. Heartily, he added, "I've been looking forward to meeting you ... Marcy's spoken so much about you ... Hey, and now that I'm here, I'll keep tabs on those meetings. I'd like to go to the next one. Can I call you?"

"Sure," Jack said, trying to sound equally enthusiastic, already dreading the excuses and strategies he would be forced to invent if he continued to believe his attendance at these frankly hostile meetings inadvisable. Once had been enough. Maybe, more than enough. He had to exercise some limit, after all. He had never planned to abandon family concerns entirely. Just to help Armand and his mother arrive at the best possible compromise ... when and if it should be necessary.

DRIVING home, Jack decided he would not call Marcia when he arrived at his Carriage House flat that evening. Nor even, perhaps, tomorrow. Nor maybe the day after that.

Steering over the twilit rises and dips of Bay view Drive; he felt suddenly, momentarily, fiercely LeClercian, solidly upper Bay. All these people, after all, were outsiders: they could not begin to understand the complex exigencies in this whole Hughesville situation. Their easy answers were all ultimately diminishing to real native-born sons and daughters.

In fact, everything was turning hurtful. His relationship with Marcia. And now this crusty, difficult, pontificating old man. And his fretful, mysterious wife, with her introspective silences and her stiff, arcane evaluations. Even Vivvy, the child he had loved as much as any other living human being, to whom he had just proven to be an afterthought ...

He had best prepare himself for yet another letdown...

NONSENSE. He was just tired. He wasn't LeClercian, nor any Bay Booster. He wasn't unloved, nor even disregarded. He was tired and becoming childlike, confronting these potentially exciting but demanding adjustments.

Once again, wisely, his prescription for himself was a good night's sleep and a few drams of honest self-examination in days to come.

But perhaps, too, a few days off, from the exactions of the whole situation.

Chapter Sixteen

MARCIA HAD decidedly noticed. A spool of weekdays had unrolled into a restful, if uncommunicative weekend, and she speculated now randomly about Jack's having been called out of town, perhaps suddenly, to confer over the sale of the LeClerc business. Or to advise his brother about some legal matter that had arisen with Allied General's people. Immediately, she found her suppositions unsustainable; he would have called in any case, especially had it been an emergency.

Monday following, she needed to do something. And she did, finally. Something she considered juvenile and believed uncharacteristic of her own more normal behavior. She called his office just when he habitually went to lunch, hoping to talk to his secretary Suzanne, at the least. As she had expected, Jack was not in. But after informing Marcia of Jack's present unavailability, Suzanne offered no other information or explanation. And despite her curiosity, Marcia could not bring herself to ask any further questions. Suzanne assured Marcia she would inform Jack of her call. But there had been no return call that day ... nor the next ... nor the next.

Midweek again, now mid-afternoon, Marcia sat at her desk reviewing meds, when her eye settled on the telephone. That last meeting at Alex's---had she said or done something Jack might have considered offensive? Hardly. It had been a perfectly impersonal afternoon, a completely ordinary family dinner, she remembered with something of a twinge of misgiving. Jack had spent a fair amount of time with Barry---but she had hoped for that meeting. Had Barry been off-putting in some way? She could not be absolutely certain, of course, but even given Barry's recent bewildering moodiness, Marcia could not imagine his ever being deliberately abrasive or woundingly hostile.

What was it, then? What ...?

Settled into bed that night, almost asleep. Marcia sat up abruptly, fully awake, thumped her pillow into shape, and turned on the bedside light. Had he considered her now "all set," with her own adopted, close-by family, Vivvy, the Center, all in place? Her own cunning, satisfying universe, everyone and everything in orbit properly ... a cosmography where Jack LeClerc had quite frankly and precipitously become irrelevant? A rush of compassionate pity took hold of her, and she saw herself under the covers shudder visibly. But, what nonsense, she protested to herself. He was more than a loving, discerning, amusing companion ... and, though more and more infrequently of late, a tender lover. He had always been there for her. She needed him in her life. And now, worse luck, an inescapable prescient anxiety replaced the compassion, shortening her breath and threatening to keep her alert and sleepless for a long while longer.

Why *did* he have to insist on marriage? They were good friends and lovers, without any unnecessary ritual formalities. And, it was so much simpler that way. Better for both of them. She allowed herself several minutes of fulmination annoyance before giving way to a full-blown, supportive anger.

Finally, she slapped the pillow flat and put out the light. But it was a long time before awareness could be annulled. Only after a prolonged siege of chest-quashing depression and a final hollow surrender to an acceptance of nerveless abandonment.

When by Friday afternoon of that week, Jack had not yet called, Marcia insensibly reached for her desk phone and called Alex.

"SURE. I'll be here tomorrow ... putting in a whole bed of alyssum in the front border. You can help. So can Vivvy. I'll just pop one of my frozen casseroles in the oven for supper. Lasagna. Keep it simple."

"Vivvy is off to an overnight Saturday with the O'Neill's, but I'd love to come ..."

"Of course, come ahead ..." Alex said. "Barry'll be off fishing for the afternoon, so I'd love the company and the help."

After seeing Vivvy off in the O'Neill van, watching the dust rise from its wheels as they made their way down the unpaved Circle Road, Marcy walked back into the house, donned her light athletic jacket, and headed for her car without stopping to make her usual routine house check. Motoring the route toward Lighthouse Point, she rolled down the car window and let the unseasonably mild air-catch at her face and hair. It must be well into the 50's she responded, remembering the first of the daffodils she'd seen along the side bed that morning.

When she pulled up to the Byrnes' tint saltbox, Alex was already dragging the last tray of starter plants onto their front sidewalk. They walked together along the front bed, Alex opining they had best set the plants in about three inches apart, indicating the approximate distance here and there with the tip of her hand trowel. They set to work then, each agreeing to complete the forward strip on either side of the main front walk. Well into her task now, leaning back to view with satisfaction the several slightly drooping plants she had just put in, Marcy was glad that talk had been kept to a minimum. It felt good just digging in the earth with her trowel, letting herself be, in the sun and air.

It was nearly five when Barry pulled into the drive and began unloading fishing gear from the rear of his lowered hatchback. Stowing his gear into the garage, he disappeared into the house. Alex and Marcy hurriedly finished the empty trays into the shed next to the garage.

When Barry descended to the living room half hour later, the lasagna was in the oven, the table set, and Alex and Marcy just settled down to a modest bourbon-on-the-rocks. Barry joined them silently, seating himself in his favorite chair by the window. Reflexively, Alex rose and poured him a drink.

"Where'd you go?" she asked, handing him a glass.

"Just the bridge over the dam." After mussing through the detritus on his side table, he took up a half-empty cigarette package, obviously deciding there was not enough time to finish a more desirably pipe bowl. "Well, it was a last-minute plan. Can't expect too much."

"Catch anything?"

"Not much luck. Couple of undersized ones." He smoked and sipped at his drink. "Had to throw them back ... in good conscience."

Barry waited and smoked until Alex returned from the kitchen, where she had sprung off momentarily to check on the lasagna. Returning, she automatically refreshed his drink with a splash more bonbon, direct from the bottle, simultaneously sliding in another ice cube into his cocktail glass.

"Got to talking with a couple of guys out there, though," Barry announced to no one in particular, seeming to address the window curtain. "Now, *that* was interesting."

Alex and Marcy sat noncommittal.

Turning to Marcy, Barry inquired, "Have you ever heard of a Paul Doran ... out there at the LeClerc plant? They tell me he's vice-president of the Local."

Marcy stared back blankly.

"Well, I didn't meet *him* out there on the bridge. It was a Jim Doyle, father of Doran's son-in-law, and, of course, the kid himself, Frank Doyle. Ever hear of either of them?"

Once again, Marcy returned his question with a quizzical shrug, as Alex rose and rushed toward the kitchen again.

A moment later, Alex's voice, "Come help me carry in dinner, would you please, Marcy?"

HAVING taken their places around the dining room table, for several minutes, they were all three caught up with the business of dinner.

"Anyway," Barry went on after helping himself to the casserole, "as I was saying, I got to talking to a couple of the guys out there on the bridge. And I can tell you; there's no love lost between them and that owner ... what's his name, Armand ... Armand LeClerc." Barry looked over at Marcia. "Now, you *do* know him, don't you?

"Not really," Marcy answered, immediately regretting the unmistakable edge of defensiveness in her tone. "I mean ... I know he's Jack's brother, of course ... I know he is president of the company ... but, as far as that goes, I've never really talked to him," she added more complaisantly, avoiding mentioning she had indeed never even met the man. Looking down into her plate, for the first time, she wondered why it had never occurred to her before to wonder why such a meeting had not taken place in the ordinary course of events.

Appearing unconscious of any adumbrating subtleties in his daughter-in-law's response, Barry addressed his lasagna and garlic break diligently, with respectful attention. "What they're particularly disturbed about is what they consider LeClerc's high-handed tactics. He won't, this Armand fellow, that is, even discuss with union leadership the status of the terms of the labor agreement still in force ..."

Alex rose to refill the water glasses. "Barry, I can't believe you," she complained as she poured water, "I'm really annoyed. Why *are* you getting involved with this ... why do you *care*? Haven't you had enough of labor-management problems? You're retired, for Heaven's sake."

"Retired, sure, Alex. But not *dead*!"

Before she could stop herself, Marcia let out an involuntary giggle at her father-in-law's dour jest, quickly sobering as he went on with his subject.

"Well now, even with this potential ESOP buyout, a long shot if ever I heard one, you see, the younger guy ... Frank ... he's worried he'll never get vested for his pension ... and he's just months away from his ten-year stint. And ... and the older guy, Jim, he's afraid with the change of ownership, he'll lose his pension. The new owners will slide out from under that commitment like oil slick rising to the surface of the bay after a marine accident. "Barry pushed his plate forward. "I sure wouldn't put that past them ... they'll do just that, you just wait and see!"

Chagrined, yet empathetically succumbing to her husband's obvious involvement in the matter, Alex poked at the remains of or salad. "But how can that work, Barry? If there were to be a worker-community buyout, how could the union function, where workers were part owners? How could they sit on both sides of the bargaining table on relevant issues?"

"It'd be tricky ... I grant," he allowed, "but I'm sure guidelines could be hammered out. It *could* be done ... with effort and goodwill ..."

A quarter of an hour later, the weather, comparisons of lasagna preparations, and Vivvy's wonderful, problematic relationship with Glory-Be, having been reviewed casually, inconclusively, in sporadic conversation, they each sat in place, silent, absorbed, comfortable in each other's company. Alex and Barry each lit a cigarette. Through the open window, the bird-song of twilight floated through the room in tuneful blessing, conferring peace, pure as grace.

"You know, for a while there, in the '60s and '70s, it looked like unions were cutting into new territory, "Barry ruminated introspectively.

"They were beginning to introduce new language into their contract negotiations about shutdowns, for instance. You know, about these being a negotiable item. Stuff like ... no shutdowns through the duration of a labor agreement; stuff like ... unions getting all pertinent information from the company in the event of possible shutdown; such as pledges of retraining and/or preferential employment should shut-down become an inevitable reality. But that's all gone by the boards now."

Barry stood up, his shoulders sagging, and mechanically began stacking dinner plated as he spoke. "In fact, it's gotten worse than it was, gone back to the '50s. Sure, workers still take part in deciding wages, hours, and some defined working conditions. As they had for two decades before. But management still abrogates to itself the exclusive right to make the big decisions about investment and plant location and plant closings, *unilaterally*. As it always has. Nowadays, union personnel are lucky to get a 90-day notice before the show finally closes down around them. And that being true, it can never be right ... or fair ... for *all* concerned. How can it be? And, of course, that's a problem." Barry started for the kitchen, carrying his small Babel of dishes. "And up to now, the Court, and public opinion, have supported just such a state of affairs."

Over the clatter of plates, his voice intoned, "I just can't understand it. I'll never understand it."

Marcia and Alex continued clearing the table when Barry popped into the doorway once more, now empty-handed. "Hey. Don't you worry. It's my turn at KP tonight, Ali. Don't give me any argument! You two ladies, go sit. It's my turn tonight."

Alex snorted as she and Marcy finished clearing. "You're not fooling me, Barry Byrnes. You just want to sulk while you feel self-righteous about stacking the dishes. I thought fishing would clear out the bad vibes. But it's just added fuel to the fire! You're just one, big, sloppy, disappointed idealist, I'll tell you," she directed pointedly toward the kitchen door.

"That may be," Barry half-shouted back, over noisily running water. "But I do stack dishes better than anybody else I know, and ... and ..." he added histrionically for their out-of-room hearing, "I indulge in a better quality sulk, too!"

ALEX and Marcia settled themselves in facing armchairs in the dimming living room; after a few minutes, Alex reached up and flicked on the floor lamp behind her chair.

"What does your ..." Alex faltered, hesitant about how to identify their relationship tactfully in current parlance, "How does Jack feel about all this?" she shifted gears.

Marcia shrugged. "I don't really know. I can't really be sure. He's not a simple man. Basically, he's a liberal like Dad, but he has intermittent spells of guilt about his LeClerc responsibilities."

"I should think so. I'd think less of him if he didn't." Alex drew the throw at the back of her chair about her shoulders. They sat silent for several more moments, listening to the flushing sound of water filling the dishwasher in the nearby kitchen.

"He wants to get married, Alex ... And, soon."

Alex shot a glance at Marcy, her eyebrow lifting imperceptively. "And how do *you* feel about it?"

"I don't know. I don't know," she repeated. "I do *care* about him. *Very* much. I enjoy his company. I depend on him ... He's a tender lover ..." she brought out with a toss of the head meant to cover her considerable embarrassment.

Alex remained silent.

"The problem is," Marcy continued, "the problem is that, right now, I believe he takes my indecision, my real indecision about the two of us, as some kind of ... oh, I don't know, conclusion ... termination. It's occurred to me that he may consider that ... with your moving here ... and all that our relationship has become ... well, irrelevant. That I have all I need now ... and, I believe, he's hurt." Marcy looked across at Alex. "He hasn't called for a couple of weeks now.

"Of course, that *isn't* it!" Marcy added, suddenly conscious her analysis carried potentially wounding implications for Alex and Barry.

Alex smiled back reassuringly, her expression tender but otherwise neutral. "I think I understand ... a little." Offhandedly, in a barely audible voice, she appended, "I would hate to think Barry and I have somehow, however inadvertently, put a spoke in his wheels ..."

With Alex's last comment, Barry had entered the room and quietly seated himself in his accustomed armchair. In the silence that followed, he relit a half-smoked pipe reclaimed from a holder beside him.

"Whose putting a spoke in someone's wheel ...?" Barry asked finally, as neither woman offered any explanation.

Marcy smiled and shook her head. After a minute, Alex said, "Well, Barry, we were talking about Jack. Seems he wants to marry Marcy."

"I'm not surprised ... Why shouldn't he ...?"

"But Marcy's not so sure ... And now Jack, Marcy thinks, might be assuming it's because ... well, because Marcy's got her life all well-arranged ... and ..."

"And, I don't care enough about him to marry him," Marcy completed.

"Well, do you?" Barry asked. "Do you care enough about him to marry him ...?"

"Oh, Barry, don't be so blunt," Alex intervened. "It's not that simple."

Barry drew deeply on his pipe. "Well, I don't see why not. When I wanted to marry you, Alex, I was all ready to carry you off like Lochinvar from the West." Barry laughed, appreciating his own good-humored nostalgia. "It sure the hell was that simple for me."

"We were so young ..." Alex whispered.

MARCIA stood up and walked to the bookcases, putting her in-laws out of sight behind her. She needed to tell them, she had needed to tell them for some time. But somehow, she dreaded it. In the face of her own indeterminate longings, guilt, grief, and pain, the nature and gravity of the subject continued to torment her.

She turned and faced them.

"This actually doesn't have to do with Jack. But it does ... now. Maybe it always did," she retracted. Marcy barely noticed Alex and Barry's polite, puzzled expressions.

"You realize ... or maybe you don't ..." she said more to herself than them, "that Vivvy, Vivvy's birth, was something of a miracle. It must have been. Because after Lu and I had not conceived for over two years, we both agreed to undergo extensive medical examinations. Well, the upshot of all that was, that I was suffering from a fairly serious case of endometriosis."

Marcy sat down at the edge of her chair. "You don't have to know about all that ..." she dismissed almost angrily, "... it isn't important now. Suffice it to say that it made conception almost impossible. Normal conception that is."

Marcy forced herself to look at Alex and then at Barry. "So ... as much as Lu found it aesthetically distasteful," she gasped into a laugh, her breath catching, "much as he found it frankly almost repugnant, we agreed with the doctor to try *in vitro* fertilization. You know, they collected Lu's sperm ... that's what he found so distasteful ..." she snorted sharply, unattractively "and they were then to collect a fresh ovum from me, which would, in due course, have been fertilized and then implanted." Marcy unconsciously wrung her fingers into a tight ball: she lowered her eyes, unwilling to be mindful of either Alex's or Barry's reactions.

"That was just before Lu's first cerebral hemorrhage from the cancer ..."

The silence in the room was palpable. Alex, Barry, and Marcy had each withdrawn into their own space. No one wished to see the others. No one wished to be aware. Of himself or anyone else. They waited for the moments to pass.

After several minutes, Barry rose and went toward Alex's chair. Gently, he pulled her to standing position and lightly, almost ineffably, as if she might separate into pieces, he embraced her. Quickly, he walked over to Marcy's chair and lifting her hand from the arm, held it in his own for several seconds. Then, he left the room.

Neither of the women spoke. Gradually the air lightened. Slowly it became breathable again. In perhaps five more minutes, Barry returned with a tray holding three lightly-filled brandy glasses. Wordlessly, he handed them round and reseated himself.

"BUT that's the problem," Marcy finally spoke in a hollow voice. "That sperm ... Lu's ... is still there. In the sperm bank. And ... and I have to make a decision about it. Soon. Very soon."

Alex's face fell into her lap like an ill-attached mask. She put down her glass with great care. "What do you mean, Marcy? What ... what problem?"

Another lacerating pause, before Marcy heard an unrecognizable voice explain, "Whether to use it or not. Whether to let it go ... to someone ... else ..."

Another unidentifiable stammer, this time from Alex. "What ... what do you mean ... to *use* it?" Now Alex stood up, shaking her head, then her shoulders, then her whole torso, pulling the throw more closely about her shoulders.

When Marcy looked up, both Barry and Alex were staring at her, Alex's face distraught almost into a simulacrum of passing lunacy. Flinging all before her, Marcy stared back at them. "I have been seriously contemplating it. Using it, for its original purpose." Alex and Barry continued staring.

"I don't care. In its way, it is a *beautiful* idea! A kind of immortality. Considering Jack and I, should we marry, will probably once again never be able to conceive—the *real* reason for the failure of his first marriage---it's something to consider. It *is*. Something *not* to be discarded lightly."

Collapsed into herself, Alex sat down again. Barry mustered a gruff question. "Jack. Jack. Have you discussed this with Jack?"

"I have," Marcy replied calmly, turning full-face toward Barry."We've discussed it quite coolly, in fact. Rationally. He says, considering our medical histories, and all the other circumstances, he would not be averse to using Lu's sperm, more so certainly than that of some totally unknown stranger." Imploringly, Marcy searched Barry's face. "For God's sake, Barry, why should he be?" She took Alex into her visual sweep. "Didn't we *love* Lu?" In a prayerful murmur, "Didn't we, all of us all, quite apart from our love and regard for him, consider him a truly superior, lovable, beautiful person?"

Barry flicked the curtain in front of him, speaking over his shoulder. "I don't know, Marcy. It's too much for me to take in all at once. I don't know. I need time."

Alex's countenance, stricken, hovered above her bodily corpus as if disembodied, floating in space. For several minutes, she sat unspeaking, working her hands. Then she levitated from her chair. "Lu doesn't *need* that kind of immortality. I won't have it!" she gasped. "I won't have it. Why, why, it's positively ghoulish! Using parts of him now that he is gone. That use, as you term it, was predicated on his living association with *you*, Marcy. On his love for you. On his wanting to create a new life with you, together. His participation was canceled ... canceled out utterly ... with his death."

After another tense silence, she continued, "And, and if this is the 'problem' with Jack, for God's sake, Marcy, how could you? Of course, he's upset. Loving him! Why it's ungodly ... unfair ... literally ghastly ..." Alex looked at both of them, then rushed out of the room, through the dining room, disappearing up the stairs.

MARCIA sat running her thoughts through her furtive mind, as it were, as she felt them, each a hard, pristine pebble, a nugget of hard-won, mostly agonized, considered rationality. Had her assessment been so ill-founded, had she been so wrong, that she would forever be adrift, never able to summon the courage for another spunky try at triangulation back to moral true course?

"Don't you worry yourself about it, Marcy. Don't worry," Barry consoled from his side of the room. "I expect you've done a lot more thinking about this than we have. It's shocking ... at first, you understand, is all." He scratched his head in burlesque dismay, emanating benevolence. "I have to admit, I'm shocked. But, then again, I haven't lived with these ideas for as long as you have. You got to give us time. We'll sort it all out."

"Do you agree with Mom about the ... the commitment being canceled ...?" Marcy asked.

It took Barry a long time to answer. "In the way, she sees the whole situation, she's right. Much as it almost kills her, she feels Lu has a sacred right to rest in peace. To be permitted to die.

"But that is not to say that it can't be seen from entirely other premises, arriving at an entirely different conclusion, just as morally supportable...

"Marcy, I've just got to live with this one for a while ..."

Without glancing at Barry, Marcy rose and reclaimed her purse and sweatshirt from the hall closet. She moved toward the front door, reflecting that the afternoon had turned out even worse than she could have imagined. As she was about to let herself out, Barry's arm enfolded her shoulder.

Standing at the door, Marcy turned and gave Barry a light kiss on the check. His elderly, handsome face bent down toward her.

"I'm not saying you're right, Marcy, and I'm not saying I'll come to agree with you, but one thing I do know. I know you didn't come to this decision lightly. And I know you to be a person who never deliberately makes a move that is *merely* self-serving ... that trashes other people's feelings. I know you too well for that."

"I love you, Barry," Marcy whispered. "But I feel so bad for Mom..."

"And I love you too, Marcy." Barry gazed out into the dark past Marcy. "And I'll think about it. I'll try to understand.

"But, Marcy," he said as she pushed open the door. "Marcy, you think it about it, too. Think it over *again*."

Coda Four: Alex

S HE CARRIED her steaming cup of coffee onto the back porch and leaned against the sill of the paned double windows opening upon the black branches of their backyard oak. Scarcely perceptible, numberless tiny green shoots swelled along the new growth from its gnarled boughs. More sensed than seen, their presence filled Alex with painful, tender sadness. Backing into the kitchen, she slowly drew out a chair she set just aside the windows. Seating herself, she stared into and past the tree, across the vacant garden, and over the reviving ocher lawn, dropping into mindless vigil for the advent of that sweet, excruciating season of rebirth.

After those two years of all-too-brief Iowa City visits, after they were reunited, settling into that ancient, shabbily furnished third floor flat in Madison, after Barry had been told that windy, stormy Spring afternoon it would require at least another year to complete his doctorate, in a mad, delirious gesture of effrontery, they had deliberately become pregnant. "They," indeed, for this financially ruinous act, this wild burning of bridges, this frantic dash into the abyss of the future was nothing if not mutual. Drunk with hopeful possibilities, they had asserted their right, finally, to be themselves. To live in a world they had helped to shape, even if in some small measure.

And on that brilliantly sparkling day of wintry frost, with temperatures well below zero, Christmas on the morrow, Lenny, Barry's Math buddy and fellow seeker after the elusive Holy Grail of the doctorate, had climbed to their third-floor digs, marched himself and his pink potted poinsettia into what they were pleased to call their living room, and, with a histrionic flourish, placed, placed it in the center of their bay window table. Now he stepped back to admire his offering, while Alex, delighted, and giggling, brushed a quick, sisterly kiss across his freeze-flushed cheek.

Responding, in full Victorian sweep, he turned to survey Alex from head to toe. Holding her hand at arm's length, he gave her an appraising inspection. Whether or not he was half in love with her, as it pleased him to pretend, he managed to generate his usual ill-disguised, affectionate excitement calculated to make her feel beautifully desirable; Barry proud, unforgiving, and a tad jealous; and himself, the swashbuckling hero of his own rendition of *The Prisoner of Zenda*. He was entirely fun, and both she and Barry enjoyed his fulsome, sanguine company.

"I think ... maybe ..." she spoke demurely, assuming her designated role. "I think maybe something will ... happen ... maybe today. I've been having ... stirrings."

He looked at her again; his head cocked to one side. "What ... what?"

"Oh, nothing *much* ..." she demurred. "Just ... some kind of ... activity ..."

He assumed an avuncular disdain, leading her to the broken-springs, brocade couch against the wall. "Now, Alex, that's not like you. You're usually so *sensible*." He caught Barry's eye. "Nothing today. Don't you think it ... She still has two more weeks to go ..." he guffawed.

But about supper time, unsure of her own perceptions, she shyly mentioned to Barry that she seemed to be feeling contractions about every twelve minutes. Dubiously, she glanced down at their dinner plates laden with uneaten modest helpings of meat and vegetables. But Barry had no such qualms: within minutes, he was on the telephone to Dr. Weigand.

"He says to get your suitcase and check-in at the hospital," Barry said, hanging up the wall phone in the kitchen.

"Really ...?" she probed uncertainly.

"Really, Alex. Get your bag and let's go!"

ABOUT eleven, she and Barry, in the midst of a game of backgammon laid out across the top of her hospital bed, greeted Dr. Weigand, who, having summarily shooed Barry into the hall, conducted an examination.

Afterwards, sitting up in bed, Alex shamefacedly confronted her physician. "It's my first, Doctor Weigand. I don't know quite what to expect. Maybe it's nothing. Maybe I should be prepared to go home?"

Dr. Weigand turned from the counter at which he stood and focused an amused stare at Alex. "I'll be back by ..." he looked at his watch, "I'd say *about* seven tomorrow morning."

SOMETIME about three and thereafter, episodes began collapsing into each other, time-evolving into an uncontrollable, plastic medium of Demerol stupor; disembodied faces, serious or gleeful, bending toward her to announce some new measurement; and periodic urgent spasms that clutched and kneaded her body into total agonized compliance.

THEN the camera began to speed. The doctor stood beside her, slipping off his coat, his chest bare, pajama bottoms held up with a knotted cord, his naked feet thrust into snowy galoshes. A controlling impulse forced her bodily self into another full, overwhelming contraction, as white-clad figures pushed her, atop a gurney, down a hall, and into a brightly-lit arena.

For a moment, the pain grew so bright, so confounding, a silver sliver of consciousness cut across the back of her eyes with a stunning consideration that had as yet never before occurred to her: she might *not* be able to survive this; she might *not* be strong enough to sustain what was coming.

"Make sure she takes a whiff of gas before each contraction," the doctor's voice ordered.

An overpowering urge again, the rubber smell of the mask, her hand pushing it aside. And then another ... and another ... surrender ... yield ... vessel of fate, instrument of destiny. An ultimate contraction empowered by every muscle in her being ... mouth, teeth, ears, hair ... pushing ... a wet cascading release of some enormous, floppy, aquatic life surging into the world there, fins ... gills, unfolding, close between her thighs.

AND as the doctor fussed at the end of the birthing table, tying off the baby's cord, wiping off this just-arrived life, Alex regarded her other self, released, ebullient, rising effortlessly above her own exhausted corpus, still there, lying northern light presences ascending like vaulting buttresses about her, above her. And she knew then she *had* prevailed: she had reached across the void and caught the chain of living life.

AND after a few short hours of dreamless sleep, the tiny bundled miracle of Lu, whose miniscule ruddy fist pressed into the flesh of her breast ...

WHAT had this to do with petri dishes and precise injection? With microscopic specimens and statistical probabilities? "Don't be simple; don't be a literalist," she advised herself. Yet she was unable to suppress the anger and anxiety, the confusion and conflict that swept across her. How had the mysterious come to be transformed into the mechanical? Romantic love diminished to medical sleight of hand?

REPLACING the kitchen chair under the table, she sighed audibly, self-sustaining, waiting for Barry to find his way down to breakfast. Already, she could hear his footsteps descending the staircase. Judiciously, she admitted she was getting old. Wasn't it true, after all, that one expired ... died ... finally, when unrepentantly, consistently, even happily, one persisted in a course so deliberately out of joint with his times?

She smiled wryly, complacently unforgiving of the present. Casting a coll glance at all these changes.

Chapter Seventeen

ALMOST FIVE, and the mid-afternoon scene had already taken on the twilit character of evening. Jack stood at his amply half-wall office window looking across the rolling, greening field that he knew dropped to the bay, the water from this location seen only as a bright, reflective burnished strip cutting athwart the rectangle of the horizon. Was April then to be his cruelest month, stirring all into a renewed clutch of resurrection, w he stagnated into nerveless immobility?

Desultorily, he began to stack sheafs of memoranda and legal documents into his briefcase. Shafts of latter day sunlight beamed otherworldly upon his desk chair and the center work area of his desk, enveloping them in splendid radiance, active with diamond dust, transforming their more readily recognized banality into unwonted significance.

Was it live and learn, then? Better perhaps, live and unlearn----if one could only manage it. What had begun as almost an involuntary hiatus in his being with Marcia had taken on a destiny and a will of its own. And now he seemed almost powerless to stop or even to change it. Something had happened, had been added to the balance of forces in this three-week lacuna in communication. Nor had she used this interval to call him, or to acknowledge his presence in any way.

Now an irascible, childish pride crusted the edges of his reflection. Something akin to a compulsive, albeit childish, game of "And everything goes double for you." Still, he would not be first to let out the long-held breath in a demeaning explosion of surrender. Or precede in lowering his eyes from this prolonged glazed eyeball mutual hypnosis.

Silly. Of course, silly. In unguarded moments, he had found himself yearning for her, responding with cramping hunger for the very sight of her self. Yet, he was here, where he had been all along, and she was still ... there, where she had been throughout. Nothing had changed.

With superhuman effort, he might vault that ledge of inertia, causing things to happen, but to what purpose, after all?

He forced himself to concentrate on tomorrow's 10 o'clock meeting scheduled at LeClerc's Industrial Conference Room. He had best call, Barry, this evening and remind him of his being picked up at 9:30 tomorrow morning. Not that he needed to, for God's sake; Barry was a grown man, a lifelong professional, for Christ's sake. Yet Jack expected he would succumb to this childish habit now sanctified by decades of cultural tolerance of immaturity. Did he need to lay out any particular or relevant materials? No, he could bring nothing more helpful than his own dubious familial self to the party.

WHEN, in the last week of February, an unprecedented call from Gary Letzger had been put through on his line, he had managed to remain *retenu*, à la Boswell. Gary had taken pains to preamble his ultimate request with a thoroughgoing explication of his having first contacted Dick Stilton, Industrial Relations Coordinator at the plant; then Zach Blaine, Personnel Manager; and, finally, Stewart Carleton, LeClerc counselor, before he, by implication and exculpating telephone delivery, had presumed to have called Jack.

Protocol having thus been disposed of, Letzger's manner at once became less self-effacing, and the union Secretary quickly proceeded to the gist of the matter. The Ecumenical Coalition had in recent weeks soul-searched and argued its way to several important decisions regarding the possible acquisition of the LeClerc Works, and their newly appointed counselor, a local man, Emil Laskovsky---whose own father, now retired, had himself been a four-decade union employee at the Works---was now anxious to present the group's detailed, well-articulated agenda regarding the governance of Community Container Corporation, the new entity's putative appellation, and a revised view of the role of union membership in the over-all projected scheme of company management. In his capacity as Acting Secretary, Gary had been charged with setting up such a meeting among Company management, the Coalition, and the Union, and delivering to all concerned parties, as soon as possible, all pertinent information. He was, therefore, eager to set up this conference directly, as close as was feasible, upon Armand's return. The question was, then, when was

Mr. Armand LeClerc expected back, so all could be moved forward as expeditiously as possible?

Years of juridical circumspection helped keep Jack's language discreet, even equivocal, as he lightly opined only on Armand's probable date of return in mid-March. He trusted his own powerlessness, even irrelevancy, in the decision-making process had been sufficiently turned aside from his auditor's direct perception.

When Armand had called then early in the second week in March, his manner had been opaque, but suitably bluffs, as usual. Jack had made a full recital of all that Letzger had communicated on his previous call, and was therefore somewhat disconcerted to learn that Gary had in the interim managed to reach Carleton after all, and set up the desired meeting for Wednesday of the following week. Dutifully, Jack agreed to show up at the appointed time and place.

He now recalled that just before the call was concluded, Armand had forced out a grudging observation. "There isn't going to be much to talk about, though."

This quip was followed by a protracted silence before his brother added pugnaciously. "Allied General's withdrawn their original offer … and their new one is … well, frankly, paltry …totally unacceptable."

Another protracted silence, before Jack, heard his own voice. "Do you have any idea what you're going to do?"

"Well, I sure the hell know what I'm *not* going to do," Armand gruffed characteristically. "I'm not going to give the business away. I'm certainly not going to knuckle under to their current offer."

Before Jack half-realized, not having been aware that the idea had even occurred to him before this telephone conversation with his brother, he had inquired if he might bring Barry along. "He's a kind of consultant. Beltway personnel. Thoroughgoing professional. Anyway, he's had lots of experience dealing with just the sort of issues I expect the Coalition will be bringing up at the meeting. I thought it might… eventually … be to our benefit. Good for us. And, of course, he's the soul of discretion," Jack assured.

Another noticeable silence, followed by an explosive guffaw. "Aw, what the hell! It's damned unorthodox, but, sure, bring him along. What'd'ye say his name was?"

"Byrnes. Barry Byrnes."

"Sure, bring him along. I'll see you on Wednesday, then, "Armand said, ringing off.

Not knowing quite what to expect, Jack had set the phone back gently in its holder, it having momentarily become the embodiment of the precarious situation before them; his present overriding concern, not to disrupt its tenuous equilibrium, however unintentionally.

IT WAS pouring rain the Wednesday morning Barry and Jack arrived at LeClerc's Administration Building. Giving up their dripping umbrellas and damp rain gear to Nels after reporting into him at his makeshift security desk, as usual, Jack disregarded the ancient elevator, turning instead toward the three flight of stairs to the Industrial Conference Room. Both men mounted these in tandem, wordlessly. Then, for another few brief moments, framed together in the Conference Room doorway, they reconnoitered the seats around the oval table, all but two or three of them already taken. Holding back another second or two, involuntarily aware that the murmur of whispered exchanges went on unabated, their own presence unacknowledged if observed at all, each, as if on signal, moved soundlessly and discreetly toward an unoccupied chair on either side of the table closet to the doorway.

Armand, too, had in no way registered their arrival, yet directly upon their being seated, gave a sign for Carleton to begin the meeting. The lawyer opened with a good-humored reference to a recent news article from Hughesville *Record,* excerpts from which he now read into the minutes, concluding with a request for general commentary and confirmation of its contents from the group at large. Jack's attention had already been fully diverted in studying the faces and expressions of his fellow attendees rather than in the proceedings themselves when he observed that McClintock, Doran, and Letzger were seated center right down the table, opposite Armand and the LeClerc management. He tried to guess the men's mood, but their looks---set, serious, and intent---presented a uniform, unrevealing mask. Ranged to the left down the table from seated Union leadership, were what Jack assumed were the rest of the Coalition's heavy artillery. Of them, he knew and recognized personally only about half: Revered Boardman, senior minister at Hughesville's First Presbyterian Church; Father Meara of St. John's Catholic Church; and Harry Warner from First Bank of Hughesville. Directly opposite Carleton sat a youngish man also unknown to Jack, but whom he now guessed was Carleton's opposite number, the Ecumenical Coalition's new counsel, Emil Laskovsky. Carleton having finally finished reprising the news article, this young man responded with a lively, upbeat rebuttal of its contents, leveling his fervent remarks at Armand primarily, though occasionally bringing Carleton into the sweep of his tightly focused view.

"You know you can't believe half of what you read in the newspaper," the Coalition's counselor concluded, laughing collegially. "We realize that you've had our proposals in your possession for only a few days ... but, you'll notice, contrary to what the article states, that we have done everything possible to attract outside investment to the enterprise. Note our statements to that effect on pages 3," he turned the leaves of the thick folder with his thumb, "41-43, 70 through 81, and then again, in the concluding summary ..." Armand lifted the substantial, blue-covered packet from before him and began leafing through it, while Carleton simultaneously adjusted his bifocals on the bridge of his nose and began peering at the referenced pages with a frown. They flipped pages, as Laskovsky appended," ... but perhaps that makes as good a starting point as any. Perhaps Father Meara could introduce the subject with a few general comments on the ... the philosophy ... the tactics of the Coalition in this matter."

Father Meara, a huge, six-and-a-half foot Irish Viking, with a shock of auburn hair and a complexion to match, self-consciously began to stand at his place, thought better of it, reseated himself, then extended his three-foot-long arm across the table in an alternative gesture of attempted communication.

"First of all," the priest intoned in a heavy bass, "at the Coalition's last meeting, after considerable," he chortled, "after considerable impassioned discussion, all parties, all parties---community members, ecumenical advisors, union leadership, workers – *all* agreed that for necessary and significant equity investment, *all* interested sources should be permitted to invest. Instead of restricting purchase of stock to local residents only, it was decided to solicit, *actively* solicit, outside capital, while still taking care to preserve local control. Toward this end, Community Container would issue nonvoting preferred stock primarily to those persons or entities wishing to invest, but living outside the immediate geographical Hughesville community." He swept the LeClerc side of the table with an intense gaze, although maintaining a countenance of sweet reasonability withal.

"And, you'll notice, too, in the Addendum, to facilitate this hoped-for-acquisition, so desirable after all, for our whole community," Presbyterian Reverend Boardman inserted, "you'll notice substantial *contributions* from the governing Boards of many of the ministries involved amounting to..." he flipped back to an Appendix, "amounting to, even at this time, to near a quarter of a million dollars have already been tendered.

"Not a negligible sum," Father Meara added modestly. "But which we hope to augment as much as fourfold with our present marketing strategies..."

At this juncture, McClintock chimed in in a no-nonsense voice. "We really had it out... all of us... about this vital investment strategy at our last several Coalition meetings. And what we came up with... how we resolved it, is that we agreed that workers would be given a veto over *certain* kinds of decisions. Like a plant closing, for instance."

Laskovsky resumed. "You have probably noted throughout the various proposals and resolutions submitted," he looked over at Carleton, who nodded back curtly in his direction, "you'll notice that that philosophy became a fundamental requirement in our total plan. The best of two worlds, in our opinion. While offering ordinary stockholders the possibility... the reality, in fact... of control, we still endeavored to assure the workers of the protection of their vital interests."

Armand grimaced at a page in his folder, his eyes flicking across the heads of his own cadre. "Well, naturally, we are still in need of more time to... to study... to review... each of these propositions in detail. I had no idea," he continued, "I had *no* idea that... that all this... had gone so far. Of course, I've followed the newspaper articles..." he looked over at Carleton. "Mr. Carleton had the local paper forwarded to me. But, as I said, I had no idea, until I returned, and Mr. Carleton and I sat down and gave an initial review to the Coalition's ideas, as put forth in these documents, I had no idea that your Coalition was so far along in preparing... actually ready to put forward a serious, negotiated bid. It will naturally require much further review... before we can give any serious response... The matter of how to work an ESOP, for instance. That alone could require months of fact-finding into means... procedures..."

"What part would your Local play in all this?" Carleton inquired dryly over Armand's left shoulder. "Seems to me, *that*, in itself, could present an insuperable difficulty. For an ESOP arrangement... that is..."

Letzger's cautious tenor rose from the other side of the table. "That's built into the structure, too, as you'll notice. It was agreed that full-time union representatives would not concurrently serve as members of the Board of Directors. Impossible conflict of interest. But, nevertheless, workers could serve on the Board. Each area or department could select a Board member to represent them, as they do on a grievance committee. Rank and file members would also be able to nominate board members by petition. And union recommendation would count, too, even though, union representatives themselves could not serve."

Laskovsky and Carleton now got down to a page-by-page, line-by-line exegesis and analysis of various sections of the pertinent submitted documents, attempting to clarify for both sides the exact status of union membership in a variety of what Carleton persisted in evaluating as untenably ambiguous relationships. After a twenty-minute go-round on this score, Zach Blaine thought to slide a copy of the relevant documents deftly under Jack's elbow. Momentarily Jack considered moving his chair next to Barry's so as to share materials but decided finally to remain in place, observing that Barry was managing by himself very well, without benefit of documentation, sitting complacent, Buddha-like, arms folded over his vest, quietly contended, appearing rather to be communing amicably with his own personal oracles.

Armand now changed the direction of the exchanges, focusing on financial considerations, as he, Warner, and, not infrequently, one or more of the clergy, with Carleton and a tax lawyer imported from Baltimore, monitored and advised various group members regarding specific, hypothesized numbers. Arguing and emending, they moved around the table, steering the members of the Coalition inexorably toward new bottom-line figures more copacetic with ownership's present expectations. Gradually, however, wearying of his half-hearted eavesdropping on these testy projections, Jack's memory relaxed into replaying snippets of scenes from the foregoing discussion.

Schemes and dreams, Jack repeated to himself. Equitable future organization... policies of workplace democracy. And all the while, the situation was, in reality, well-nigh hopeless.

For all this would turn out to be, as it always had been before, about money. And about money exclusively. Money for Armand. And the power Armand could command with this money. The Conference and the Coalition would turn out to have been a diverting charade only, whereby Armand could initiate an interesting bidding war with Allied General. And it now appeared that Armand considered himself more than equal to such a wily and cynical ploy. His brother wasn't considering the Coalition's propositions seriously. He wasn't trying to connect with these people. Or open himself to their ideas. Jack sat up straighter in his chair and forced himself to tune into the content of ongoing ambient discussion.

Nels now wheeled in a cart stacked with submarine sandwiches, coffee urn, and mugs, napkins, and condiments, which he propelled around the table unobserved, hardly disturbing the ongoing fervent discussions of the smaller enclaves into which the larger group had reformed. Jack picked up a sandwich and moved toward Barry. They stood next to each other for ten minutes, companionably munching at their packaged savory bundles, smiling nervously but mostly silent, mindful that more telling private conversation in this closed space could not only be overheard but possibly hazardous.

After lunch, individuals in both groups gradually resettled into their former seats, and the two integrated sides faced each other as before. Laskovsky scanned his army circumspectly, smiled at both Armand and Carleton, and began speaking. "Before we adjourn, I can only urge again that management and management's counsel pay particular attention to the model for the proposed corporation. And, in conclusion, with your indulgence, and for the benefit of all of us, I would like to summarize briefly its major tenets.

"One: The Corporation would be headed by a 3:3:1 ratio of management – stockholders electing three directors; employees; three directors, and the community corporation, one.

"Two: Nominations of Directors: Employee directors would be nominated in two ways: by a nominating committee from the Local and by petition. Full-time union representatives could not serve as employee directors – as already pointed out, to avoid being on both sides of the bargaining table.

"Three: Any major change in operations would require 75% approval of each group of stockholders. No corporate layoff of more than 10% of employees could occur without such an approval.

"Four: Money raised through sales or contributions would be loaned to the ESOP trust for purchase of stock. As the company paid back its loan to the trust from operating income, a corresponding amount of the stock would be allocated to the accounts of individual employees, who would then received it upon their retirement from the corporation.

"Those essentially make up our proposed tenets of governance. And, on that note, the Coalition resubmits this Proposal to the consideration of the LeClerc Company for final review and, hopefully, opening negotiations toward effecting a binding acquisition." With a final glance at Armand and Carleton, Laskovsky quietly reseated himself.

Armand waited a full minute but remained seated. Finally, lifting his head, he smiled amicably across the table at no one in particular and everyone in general. "Well, gentlemen, you've certainly put together a... a coherent, complete package. And, as it so happens, at just the right time. Allied General, our putative current buyer, has just completed several appraisals and various feasibility studies and is about to submit its final considered offer. So..." he raised his palm, opened his hand, fingers slightly splayed, allowed a quizzical expression to drift across his features, and then, humbly averting his gaze, smiled again into the table.

Surreptitiously, Jack glanced at Barry, who still sat abstracted and removed, in his own neutral no-man's land.

Armand suddenly stood up, shook hands with half a dozen union and Coalition members down the table, followed in suit by the remainder of LeClerc management. He then moved toward the door, as Father Meara impetuously cried out toward Carleton following behind Armand, "It's an ambitious... but, you'll agree, an exciting idea, Mr. Carleton. Worthy of careful consideration."

Carleton mumbled something in reply, smiled up at the wall, and trailed Armand own the hall to the elevator.

JACK decided to saunter over his brother's office before joining Barry, who had summarily excused himself at the end of the meeting to wait for him in their parked car. Having used the stairs again, Jack was surprised and gratified to meet his brother, just exiting the elevator on the first floor. He fell into stride with him as they make their way in the direction of Armand's office.

They were halfway to their destination before Armand observed dourly: "I don't know how seriously to take all this... I can't decide if it's a monumental gesture of effrontery or just an unworkable pipe dream.

At this juncture, Carleton caught up with them, and they all walked on together. "I heard what you said... just a moment ago..." Carleton remarked, slightly out of breath, to Armand. "But I can't help but think it might be excellent strategy to lay some of this out for Allied General. You know. It's bound to pique their interest. It's never a bad idea to let be known there's action in the field... that there's another interested party... another potential buyer."

Armand did not slacken his athletic pace. He turned in at the door of the building housing his office. "Set up a meeting for 10 on Tuesday," he murmured to Carleton. "That'll give us a long weekend for final review... and time to get in touch with Allied General's people."

Without any response from Armand, Jack excused himself, watching Armand and Carleton disappear down the hall. Jack slowly recrossed the parking lot and joined Barry, eyes closed, dumped into the front passenger seat. Jack entered the car, started the engine, and slowly pulled out of the lot. "Home?" he inquired of Barry. Barry nodded. "How about another coffee at the diner first? I can't linger. I've got some work to finish up at the office this afternoon... Just to unwind,' he added redundantly.

Barry shrugged. "Why not? But, man," he laughed, "I'm all the way unwound already. Practically a zombie."

Almost at the diner, Jack quipped. "Well, what?... What?"

The older man sat up and pushed his cap back over his forehead. "Well, the committee seems to have mobilized successfully in this effort. Over-all, I think they made a realistic and challenging presentation."

"But..." Jack added, "That sounds like a sentence that has to end in a 'but...'"

Barry did not answer; just looked back at Jack.

"I think you're in a better position to comment on that one than I am, Jack..."

"Last weekend, my brother received what he calls a totally unacceptable offer from Allied General..." Jack said.

"Interesting... more and more interesting," Barry mused.

"You think anything will come of it?"

"I don't know," Barry said warily. "What do you think?"

Jack, in turn, shrugged. They exited the car and made their way toward the diner. Neither man felt willing or able quite to empty himself of the complexity of hopes, doubts, second thoughts, reservations, ambiguities, and anxieties he felt at that moment.

Over coffee, they talked of the weather.

Chapter Eighteen

I N A routine midweek call to Alex, Marcy was more than a little surprised to learn that Barry had been picked up by Jack that very morning, the pair bound for a meeting of management, and the recently formed community Coalition to be held at the plant itself. She assumed she had exhibited to exaggerated interest or excitement at this piece of discomforting news, scarcely having made more than a single perfunctory comment about it in passing, though the circumstance of the meeting, its agenda, its participants, and most particularly, Barry's unexpected attendance at it, more than piqued her curiosity. Almost simultaneously, it had occurred to Marcy, that on her side, Alex had demonstrated a comparable cautious circumspection, discouraging further gratuitous questions or speculations, by an assumption of an unmistakably flat, matter-of-fact tone, clearly aimed at deflecting, if not squelching altogether, any supererogatory curiosity.

Since that last painful and probing encounter between herself and Alex, Alex's disposition and demeanor seemed to have cleared completely, presenting a lucid summer morning after that turbulent evening storm. So entirely transformed, in fact, that her mother-in-law's present equanimity obliterated almost for Marcy even the memory of the precedent explosion, let alone its possible recurrence.

Through the latter hours of the Thursday afternoon following, Marcy performed her needful mental and manual duties at the Center, conscientiously, automatically, yet with a growing perception of a japing, troubling incubus that had entered her space and had ensconced itself firmly upon her shoulder. She was aware she had carried the creature home, where though shifting into her domestic role, preparing a light supper for Vivvy, desultorily putting together a sandwich for herself afterwards, it sat unperturbed. Calling her daughter from homework to supper table, Marcy took up a plate with her own sandwich and mechanically made her way up the stairs to her own second-floor study. Without flicking on the light, hardly aware of what she was about, she stepped to the desk, lifted the phone from its cradle and dialed her neighbor Elaine's number.

She was startled nearly to hear Elaine's voice so close, intervening between the corpus of the phone and the incubus, the creature's presence temporarily expunged, while her own cranking responses of innocuous pleasantries created meanwhile a neutral interval into which the gravamen of the call would have finally to be introduced.

"Something's come up, Elaine," she heard herself say at last. "It may be necessary... or, at least, convenient for me to be away tonight. Quite late, in fact. Maybe, even into the wee hours... If I got Vivvy's night things and her clothes for school tomorrow together, could I, could I impose on you to have her over for the night? And to get her on the bus tomorrow morning? With Jean, of course, baby-sitting, as usual.

In the hardly perceptible hiatus that followed, Marcy scarcely suppressed a rising titer of nervous anxiety, feeling a teenager about to be third-degreed regarding smoking or something equally if momentously insignificant. She steeled herself for Elaine's concern, followed by a trove of sympathetic inquiries. What should she say? What use as an excuse? Should it be oversight of the Center's night personnel or something to do with Alex and Barry?

Elaine's unanticipated detachment, though filtered through a mild distinguishable lilt of curiosity, was immediately forthcoming.

"Of course. No prob*lem*-o! When should Jean come over for Vivvy? ... In about half an hour? ... She'll be finished with dinner by then."

"Oh, I'm sorry, Elaine."

"Don't be silly. We're essentially almost through right now."

And without there being time to thank her, or to go into any further explanation, Elaine rung off with, "OK. Jeannie'll be there in half an hour, then."

Unconsciously taking a bite of her sandwich, carrying the plate with her out of the room, Marcy made her way toward Vivvy's bedroom, placed the sandwich plate down on the child's bureau, slid an overnighter from under the bed, and began filling it with Vivvy's night things and school clothes for the next day. She felt half herself programmed into robot efficiency, while the other half continued standing apart, abstracted, nonjudgmental, almost disinterested in the ongoing proceedings. Her task completed, she snapped shut the diminutive case and carried it and the plate with her still uneaten sandwich down to the kitchen.

"Vivvy, dear," Marcia said, 'I'm going to haven't stop back at the office for a while tonight, and then, maybe drop in at a few of the cottages." She shook her head as if to dislodge her own rising need to invent further incidental details. "Because I expect it will turn out to be pretty late before I can get back, I've arranged for you to stay at the Ruskin's tonight. Jean will be here for you in about fifteen minutes. I've packed your night things and your school clothes for the morning..." Marcy patted the case. "How're you coming with your homework?"

"Oh, I'm almost through." Vivvy skipped the closet for a jacket. "Oh, goodie, I'll get to beat Andy at *Mario* yet! Oh, I can't wait to..." Vivvy's voice trailed off. As she began piling books and papers into her backpack, when only minutes later, upon Jean's unexpectedly early appearance, the two began chatting at each other so concentratedly regarding plans for the evening, there was hardly time for good-bye's, let alone any opportunity for prolonged or protracted explanations.

THROUGH the wistful long-rayed beams of approaching dusk, sunlit sides of houses and barns presented themselves in dazzling architectural relief, standing apart and freed of their muted nurturing verdant enclosures. Marcy sighed involuntarily at this most favored time of day and most astonishing miracle of light: instantaneously stanching the yielding vulnerability this loveliness always engendered. She must concentrate instead on nothing but her present active goal.

She drove into the Center's lot, parked in her usual slot, let herself in at the Center's service entrance, and walked into the building that had become her second home. Briefly standing still in the hallway, she flicked on the master light, feeling neither her usual surge of warm association for these familiar surroundings nor a contrary anxious melancholy at their present foreboding abandonment. Nothing. She was nearly hollow, suitably cleared.

From a hall phone, she dialed the local Hughesville cab company the Center occasionally utilized, asking to be picked up as soon as a cab were free. Enroute to the Center, she had already decided neither to provoke Amanda's curiosity with the appearance of her Saturn on LeClerc grounds nor signal Jack of her arrival by parking her vehicle before his Palladian garage door.

Having entered the cab and indicated a destination well-known to the cabbie, she tried to settle into nonchalant relaxedness in the back seat. Yet, she could not suppress an escalating nervous excitement, though she remained unable to construct even the least schedule of what she was going to do, or what she was going to say once there. As the cab pulled in front of Jack's Carriage House, turning around into the exiting loop that put the vehicle once more facing the bay, she felt nothing so much as joyous relief at seeing total darkness in all the windows above.

Sleepwalking, she exited the cab, paid her fare to the cabbie, climbed the stairs to Jack's front entrance, and let herself in with her own key. She switched on the nearest living room lamp only, hung her coat in his vestibule closet, tucking her own overnighter neatly into a dark corner under the longer coats. For another full minute, she stood in the anteroom, listening.

Her watch said 8:10. She turned off the one lamp she had lit and maneuvering by the light coming in at the opposite French doors only, seated herself in a corner white armchair that faced the front entrance.

For a matter of perhaps another ten minutes, she alternately turned to stare through the French doors behind her or tried to piece together some scenario of what she would say, what she would do, when Jack arrived. Finally, giving up both, she fell into an open-eyed daze approximating sleep.

AN INDEFINITE hiatus, when she barely heard light, almost hurried footsteps outside, a key scraping in the lock, saw the outer door swing open, wincing involuntarily at the rush of light to vestibule and living room, concurrently just discerning dark sheathed figure moving toward the closet. Another door clicking, and suddenly Jack was there, framed, frozen in the archway of the living room.

Her first instinct was to rise, but she was unable to make her right leg tucked under her function. Though she tried to move, it remained inert, coming alive only slowly into prickling waves of cramping immobility.

Jack advanced a few steps into the room before he saw her. "What are you doing here, Marcy?" his hushed voice finally sounded. "Why... why are you sitting here... in the dark...?"

She was ashamed to hear her own halting, circumlocutory, childlike response. "I just wanted to see you... be with you..."

Instantly, she knew what she had to say...

Without looking at him, head averted, she murmured, "I know what we ought to do now, Jack. I know. I've had plenty of time to think things over... these past few weeks. To think about a lot of things, in fact." She turned to face him. "I think we should get married."

"Tomorrow... the day after..." Jack said immediately, sitting bolt upright.

"I don't want to discuss time... logistics... right now, Jack. But yes. Soon... very soon."

"That's the best way, Marcy. You'll see..." Jack insisted, breathless. "We'll get a license and physicals tomorrow and be married on Friday. No explanations. No long, drawn-out excuses and adjustments. Just present ourselves... next Monday... married! *Fait accompli. Finis.* End of story." Jack was now standing beside her, his right fist grinding into his open left palm, appearing ready to spring out any available exit at a moment's notice.

Marcy looked up into his flushed countenance; her arm lifted, and her index finger instinctively traced the line of his jaw. She felt weary , heavy with echoes of the voice of reason, of circumspection and restraint. Recklessly, she willed mounting this tidal wave at her lover's side, with him, freeing herself to be spontaneously, gloriously happy.

They stood together, embracing, succumbing o a timeless fulfilling kiss. "Jack, Jack, Jack," Marcy crooned finally. She cradled his face. "Jack, I *do* love you. I *do*," she repeated, whispering beneath his ear.

His eyes shone as he bent to kiss each of her eyelids in turn.

After measureless interval, she murmured into his shoulder. "I brought my things... for the night. I've arranged for Vivvy to say with the Ruskins..."

He tightened his clasp, pulling her into his chest. "I'm so... glad... So grateful... my dearest, dearest love..."

THEY surfaced sometime after midnight, momentarily sitting up in bed, blue-white moonlight, unbeknownst to either, sculpting their faces and bodies anew, strewing brilliant encircling parabolas across the warm bedclothes between them. Once again, supine and replete, they lay back, quiet, and childlike, side by side, aureoled between sleep and waking.

HAVING finally arisen, they sat facing each other over the kitchen table and a cup of Jack's own special clam bisque. He poured each of them a sniffer of brandy.

With her free hand, Marcy reached across the table and covered Jack's with her own. "Serious, now, Jack. Real. We can get the license tomorrow... today... and the physicals, too, if that can be managed. But we can't get married, even if we should decide to elope before I've had time to speak to Vivvy. At least. You can't just move in... like that... come Monday."

Jack stiffened visibly. "For Christ's sake, Marcia, give me some credit, at least. I'm not a brute, after all..." He guffawed, his lowered eyes sparkling with pain. "I didn't expect to move in... right away... Perhaps not for several weeks. I thought you could speak to Vivvy in that time... and any relatives you cared to tell..." His expression brightened. "We might even have a small at-home to commemorate the event..."

"No, Jack, I didn't really mean *on* Monday. But... without adequate preparation. Let's do this in the right order. I feel it is too important not to do it right, the first time. Too important for us. For our relationship. For getting the absolute best right start."

They sat looking at each other. "If you feel so strongly about it..." Jack reneged without conviction. "You could have held off making an announcement to the family until Vivvy felt ready. I was prepared for that..."

"I know, Jack. I know... you're afraid. You're afraid I'm going to back out at the last minute. That I'm putting it off... stalling..." Marcy stood up and carried her cup to the sink. "I can't absolutely promise you that I'm not, either. That my motives are altogether clear to me or under my control. But I can assure you that I don't *believe* I'm deceiving myself." She reseated herself across from him. "I signed off on Lu's sperm yesterday... It goes into the general sperm bank now..."Another flash of pain cut across Jack's eye. "Not because of me surely..." he breathed.

"Yes. Because of you." She squeezed Jack's hand again. "Because of you... and because of me... because of *us*." She forced him to look at her. "Because we *deserve* our own fresh start. Our own mutual life ... whatever it may bring..."

"Marcy," he whispered. "Marcy, Marcy..." inclining his head afraid to examine her face for the implications of this terrifying revelation.

THEY sat holding hands across the table for an indefinite time. The mundanity of the scene in no way intimated the profound gravity of their silent, mutual commitment.

"JACK, my love," Marcy spoke finally. "Perhaps we should have another few hours of real sleep... before... before we take those initial steps... tomorrow."

They both laughed aloud, joyously, as they left the kitchen, snapping off the light fixture enroute, making for bed... and sleep.

BOTH having showered and dressed, Marcia first checked in with Elaine to see that all had gone according to schedule with Vivvy, and then, assuming their staffs to have at last clocked in, each called to report their expected full-day absence.

Breakfasting at a small diner on the edge of town, where neither of them were known, they went to the City Hall and then the Court House, to initiate proceedings for obtaining a marriage license. Shortly before lunch, they had already visited the several offices and signed the many requisite forms toward the issuance of their license and were now ready for the municipally approved physician to put them through the perfunctory examination that would satisfy their last legal requirement. By mid-afternoon, license secure, they drove to Shore House for a late lunch and a celebratory bottle of champagne.

LUNCH completed, at the risk of appearing devious or even unnecessarily mystifying, Marcy insisted on taking a cab from Shore House to the Center. She would have to be home by dinner time or make fresh arrangements for Vivvy. Jack did not protest her decision. Glancing at him, she suspected he felt worn, as did she, and more than mildly depressed. Throughout the subsequent leave-taking, they talked at each other, volubly, inconsequentially, avoiding pockets of silence, fussing over the many complicated mundanities they anticipated in upcoming business days. They avoided looking at each other.

Standing in the Shore House parking lot, they caught sight of the cab beginning its long ascent up the winding road leading to the restaurant. Tentatively, Jack drew Marcia to him, kissing her lightly, self-consciously, on the mouth.

"Naturally, I'll call tomorrow..." he said, leaning away from her.

"Not tomorrow," Marcia demurred. "Not... please, Jack, please understand. Give me 'til midweek, at least. Maybe, by Friday, we can have lunch. Maybe, I'll have talked to Vivvy by then... and we can put our heads together for what to do next... Some new strategy, perhaps, with all of us participating... together..."

The cab swung into the circular drive in front of the Shore House. Upon its approach, Marcia had immediately identified herself as the prospective passenger by waving energetically in its direction. The vehicle swerved gracefully around the curve, stopping soundlessly, inches from where she stood.

She entered the cab, rolling down the rear window as she seated herself. Though assessing herself a poor imitation of a high-school prom queen or a contestant in a beauty pageant, she felt nevertheless compelled at this moment to produce just their brand of predictable, generic exit: she thrust her face out the window, produced what she could be described only as a radiant smile, cocked her head playfully in Jack's direction, and lilted, "Now, don't you forget me, Mr. Jack. I'll be waiting to hear from you, d'y'hear...?" Serving as a perfect supportive prop, on cue, the cab pulled away, churning up exactly the right amount of gravel, Marcia's wave out the window completing this consummate histrionic moment.

Cinderella-like, she faced forward, eyes smarting. She choked down a hiccough, the first of many wrenching spasms that she was to endure on that dismal return journey to the Center, nature's cruel exaction for tears too deep to shed.

Jack was not successful. His features twisted into an expression of sarcastic contempt, for himself, for his situation, for them. "Some honeymoon," he snarled. The cab out of sight, he turned to plunge back into the restaurant for coat and briefcase, vacating without his usual parting acknowledgment to the hostess, or chatting with his longtime friend and client Charlie, the proprietor, who stood with hand outstretched, quizzically watching as Jack banged out the door.

"WE SHOULD have married. Today. Right off. Like I said," he muttered to himself on his way to his car, at this moment, hating Marcy, Vivvy, and himself, as well as the whole miserable wide world out there. But more even than that, anguished at his own seizure of regressive, childish anger.

Chapter Nineteen

F RIDAY, MARCY came back for a disconcertingly routine day at the Center. No questions about yesterday, not even from Ginny, after hours spent together on meds. Nor scarcely an inquisitive glance from Marie, or Jonesey, busy inspecting Gloria's most recent set of braces, Jonesey on her knees palpating the child's right boot, checking the fit of brace to slot. "They're not right," Jonesey diagnosed to no one in particular. "They shouldn't hurt so much as that," she muttered in Marcia's direction. But, though Marcy stood in the doorway for several more minutes, neither staff member paid her any further attention. She went on to make a routine daily tour of inspection physical therapy room, activity center, kitchen, returning to her own office, finally, only half-aware that it would have been gratifying to have been able to tell someone about yesterday.

But it did give her time that afternoon to think. What would be the best way to break the news to Vivvy? A day trip away to Baltimore? With something special planned? Perhaps a night spent in a motel with late evening time for discussing this fragile matter privately, intimately? Or, more simply, just a long Saturday afternoon picnic somewhere together? Where they could be alone, uninterrupted? The weather was getting warm enough for that to be possible.

When Marcy stopped to fetch Vivvy from her after-school nursery "babysitting," she hoped to broach some half-formed ideas on this score and sound Vivvy out as to her preference. But as her daughter gathered books from the stair-hideaway and grabbed up her sweater, making her perfunctory good-bye's to Ellen, she was already deep into plans for tomorrow.

"I got the birthday invitation on Thursday, Moms. The day you were gone," she explained unnecessarily. "You remember..."

In the car on the way home, Vivvy extracted an obviously homemade invitation to Glory-Be's birthday party tomorrow, Saturday, waving it just aside the steering wheel.

"I'll look at it in a minute, dear," Marcia said, trying not to let a critical edge creep into her voice. "You mustn't wave that thing in front of me when I'm driving..." she added more softly.

"Oh, Moms, I'm sorry." Vivvy sat back. "But we shouldn't go home yet. We need to buy Glory a present. I haven't got her any present... And I know a perfect one to get!" Before Marcy could respond, Vivvy was wriggling on her seat. "A typewriter, Moms! A typewriter. She could *write* if she had a typewriter."

"We'll just stop at home, and I'll give Samantha O'Neill a call," Marcy answered as soothingly as she could manage. "Then, we'll go out and buy a gift and have supper at Delmonico's afterward."

Vivvy was out the car, running into the house before Marcy had caught up with her at the side door with the key.

SAMANTHA O'Neill was immediately apologetic, making Marcy feel instantly even more depressed and disconnected to events as they falling out. "I'm sorry about the lateness of the invitations," she apologized. "The kids *insisted* that they had to make the invitations themselves, personalize them, you know, with Gloria coloring in some of the designs... Her own special touch, you see. And before we had them mailed, and everything... At any rate," she recovered herself sensibly, "I know Gloria will be looking forward to Vivvy's being here... her very *best* friend."

Embarrassed, Marcy asked if she had any suggestion for a gift. While Marcy knew a full-fledged typewriter was an unreasonably expensive option, she tried to explore the subject of some limited key-board play equipment, suggesting a brand name writer-printer-computer type of apparatus she'd considered for Vivvy last Christmas.

"Well, that's more than thoughtful. In fact, that same thought had occurred to me some months ago... I even broached the subject with Marie. Frankly, I was surprised... well, maybe on second thought, not *so* surprised when she said, 'Nothing doing. That'll just give her an out not to work on her pencil skills. It's too easy an out.'"

"I see," Marcy heard herself reply.

"But, heavens, Marcy, anything will be fine. Anything! We'll just be delighted to have Vivvy come," Sam added gracefully, sounding just a bit harried and hopeful for closure to this bread-and-butter conversation.

ALL this was conveyed tactfully to Vivvy on their trip to the mall. While Vivvy let go of the typewriter suggestion, at last, she next insisted on the purchase of a pair of patent leather slippers because Glory was so-o-o tired of those ugly brown boots she always had to wear. Marcy used her most facile tactics to disengage her daughter from that heartfelt, truly irrational notion, and in the end, they settled on two beautifully illustrated children's classics, Sewell's *Black Beauty* and Grahame's *The Wind in the Willows*, chosen at Donovan's, because Glory was recognizably such an apt and outstanding reader.

BY THE time they reached home and were finished with the bathing routine, choosing tomorrow's prettiest party dress, and wrapping the presents with special care, Marcy had altogether forgotten the original burden she had set herself for the evening and was glad to climb into bed without even turning on the eleven o'clock news.

MORE thinking through Saturday afternoon while Vivvy attended Gloria's party. As Marcy assembled a casserole for Sunday's dinner, she decided that her former ideas on how to handle this situation were all too "worked." Too deliberate. Too artificial. The initial conversation should just be "natural," in their home setting, nothing "prepared," in the normal course of things, as it were. Of course, after the enervating events of a birthday party afternoon, tonight would not be the best night for such a talk. Perhaps tomorrow morning after brunch, after homework, during the long, often dismal hours of a sleepy Sunday afternoon.

Storing the ready-to-bake casserole in the refrigerator, Marcia felt more or less relieved of the problem of having to choose an optimal strategy for the morrow. She had barely settled into a kitchen chair and unfolded the evening newspaper when Vivvy burst in at the back door with handfuls of frilled paper basket, candies, and small toys escaping their cellophane wrappers, all of which she dumped in the middle of the kitchen table.

"Moms, you'll never gu-e-ss what happened."

Marcy was not kept waiting. "Before Glory was to open all her presents, her Dad carried her downstairs to the den so that her Mom and sisters could put all the presents out of the dining room table and everything... And when they were ready, her Dad went down to get her, and she came out of the den, and, guess what?" Vivvy hopped from one foot to the other behind the kitchen chair. "He set her foot on the bottom step sideways to the wall, and put her hand on the railing. And then, she *pulled* herself up to the next step! Her Dad stood behind her all the while, of course, and she did it all over and over again... every step... one by one... it took her a long, long time of course, and her Mom was sitting on the top step, and when Glory *finally* made it to the top step, her Mom was crying, and her Dad was crying, and everybody, all of us were cheering and laughing, and then d'you know what happened? Her Uncle Fred picked her up and carried her to the dining room table and put a big box in front of her, and she opened it and took out the most beautiful white silk dress and cap and matching shoes because Glory's going to be confirmed next month and..." Unable to repress herself, Vivvy did a little jig behind the chair. "Isn't that wonderful?" She threw out both her arms and spoke heavenward. "Isn't that wonderful, Moms?"

Marcy walked over to her daughter and enfolded her in her arms. "*You're* wonderful, Vivvy." She held her daughter at arm's length and beamed upon her. 'You're a wonderful girl and a very special daughter."

VIVVY had just completed impromptu oral responses to the study guide questions at the end of the chapter on hemispheres; torrid temperate, and frigid zones; latitude and longitude; time zones and the International Date Line, directing her answers to Marcy, who held the oversized text in her lap, only infrequently flipping back into the text to check on a fact or the wording of an explanation. Marcy could not help feeling just a bit complacent about the daughter, who had been identified as "gifted" in last year's third grade mandatory testing on a standard intelligence test. But, gifted or no, Marcy told herself, thoroughness, ability to relate data to other pertinent data, to generalize accurately, and to pose questions not specifically delineated in the printed matter at hand, these skills more accurately constituted real learning, and required of everyone, especially perhaps the talented, disciplined, even repetitive exercise, manipulation, and restructuring, until particular knowledge became personalized into one's own *gestalt.*

"OK, kiddo, I guess, like the song says, 'You've got the world on a string... The string around your finger,'" Marcy sang, tangoing up to Vivvy's backpack perched in the window seat and, on beat, thrusting Vivvy's social studies text into the bag.

Vivvvy giggled. "Boy, Moms, you're funny... You really *are...*"

Marcy negotiated a spontaneous staccato flamenco heel tap, simultaneously lifting her arms in finger-snapping accompaniment.

"Boy, Mom," Vivvy giggled, hurtling out her armchair now to imitate her Mother's flamenco extravaganza.

They danced for several uninhibited minutes, facing each other, now turning away, assuming exaggerated, histrionic poses, until each fell into a corner of the sofa and gave way to bursts of unrestrained hilarity.

When they had subsided, Marcy reached over to Vivvy and gently pinched her cheek. "So... you really had a good time at Glory's party yesterday?"

"Oh, yeah..." Vivvy exhaled. "Yeah."

Marcy grew serious. "Glory is a wonderful little girl, too. Wonderful... and *brave.*" Marcy sighed. "But she's lucky, too. Lucky to have a wonderful, supportive mother and father.

"Oh, sure," Vivvy acceded.

"And it takes a mother *and* a father to carry the... to make the constant effort... of so much loving care. Of course, you know that, Vivvy. It almost can't be done by one parent... alone."

"I guess so." Vivvy acquiesced. "Mr. O'Neill *is* awfully nice and helpful and *good,*" Vivvy agreed obligingly.

"Do you ever miss having a Daddy?" Marcia ventured.

It was a considerable time before Vivvy responded. "No, I don't. Of course, I *loved* Lu. He was always my *real* Daddy. I love Lu right now, and I'll always, always love Lu. I even used to wish," her voice grew distant, "all the time, I used to pretend that if I wished it so hard that I could feel it... here," she said, pressing her thumb against her diaphragm, "so real, he might appear. Come back to us. Just as he used to." Vivvy shook her head. "But, I was only a child then. What can you expect?" she mused, catching her mother's eye and nodding complicitly. "No. I don't do that anymore."

They both sat quietly, staring across the room at the cold fireplace on the opposite den wall. Vivvy said, "But I don't want any *other* Daddy. And besides," she added, "if I did, there's Pop-pop. He's my second Daddy. I love him as much as Lu."

Marcy had almost forgotten about Ned, Vivvy's genetic father. Ned's peregrinations had begun so early and were so well established before Vivvy had scarcely celebrated her first birthday, only the bitter aftertaste of their divorce litigation retained a bright edge of reality for Marcy. In fact, she could hardly remember anything else about Ned at all. And, of course, to Vivvy, he was a complete unknown. He had never even asked for visiting privileged or ever, ever contributed a cent toward her support... Marcy's mind twisted off any further recall of this, her first disastrous venture into marriage.

And then there was Lu. So reserved, even standoffish at first. So different from Ned's Hail-fellow-well-met, I'm-here-for-you-baby persona. Well, Lu had had his own problems with Andrea. But by the time Lu had moved in with them, three-year-old Vivvy was his sworn buddy. Marrying, as they had finally, had been almost an afterthought. It had made absolutely no difference to Vivvy's experience of him as a parent.

Without hearing herself, Marcy let out a deep sigh and turned to face her daughter.

"Well, you know, Vivvy, Daddy's are usually someone's husband, too."

Vivvy flicked a quizzical glance at her mother. "I know *that*, Moms," she retorted deprecatingly.

"Well, Viv, what if *I'd* like a grown-up companion... a real friend... a partner..."

Vivvy faced Marcy. Marcy watched a succession of responses pass over the child's face – mild surprise, curiosity, disbelief until Vivvy's lips pursed at last, and a steely distaste cut across the irises of her bright eyes.

"Why do you need *him* if you've got me?" Vivvy indicated.

"You like Jack, don't you, Viv?" Marcy changed venue, reaching across the sofa and laying her hand on Vivvy's arm. "I think I love Jack, Vivvy, and he's asked me to marry him."

Vivvy rose abruptly and walked toward the door between den and kitchen. "Do you love *him* more than *me*?" she accused. At the doorway, she paused momentarily, and without even glancing back at her mother, flung out, "Because if you loved me best, you wouldn't want anybody else. Just like... I never, ever, want anybody else. Ever." Now Vivvy turned and faced Marcia again. "And besides, he'll *never, never*, be as good as Lu, and, and," she ran through the doorway into the interior of the house. "he can't *make* me love him... ever," she shouted somewhere from the vicinity of the dining-room.

Marcia rose and walked to the window seat. Instinctively, she knew to leave Vivvy alone for now. She could hear her daughter slamming drawers, probably at the living-room chest, where they had together, lovingly, longingly, years ago, finally collated and entered all the photographs of Lu in a large dedicated leather-bound album, photos that, until his death, had been slipped carelessly, casually into overflowing envelopes, and stuffed into various desk drawers, but which had never, until then, been sorted, arranged, and affixed, deliberately, and for all time. After Lu's death, after the album had been assembled, Vivvy had spent whole half-hours sitting alone in the living room, late Sunday afternoons, evenings sometimes, sadly, a wistful smile often invading her face, the oversized leather volume in her lap, slowly turning its pages. No, best leave her alone.

Marcia went into the kitchen, removed the casserole from the refrigerator, and slid it into the oven. Mindlessly, she reached down two salad plates from the cupboard and began arranging lettuce leaves on each. A quarter of an hour later, as she had just begun to set the table, Vivvy suddenly flashed past her through the kitchen toward the backdoor and, before Marcia was able to turn around, shouted, "I'm going over to the Ruskins for just a minute, Moms. I'll be back in just a minute. OK?" And never having intended to wait for an answer slammed out the door.

SOMEHOW they both got through the evening meal. One in which their every remark shone with icy politeness. And through which mother and daughter avoided each other's eyes, smarting as they were with painful constraint. Having helped clear the table, Vivvy departed the kitchen as silently as a wraith. Moments later, Marcia heard bathwater being drawn in an upstairs bathroom. And more than an hour after that, Marcy heard her daughter call from her bedroom. "Do you want to tuck me in, Moms...?"

As she climbed the stairs, a smile of resignation and affection crowded out all other incipient expressions on Marcy's weary countenance. Vivvy's hug and kiss were just as warm, just as sweet and fresh as always. As she snapped out the light, Marcia allowed her hand to linger lightly, briefly, upon her lovely daughter's damp and fragrant forehead.

SHE picked up the phone just after the second ring, hoping the sound had not carried enough to wake Vivvy.

Immediately, Jack spoke. "I know I wasn't supposed to call until later in the week... But on the off-chance that *you* might call me, I thought I'd let you know; I'll be out for the rest of the evening... at the Big House. I promised Armand. I don't know what the hell he wants to talk about! I haven't been at the House..." he trailed off inconsequentially.

"I'm glad you did," Marcia dissimulated. "You make it sound like a penitentiary," she quipped flippantly, hoping to avoid telegraphing anything of her disappointing confrontation with Vivvy. If he asked outright, she'd already decided, on the instant, she would just have to lie; she could not bring herself to deal out such a wantonly cruel blow. Innately, Jack spared her any accounting, as he had already promised he would.

"OK, Marcy. You all right? Everything OK?" he dismissed. She was grateful.

"I'm fine, Jack... Just fine. I miss you," she added.

"And I *love* you." He whistled under his breath. "I'd better get over there, Marcia. Damn. Damn,' he repeated. "Marcia, I'll call again, *much* later in the week. Unless something comes up, of course."

"OK, Jack," Marcia acknowledged.

FROM the coffee table, she lifted the Sunday copy of *The Times* and began sorting sections onto the free sofa cushions. She glanced at a few headlines on the front page, went on to read through two of the lead articles, then turned to the editorial page. In a few moments, the paper sank onto the sofa, and Marcia dropped into a wide-eyed musing daze. It was uncanny that considering all the persons she knew, at this moment, for one reason or another, there was no one she felt entirely comfortable talking to about her immediate dilemma. Unconsciously, her eyes flicked up to the wall clock above the fireplace, and her hand reached automatically for the telephone. She dialed Alex and Barry's number.

A gravelly, tired female voice identified itself as Alex.

"I hope I didn't wake you," Marcia apologized. "I know it's a bit late."

"No, no," Alex's voice assured, beginning to take on Alex's more natural timbre and evidencing a more familiar cadence. "I guess I must have fallen into a muddle. *Half* asleep, maybe."

"Alex, I've taken a kind of a step. About Jack..."

Marcia listened to the silence at the other end of the line. After a full half-minute, she continued.

"Thursday, Jack and I got our marriage license... completed all the requirements."

Another silence. A flash of resentment passed through Marcia. Might this be Alex's ultimate revenge: to make everything now as difficult as possible?

But, after a prolonged clearing of the throat at the other end, Alex's voice came through clear and profoundly serious. "Marcia, you know I wish you... both of you... wee. I'm fond of Jack, although I think he thinks me something of an ogre... albeit a mysterious and somewhat interesting ogre." She chortled. "But... however, that may be... you also know how I feel about... about other relevant matters in this situation..."

"Alex... I released the... My holding in the sperm bank has been released for anonymous usage...Last week. Before all of this ever happened," Marcia said.

Another long silence. "I'm glad," Alex said simply, without overtone, almost resigned.

"I wish I could speak to you, Alex, face to face," Marcia said. "This all seems so impersonal." She fidgeted. "But I just had to talk to someone... and, of course, it's not possible with Vivvy..."

"Maybe, it's just as well." Another hiatus. "Sometimes... sometimes," Alex mulled. "Maybe, it's sometimes better to let things lie there for a bit... while the 'other self' if you'll excuse the term, our darker, deeper half, takes it all in. processes it, so to speak."

It was Marcia's turn for ruminating. "I guess so, Alex. But, there's going to be a problem. One didn't really think would come up..."

When Alex failed to respond, Marcia went on. "I broached the whole topic of marriage to Jack with Vivvy... and, quite frankly, she *hates* the idea." Marcia's voice trembled. "She was positively hostile."

Alex sighed audibly. "Well, consider, Marcia. She's got a darker side to reconcile, too."

"But it's so unlike Vivvy," Marcia protested. "And she's never before shown any dislike of Jack. Quite the contrary. I always thought they got along well."

"Yes, sure, but that was then, and this is now. This is different. It's serious. It'll mean a realignment of everyone's position. Hers, yours, Jack's... even ours."

"Lu's, too," Marcia whispered.

"And Lu's too." A rapping sound from Alex's end carried over the wire. "It's a lot to take in. For Vivvy, surely. For all of us." Alex paused. "Give her time."

Finally, in a muffled voice, Marcia said, "Jack was hoping to be married soon. He had even urged doing it right then. On Friday... the next day."

Again, Alex said nothing, Marcia envisioning her former mother-in-law's distant look, her inscrutable shrug.

"Will you tell Barry?" Marcia asked finally.

"I will if you want me to." In the interim, small unidentifiable sounds of the movement of objects transmitted themselves. "He left for Alexandria late afternoon. Lindquist had called him to show up for a staff meeting early Monday morning. He thought he'd take a motel room down there. Be well-rested. Sure to be on time... I think it's merely some routine business," she said uncertainly. "But I'll be sure to tell him when he gets back."

'When's that, Alex?"

"Well, I'm not entirely sure about that, either. I expect maybe even tomorrow evening."

FRESHLY disconcerted about Alex's estimate of her sincerity, her genuine reconciliation in this recently conflicted decision regarding Lu, now frankly worried also – probably unnecessarily so – about Barry's and Alex's fluctuating economic status, Marcia instinctively conceded the call had not been such a good idea, after all. It had certainly not been a relief.

"Well, Alex, I'll be in touch. Will you be calling me when Barry's returned?"

'We'll be in touch, dear," Alex said mildly, reverting to an older, more familiar motherly role. "And don't worry. You'll see. It'll all come outright. Just keep the faith, baby," she wisecracked, her slightly oddball, generationally inspired, linguistic catch-up, putting a curious, melancholy smile on Marcia's face.

Chapter Twenty

O N THE Thursday morning that Marcia and Jack had initiated efforts toward obtaining a marriage license at the various public edifices of downtown Hughesville, on the bay, considerably further uptown, in a building immediately recognizable as vintage nineteenth-century Industrial, Carleton distributed Allied General's handsome, leather-bound, book-length Memorandum and Document of Agreement. This compendium of neatly formatted background analyses, valuations of comparables, and market value ratios of the LeClerc Works concluded with a final, illuminating chapter, evaluating the company's present fair market value and a proposed sales price for the Works Allied was currently prepared to offer. Fewer than eight persons sat around the oval table in the Conference Room; six assorted tax and corporate lawyers, fiscal consultants, and appraisers, representing Allied's interests; Armand and Carleton alone for the LeClerc's.

Although Armand had informed Carleton early in the week that, indeed, the anticipated conference with the Coalition and union leadership should take place on Wednesday as scheduled, the news of this latter Thursday meeting with Allied General personnel would remain strictly confidential between them.

After Allied's lawyers had made a synoptic oral presentation of this Memorandum and Document of Agreement, their fiduciaries took over. Their appraisers' claims that almost a million dollars would be required for LeClerc plant remodeling and manufacturing upgrades were closely evaluated. The company's long-term trend of operations attesting to steadily declining sales and income, its markets exhibiting dependence upon too few, themselves market-stressed customers, were meticulously scrutinized. This painstaking analysis of the company's present viability was hardly conducive toward putting

Armand in a genial frame of mind. He would have been stupid, indeed, not to have anticipated what came next. But, braced as he was, he was nevertheless disappointed, if not confounded, by Allied's final bottom line purchase offer of under three million, with an $875,000 cash down payment only upfront, and seller financing over a protracted period of seven years. Allied's offer was further tethered to a three-month deadline, with a lengthy list of codicils to satisfy, including successful resolution of current ongoing union labor negotiations and a lock-in of a labor contract acceptable to them, to assurances that local government would not for an indefinite period alter certain desirable traffic patterns and zoning regulations now in place. All in all, as Armand, having at last completed his departure ritual with Allied General's representatives, demonstrating throughout, a seamless bravado and confident equanimity, finally strode out of the room, quitting his tormentor, he felt grim – disgusted and trapped.

A quarter of an hour later, when Carleton hustled through the door of his office, Armand was more than ready to attack anyone who had been present to witness the opening salvoes of what now appeared would terminate in his own distressed capitulation, and, ally though he may have been, his presence offended, smirking and self-possessed now, looking as if nothing had happened.

"What the hell do *you* want?" Armand barked unceremoniously in his direction, before turning his back on him altogether and advancing toward the wall safe.

Ever the judicious counselor, a mere twitching lift of a left eyebrow evidenced his having heard this last unwarranted attack by his near lifelong employer. Calmly, he took a seat in one of the leather armchairs facing Armand's desk and waited for him to reseat himself.

Armand in place behind the desk, Carleton proceeded. "I think this will interest you..." he articulated in his measured way, aware he had already focused Armand's attention.

"I don't know if you were aware that, at the very end of the meeting, my pager commenced buzzing repeatedly...?' Carleton looked across the desk at Armand. Armand looked back, silent and unresponsive.

Carleton went on. "When I got to my office and took the message, which... by the way... was to call Jamie McClintock at union headquarters... I must say, I *was* a bit surprised..."

"Get on with it, will you, Carleton? What the hell did *he* want?" Armand snarled.

"After some little fishing about... Jamie allowed as how it had come to his attention that a meeting with potential buyers might be in the works, and, and... here's where it gets interesting... union leadership was proposing they be given an allotment of time at the end of our session... to present some important labor concessions the union was prepared to make. He hinted broadly that... that it might even help our cause... help us with the sale of the company."

"Why, that insufferable pup! How the hell did he find out about the meeting?" Armand spat out.

"Yes. That's exactly what's interesting," Carleton agreed, bringing the fingertips of both hands together, holding them balanced before his face. "How *did* he find out about the meeting?"

"Don't play cat and mouse with me, Carleton! I'm not in the mood. Are you telling me the union has *spies*, for Christ's sake?"

"I don't know," Carleton said thoughtfully. "I *don't know*," But someone must have noticed something." He paused. "Of course, it isn't that hard to catch sight of a veritable convoy of limousines wheeling into the parking lot."

"Yeah..." Armand said, dispirited.

"And to put two and two together," Carleton continued. "What bothers me is that the union was prepared to *act*. On such short notice... Means they must already have had some strategy in mind. Some tactic they're already prepared to play out..."

"Whatever they may have had in mind, I still *own* the company," Armand's voice rapped out harshly. "And I still *run* the business. You can tell you McClintock, and any others of that union mob... I'll handle all concessions. *And* negotiation. *And* labor contracts... for the foreseeable future." Armand stood up, clearly indicating Carleton's dismissal.

Carleton, in turn, stood and quietly turned toward the door, his dignity intact.

CARLETON'S visit had just made things worse. Much worse. Armand felt as if the air was being sucked out of the room. The walls closing in.

Abruptly, he walked to his wall closet and pulled his coat off its hanger. Hell, he didn't have to stay here. He'd had enough, more than enough, for one day. From nowhere, it occurred to him to call on Harry Warner at First Bank. Find out how the Coalition's ambitious plans were faring, but, on second thought, he decided, what the hell, why fool around with underlings? Why not get in touch with Jeb Murray instead? The mayor was his lifelong friend and gold buddy, after all; he had dated Eliza Murray before she'd ever decided to marry Jeb... a hot romance, too; attended dozens of country club affairs with the Murrays over the years; supported Jeb's campaigns over lo! These many elections, not only with his considerable political heft but with substantial monetary contributions. *Very* substantial contributions, at that. After all, the sonofabitch owed him?

Feeling slightly better humor, finally doing something about his situation, taking decisive action, Armand put in a call to Jeb's office. In seconds, he had Jeb himself on the line and was told to stop in at four, when Jeb would be free for the day.

FORMER fullback, Murray stood solidly behind his desk. With a welcoming sweep of his arms, he motioned Armand into a facing chair.

"It's been too long since we did the course..." he grumbled amiably. "Too *damned* long!" He held out a black walnut cigar humidor and watched Armand slowly lift out a cigar. Deftly, the mayor held a Stall silver lighter to the working end.

"What's on your mind, Armand?" he said finally, sitting back and neatly severing the end of his own cigar into an ashtray.

It was some minutes before Armand could bring himself to speak out. He realized again what he already knew about himself – he hated talking about his business to anyone, ever than mayor – maybe especially the mayor. He didn't like the position it put him in immediately: a weak position: the position of a suppliant. And having to ask for concealment was even worse. Too hole-and-corner altogether. Armand rolled the cigar between his fingers appraisingly.

"Well, I've got a few... concerns, Jeb. But, you realize, for all kinds of reasons, I'd appreciate my inquiries be kept... confidential."

"Of course," Jeb responded before Armand had finished his sentence. "Of course.' Jeb's eyebrows drew together concernedly, his smile deepened unctuously.

"Just how extensively are you involved with this local Coalition?" Armand asked at last. "And, just how much chance of success do you think they have?"

To Armand, Jeb's answering chuckle sounded hollow. Yeah, hollow. Jeb was taking his time.

"Well, Armand, now I'm going to have to ask you something. To extend to our conversation, the same privilege of... of discretion... you just asked me." Jeb sat forward in his chair, his gaze focused somewhere past Armand's shoulder. "You know, when the LeClerc Works was fully operative, employing four... five hundred people, when business was perking along... I grant that's some time back now... in the 50's and 60's you'll recall, Hughesville had a fair contingent of blue-collar workers on the City council. That was before the time of my mayoralty, of course." He laughed reflexively. "And, though I'd never throw it up to the old buggers at the plant – the guys who served in that period, the township was going, well, nowhere then. My uncle Ed, who sat on the Council for decades, still remembers how they typically controlled negotiations for contracts for county and city employees. Awarding them some of the highest compensations in the state. Because they brought that same kind of labor union mentality to everything they did. They didn't want to hear about new business. Or about local commercial development. Not unless it helped lower their taxes. They weren't willing to spend an extra dime on roads or parks or civic improvements. No. Their record proved they certainly didn't run the town with the interests of the majority in mind." He stopped, turning his chair to face the wall of windows opposite. He continued smoking for several long minutes.

"By the '80s, downstate fisheries were beginning to feel the pinch of bay pollution, of diminishing incomes. My uncle's marina offered free dock space to whatever watermen and workboats showed.

up from the lower bay. But, except for the Pennsylvania Navy that came down to his place every summer, regular as clockwork, Ed and his son John were virtually without a sustaining income. They finally had to recognize that what they were actually running was a resort facility. So, eventually, they put up Watermen's Wharf, restaurant, and gift shop, which has been going like gangbusters ever since it opened. Throughout every season and beyond. Put in a lot of extras. But the old bucks… the diehards, well, you know, they figured LeClerc's, it'd be there for them forever. They'd be producing containers for shipment down the bay 'til the end of time. And you know better than I, for years now, the whole town's done nothing but go up and down with every change at LeClerc's. Bad. Good. Up. Down. Layoffs coming pretty steady now. But the old-timers wouldn't face reality. They just couldn't see our local industry was essentially…" He shrugged.

"So… when you ask me if I'm *for* the Coalition… I can't say… 'Yes, I am.' But I'm not *against* it either. I just don't think it's going to solve anything, that's all. Not in the long run." Jeb sat up straighter and looked directly at Armand. "I think you'll have to agree with me about that, won't you, Armand?"

Armand took a long time to answer. "That business you're writing off, Jeb… that business… LeClerc's… has been in the family for almost 150 years. Great House dates back to pre-Civil Wars days…" her recited reverently.

By way of response, Jeb Stood up and walked over to an oversize glossy photographic layout of a scenic bayfront installation hanging on the wall. He inspected it carefully for a few minutes, before speaking levelly, over his shoulder.

"Ever hear of Windrift Keys?" he asked, just slightly inclining his head toward the reproduction beside him. "These luxury bayfront condos are selling $250 to $350 thou, right now. Offering life on the Chesapeake. Serene. Beautiful. 'Convenient distance to the cultural and business activities of either Baltimore or Washington,' he read from the printed legend posted beneath the wall-size illustration.

Disinterestedly, Armand's glance slid over to the pictorial layout at Jeb's shoulder. "All right,' he conceded. "I hear what you're saying. But they're 'conveniently located close to Baltimore and Washington.' Not stuck up here… on the last swampy inlet of bay… is the sticks," he added morosely. "Close to… nothing at all.

"No… Since Great-Granddaddy converted the plant from an infant steel rolling mill to a more manageable tin container manufactury, we've continued making necessary changes… when they've been called for. Adjusting to evolving times and shifting needs. We haven't just been sitting still. Hell, no! We're always trying to trim our sails to a more realistic estimate of the our total economic situation.

"OK. Let's explore that," Jeb said. "Remember the St. Clair Oyster Company?" Jeb walked over to a window, looked out at the lawn below as if he were viewing the plant taking shape directly before him. "When it closed its doors in '89, it was the last oyster shucking house operating on the Western Shore. There's been some attempt by the locals to reopen it as a cooperative recently, but what the hell... oyster fisheries just won't support a serious comeback."

"Sure, I know it,' Armand said. "We lost a big contract when it went under..."

"And I don't know if you ever did any business with the Woodbridge Fish and Oyster Company in Hansford? Now, it specializes in making ice for marinas! Local schools've shut down. Older homes being bought up for vacation retreats... at outrageous prices! Half the locals employed by a recently built penitentiary in the area. And a Delaware developer right now knocking himself out to put up a condominium complex there. Build a marina, even lay in an airstrip. Come to think of it, his is a kind of Coalition, too! The developer is trying to gain local support by bringing in townspeople as shareholders." Jeb laughed ironically. "You getting the picture?" he said, turning toward Armand.

"They were another of our customers..." Armand replied. "But I don't see how all this has anything to do with me... Not *directly.*"

"Oh, come one, Armand. You can't be that dense. Cunningham's talked to you about your... your facility... the potential land value of LeClerc commercial land for real estate development... some three years ago now. Before his Consortium ever started working on an alternate master plan." Jeb strode over to another large wall representation mounted to the right of his desk, this time of Plexiglas overlay superimposed on a pictorial replica of present-day Hughesville. The overlay included architectural renderings of a marina, boardwalk, and municipal park; all ranged attractively within easy walking distance of an array of townhouses stretching across the right bank of Boar's Head Inlet north of town. "But this is nothing compared to what they had in mind originally... what they could *still* do... if they could enclose the whole inlet... get possession of this LeClerc bay frontage." Jeb guided his index finger around the appropriate shores. "Why... why it could be one of the gems of the upper bay... a paradise for Philadelphians... Baltimoreans... affluent retirees... With, needless to say, *gem* prices to match." Jeb resumed his desk chair. "Of course, *you* were never interested."

"I can only repeat," Armand said more stiffly, "the business has been in the family for almost 150 years."

Jeb let his hands fall heavily upon each of the arms of his leather desk chair. "Have it your own way, Armand! I'm not going to argue with you. I'm just going to point out once more, that times change. Change! Predicting change, taking advantage of it, that's where the smart businessman shows his real flair."

Despite his rhetorical protestations, Jeb couldn't let the big one get away without a fight. 'I'm not going to argue with you, as I've said, but I'd just like you to listen for a minute. I *know* Cunningham is still interested... very *interested*. If I could arrange for all of us to meet here and talk... just go over the possibilities, one last time. Say tomorrow... midmorning... about 10:30? With lunch at the Shore House afterwards. What'd'ye say?"

Armand considered for a decent interval. Firmly, but unenthusiastically, he agreed to be at Jeb's office at 10:30 the next morning.

Jeb shook Armand's hand all the way to the door. When not pumping it up and down, he held it in his massive to the door. When not it amusing, if depressing. What he himself lacked in fervor over this potential deal was certainly being amply supplied by the mayor. "Armand, there's a gold mine in it for you," Jeb encouraged. "You can travel, you can live here. Or anywhere... become a world traveler, if you like. You can write your own ticket."

Armand felt relieved to finally escape the mayor's City Hall office and his encroaching tide of humid ardor.

AFTER supper, which was served to him on a tray in the family room while he watched television news, Armand decided for the first time in months to take a walk around the property. Happily, Blanche was on a week-long shopping trip to New York City with her sister, and, for once, he didn't chafe at the extravagant bills he anticipated would roll in after this, her latest sortie on department store and boutique. These were but a small price to pay for being let off the hook of his wife's well-meaning interrogations. Her persistent, prodding questions about plant activities, followed by her invariably well-intentioned, but garbled, insistent, and inappropriate advice.

He circled the periphery of the grounds, feeling good, allowing himself to breathe in the Spring air deeply, placing his feet solidity and undeniably down upon the turf, his turf, where centuries ago, he ex-possession on this mild, overgrown Maryland inlet. An innervating sense of ownership intensified into an overall sense of well-being rubbing russet vigor into his cheeks, His trek led him finally to the furthest west garden, with its continuous, trimmed bow wood hedges arranged in an ingenious, carefully interlocking maze.

As a child, this was his favorite place for play, once he had been allowed this big boy privilege. Because, until reaching the age of eight, he had been strictly forbidden these premises. But, having satisfied the required age limit, at last, the maze had become his ultimate Oddyssean challenge. His and his chosen friends' most wonderful, best theatre for scoring those repeated total victories over the fiercest Indian tribes. The scene of their innumerable outflanking and outmaneuvering of the wiliest generals, sometimes British, other times, German.

He walked the course of the entire maze once, rapidly. All the way trough. To the end. In record time. Then, he allowed himself in repeat the excursion. But this time, he stopped to rest at the last of the several picturesque way-stations placed at significant junctures in the maze. At these particularly difficult twists or turns, slatted wooden benches had been positioned to invite the bemused questor to rest and consider.

In the diminishing light, a lone sparrow flew inches past his ear and perched, momentarily, posing absolutely still upon a thick impenetrable leafy branch of box. With a mere two or three flutters and flourishes, the bird disappeared utterly. At that moment, eventide shifted into deeper shadow. The air filled with silence.

A flick of fear, alien and exciting, stirred Armand to rise. Standing still, he instantly spurned the tableau of the small wrapped body supine on the sled pressing into his memory. He scorned the vision of the sleigh drawn by elder Nels across an endless hypotenuse of snowy lawn, leaving painful, telltale parallel runnels all the way to the garage door. He was to sustain days of fretful anxiety before Amanda visited his bedroom to tell him Jack-Jack would be all right. That he had passed the "crisis." She had never accused him of not preventing his four-year-old brother from following them into the maze. Nor had father. But her eyes spoke it. With a grunt of rejection, Armand started across the lawn, duplicating the very hypotenuse old Nels had imprinted in the snow more than four decades ago.

WHAT the hell! What had he got to lose? He hadn't seen old ... well, not so old, some to think of it ... his own age ... old Cunningham for ... what ... three years now? If he and Jeb were bent on putting on a dog-and-pony show for his benefit, why should he object? It'd provide a morning's entertainment. And, Christ knows, he was in need of some diversion!

After half an hour of shuffling expensive and impressive architectural renderings and overlays from easel to floor. Cunningham got down to business, and Armand's interest perked up. Cunningham was talking directly to him: "You know, ever since the Chesapeake Critical Areas Act was passed in '84, setting off---as you might or might not have realized---a land rush among developers, any property grandfathered under this Act automatically became premium. We took note when the Coalition became active in Hughesville. After the first of their meetings down here, our interest got fired up. At several of our subsequent meetings, we reopened the matter of inclusion of LeClerc property into a revised master plan. With a real view to making you another offer, Armand." Cunningham looked at Armand deliberately, not without a glint of humor around his eyes. "So, you see, we weren't totally unprepared for today's meeting."

Before Armand could add anything to this admission, or comment in any other way, Cunningham went on. "The important point here, Armand, *important* to us, is that LeClerc land, and that includes the wide swath of adjacent acreage from the creek to the inlet, still enjoys its original zoning. We looked into *that* carefully. Should we acquire the property, it would automatically be grandfathered under the present law. For us, this would mean a much, much wider waterfront area for development. Enough to build as many as three times the units we originally envisioned with the Boar's Head Inlet plan. Enough, too, to put in a *real* marina. And park. And *proper* internal roads. There'd be no comparison!

"But whatever turns out to be the final housing mix in the ultimate development of our master plan, we are prepared to make you an offer right now. Today. We're prepared to offer a sales price of no less than three million, or very close to it. That offer exceeds our original one of three years ago by a considerable margin, you'll agree. Of course, the numbers would need further refinement by our key advisors, but, nevertheless, top management has agreed unanimously, as of now, unanimously, I emphasize, on a figure very close to the one I just quoted."

"On what terms?" Armand inquired.

"Well, that, too, would have to be negotiated. Probably something like a million in an original cash down payment, with, let's say, two additional notes of equal value to be paid off over a three-year period. All this, of course, subject to further input and refinement from our own people."

"What about the capital assets of the Company? Who gets the revenue from these?... I am assuming, of course, that you're going to clear away the whole facility?" Armand observed stonily.

"The municipal government has already agreed to share the expense of dismantling the bayfront plant with us," Cunningham said formally. "Sale proceeds of assets would be LeClerc's."

A tap at the door and the head of the mayor's secretary appeared. "Councilman Edwards wondered if he could have a word with you, Mayor? He said it won't take but a minute. He's out here... now... in my office." The head bobbed ingratiatingly and disappeared once again. The mayor rose and left the room.

"Of course, I'm sure you understand this is only a first cut," Cunningham added after Jeb had left. "But, I wanted you to know we are serious. *Very serious.* We wanted you to know this, and to get in our opening bid. For your consideration... of the *whole* situation. Before you've made any final decision as to the disposal of LeClerc's. Naturally, if you wanted to make a capital investment in our Consortium, the arrangement would be altered and made commensurate with your participation. Terms could be negotiated. With a larger profit margin, naturally, in the long run. But, if you were interested, something could be worked out in that regard, too, I'm sure."

Armand responded instantly. 'I'm not interested in any ongoing deals. When I sell the property... *if* I sell the property... I want *out... all* the way out. With adequate assurances."

"Anything you say," Cunningham assented agreeably.

HE WOULD have declined lunch, but such an action could not be seen as anything but churlish. He went along, as did Cunningham, both of them individually nursing their single Scotch and sodas throughout the meal, while Jeb, on his third frozen daiquiri, slipped into the role of mine-host with ever-mounting flushed enthusiasm. 'A lot of people would call Hughesville a cultural backwater," the mayor said. "Now, this attitude has developed from generation to generation in Hughesville..." he confided, leaning forward, his voice thick with emotion, his eyes just beginning to glaze. He motioned the waitress and ordered a fourth daiquiri. "I love this community. Much as anyone. More. But it's time to move on. I really think the plant closing will redound to the benefit of all the people of Hughesville... in the *long* run. And their children. They'll be able to have better hopes, bigger dreams." Jeb looked around the table at all two of his audience. "And gentleman, we are the ones making it happen. All of us together. On the threshold of a new millennium."

At the door of the Shore House, Cunningham shook hands with Armand. He looked through his eyes before reaching up to touch his shoulder lightly. "We'll be in touch. Soon. Perhaps we can set something up in Wilmington for midweek, next week? If you're still interested, that is."

"You can call me either at my office or at home," Armand said. With something between a wave and a salute, he made his good-bye's and walked briskly out the door.

ON THE Sunday evening following, the diminutive Filipino housekeeper, wife of Big House's present general factotum, answered Jack's ring. Her large smile preceded a gesture of welcome, as she swept an arm forward, indicating Jack's route through the dim foyer. 'He's in the library, Meester Jack. You find your way?" she said demurely, smiling again, and hurrying away down the hall. Jack turned and deliberately, quietly, shut the heavy entrance door behind him.

He took in the deep and spacious foyer of his 18th century natal home, with its familiar blockfront chest bearing one of Blanche's prize Chinese bowls, replete with daylilies, roses, and other varietal exotics unavailable in local gardens. The facing wall exhibited mother's fascinating *trompe l'oeil,* which she had long ago imported from somewhere in France to the amazement of her friends and her personal proof of instinctual *haute mode*. He stepped quickly across the muted sheen of the wood floor, over the soft blue-patterned Chinese Oriental, into the living room.

Here, too, all was quiet elegance, nonetheless, past the vast space of fine paneling, molding, and wainscoting, past the Queen Anne sofas with their tiny worked gold pattern, past the wing, Windsor ad Heppelwhite chairs, all ranged about the impressive decorative centerpiece of the fireplace, he could spy his favorite adjoining alcove ... decently large, floor-to-ceiling glass enclosure, furnished cheerfully in bold flower prints and informal comfort, positioned to invite the visitor to enjoy a breathtaking view of garden, gently descending to an arresting sweep of inlet.

This retreat had always been one of his favorite haunts as he stood now at its edge, gazing out at the treasured scene below, he unconsciously calculated when he had been here last, here in Big House, his childhood name for Old Homestead, or as his father preferred calling it, "Great House." Not last Christmas, he remembered.

Could it have been the Christmas before that? So long as that? Shaking his head, he turned down an adjacent short passageway that led to an adjoining study. He tapped lightly, entering the dark, rich room.

The figure at the oversized desk was backlit even in this fading light, which streamed through the bank of French doors behind him. Antipodally, an enormous hurricane lamp seated at one corner of the secretary, highlighted the most salient features of his bent head.

Without speaking, Jack settled into an ample wing chair, facing the wall of floor-to-ceiling glassed-in bookcases at right angles to a deep claret-hued velvet couch.

"Evening, Jacques. You're right on time," came from the shadows. The figure rose. "Would you like a drink ... Scotch ... brandy?"

"A little brandy would be nice...."

The figure disappeared momentarily toward one end of the bookcases, reappearing in a few minutes. Armand handed Jack a snifter, then settled himself on the couch. A few more seconds and he reached up and snapped on a table lamp, barely affecting the over-all dusk in the room.

"I guess you're wondering why I asked you ... specifically ... to stop by ..."

Jack inclined his head once, then shrugged.

Armand leaned back into the sofa cushions. "Maybe I'd best start by summarizing Thursday's meeting with Allied's people,"

"I didn't realize you were having another meeting on Thursday," Jack remarked before he wished he had not responded.

"Yes. Well, no one did. It was to be just me and Carleton. We kept it very close."

Carefully, with a remarkable degree of objectivity, but not without a certain saturnine edge, Armand laid out the progress of that meeting with Allied, chronologically and in detail, summarizing the Company's immediate cash offer and ultimate projected settlement. He concluded with an explication of Allied's imposition of the three-month deadline, and the extensive, difficult contingencies they had further prescribed before conclusive realization of final sale would be possible.

"Difficult ... vexing ..." Jack mumbled, unheard.

Armand was not a heavy toper ever, but he lifted his glass now and automatically rose to collect Jack's.

"All this doesn't surprise me," Armand said reasonably, reseating himself on the couch. "To be expected. No, what bothered me was what happened later ..." He leaned back and balanced his tumbler of scotch between thumb and forefinger. He rocked the glass and its contents gently, hypnotically, back and forth. For a moment, Jack wondered if his brother intended ever to conclude his narrative.

"Carleton came rushing in some quarter of an hour after the meeting with news of a telephone call. From Jamie McClintock. To announce some kind of union request for a meeting with the potential buyers. To discuss labor concessions!" Armand's laugh was harsh, ugly. Uncharacteristically, he averted his head and rubbed his knuckles into his scalp. "I won't have it! I won't have those louts sniffing around my office ... trying to set the agenda. Whatever else I've done or haven't done, it's still my company."

Jack said nothing. His omnipresent other self was literally struck dumb. Briefly, he warmed with sympathy for Armand, then cooled into contempt. Mostly, he struggled to save himself from a swamping melancholy.

"There's more. Much, much more." Armand chortled, in a lighter, deadlier vein. "Do you remember ... oh, perhaps some three years ago ... do you remember that developer ... Cunningham ... who offered a bid on our bayshore land? He wasn't interested in the business. He wanted the land for marina and condominium development."

Jack could barely recall the event. Nothing had come of it, in any case, and he had forgotten about it entirely since then.

"Well, without going into the politics, and the whys and wherefores, he got in touch with me again ... Friday ... and make me another offer. A new one. A million upfront, and two to follow. Clear and clean. No strings attached. Furthermore, he's prepared to pay up over a *three-*year period instead of Allied's seven. And proceeds from assets ... machinery, inventory, et cetera ... ours,"

The brothers sat facing each other, Neither spoke.

"Why?" Jack finally murmured, stunned.

"Why *not*?" Armand cracked, then let out a horselaugh, "Why the hell *not*, Jack?"

"Wouldn't that mean ... dismantling the plan? Junking it?" Jack asked, sounding dazed.

"Yes, it would," Armand answered straightforwardly. "It would mean just *that* ... And, I don't know how the sonofabitch managed it, but he's got the city picking up half the tab for that caper, too,"

Unconsciously, Jack shook his head. He couldn't take it in. "But ... the business has been in the family for almost ... almost 150 years," he heard himself say.

"Yes, it has. But facts are facts. The business has been only marginal now... for... for at least two decades. But, you know the score! You *must*. You've seen the books. And with the loss of some of our best and biggest customers... Why, hell, you know what's happening to fisheries all along the bay! It just isn't there anymore, Jack. It's not there." He stepped over toward the bookcase and poured himself another unprecedented small one.

Jack looked at his brother as if they had sustained a prolonged separation. He studied him a good long time. "You're serious about this, aren't you, Armand? You're serious. You *want* to pursue this deal!"

"I'm serious, all right. I'm meeting with Cunningham midweek next week."

"*Why* is he matching... exceeding... Allied's price? And, no plant?" Jack persisted.

"That's what I've been trying to tell you, Jack. The land that old plant stands on is worth more today than the business itself. Hell, the business is well-nigh *worthless*! But the ground it sits on... that's another story entirely. Cunningham explained that the advantageous zoning of our area has been grandfathered under the Critical Areas Act. That makes a whole lot of difference to its profitable development. A *whole* lot. And, he's willing to pay us for that advantage."

"Bastard!" Jack hissed.

"Oh, come off it, Jack. Cunningham's plans are pretty impressive. And Jeb Murray, that old reprobate, is ecstatic over them. He thinks it'll put Hughesville on the map."

"If a lawsuit doesn't stop Cunningham first."

"You don't *want* that to happen, do you, Jack? Surely, you don't want that to happen!"

Jack did not answer.

"I'd better get cracking then, hadn't I?" Armand quipped. "Take the money and..." He snorted, then added more seriously. "Hey, was that old rust-bucket of a plant such a beauty on the landscape, I ask you? And, despite all our efforts, didn't it add, continue to add, year after year, significant pollution to the upper Bay? Be fair, Jack! Jeb's right. It'll be a lot better... an improvement, with the condos. Cunningham even sees himself as something of an environmentalist. And, hell, you wouldn't want to keep me from doing my civic duty, would you?"

"What about the Coalition?" Jack asked darkly, finally.

"What *about* them?" Armand snapped back.

Stupidly, as if reciting a lesson he did not understand, Jack repeated. "What are you going to do about the Coalition? All those plans?"

"Tell them they can go straight to hell! Don't pass Go. Straight to hell! You're not going to wet my shoulder over that bunch of self-serving unionists, are you?" Armand rose and walked toward his desk for want of something to do. He stood fiddling with some item he had picked up without noticing. "Cut me a break, Jack. Why the hell should I care about *them*?"

Jack felt overwhelmed. In his present state, he did not trust himself to agree or disagree with Armand. To ask questions. To bring forth opinions. To make judgments. He just wanted to be left alone... to sort things out.

Armand walked toward Jack, then turned and took his seat on the couch once more. "Christ, I knew you'd be surprised, Jack. But I didn't bargain on this. You're bowled over!"

Smiling feebly, Jack waved his hand in a deprecating gesture. "I can take it," he said.

"Yeah," Armand responded gruffly, unconvinced. He stood, walked to the French doors, and looked out at the dark.

"Have you mentioned any of this to... to Amanda?" Jack asked from behind his brother.

Armand turned and walked back into the half-light of the room. "No. Nor to Blanche. Nor to anyone in the family. And I'm counting on you to keep your mouth shut about it. Surely, you can see that you *must*. Until everything is wrapped and tied up solid. A *done* deal."

"Of course," Jack said.

SOMEHOW they got through another quarter-hour of small talk and incidental family gossip before Jack felt he could decently escape the seriousness of this encounter. Armand walked him through the house to the door. This time Jack shamed through empty space. Noticing nothing.

Armand opened the door and stepped out onto the portico with his brother. At the top of the steps, they both scanned the sky for several minutes. Brilliant with nebula, starts and mysterious glowing smudges, alive with light. They stood within reaching distance of each other, silent.

"You know, Jack. I've never been a complainer. I hate whiners. At first, I enjoyed the business. I didn't mind stepping into Dad's shoes... they were big shoes, important shoes. But I loved being boss. Calling the shots. Solving problems. Difficult, challenging problems. Man-size. But, lately, it's been different. I'm not in charge anymore. Not like I used to be. I'm pussyfooting around every God damned labor official. Listening to endless Union double-talk. Hustling to satisfy OSHA's endless regulations. And... Christ... regulations in general. Federal. State. Local. Everybody telling me what to do with *my* business. I'm just *not* in charge anymore. Not like I'd like to be. Not like I *insist* on being if I'm going to stay in the game." Armand slipped his arm across Jack's shoulder. "Maybe, I'm just getting old, Jack, old and *tired* of the whole damned thing."

"Sure, Armand. I understand. Sure," Jack said, finding and then shaking his brother's hand. He didn't know what else to do. It occurred to him that it wasn't true that, with goodwill and intelligent effort, anyone could eventually communicate... meaningfully... with anyone else. There *was* no way to Go.

HALFWAY down the walk, Jack turned and saw Armand standing there, waving at him. He waved back. Having reached Carriage House, he realized that he had never mentioned getting a marriage license on Thursday or planning to get married as soon as..." Just keep your mouth shut until everything is wrapped and tied up solid," he commented dourly to himself.

ARMAND washed his face and poured some aftershave into the palm of his hand, slapping it smartly, painfully, against his cheeks and temples. Although he had dressed to go to the club, once in the study, he decided against it. He looked through *Forbes* and the *Wall Street Journal*. He found himself staring into the dark, unable to remember anything he had just read. Sighing, he lumbered up the steps to his room. He turned on the television, surfed onto an old movie on a premium channel, adjusted the volume to just below intelligible level, and settled deep into the pillows. Despite the coziness of ambient white noise and warmth, he could not obliterate the recurrent image: his brother's small, steamy body, mummified under fresh sheets, his mother whimpering meaninglessly beside the oversize enveloping bed. "Can't I come too, Armand?" his tiny falsetto pleaded. "Can't I come? I won't *bother* you. Just this *once*?"

HE SAW himself walking into the depths of the maze without ever looking back.

Chapter Twenty-one

A LL WEEKEND long, Alex was drearily aware of Barry's absence. In spasmodic presentiments, tag ends of carefully rehearsed speeches in Lindquist's glass and leather suite, between Lindquist and Barry, John Blum, and Barry and Lindquist, Lindquist, and John spun themselves out with moot foreboding. It was all too silly and childish. Unworthy of someone her age.

When Barry had finally tiptoed into the bedroom last night somewhere close after eleven, she had just entered that dense, furtive, undeniable sleep that came as a blessing after two nights of tossing anxiety, and when she felt his slight weight bending to kiss her cheek, she had not sat up. She had not been able to exert herself to welcome him properly. Instead, she recalled smiling only, mumbling something about tomorrow, and deliberately shifting her position to face away from his glowing night-table lamp.

Now she let him sleep "in," as she showered and dressed. She took the stairs down, donned an old jacket, and let herself out the back door into the startling brilliance and freshness of the back garden.

SHE lost track of time, digging a shallow trench around the backside, weeding painstakingly around the choked stands of lilies-of-the-valley, peonies, daylilies, and primrose. Already erotically suggestive rows of ruby peony shoots pushed their way out of the ground, insistent through the tangle of competitive flora. Whatever growth-restoring surgery might be advisable here would have to wait until Autumn now. There was no stopping this Spring surge. She stood up, bending backwards, alleviating the rippling tension in back and buttocks.

She felt his hand at the small of her back. She heard his voice before she saw him.

"O.K., LUTHER. How about knocking it off... and we go to lunch? Brunch? What have you..."

"Just cause I'm only on my knees doesn't mean I'm praying. But I assume you meant Burbank... not Martin..."

"You got it..." Barry picked up the hand trowel, hand rake, and basket of weeds. He headed for the garage, Alex following.

"I was about to finish for the morning anyway," Alex said to his back.

THEY drove toward Hughesville, almost silent. It was too beautiful to talk. Everywhere the painful green of new tree bloom, the curving road, giving way to always unexpected small and then larger vistas of river, bay and undulating awakening countryside. They ate at MacTiffen's on the river, the sourceless Susquehanna. Appreciatively, become hungry and young. Young as needful lovers. Stalwart proven veterans of ancient affection.

Glancing past Alex's shoulder at the stretch of river in the near distance, Barry smiled. "This is the life, isn't it? Here it is," he nodded toward the antique wall clock on MacTiffen's west wall, "nearly twelve, and we're just thinking our first meal of the day." He laughed aloud. "Perpetual weekend."

Alex blotted her lips carefully and laid her napkin precisely next to her plate.

"I assume you're speaking of yourself," she said sharply. "Because, Just this last Monday, I interviewed with the Editor of the Hughesville *Record*. And... you might be interested to know, I have agreed to write up a series of articles, yes, more or less stimulated by the recent activities of the Coalition, a series of articles, at any rate, beginning with the establishment of the LeClerc Works in this area after the Civil War and coming forward to current employee buy-out plans, here and elsewhere. Prognosis for their success based on available records of performance, and that sort of thing. Et cetera. Et cetera. The series would be open-ended, as Enoch and I see it now. He wants to be able to judge what community reaction will be... and..."

"Enoch," Barry guffawed. "So it's Enoch, is it? Christ, Alex, do they still name people Enoch?"

Alex's lips pursed, but there was a twinkle in her eye. "Don't be naughty, Barry. Just remember... he's of *our* generation."

"Well, Alex, that's *great*! I had no idea you were cooking up such a scheme. Damn clever... and ambitious... old girl."

"Old girl, yourself. I don't tell you everything. Some of that old Los Angeles marketing material stood me in good stead. Got me in the door. Then, a couple of weeks ago, I took my first best shot at a lead article for such a series. Accompanied by a prospectus for several projected future articles. We talked, and Enoch liked the idea."

"That's super. But, what about your substitute teaching? I thought that was what..."

"Well, that's always a mug's game, you know. Nothing but picking up pieces and playing the heavy. Of course, I'll do it, if nothing else prevails. But, to tell the truth, that's been a large part of my motivation. That, and being genuinely more interested in the autonomy, the self-direction, of writing, as opposed to school-sitting."

Barry looked at his partner critically. "Hey, Alex, if you hate it that much... you don't have to *force* yourself to do it."

"I may have to..." she said resignedly. Then perked up. "But, right now, I'm dying to try this. And, Barry, I've even thought that the copy... with suitable extended developments here and there... might eventually be worked up into a kind of short case history. A timely portrait of a fairly typical current American town undergoing an unfortunately fairly typical present-day industrial adjustment."

"Yeah. That's a nice way of putting it. You mean being blown out of the water! But, it *should* make relevant copy. No doubt about it." Barry picked up the bill and slapped the edge of the table. "But, hey, Alex, I'm delighted for you. I really am. It sounds like a great idea. And I can't wait to see your first installment in the *Record*."

IT WASN'T until their second pass along the MacTiffen shoreline of the Susquehanna that Barry motioned them toward two of the deck chairs placed at regular intervals along the Strand. He and Alex seated, almost at once Barry began to unburden himself of his weekend encounters.

"What goes around, comes around," he pronounced, enigmatically.

"Remember what we were doing when we first met?" he asked, not waiting for a response. "Remember we were working on that Anthropometric Survey at Corinth? In conjunction with the Air Force?

Evaluating data on length of fingers, distance between ears, all that good stuff... remember?"

"Sure, Barry. Of course."

"Well, believe it or not, I'm to meet John Blum tomorrow at Aberdeen to accompany him for a scheduled presentation to the military brass to layout Alcon's current master plan for setting up just such another survey. Sure, I still know a few people at Aberdeen. From the old days. Not many, you understand. A few. But Lindquist insisted that was the way to go. So, what the hell..." Barry turned his right-hand palm upward, then dropped it between his knees.

Alex looked puzzled. "I don't understand, Barry. Are the statistics the Air Force so painstakingly gathered and we so methodically correlated already out of date? Surely," she objected, self-conscious in this technical arena, "surely, we haven't sustained an evolutionary change of any major proportions in just *one* generation? It isn't reasonable."

"Small, but measurably significant differences. Yes. We haven't evolved a sixth finger or a third eye, of course, but small, significant, persistent differences have been determined to exist. Yes. Significant enough, it is felt, to justify a new study."

Alex nodded, her expression uncertain.

"Then, on Friday," Barry continued, "Lindquist wants me to take John around to the University, and introduce him to several assorted deans and heads of departments. I told him my associations at the college were really rusty. Nelson, for example, isn't even there anymore. In fact, I think he may have died," Barry murmured aside lugubriously. "And a lot of the people I dealt with formerly, even as late as Pittsburgh days, have long gone." Barry shook his head. "But, again, Lindquist insisted."

"Why the University?" Alex inquired.

"Well, that's another good one. Alcon thinks there's a big potential market... with local and federal government financing... for employee retraining programs. Right now, Alcon's working on a number of different strategies. They've got connections all over Academia. Netting in and evaluating all kinds of input." He sighed. "But, thank God, that's not my problem. That'll be John's... and a host of others, of course."

"Like what, Barry?"

"Like, I suppose, all kinds of programs for upgrading mechanical and technical skills, using a variety of self-directed computer courses."

"I see," Alex murmured, dubiously.

"But, for instance, Barry. Just suppose LeClerc's closes its doors. What are all those people going to do for jobs?" She let her gaze wander across the river. "Even if they were retrained? Where would they be employed?"

"Well, some of them would obviously have to move. To cities and towns with available jobs. Then, again, if Hughesville got its act together, like the mayor is always threatening, gentrifying like the rest of the lower bay, they'd be service jobs. Maybe, plenty of service jobs."

"I see. And would these require retraining?"

Barry's voice rose in rising irrepressible pique. "Don't diddle me now, Alex! I know what you're thinking. They don't have to send them to school to learn how to make beds and push a vacuum cleaner around."

"I'm not diddling you, Barry. I'm just trying to be informed... and honest," Alex said defensively.

"Look, Alex. They didn't make me Lord of the Universe. We're still operating with a mindset calibrated at circa 1900. When economic expansion and world domination were the ticket. When all-out production, the devil take the hindmost, prevailed. But the situation has changed enormously since then – calling for economic decisions on a global scale and all-round greater cooperation. And, at home, there's still plenty of work that hasn't been addressed adequately. Good work. Needful work. Physically hard and labor-intensive work. Cleaning streets and parks, caring for children, old people, the sick. Rebuilding the infrastructure. But who wants to fund it? Why, hell, the trend is all in the other direction. And getting stronger all the time. And then who wants to do this work? It's not fair or reasonable that one class of persons be permanently assigned these jobs. It's only fair that there be task equalization, every person obliged to perform some of the least desirable jobs for some time, regardless of accumulated credentials. And 'mental work,' redistributed amongst a much broader portion of the 'labor' force. Bu all this calls for reshuffling priorities, a genuinely different perspective, a whole new orientation in our education. Our thinking. Our society. And more money, too." Barry shook his head, looking suddenly despondent.

"Don't get me started, Alex. It's like picking up one strand of seaweed. It can't be done! Once you start being honest, as you call it, so many things come into question, it makes your head spin..."

"Like what, Barry? Like what comes into question, just for an example?" she insisted.

"Like reducing the workweek to thirty hours and not permitting over time, with no reduction in pay. That'd create jobs, for instance. There hasn't been a reduction of work hours since 1938, for Christ's sake, and you can bet that idea was fought tooth and nail then. Like making qualified students able to attend college cost-free to produce that increased number of technically trained people we so sorely need. But I do mean qualified, the way many European countries set high standards to be met, but provide free post-secondary education. Like genuinely reevaluating the social cost of unbridled private enterprise, with an eye toward ecological improvement. In fact, taking a good hard look at the whole job culture society of consumerism we hold so dear, and that has us so shackled to so many outmoded, destructive concepts." Abruptly, unexpectedly, Barry heard and saw himself outside his own psyche and skin: a lone ridiculous kook reformer, ranting to himself. Instantly, he shifted his position into audience mode and joined in the laughter at himself.

"I told you not to get me started, Alex..." he said by way of explanation and apology.

Alex laid her hand on his jacketed arm. "It's all going the other way, isn't it, Barry? Everyone whose listened to at all these days is a staunch defender of the status quo. But why should those in power push for shorter hours, better health and education, and greater participation in the good life for all? That's what I mean by being honest, Barry. And realistic." She patted Barry's sleeve again, thoughtfully, resignedly. "I'm afraid I see it as a fairly simple matter. It's not to their advantage to share. And change is difficult. Even for the overworked and the underprivileged. For the truly privileged, it's almost an impossibility," she concluded.

"That's why social Darwinism is still alive and kicking... it's just a pseudo-scientific excuse for taking more than your fair share..."

Barry remarked ruefully, standing and pulling Alex to her feet from her deck chair.

"And why the eye of the needle parable is as relevant today as it was when first spoken," she concurred, dismally.

THEY walked along the Strand arm-in-arm, private ruminations submerged in the sheer dominance of sunlight, Spring, and natural beauty.

"So... you'll help me with articles, then?" Alex seemed to remind from far away. "Let me bounce my copy off your special brand of crusty philosophical speculation...?

"You bet. In fact, you won't be able to stop it. You should know that by now. Better than that," he slipped his arm around her waist. "Better than that. I'll listen to you bitch when things go wrong, and hug you regularly, right or wrong."

"There you go," she said, flashing him an appreciate, companionable smile and slipping her arm around his waist in turn.

HOME again, Alex decamped to her computer for an afternoon session of hard confrontation with her material, while Barry disappeared to the second floor with the portable telephone to fine-tune arrangements with John, Aberdeen, and various University personnel. She had lost track of the time again when some minutes after five she heard evocative noises from the kitchen. At five-thirty, Barry appeared at her computer in his oversized barbecue apron. "I just rustled up some tuna salad ... with apples and cashews, like you like it ... and some soup. Ready by six?"

Sure thing, Barry." She turned to edit a phrase in her last sentence. "And, thanks, honey."

"I SHOULD tell you," Alex recalled, "Madi called mid-afternoon. I was surprised the call came through at the desk since you had the portable. I thought you'd have gotten it."

Barry helped himself to another portion of tuna. "Must've just been making a pit stop ... Then I did take about fifteen more minutes to look up some phone numbers at the college. And dig out those Alcon materials Lindquist had ginned up about retraining programs to take along." Barry looked across the table at Alex. "Everything OK?"

"Oh, yes. Nothing like that. She's fine. In fact, *very* fine. She called to say she and her new 'friend,' Toda Yamashigi, I wrote it down somewhere, in fact, so as to make sure to get it right," Alex rummaged through her jacket pocket. "She and Toda will be coming up this next weekend. They expect to be in on Saturday, about noon. She made a point, Barry, of saying she was anxious, those were her words, anxious for us to meet him."

Alex and Barry exchanged concerned, not quite apprehensive, glances.

"Oh yeah?" Barry said. "Her 'friend ...?'"

"He works there in the lab. Not with her exactly, but on the same problem."

"Is she going to stay over? In the guest room?" Barry asked as he poured himself another coffee from the decanter. "Or what?" he added.

Alex smiled. "She said they had their accommodations all taken care of. Not to worry." Alex rose and carried her plate into the kitchen, returning immediately. "So, I'm not worrying," she remarked with unmistakable Borys' pungency.

"Yeah," Barry said, preoccupied, while he began stacking remaining soiled plates mechanically.

Alex followed her husband into the kitchen. "Do you think I should have Marcy and Jack over for dinner on Saturday night? Sort of a party to mark the occasion? Oh, and I haven't told you another piece of good news I've been carrying around! I'm really getting hopeless! Marcy called, too ... oh, several days ago ... when you were in Alexandria, to tell us she and Jack have taken out a marriage license. They haven't set a date or anything ... they want to wait until Vivvy's gotten used to the idea. And all. That sort of thing." Alex looked out the kitchen window at the dusk, while Barry continued rinsing and stacking plates into the dishwasher. "And, Barry, she's released Lu's sperm from the sperm bank."

Barry unbent from over the machine, standing erect, plate poised in midair for several minutes. "Well, I'll be damned," he said finally in hushed tones. "I'll just be damned." With a brief shake of his head, he resumed stacking plates.

"This is all going too fast for me. I'm an old man, after all," he complained to himself, unconvinced, unheard by Alex. "I need to take my time ..."

"What do you think about Saturday?" Alex repeated.

"What?"

"About having everyone here on Saturday evening?"

"I wouldn't," Barry answered after a noticeable pause.

"Why not?" Alex protested. "Everyone like a little fuss made over them ..."

"Make it Sunday brunch then," Barry said at last. He set the controls on the dishwasher and turned to face Alex. "Maybe the kids'll want to talk to us ... privately ... that first dinnertime. I'd leave it open."

"O-o-h?" Alex retorted, almost archly, not quite successfully camouflaging her genuine surprise. "You think so?"

"I think there's a good possibility," Barry said flatly.

"Maybe you're right, Barry."

They walked out of the kitchen toward the living room. "You may just be right."

She flicked on the outside porch light, and then the living room overhead fixture.

Alex sat down to her computer and brought up the copy she had generated that afternoon. She meant to edit it only cursorily, while Barry settled down to reading today's Record. A quarter-hour later, she winced as the telephone on the desk rang sharply, interrupting her train of thought. With effort, hoping to clear her voice of the exasperation she could barely suppress, she picked up the instrument. It was Jack, and after a few innocuous pleasantries, she slid her palm over the speaker, gesturing that Barry was to pick up the portable phone.

"CONGRATS on the marriage license. Great news, Jack! Great news!" Alex heard Barry say, as she gratefully returned to her work.

"Thanks," Jack murmured dismissively. "Barry, what do you hear on the grapevine about the Coalition? Anything new? What're your old fishing buddies saying?" Jack asked with unmistakable, almost breathy, curiosity.

"Why, nothing, Jack. I don't know. I've been out of town. And I haven't been fishing lately." Over the silence on the other end, Barry inserted, "You're in a much better position to know what's going on there than I am, Jack."

"Yeah," Barry heard.

"Well, I guess so," Barry said. "I guess so. I don't rightly know. Why, Jack?"

"Ooh, nothing definite. Nothing definite." After a while, "Just a kind of hunch." He let out something between a snort and a laugh. "I just get a kind of feeling that my brother may be looking around for other alternatives. Other than allied, that is. Maybe even other than the Coalition." Another laugh. "You know, Armand doesn't cotton to the whole idea of the Coalition. He just doesn't buy it."

"Well, I'm not entirely surprised," Barry acknowledged.

"What would happen ..." Jack interrupted, "what would happen to the whole matter ... you know, the money already raised, all that organization, if it all fell through ..."

It was now Barry's turn to deal with this stunning possibility. "I suppose it would depend on what you meant by 'fell through,'" he equivocated, clearing his throat. "You're the counselor, Jack. With all the legal expertise." After non-responsive silence, Barry insisted, "What's happened, Jack?"

"Nothing. Actually, nothing." Jack said, inspiring neither Barry's credibility nor his assurance. "Have you heard when the Coalition is having its next public meeting?" Jack persisted.

"No, I haven't, Jack. Hold on ..." Alex was motioning a time-out signal to Barry. "Jack, Alex would like to speak to you for just a minute," Barry said, handing the phone into her waiting hand. Her intrusion was amiable and lighthearted, an invitation to Jack and Marcy to join them and their out of town guests for brunch at eleven on Sunday. Another congratulations on Marcy's and Jack's marriage license, and the receiver was handed back to Barry.

"Once again, congratulations on the marriage license," Barry repeated, warning to a subject he would much have preferred pursuing. "Will it be soon? The two of you?"

"As soon as Marcy feels comfortable with it. I want that more than anything, Barry." Another hiatus. "Believe it, Barry. More than anything."

Having stumbled into something that felt like another landmine, Barry retreated. "About the Coalition ..." he remarked breezily.

"Dunno, Hope for the best, I guess. I sure the hell would like to see it succeed," he concluded earnestly.

"I'll talk to you on Sunday," Jack responded balefully. "Oh, and I'm looking forward to meeting your daughter ... Madi."

"Sure thing," Barry said. "Til Sunday, then."

HE WENT back to his paper, watching Alex focused at the computer in what he hoped were, for her, productive, revelatory bursts. When she woke him two hours later, he was as tired as if he had been digging in the ground the entire afternoon.

AS THEY locked doors, adjusted the thermostat, and turned off lights for the night, Barry reconsidered. "I take it back, Alex. I'm as tired as a stevedore. This ain't no weekend."

They followed each other up the stairs. "Hell, there just isn't any abdicating from the human race, is there? There are just so many ... people ... Alex. So many people ..."

ALEX looked young and fresh as she threw the bedcovers from her side of the bed and slid under the sheet. "It's only for a few more months, Barry." she offered conciliatorily, sliding into prone position.

"And a good thing, too!"

He looked at the contour of his wife's still serpentine back, sexy and inviting, even at this latter date. Before he had finished his last cigarette, cleared his mind, and slipped in next to her, her breathing had become steady, regular as heartbeat. Turning to his other side, aware he would not, in any case, have been able to perform his conjugal duty tonight (he smiled at the persistence of these damned arcane phrases), he denied feeling defunct, superannuated, or indeed, a man without a country (there ---that was another one of those worn-out school phrases) ... dedicated as he had been to Human Resources, (yeah yeah), unable to mount entirely this postmodern world of Internet idiom and virtual reality.

Despite his bone-weary exhaustion, it seemed an endless interim before he finally dropped off into muffled sleep.

Chapter Twenty-two

M ADI HAD not actually met or spoken to Toda until she had been at the Lab for over a month. Several weeks before her arrival, she had later pieced together from random Lab scuttlebutt, Rafe Sunsteen, their excitable, unkempt, lovable, intellectually unforgiving Lab supervisor, one of the Rosenfield's half-dozen picked cadre of stellar young post-docs, had waxed ecstatic upon Toda's having finally isolated a certain protein precipitated from a gene transfected from original neuroblastoma cells. Toda had subsequently managed to determine the location within that protein of something with at least one characteristic of a "receptor." Even in the face of his supervisor's synergistic enthusiasm, Toda had continued circumspect, if not skeptical, discreetly pointing out that the protein derived from the pulsing clusters of T-cells may have indeed been synthesized from the neuroblastoma oncogene as Rafe assumed, but, too, it may just as well have been a piece of "garbage" picked up in one his many precipitations on the focal cell. But Rafe was not to be diverted. Hadn't the orphan protein, he argued, consistently shown part of its head above the surface of the membrane, as if to catch a hormone or other growth factor in the bloodstream? And, if this protein turned out, in fact, to be a "receptor," a perverted version of a normal membrane receptor, wouldn't the Lab be well on its way to an important forward thrust in its current research? The situation was altogether too provocative for him to overlook or neglect. The potential breakthrough for the Lab, too stunning to spurn.

Toda continued to demur, even allowing himself to become argumentative on many occasions. He had no assurance that the membrane receptor produced by the neuroblastoma oncogene would have anything to do with the tumor in question. The difference between a normal protein and the cancerous protein might well be too subtle to detect experimentally. And, were he to begin a genomic cloning from the neuroblastoma oncogene in order to resolve the matter conclusively, as Rafe now insisted, such as course would commit him to years of investigation of a single oncogene and a single protein. It was a gamble sure to tie him up on this one facet of their research for the next several months, if not for years.

That afternoon she had finally slipped down to the lunch-room located in a small annex attached to the first-floor lab, purchased herself a hot chocolate from the machine to sip along with her single bologna sandwich brought from home, and found a seat. Minutes later, he had rushed into the room carrying his requisite brown bag, fed in coins at an adjacent machine, claimed a bottle of iced tea, seated himself two tables away, completely oblivious of her, and was soon fully absorbed in studying the pages of a dog-eared folder. Ten minutes after that, just as suddenly, he slammed the folder shut, scrunched the waxed paper under the sandwich he had finished eating, looked across the room, and immediately broke into a broad smile in her direction. She noted the stray strip of glossy black hair across his forehead, his rather heavy but pleasant octagonal face, in which, however, pristine, sculpted, almost delicate features were carefully, even aesthetically, arranged. "Hi," he said simply. "I'm Toda Yamashigi. Are you up in Sunsteen's section? I don't remember seeing you."

"I'm a postgraduate student from Hopkins," she responded, equally simple, having repressed the need to say "just." "I've heard about you ... And your work." She proceeded to worry her brown paper bag into several careful, redundant folds. "I know you're trying to precipitate a normal, noncancerous protein from your cell line. To determine ... ultimately ... whether the protein receptors synthesized from the oncogene membrane are really ... distinct."

"Yeah," he said. "Yeah," he repeated, pleased, and gratified. Studying her more closely now, he politely reiterated his original question. "And you? What are you working on?"

"Well, I'm hardly a maestro," she succumbed now self-consciously, immediately disapproving of her self-deprecation as disingenuous. "Understand, I'm not putting myself down ... just being realistic. "I'm working on a post-doc ... maybe. Hopefully, in molecular biology. Hopefully, in less than three or four years. I'm hoping to share a piece of the action. More or less, so far, I've been attached to Hatty. She's cloning a complementary DNA version of your gene. The one with exons, only. "Now it was her turn to smile at him. "That's how I come to know so much about what you're doing."

For a moment, his expressions furrowed, a wincing discomfort swept briefly across his lowered glance.

"Yeah. I guess I've been at it for quite some time now. I've encountered some difficult problems," he added defensively, with a barely discernible noted of stiffness. "Why molecular biology?" smiling once more, he asked, abruptly changing the subject, seeming to have again fully regained his good humor.

"Well, like all of us, I've always been interested in science."

She looked at him full-face. She did not wish to leave an impression of mawkish adolescence. "But ... I made a kind of final decision a few years ago. When my older brother ... not so much older, really ... died suddenly. Of a metastasized brain cancer." Involuntarily, her fingers clenched into a taut grip on each other. "It was all over in just a few months. Three or four only." She looked at Toda again. He was looking right back at her. "It was awful. Shocking. Unacceptable."

"Yeah. It's like that sometimes," he agreed simply. He straightened himself against the scrolled back of the rickety dinette chair. "I think I understand." For a few minutes, he toyed with the twisted brown bag that had held his lunch.

"Before you came, this summer, even with everything going on," he moved his hand in the air in an indefinite, exculpatory gesture, "I had to take time off. Half or partial days for at least four months. To take care of my mother. I'm the oldest son," he explained, "and Dad had died the year before. Mother is a very serious diabetic. She'd lost a leg recently. At the time, she was bedridden." He stood up, walked to the trash can, and let his brown bag drop. He leaned against the wall.

"And though I was under this terrific time pressure here from Rafe ... you know he is ... it was my responsibility. I *had* to be there. To help." She noticed his upper lip was beaded with sweat, his voice having fallen to a whisper.

But, unexpectedly, once again, he smiled, walking toward her. "So that's the way it is. 'Family considerations.' I understand.

"Yeah," he laughed as they started out of the room and down the hall. "But it turned out my mother did more worrying about me in those four months than I did about her. She was worried that I was earning less than either of my two younger brothers ... one in business, the other in real estate."

"But isn't she proud to have a son in basic, cutting-edge research?" Madi could not help asking, unable to mask the incredulity in her voice.

"Sure. Of course," Toda laughed a noiseless giggle, his shoulders heaving into a rueful shrug.

WHEN the elevator reached the second floor, they debarked and stood facing each other for a moment. "I and my brothers finally set her up with a younger female cousin for a prolonged visit to Key West. I can work nights now. Extra hard. And catch up ... maybe," he concluded, amiable, turning his office, in a direction opposite to her cubicle. Halfway down the hall, he swung about and waved at her.

SHE watched until he disappeared into a doorway. She wondered how she was so sure he would seek her out again. She simply knew he would. And, if he did not, she would make an opportunity, somehow, to find him.

AND that is how it began. And grew. She could hardly remember any formal "dates," as such. Their relationship just happened.

By tacit mutual agreement, lunches became habitual on Conference Tuesdays and then on end-of-the-week Fridays. Gradually all the days in between filled in. One late evening when her Volkswagen was in the shop, he suggested he drive her home. Soon after, it became every evening she worked late at the Lab. She would come in after supper with Vicky or Jean, and he would be there to chauffeur her home later. He was always easy, unstintingly attentive and interested in her work and her ideas, unselfconsciously but markedly respectful toward her sex. Of course, their conversations were frequently about matters at the Lab, but they were just as likely to be explorations of life values, ethnic differences, persons; or religious, political, or purely personal beliefs. She came to admire his ironic, off-sides, nonjudgmental observations and insights, often tinged with affectionate humor. To cherish his unflinching honesty. To rely on his trustworthy friendship.

One evening after weeks of anxious calculations and refinements in the conditions of his experimental setup, he remained uncharacteristically silent on their nightly ride home to her apartment. She knew he had thus far managed to clone the genomic gene, but had as yet been unable to construct the cell line that Rafe and Hatty had expected by now. Early on the ride, he had mumbled something to that effect, but instinctively, she knew he did not want to talk about this matter, maybe ever, but certainly not tonight. Without having thought of it before, for whatever reason she could not now really guess when they reached her apartment, she impulsively invited him in. "I'd be surprised if either Vicky or Jean are in yet," she said, having consulted her watch. "We two left early tonight. Well before our usual time. So, we'll have a little time by ourselves." She giggled inconsequentially, aware that her quip could be interpreted suggestively, even provocatively.

They shared a pot of tea, comfortable, desultory chat, and a new CD of Brandenburg Concertos she had just treated herself to. After about an hour, Vicky and Jean still away, Toda put on his jacket in preparation for leaving.

At the door, he asked, "Do you like Japanese food?"

"I think so," she said. "I've really not eaten it that often."

"Would you have dinner with me in my apartment this Saturday evening?" he asked decorously.

"I would be pleased to do so," she twinkled back at him, equally serious.

"Then, good," he answered, breaking into a grin. "Good."

He took the steps down from her apartment, two at a time.

IN FACT, the meal he served was delicious and beautifully presented. As a centerpiece, he had arranged a single branch of forsythia, which arrested attention and invited frequent admiring glances between quietly laid courses.

Well, after the conclusion of dinner, he had touched her for the first time. He took up her hand, his palm still warm from his teacup, perhaps just detectably moist from nervousness. He looked down at the low tabletop between them. "Would you mind if we began keeping company?" he asked. "If we began to see each other ..." he hesitated, "more seriously?"

She was confused by her conflicting respect for him, his obvious sincerity, his brilliance, the comforting reliability of his friendship, and her utter inability to project, to image any possibility of physical intimacy with this person. In their relationship, this whole complicated aspect had been unexplored ... an inchoate blank. "I realize this is a serious kind of commitment," he continued differently, replacing her hand on her knee. "And, as we have so often discussed, we are of such different cultures," he preserved, even more quietly.

"Oh, that's not it," she said almost too quickly. "No. No. That has nothing to do with it." She looked across the short length of table at him. He dropped so dispiritedly, hunched across from her so absolutely hangdog, she leaned over and kissed him on the check.

IN THE next two or three months, as he doggedly mixed and matched his several DNA segments, his spirits alternately rose in enthusiastic anticipation and dropped into mute despair as his sequences failed to produce the hoped-for results. They continued to read to each other, to talk, to take long walks, to eat together, to shop and do laundry, but, concurrently, separately, their sexual relationship grew with astonishing spontaneity into burgeoning pleasure and pure joy, setting its own pattern into unquestioned regularity. One evening, after appreciating a new Mozart CD and *Don Giovanni*, she could not help but see he was more than normally dejected. At these times, she had previously always tried to be close, but not intrusive: she avoided questioning him. And, usually, he would slowly regain his equanimity, if not his entire sanguine good humor.

"The experiment?" she allowed herself finally, looking up at him through her eyelashes.

"Rafe put Andy onto the project. He's to develop the cell line."

She could not look at him. This was much more serious than she had even anticipated.

"But, in a way, it's helped me reach a decision I should have made a long time ago. I've accepted a scholarship to a medical school,"

She tried not to move. Not to appear surprised, relieved, or disappointed. Anything.

"You know, like all people who love science, who have always loved it, I can't resist trying to solve a puzzle. But, in the end, besides the high stakes and the exciting risks, it is a game. The most serious game around. And one I've allowed myself to play for a long time. Maybe, too long. Oh, I know Rafe will be ... furious ... disappointed when I tell him. He'll think it's because of what just happened, that he gave the project to Andy, and, in a way, that can't be discounted. But that's not it!" he remonstrated. "Not really."

He walked over to the sofa and kissed her lightly on the cheek, then resumed his own chair at the desk. "It's more complicated than that. It's too expensive a game. At least, for me. Pure science is too jealous a master. A tyrant, really. Your ego has to be totally dedicated at all times. You have to be obsessive about your work. That last experiment just revealed something to me that I have been pushing aside for a long time. I'm not willing to put my whole life on the line for years and years with little or no assurance of success. Call it cowardly. Say I don't have the right stuff. But that's the way it is, and I may as well face it now, as later. I want a more normal, happier life. With some regular feeling of achievement ... of doing some good in the world ... all along."

Neither of them moved nor spoke. "With you, if you'll agree," he proposed tentatively. "I hadn't told you, but recently, I was accepted at John Hopkins as a pre-med. With a substantial ... or at least, a livable stipend. You could still continue your own work at the Lab. Nothing would have to change between us."

Once again, she faced the unknowable, and despite all the positive evidence that should stand as her assurance, she felt adrift, frightened.

Instead, startling herself, she heard herself speaking from an intuition as passionate as his own. "When I saw my brother ... dying ... because I knew enough to know that his case was well nigh hopeless, that he was going to die, although my resolve was always strong and didn't need bolstering, I *knew*, I knew as fully and clearly as if ... as if..." Her hand brushed across her forehead. She shook her head in hopeless recall. "And that's why I'm doing what I'm doing. I know that only basic research can solve his horrible death. This horrible death." She looked across at Toda. "I'm *sure* of it."

"But what I spoke of is *my* decision," Toda said without looking at her. "It's for myself only. I would not even wish to influence your decision, ever, even if I could."

In a few minutes, he walked over to her and squeezed her hand. "You don't have to answer now. It's a big step, I know."

MORE latterly, Toda's younger married sister had invited Madi and Toda to a family dinner. Over gingered beef, his two younger brothers and his mother made amiable conversations and exerted every effort to be as sensitivity inclusive in their every comment and in all their conversation as their own suppressed sense of historic social rejection, and their own best intentions could manage. Only later, as Madi carried a tray of platters from the dining room into the kitchen, had she heard Toda's mother's sibilant whisper, suddenly stilled. "*Hakuyin*," his mother had hissed under her breath. Madi had pretended not to have heard, as his brother's wives interposed fresh observations and cheery remarks, all smiles, and helpfulness as they refurbished Madi's tray with teacups, assorted dumplings, and sweetmeats.

"You survived," Toda had said on their drive home. "More than that. You were gracious. Demure."

At her usual stop at his apartment before leaving for her own, she desultorily pushed in a CD and sat next to Toda on the couch. He took up her nearer hand.

"Yes, you were great. Just right," he repeated.

"Toda, what does *hakuyin* mean?"

He flushed to the roots of his hair. His hand twitched. In a whisper, he responded, "It means 'white.'"

They sat silent, staring through his mini-picture window out across the postage-stamp-sized deck at a darkening patch of sky. "You are the most natural, the most perfect, the most beautiful thing that has ever happened to me," he said, addressing the air. "I don't want anyone else, or anyone else's feelings or ideas, to come between us, to spoil anything that we have." He lifted her hand, examining the fingers, then brushed the fingertips against his lips. "I have known for a very long time that I wanted to marry you. But you haven't ever told me that you wished to marry me."

She kissed him passionately then but was still unable to say the words.

AT THE door, before she left the building, she touched his cheek. "I'm just happy. Happy to be with you. But I don't share your mystic certainty. I'm just grateful. For you. For us. But I'm frightened." She pulled open the door. "Marriage is so *final*," she whispered under her breath, as much to herself as to him, starting down the stairs.

ONLY a week later, Madi initiated discussion with Alex about a possible upcoming visit with Toda as her designated guest. In her several calls to her mother, Madi avoided all talk, let alone revelation, of her relationship with her new companion. Because Madi's and Toda's individual Monday schedules made return to Baltimore no later than mid-afternoon Sunday advisable, Alex scrapped her original plan for Sunday brunch, re- inviting Marcy, Jack, and Vivvy; Ginny and John from the Center; the O'Neills's and their three daughters; and the Ruskins and their two children instead, to an adult happy hour with a buffet supper for everyone following, late Saturday afternoon, setting the duration of the "party" at approximately 4-8 p.m. Alex hoped that inclusion of the children would discreetly insure her guests' timely departure more or less within suggested time parameters. An informal menu of hamburgers and hot dogs, salads and beans, concluding with a wonderful birthday cake for Jean, baked and brought by her mother, helped the whole party remain, though noisy and often even slightly obstreperous, and unpretentious, comfortable and finally genuinely enjoyable affair for both children and adults.

Around an oversized picnic table on the deck, constructed by pushing two standard-sized picnics tables together, Marcy and Alex, Madi and Toda, Jack and Barry, Vivvy and Gloria, and Mr. and Mrs. O'Neill had all settled along the rightmost end. The O'Neil's special duties involving their daughter's physical oversight and Alex's and Barry's responsibilities for hospitality and cookery had kept them all busy until most other guests had already seated themselves – but the somewhat unlikely, accidental arrangement that has resulted proved remarkably, satisfyingly congenial for their end of the table.

Madi sat next to Alex, enjoying the exchange of small talk with her mother, watching the play of interest and reaction on what to her was her mother's unalterably exquisite face, realizing wistfully, yearningly, how much she has missed her, warning now in the unique quality of her parent's simple nurturing acceptance and affection. Across the table, though deep in mostly murmured exchanges with Jack over the Coalition and like community matters, Barry kept his wife and daughter in view, his occasional unguarded, tender glances betraying him overcome, if not ravished, by these two most loved women in his life.

Gradually, Madi's magnetic focus on Alex relaxed, and she became more globally aware of other guests around her. Now she observed that Vivvy, while astonishingly replicating her mother's slender dark good looks, was growing into a kind of ineffable spiritualized version of her more earthly parent. She puzzled as the child's arm passed frequently through Marcy's, claiming quiet possessions of her, especially when Jack had just managed a special *bon mot*, incisive observation, or subtle affectionate glance at Marcy, all apparently authentic natural expressions for him. But, at the same time, she noticed the child also watching others. Especially in their reactions to Jack. She observed Vivvy's pride at his patent knowledgeability about community affairs with the O'Neill's and Barry, the effect of his unimpeacheable personal standards upon Toda, his incisive humor with Marcy and Alex.

Madi also noted how gently, how solicitously, Toda responded to Glory sitting next to him. It was more than politeness, more than decorum. He appeared to have spontaneously bonded with that charming, handicapped young person. Reluctantly, Madi remembered their infrequent discussions about having children. Always touched with humor, always explored in an abstract, theoretical sort of way. She had been fairly convinced that, like herself, he felt deeply, that there were already enough abandoned children, children deprived of love and nurture, throughout this sad wide world, that, should they ever in future feel the need to broaden their horizons, refresh their present commitment in e new direction, adoption would stand as the primary, the most preferred option. Having one's own children under present circumstances, they had understood, she had thought, was nothing more than a kind of egotistical self-indulgence fundamentally, contrary to a more selfless enlightened, humane understanding. But, as she now observed Toda, fully and unselfconsciously entered into Glory's universe of discourse, she was impressed, and frankly, disconcerted.

When toward the end of the meal, Vivvy led Glory away to other activities; a fresh interlocutory conversation sprang up between Barry, Jack, and Toda. Madi was proud that Toda made no attempt to impressive or memorable in responding to Barry's in-depth probings about his medical school decision, his background, or even his parents' family internment during World War II, invariably answering her father's and Jack's questions diffidently, but with lucid simplicity and honesty. At no time did he shape even simple responses to fit the perceived emotional bias or expectation of his auditor. Madi could not help feeling gratified at her father's evident growing admiration and respect for her fiancé. Nor Jack's equally buoyant enthusiasm for him throughout the interchange.

WHEN the uncommonly congenial evening came to a close, many warm embraces and good-bye's over; Barry stoked up a pleasant fire in the den fireplace, Toda sitting next to Madi on the sofa, unobtrusively holding her hand, half-buried between the couch cushions.

When Barry finally seated himself in his favorite wing chair in front of the fire, he chose to play the bluff parental. "So, what are your plans, kids?" he half-chided, reaching for a pipe.

It was Toda who answered quietly. "We are very serious about each other, Mr. Byrnes."

Alex directed a glance from under hooded eyelids, raised momentarily from the newspaper on her lap. "And, Madi, what do you say? She probed gently.

Madi sighed. "It's true, Mother. We are serious. Now that Toda's been accepted to medical school with a stipend. It seems a good time."

"What do you mean?" her mother asked.

"Well, *Toda* thinks we should be married ... soon. That it would not alter either of our plans. I could continue working toward my post-doc at the Lab, while he ..."

"And what do *you* think?" Alex pressed.

Madi shrugged, giggled, and nervously pressed Toda's hand under the cushions.

"We are both very private persons," Toda interposed quietly. "I and Madi. You could even say, I suppose, that with our particular intellectual and scientific interests, we chose activities and careers that are not exactly commonplace ... or popular." His voice dropped to bare audibility. "Sexually, we were both ... innocent ... inexperienced." He looked over at Barry. "To my brothers and sister, who don't want to take many pains to conceal their opinions, I know I am just a big grown-up boy. An *indulged* grown-up boy. And Madi, too," his eyes settled on her face. "She's like my female counterpart. She's the same kind of innocent girl as I am an unproven boy." Toda looked at Alex. "But, we truly love each other. That I know. And, we suit each other. That I know, too. But ... naturally, she is afraid." He was speaking now to himself. "I am afraid, too, but not as afraid as she is." Again, he looked over at Alex. "But I think it will work out. We suit each other." He laughed ingenuously, boyishly. "None better." Under the cushions, he once more double-squeezed Madi's hand.

Confused, Alex set her stare on Barry, who poked at his pipe and glanced down at his shoes. Upon the conclusion of Toda's ... what ... declaration, for Heaven's sake? She had felt her throat constrict and then thicken and, biting her lower lip, she hoped her cheeks were not visibly flushed. If she could have read his maundering thoughts, she would have heard Barry congratulating himself on not having blundered into a desperately insensitive remark already on his lips, "Ancient Oriental Wisdom."

NOTHING was decided. Everyone just dropped the subject. As if they all needed to come up for air. The evening ended quietly, amiably, Madi going off with Toda at about midnight.

SUNDAY afternoon, as she watched Madi climb into the car next to Toda, Alex was revisited with the same choking ache and insuperable need to cry out. Instead, she fussed over her daughter through the passenger car window, posing nervous rhetorical questions about her baggage, their route, Madi's Monday schedule. Having stowed their goods into the trunk, Toda walked deliberately over to Barry and, with dignity, almost gravity, shook his hand. Madi kissed her mother's cheek. "I'll call, Mom. And I'll write." She looked wistfully at her parent. "Don't worry, Mom. Just don't worry." Toda then swung into the driver's seat, waved, and pulled out into the connecting road.

FOR the balance of Sunday afternoon, Barry and Alex each seemed to have innumerable small chores and errands that kept them busy and out of each other's way.

Dinnertime approached, and Barry saw that Alex was nowhere near the kitchen. When she descended from the second floor after six and fussily settled down to the newspaper, Barry let matters drift for a quarter of an hour before suggesting they go out for supper, somewhere simple, nearby.

Alex did not answer, simply rose and headed for the coat closet. Desultorily, he followed.

"You OK, Alex?"

She just nodded.

"You sure?"

She thrust her arm through a jacket sleeve and glared back at him. "Of course, I'm sure. Why shouldn't I be OK?"

He reached for his own jacket. As he snapped off the closet light and shut the door, he saw her propped up against the wall, staring into space, her eyes suspiciously glazed.

Just as suddenly, she snapped herself erect and laughed. "Silly, Silly, silly, silly ..." she chanted.

"HE SEEMS a ... wonderful ... chap," Barry said stiffly, as he pulled the car out of the driveway. Though Alex nodded her head, she kept it firmly turned from him, toward the car window.

BARRY drove toward Hughesville slowly, not commenting on her silence.

"I'm not ready, Barry. I'm not ready for this," she protested finally. "Are you?" she added accusatorily.

He took his time answering. "It's not about you and me, Alex," he said quietly.

"For Heaven's Sake, why not? We're her parents," she burst out.

He shrugged. "Yeah, Alex, we are ..." he intoned. "We're her parents," reciting the phrase like a mantra, to himself, prescient of all the fated helplessness in the undeniable relationship of blood and bone.

Chapter Twenty-three

THROUGH THE latter half of March, although Carleton remained meticulously responsive to Allied's repeated demands for voluminous, time-consuming and painstaking legal, financial and business documentation, most weekdays, Armand calmly drove to Cunningham's Wilmington office, for week the pair becoming inseparable, invariably spearing in each other's company, as Consortium feasibility studies for the new Baywater Inlet Condominium Project, to be situated on the present LeClerc site, were developed. In the first instance, LeClerc employees evinced surprise and innocent curiosity only, good-naturedly reparking their vehicles in their designated reassigned parking slots in the Employee Parking lot, untroubled in accommodating the several small, young, fresh-faced bands of surveyors industriously setting up their tripods and going about their business. Most assumed their activity had something to do with the sale to Allied. Then, when stretch limos had occasionally been observed pulling up to the doors of the Conference Building, LeClerc workers assumed again these were Allied people, as, indeed, they were. The Coalition had remained active, additional growing investments were encouraging, Coalition leadership was in place and energetic, and the continued presence of the chief outside suitor was observed and regarded impassively as entirely normal.

Meanwhile, after Consortium-contracted surveyors had calculated the total square footage of the property, their site maps then submitted to environmental engineers for evaluation toward final determination of actual usable, buildable space, Consortium's architectural affiliates next took over, adapting and expanding original Boar's Head site construction plans to incorporate the larger, more varied addition of LeClerc acreage. For Armand, it was all working out well: by the end of April, Cunningham was able to assure him the Consortium's original offer and terms still held: a million upfront, with two to follow over a three-year period, while plant disposal remained the negotiated responsibility of the Consortium and Hughesville. Throughout the process, the mayor had been kept apprised, in a general way, of the Consortium's extended feasibility studies, knew they were on schedule and going well, but had tacitly agreed to "keep it under his hat" until such time as their projected plans should have to be presented to the City Council and state authorities should confirm the area's original zoning under the Chesapeake Critical Areas Act.

ALEX had been gratified to read her own historical, nonetheless piquantly picturesque, rendition of the mid-nineteenth century establishment of the LeClerc rolling mill on the present site, a second following, presenting evolving company adjustments to the exigencies of changing markets, regional needs, and the personal vision of the successive family managers, inevitably trending away from the original conception of an ambitious basic steel manufactory to a more limited, more manageably efficient canning and container facility. These articles roused mild interest only, Jack looking pensive and proud in his conversational acknowledgment of her efforts, but no comment or recognizing calls were forthcoming from any of the title-holding LeClerc's, their management, or even Coalition members. Barry carried copies of the first article, then the second, in his jacket pocket for a full week after each publication. He whipped them out upon expression of the auditor's mildest interest in the subject.

LATER, much later, when he came to review and puzzle over the accretion of events that erupted into Hughesville's major port World War II crisis, and its chrysalis emergence as one of North Shore's more exclusive addresses, Jack was forced to admit he had then temporarily not inhabited the same world as his brother. Until that fateful afternoon in the LeClerc Employee Parking lot, he, along with Marcy, had been concerned so exclusively with the best time for his moving into Marcy's house; when and how to formalize the marriage legally; how to manage the inescapable corporeality of his very presence in Vivvy's heretofore exclusive domain – his clothing, his gear, his car parked next to Marcy's daily in the adjoining garage, he had scarcely noticed Armand's comings and goings, nor had been aware of the hiatus in his brother's routing bread-and-butter weekly telephone calls.

Marcy and Vivvy had already decided that this year would be Viccy's first at a grown-up, overnight, go-away camp. At considerable sacrifice to Marcy's budget, the price of more than a year's tuition and fees at State College, Marcy ruefully noted, early in the Spring, Vivvy had been enrolled at Camp Oquaka in Maine for the month of July. That had seemed to Marcy and Jack the ideal time for Jack's move-in. But, after more ruminative discussion and just living with that hypothetical solution, they decided mutually that such a move without considerable preparation might well be viewed by Vivvy as a sneak invasion when her defenses were down, exacerbating potential resentment and fixing alienation for possibly a long time to come.

So, although they had continued to agree about keeping the wedding date firmly locked into Memorial Day weekend, planning a quiet civil ceremony in Hughesville only, with close family sharing a festive dinner at Logan Inn afterward, they now conceived and scheduled an exciting, child-oriented ten-day vacation tour together in Marcy's RV to Walt Disney World, Busch Gardens and other points of interest in Florida directly upon Vivvy's end of school term. Until that time, Jack would retain his present residence at Carriage House. Then, upon the conclusion of their Florida sojourn, Marcy and Jack would together drive Vivvy to camp in Maine, rewarding themselves with a long weekend at Martha's Vineyard on their return trip to Maryland by way of a deserved, if brief, honeymoon. Now, though Jack would be taking up permanent residence and full membership in the household, even as originally planned, Vivvy would have been more fully apprised and hopefully better prepared to accept its occurrence with equanimity.

Barry's call on that fateful Friday had literally come as "a bolt from the blue."

THE first week in May, the second City Council meeting on the subject had been held, the first having been a "closed session" that had almost immediately broken down into a faction of Hughesville Boosters, enthusiastic over Cunningham's presentation of construction plans and another comprised chiefly of a minority of labor-oriented oldsters and longtime indigenous merchants who branded the whole scheme as at the least irresponsible, if not deceptive, or even criminal. This second meeting was technically "open" (although called at the last minute and unannounced in the *Record*), formal and legalistic, concluding with a firm majority vote for allowing Cunningham's project to go forward. Enoch Blaine had been notified only the day before of Tuesday's Council meeting and had duly sent a brace of his regular news reporter to cover the story. Upon submission of their copy for Wednesday's first biweekly publication of the *Record*, he knew he was sitting on a time bomb. But he called no one except Alex, to tell her he would have to temporarily hold back her third installment – dealing with the formation of the Coalition --- until next week's issue. In answer to her bewildered questions, his ambiguous, noncommittal, "Something has come up," left only more nonplussed than she had been before any explanation had been proffered.

THE first of the weekly publications of the *Record* was timely placed in subscribers' newspaper boxes on Wednesday afternoon. The usual bundled deliveries were made to all the customary locations and at all designated places of business as well.

AS IT happened, the Coalition had also scheduled a meeting for this very evening, to be held in Harry Warner's First Bank Conference Room. But as Gary Letzger walked up his front walk after shift, his wife was already hallooing him from their open front doorway, waving a newspaper above her head. Before he was half-way through supper, he himself had jumped up to get the burring telephone off the kitchen wall. It was Paul Doran. A very disturbed, angry Paul Doran.

"What the hell do you make of *this*?" Paul had bellowed, as if he, Letzger, had created the entire debacle.

"Just *what* the hell do you make of this?" Paul had repeated, roaring.

Letzger had barely gotten him to quiet down long enough to assure him they would all talk about it, talk it all out, at the meeting tonight.

More than half of the Coalition regulars had already read tonight's paper before they'd arrived at the meeting. The other half were quickly drawn into discussion after scanning the lead article in one of the many copies of the *Record* scattered haphazardly over the length of the Conference table.

Laskovsky got there late and had not yet read the article. Perusing it, he sat listening to the escalating agitation and exasperation in the exchanges amongst the discussants around the table. Finally, *sole voce,* as a body, they insisted he call Armand at home, now, and find out what it all meant for them. Though he advised against it, his better judgment capitulated in the face of their aggrieved uproar. But, it proved to no avail. LeClerc's housekeeper meticulously whispered that Mr. LeClerc was "out of town" this evening. Upon further request for Mrs. Amanda LeClerc, he was similarly informed that she likewise was not in town.

The group attention then shifted to Harry, and they insisted he call the mayor at home. He did and was told the mayor was not there. However, five minutes later, the mayor called Harry on his cell phone from his car.

"Jeb, this Cunningham business. What are we supposed to think about it all?"

A chuckle. A pause. "Why I think it's fairly clear. I think it will go through." Phone static-filled a brief interval. "In fact, if you'll read the *Record* article carefully, you'll see it more or less already has."

More phone static. Harry's choked voice. "I don't understand it, Jeb. I just don't understand it." Second wind. "Why weren't any of us ... me, Laskovsky, Reverend Boardman, Father Meara ... not to mention McClintock and Doran ... why wasn't *anybody* told this was about to happen?" His guffaw sounded as if it might well end in a sob.

"Don't you think *someone* had the responsibility for letting the Coalition know?"

The pause was so long; Harry thought the connection had been broken or that Jeb had hung up. "Why?" the mayor's voice crackled.

"Why...?" Harry spluttered in disbelief.

"Yes, why? Seems to me, as entrepreneur-owner, Mr. LeClerc has every right to examine *all* his potions. *Any* deal advantageous to him. In privacy. On his own schedule." Harry could almost see Jeb's rueful smile. "As it so happens, such a development will be wonderful for the city."

"The hell you say," Harry could not contain his riotous emotions any longer, his sense of personal outrage. "The hell you say!" he shouted. "Whose city, for God's sake? What city?" Harry's face shook. "Listen, you, you... I voted for you in the last election." His laugh became dangerously close to lachrymose. "I voted for you," he repeated, defeated.

"Maybe, you'll think better of it. In time. When you've had the opportunity to sort it all out," Jeb said cheerfully. He hung up.

Off the phone, Harry dejectedly reported everything they had all already heard. Father Meara let out something like a bleat. Laskovsky looked as if he had been cast in stone. Paul Doran presented a convincing replica of a high blood pressure victim about to suffer a stroke. Only McClintock remained impassive and grim. He stood up and spoke in loud, even tones. "The first step here is to call a mass meeting of our local for tomorrow," he said. "I will recommend a picket line be organized, and team leaders appointed for Friday. The mandatory vote will be taken, of course. But I don't need to tell all of you that there isn't a chance in hell we won't be out in force come Friday." Without looking back at any of his colleagues, he stalked out of the room.

WHEN Alex awoke the next morning, she stared out the bedroom window for long minutes observing the cold, almost sleety rain, at a morning that threatened to be nature's last attempt to hold off Summer's insistent arrival. She felt headachy and slightly sickish. Although she herself had gone to bed at more or less usual hour, she had awakened several times during the night, the last time sometime around 2:30 in the morning, to hear an unbroken, tense stream of dialogue, intermittently audible, flowing relentlessly from the first floor up to the upper reaches of the house.

Jack had called at about ten o'clock last night, unprecedentedly late for him, Barry having taken the call. Afterward, Barry had tried to appear casual, mentioning that Jack would be stopping over this evening and broadly hinting they would appreciate the living room being reserved to themselves. Considering the late hour of Jack's visit, and the likely subject for discussion to follow, Alex was more than happy to have an excuse to escape.

Now she bathed and dressed, noting as she left for the kitchen downstairs, that Barry was still deeply asleep. Trying to preserve this midmorning untimely quietude, she had snatched the kitchen telephone off the wall after a single ring. It was Enoch from the *Record*. Inquiring if she wanted Hugh to pick her up in the *Record's* van as he and Jerry swung down to the LeClerc Employee Parking lot where they were being dispatched to cover the picketing. Enoch had thought that, despite her more-historically-oriented feature series on the broader topic, she might wish to accompany their regular firsthand news coverage for her own later more responsive reportage. She agreed with alacrity.

Tiptoeing up to the bedroom, she saw that Barry was still sound asleep. She propped a note up against the bedroom television set, but left one on the kitchen table downstairs as well, for good measure. Unconsciously, she sensed and simultaneously wished to avoid future confrontation with Barry on this issue. Whether from an instinct of self-protection, desire to save Barry unnecessary concern, or simple willfulness, she had kept both notes vague and generic, indicating only that she was off with two of the *Record's* news reporters to cover a story, at last, first hand.

HUGH parked the van on the nearer side of the parking lot, adjacent to the street. He and Jerry confabbed for about ten hectic minutes before dismounting together – Hugh prepared to interview strikers on the forward picket line, Jerry following close behind to get the arresting, corroborating photos he always hoped for. The drizzle had thickened into a steady, dismal rain, not a downpour exactly, but drenching, bone-chilling, and off-putting nonetheless. Jerry and Hugh had decorously presented Alex with a halfhearted offer to tag along, but she had declined.

She watched now as Hugh penciled notes, shaking his head now and again, all the while scribbling on his chest-anchored pad. Jerry dodged, weaved, and crouched around and behind Hugh, calculating his most effective angle. At first, only a few, then small clusters, of colorful umbrellas began to appear at unequal intervals within and along the long scraggly line of homemade picket sign carriers. Even at this distance, their messages were clearly visible. (Puns): "Don't *Care* Us, LeClerc!" – (historical): "Pearl Harbor on the Chesapeake!" – (alliterative): "Coalition, Not Consortium" – and (most distressing, heartfelt, and predominant): "Save Our Jobs! Save our Community! Save our Lives!"

Hugh and Jerry had just returned to the van briefly, shaking off their wet slickers and rooting amongst their gear for the oversized thermos of coffee they had brought along, when Wilmington's Channel 11 van pulled into the lot, followed scarcely five minutes later by another van identified with Wilmington *Times* name and logo. Handling her a half-filled styrofoam cup of coffee, Jerry pointed at the newcomers, "I guess Hughesville's hit the big time," he chuckled. Before his comment was out of his mouth, three more vans, two labeled as Baltimore's Channels 6 and 8, another from the Baltimore *Herald*, pulled up and zigzagged jauntily between the picketeers, across the lot, settling down along the innermost rim, furthest from the street.

As Alex continued peering through the van windows at the action outside, a milling crowd seemed suddenly to have gathered, pressing ominously nearer the Conference room doors. Hugh and Jerry grunted at each other, Hugh flinging his now empty styrofoam cup to the floor, and, in a single bound, tearing on his jacket and negotiating a vaulting leap from the van, minutes before Jerry was able to collect his camera and equipment and scramble after him. Watching mesmerized, Alex now saw the human mass before her sway – forward, backward – in a kind of convulsive rhythmic pulsation. She hardly realized she had descended from the van, hypnotized and baffled by the scene before her when a Lincoln Towncar pulled up to the end of the picket line and a tall, dignified, behatted man emerged smartly and deftly manipulated a folding umbrella unto upright position. Immediately, a second figure, shorter, stockier, also wearing overcoat and hat, emerged jerkily, obviously angry, and for a brief moment only, narrowly scrutinized the crowd around him. The two figures, followed by a dark-coated entourage, then moved as a self-enclosed cluster, swiftly and directly, toward the Conference Room doors. Upon their near approach, miraculously, the doors were flung open from the inside and then just as miraculously were pulled shut. For several minutes thereafter, an amorphous, moving blur, indistinguishable and nonrecognizable, stirred behind the glass, fussing with and double-checking locks.

She saw that the tan-raincoated media people had near sandwiched in the picketeers whose line had broken into disarray, and who, in helpless rage, now bawled at the doors, or at each other, or at the reporters. As the controlling executives had disappeared into the building, the crowd's muttering had swelled into a yell, tentatively at first, the cresting into a thunderous roar. "That's him. That's him."

- "Are you going to yell?" the reporters encouraged.

- "Are you going to chant?"

- "Are you going to storm the doors – force yourself in?"

- "Are you going to block their way out? Throw yourself in their path?"

The crowd shifted like a dumb beast, befuddled, and in despair.

All at once, everybody was in motion. Someone from the picket line screamed, "Why don't *you* ask them to come out and talk?" "Yeah, why don't you *help* instead of looking for a good show!" someone else taunted. A stray figure lurched from amongst the strikers and pulled a camera from a photographer's neck. "Troublemakers," a voice shrilled. "Troublemakers," a woman's hysterical voice screeched. "Troublemakers," the crowd resonated, coming toward the phalanxed media.

The Hughesville Police, who until then had quietly and inconspicuously stood watch along the periphery of the parking lot, instantly mobilized and moved forward. Swinging batons, pushing themselves between the strikers and media personnel, they attempted separating the motley human tangle into its original components. Alex watched from the edge of one of the further-flung groups. She stared at the thrusting advance of the police, then heard the global unearthly war-whoop. All around, there were persons, people, bodies – shoving, kicking, stumbling, falling. With a thump, she realized she was on the ground. She half-turned to protest. A body ran across her chest. She could feel boot heels cutting into her jacket, the fabric twisting. She tried to sit up. The searing pain knocked her breath out in a heaving gasp. She folded back and down, supine. And, then, nothing.

SHE was staring into Jerry's wide-open, anxious brown eyes. He looked so frightened, so stricken; she couldn't help herself. "What's the matter, Jerry? What's the matter?"

"What's the matter?" he near sobbed. "What's happened to you, Mrs. Byrnes? What happened?"

"Don't cry, Jerry," she said soothingly, remembering now that she was still prone, and on the ground, her fingers reaching down to her lower rib cage, trying to find the place where the sharp pain had come from before. The pain that had sent her back down.

"You must have fainted," Hugh's voice reached down from a great height. She forced her head backward, her eyes upward, straining to see his horsy, handsome blond head. He looked grim, his mouth, a straight line. "We've called the ambulance. They'll be here any minute now." Alex stirred. "Don't move, Mrs. Byrnes. It's probably nothing serious. But, until the ambulance crew check you out, I don't think you should move."

"I guess you're right," she said obediently.

"My husband... Barry... he doesn't really know..."

Kneeling beside her, Jerry shifted to reach his pocket. "What's your home number, Mrs. Byrnes?"

"No," Hugh's voice interposed. "No. As soon as the ambulance picks Mrs. Byrnes up and we know for sure whether she's to be taken to the Hughesville Hospital or the Chesapeake Regional Center, we'll call Mr. Blaine. He'll want to handle this."

"OK, if you think that's best," Jerry said reluctantly, looking down again at Alex, giving her hand a squeeze.

"Here they are..." Hugh's voice.

Several rushing persons crowded about, examining, palpating, fussing over her, finally lifting her onto a gurney, strapping her. "You'll be fine." Someone said equably. "We'll have you at the Regional Center in no time."

Jerry and Hugh followed the gurney. Jerry asked if he could go along in the ambulance, but one of the ambulance crew said it would be impossible as they had at least one other gurney to load into the van before taking off. Hugh reinforced this prohibition by saying that, under the circumstances, he thought they should get back to the *Record* office as soon as possible.

As they lifted Alex's gurney into the ambulance, she heard Jerry say something. Something urgent. Something reassuring. She carefully adjusted her breathing to shallow, shallower, as the pain of inhalation persisted and grew more intense, and she wanted above all else, to avoid any second embarrassing blackout.

Chapter Twenty-four

B ARRY REACHED out instinctively, palmed the portable phone, his thumb simultaneously pushing down the talk button.

"Good morning, Barry," a voice he could not immediately identify announced at the other end. "This is Dean Crandall... at the University." Another chuckle. "Your junior colleague, John Blum, is sitting right across from me at this very minute. We're about to go into a work session with our Computer Science and Measurements people. You remember we talked about getting up a prototypical course in CAD/CAM... and related skills... for ultimate incorporation into that projected Employee Retraining Program? Anyway, I realize this is sort of short notice. But we wondered if you could join us for lunch and an afternoon work session?"

Barry's arm had already gone on automatic pilot, scrambling for the alarm clock, upsetting an ashtray enroute, pushing the bedclothes to the foot of the bed. It was a minute or so after 10 a.m. His mind scrambled for plausible excuses to beg off this one, dimly resentful that Alex had not waked him earlier.

"If you could fit it into your schedule, it would be helpful. Actually, Mr. Lindquist called earlier, and mentioned that he thought, with your broad experience, your input would be invaluable." Was the dean being dryly sarcastic? "If you could fit it into your schedule" – the sonafabitch knew he was retired. And that final turn of the screw about Lindquist.

"I believe I can make it," Barry answered simply, without flourishes. "It'll be about an hour before I can get there, though. You'd better give me a phone number where I can reach you, just in case."

The Dean gave him instructions as to the building and room number of their current meeting, adding a couple of telephone numbers where he could be reached until noon.

HE FOUND Alex's first note perched up against the TV screen on the bureau. It said she was going out on a story for the *Record* with a couple of reporters. She'd be back sometime late in the afternoon.

Downstairs, he found a second note. It repeated the same message. Before leaving the house, he lifted the kitchen phone and called the *Record* office. Checking the roster, the receptionist recited Alex's message essentially as stated. Barry asked to speak to Mr. Blaine, but he was out. So, thinking better of it, Barry similarly penned a brief note advising only of his going to the University for the day and laid it next to the answering machine in the study.

INTERFACING with all that technical talent had proved totally fatiguing. Besides the oblique, arcane, and near-mystical math wizards and the canny computer gurus, there had been an hour or more of flatulent management analysis by Human Resources experts like himself, enough to give any normally strung-together human being something closely resembling a stuporous headache. Now, at four, after Dean Crandall had suggested a drink at the Faculty Club down the street, John had wisely begged off with the convincing excuse of Beltway rush hour traffic. Out of a misplaced instinct of common affability, and because he was the last remaining body still standing there, Barry agreed to a very short snort.

BARRY was served his bourbon on the rocks and the Dean his scotch and soda. The Dean, looking relaxed and comfortable, grinned across the table at Barry. "You're not so enthusiastic about this whole effort, are you?" he questioned rhetorically. "Or I mistake my man."

Barry shrugged, trying not to bristle at the Dean's manly presumption.

The Dean's smile dropped away, he grew serious, studying the side of his glass. "I'll agree ... it's difficult ... for anyone to find a new identity. Essentially a new life." He took his swig." But, hey, it's a fascinating, changing, and cruel world out there. Always was, in fact."

Barry smiled responsively, sensing a lecture in the offing and unable to rid himself of a childish tactile urge to reach across the space between them and snap his fingers in front of the Dean's face.

"Of course, Barry, you've got to admit, those LeClerc employees should have known better. Our heavy industries have been losing out for decades now, and LeClerc has been limping along for ... Well, for a long time. Anyone with his eyes open knew it couldn't last forever."

Barry took a long pull on his bourbon. He hoped he could finish up fast. Instead, he heard his own unmistakably angry tones.

"Well, sure. Working for LeClerc never could be represented as the acme of ambition. But, for some, especially the academically challenged," he guffawed, "it might have seemed a good enough deal. After all, their Dad's their uncles, many of them it *did* represent security, You'll have to agree, Dean, there are a lot of factors determining long-term successful survival. Family and education, to begin with, general motivation and opportunity. Not to mention luck, contacts those jobs that've gone glimmering to Mexico or Taiwan are being picked up by the well-educated!"

"Oh, those poor devils are working for nothing, I grant. But still, these Americans, they took the easy way out. Right upfront. They did the easy thing. They didn't acquire the skills. They didn't stay the course and get what they needed to survive. To prosper."

Knowing the Dean to be the third or fourth generation of one of Delaware's most well-established and affluent families, having survived the '60's unscathed-one of Kennedy's bright-eyed peace Corps veterans, that generation riskier form of the Gilded Age's Grand Tour, married to an equally well-connected descendant of old Virginia tobacco money, Barry felt something akin to ludicrousness in this whole discussion.

Instead, he said, "There you have it, Dean. The same old protestant ethic of meritocratic class structure. It's not really only about work and jobs, is it? It's about the right ordering of the universe. Your place in society is actually only a reflection of your basic moral character? Right? Right?" Though Barry had double-dipped his phrases in sarcastic irony, the Dean, eyebrows raised and breaking into a full laugh, was taking Barry's meaning absolutely literally, at that, Barry sat straighter, having a sustained a turn.

"You betcha. How else can we determine the winners and losers?" he postulated. "It's true. The quick, the smart, and the strong translate hardships and challenges into *progress*. The slow, the stupid, and the weak, just wash out. Fall by the wayside."

One more long pull and he'd be finished. "Seems to me, Dean, you've just delivered an almost perfect argument for Economic Darwinism. Survival of the fittest. Feeling the way you do," Barry added more insinuatingly, "feeling the way you do, Dean Do *you* think retaining is the way to go?"

The Dean let out another mighty, laughing huff. "Of course. Of course. We're not barbarians." With solicitous *noblesse oblige*, he added, "A society is also measured by how it treats its disadvantaged. We're doing the right thing. We're giving each individual another chance ... another chance to pick himself up and put himself back in the race. To make good. Nothing fairer than that!"

As an afterthought, the Dean appended. "And this situation is going to become more and more common. What we're doing isn't charity. That would be wrong. *Dead* wrong. You know the statistics. In any ordinary life span, they tell us, most of us will be retraining for, maybe, three, four different jobs. We're moving on to a whole new cultural arrangement."

"Then, we're lucky, Dean, because we'll have checked out by then. Maybe. If we're lucky." Although the Dean was his junior by at least a decade and had held his present position for at least twenty years, Barry's dour quip aroused neither his ire nor his anxiety.

"Oh, I don't know," the Dean answered reasonably. "I'm sure both of us would be up to it. Up to the challenge of changing venue." He took another sip. "You underestimated yourself. And, that brings me to my next question. Will you be joining us for some of our other sessions? We could really use your help."

Barry's reply was purposely ambiguous.

ON HIS drive back on Hughesville, Barry had plenty of time to think over what the Dean had said. It wasn't so much his culpably simplistic economic ideas, as the self-protective blindness that underlay his persistent, solid, obdurate smugness. He was like a person who had never suffered anything more serious than a cold pontifically advising terminally-ill cancer patient, struggling in chemotherapy, to "Buck Up" to "Give It His All." Besides, Barry recalled dourly, his good friend Victor Deitz was right in his apt observation that "A gentleman always knows when he is being insulated." Instead, recalling Lu's album cover. Barry could only assess Dean Crandall's psyche as "Thick as a Brick."

As he approached the highway intersection to Hughesville's business district, on impulse, he decided to turn off and pull into the nearest gas station on the way. He'd call home, and should Alex still not have arrived there; he'd still be conveniently close to drive to the *Record* office from here. He held the phone until the messages machine clicked on, then promptly hung up, reentered his car, and headed towards the newspaper office.

AS HE walked into the *Record* office and approached the receptionist's counter, Barry saw that Enoch Blaine was already descending the stairs from his second-floor office. He sensed immediately that something was wrong.

Enoch walked towards him slowly. He nodded. "Barry. Barry, would you step into my office?" he said, turning to remount the stairs. Barry's breath caught: as bad as that ...?

Once in Enoch's office, instead of taking the chair behind his desk, Enoch motioned Barry to one of the armchairs in front of the desk and seated himself in another, facing it, next to Barry.

"Barry, this morning Alex went along with Hugh and Jerry to cover what we thought was a demonstration at the LeClerc Employee Parking lot. We'd been told by union leaders that it was to be a local protest. We figured it was of limited hometown interest." Enoch looked at Barry. His eyes dropped. "I don't quite know what happened. I can't get any sensible, coherent story out of either Hugh or Jerry. What they said was ... is that ... suddenly everyone was pushing and shoving ... and, and I don't know, but Alex must-have ..." Enoch sighed and looked up at Barry again. "Barry, she's at the Regional Medical Center right now. I've already been up to see her. She's all right. I mean ... it's nothing serious, as those things go. The doctor assured me that she'll be fine. She's sustained a couple of broken ribs, but the doctor wants her to stay put at the Center tonight so as to be able to watch for any possible adverse reactions to the concussion she's also sustained. He said he expects no reactions whatsoever." Enoch got up and walked to Barry's chair. Silently, he placed his long, thin hand lightly on Barry's shoulder. "I'm awfully sorry, Barry."

A rushing sense of relief that it wasn't something fatal, a heart attack, or a serious auto accident, was almost instantly replaced by a flaming angry exasperation at Enoch's bad judgment.

"Why did you *send* her," he bit off. "What could you have been thinking of, to send her – " his sigh turned into a strangled yelp, "on a such a..."

Enoch shook his head and looked down at the floor. "I didn't *send* her, Barry... but that's not relevant now anyway. She's wanted to follow this LeClerc story more closely... have something current to move into with her series. But, as I say, that's not relevant. I asked her if she wanted to go... it was a mistake, I know now... and she jumped at the chance."

Barry had no more patience for this useless equivocation. "What room is she in?" he said at the door.

"Ward H. Room 432."

"Would you like a lift?" Enoch called after Barry, already halfway down the stairs into the lobby.

Enoch saw him slam out the glass doors and disappear around the front of the building. He hoped he was not too agitated to drive with at least a modicum of self-preservation.

As HE swirled past a half-wall-sized portrait of Doctor Somebody-or-Other, founder and benefactor of the present modern medical facility, toward a nearer bank of elevators and a wall schemata of the floor plan of the Center, he could barely suppress a revulsion that rose and clogged his throat. His mind was just free enough to decipher the neatly rendered drawing sufficiently to recognize Ward H to be in the opposite East wing, clear across the facility. His legs began pumping automatically in that direction, while his repugnance settled down to a dull, persistent, but sustainable nausea. Finally, the elevator doors yawed open at the fourth floor, and once again, he could scarcely move against the sense of dread and foreboding that overcame him. At last, he stepped out, having forced himself to realize he was recycling all those nightmare weeks of vigil at Lu's hospital bed. His son's deathbed. He found Room 432, but before entering, he halted abruptly and tried to douse himself in a self-generated, cold, practical shower of rationality. Gradually, he forced his mouth and jowls into something resembling a grin and marched into the room.

THE nearer of the beds in this semiprivate was empty. A small figure, back slightly elevated, sat in the other bed staring out the window. At his approach in the twilit darkness, the head turned slowly, and a gentle, compassionate smile overtook the features. The eyebrows raised, and Alex extended both arms toward Barry.

"My God, Barry, you look awful! What happened? You're grinning like a death's head. It's positively frightening."

Not really able to control himself, he buried his face against her still lithesome bosom, thinly covered by the regulation layer of faded cotton gown. "My God, girl," he tried mightily to keep from weeping. "My God, what did you do to yourself!"

They both laughed, looking at each other, relieved, together, rejuvenated, growing stronger.

IN THE next quarter-hour, despite Barry's many emotional interruptions with questions, grunts, and groans, Alex was able to craft a disjointed narrative of the day's events but scarcely more cogent than Enoch's earlier bemused recollections. Soon afterward, a nurses' aide bustled in with a supper tray, and Barry, somewhat purged of his initial intense anxiety, could sit now, more or less quietly, in a chair at the foot of Alex's bed, and watch her pick disinterestedly at the contents of the various dishes before her. Ten minutes of this, and she pushed the hospital bed table away and sank back into her pillows. "I guess it's what Lu and his friends would have called a 'happening.'" She sighed, realizing that it had become for her by now a very long day.

"I guess," Barry echoed. "One never to be repeated... God willing!"

TWO heads, one above the other, preceded by a huge bouquet of mixed spring blossoms, poked their way just inside Alex's half-open hospital room door. Marcy and Jack. Automatically, Barry flicked a glance at this watch: just past seven and regular visiting hours in force. They approached Alex's bed hesitantly, Marcy smiling a fixed, sun-drenched smile, but Jack making no attempt to alter a grim, indicating expression.

ONCE again, more haltingly, more wearily, Alex reconstructed the main lineaments of her day's fate. Marcy and Jack stood at her bedside, their faces cast in attentive, sympathetic mold, neither thankfully, pressing for details.

Finally, Jack caught Barry's eye. 'McClintock called me... near five. After trying to get hold of Armand all afternoon," he said stonily. "I drove home right away. Went over to the Big house before stopping at my apartment and tried to flush the bas-... him... out. He wasn't home." Jack stared at Barry significantly. "*No one* was home. Not Amanda, nor Blanche, nor the kids." Jack drew in a sonorous breath. "So, I bunnied back to my place and, on a hunch, called Enoch. At *home*. That's the first I heard about Alex."

"And then he called me," Marcy added more cheerfully.

"And here we are," she concluded lightheartedly, extending an arm around Alex's shoulder and carefully giving her a mock-hug, unwilling to put any pressure on any part of her injured frame.

But Jack continued to stare fixedly at that point in the sheet where Alex's toes described a tiny aerial pyramid.

ON THEIR way out, Barry excused himself and waylaid Alex's doctor at the central floor desk for a solid chat. He was relieved to have the day's spongy data thus presented to him, confirmed by the doctor's firm, clear and unequivocal information. He was especially grateful that things were much as they were imperfectly reported to be and, more than keenly attentive to the doctor's meticulous instructions for Alex's follow-up home care after picking her up at noon tomorrow.

NEXT day, Jack stood at the window of his Carriage House apartment, sipping coffee and staring at the dismal drizzle hanging in the atmosphere before him like cheap theatrical gauze left over from a last evening's performance. From his protected niche, he felt companionably desolate.

All afternoon he had worked desultorily, fitfully, at a couple of briefs, rearing up suddenly upon some internalized visceral cue and advancing to one of the forward windows. His eyes swept the drive, the lawn, for any sign of activity. For possible comings and goings. Nothing.

By five-thirty, he prepared to join Marcy and Vivvy for dinner at Marcy's. The meal was relaxed to the point of lassitude. After dinner,

Jack played several games of Mario with Vivvy, Vivvy winning easily every time.

Before he left at approximately eleven, he and Marcy fell into a near argument over their Memorial Day wedding. She had fixed him in a steady, subdued gaze. "I don't know, Jack. I don't know. Maybe we ought to postpone the wedding. With Alex's injuries... and all..." she trailed off.

"No, Marcy. That's nonsense! She'll be up to coming to dinner at the Logan... Besides, we've planned everything carefully. It all dovetails. I don't want to unravel the whole scheme and have to start all over again."

"We haven't *been* together... for quite some time," she observed inconsequentially but pointedly, looking sad. "I don't know. Nothing seems to be going *right.*"

He leaned over and gave her an answering snuggle. "It'll be all right, Marcy. You'll see," he reassured with fake energy, attempting to galvanize himself with his own words.

AS HE pulled into the drive toward Carriage House, a responding set of low beams flashed toward him from behind the wall of shrubbery around the West wing of Big House. Startled and instinctively on guard, he drove down the driveway in slow motion, soon able to discern, however, that it was a police prowl car behind him. Relieved, but unable to resist giving in to a growing mulishness in himself, he operated the automatic garage door with time-consuming deliberation and proceeded to park his car with meticulous precision next to his mother's vacant Lincoln, cognizant that all the while the police vehicle waited patiently for him outside in the turning circle.

As Jack approached, Officer Squires put his head out the driver's seat window. "Just checking the house, regular," As an afterthought. He added, "Whole family's gone."

"Yeah, I know," Jack said. "Well, it's probably a good idea. Did he mention when he'd be back?"

"Not in so many words. He said something about being gone for the weekend."

"I see. Well, thanks, "Jack said. "I guess I'll be turning in..." Jack turned toward his own door.

"Just didn't want to surprise you in the middle of the night... with our lights and all..." Squires shouted after him civilly.

LATE next forenoon, barely having dressed and shaved, Jack felt, then heard, the resonating purr of a motor below him. Stepping once again to his front window, he saw Armand just entering at the kitchen door of Big House.

His impulse was to run out of his digs directly and waylay his brother before he should getaway. For this very reason, he forced himself to sit down, finish his coffee, and put the Sunday New York *Times* into its successive sections on the sofa cushions before him. He could not deny the steel girder that rose in his chest, up through his neck and head, pushing back his shoulders and making his head buzz indiscriminately. He felt aggrieved, deceived, injured, and furious.

But, why? What had *he* to complain of? Armand had told him about the very real possibility of this development. Weeks ago. Was he prepared to inveigh against his brother for some vague guilt he should be feeling about not having shared with the Coalition the emerging details of his plan with Cunningham? What if the deal with the Consortium had fallen through? Deals did that. All the time. Did Armand business deal much more remunerative, much more secure for himself and the LeClerc Company than anything the Coalition had ever, or could ever offer? And, even if Armand, responding to some ancient loyalty to the Company and its employees, had been willing to enter a less advantageous deal with the Coalition, what assurance was there that their projected ESOP plan would work out, keep the business afloat for even a few more years?

He walked to the hall closet and slid a thin waterproof nylon jacket off a hanger. He wasn't justified in doing anything but keeping this meeting with Armand, non-incriminating. Non-accusatory. Light... that was the ticket... no matter how he felt about all that had happened. There was always the wedding to tell him about. It was high time he had told Armand about his upcoming marriage.

WHEN Armand answered jack's ring at the front door of Big House, he appeared in good spirits, stepping lively and motioning Jack toward the kitchen.

"Ning is just finishing putting a snack together for me. Skipped breakfast this morning. Would you like something? Tuna salad... deviled egg? I'll just see if my tray is ready. We can go into the study..."

"Nothing, thanks," Jack answered, heading for the study. He snapped on a few floor lamps and seated himself in one of the armchairs.

"You've been gone..." Jack began. "I tried to find you on Friday... after the 'incident.' No one around..."

Armand poured himself a coffee. "I just thought we'd all be better off not being here. At least, until things cooled off...' He bit into a sandwich and chewed abstractedly, staring before him. "I'll admit... that was a shock. A real *shock.*"

"It was the *Record* story did it. Wednesday's evening paper."

"Yeah, sure," Armand lifted his coffee cup. "But, damn, I'd given the regulation 90-day layoff notice to all employees over a month ago. And the surveyors, the architects, they've all been creeping around the grounds all Spring... Limos coming and going all day long..."

"But everyone thought you were only going through the motions because of *Allied.* You know, they *never* figured on *this...*"

Armand banged his cup into its saucer. A little coffee dribbled over the edge. "So, is that why you're here? Now? To let me know, I'm a treacherous shit...?" His laugh gurgled low in his throat. "Is that *it*? Because if it is, Jacques, I'm..."

"Hold the Jacques stuff, will you?" Then Jack backed up and began again, this time in another key. "No, Armand. I was actually concerned about you... and Amanda... and Blanche."

Armand took another estimate of his brother and decided to follow suit in changing tone. "There isn't anything to worry about, Jack. They're all sitting there, right now, in a cozy suite in the penthouse of the Hotel DuPont. There wasn't time, for Christ's sake, to make any other more complicated arrangements. I just tried to get us out of here, pronto..."

"I know," Jack acknowledged quietly. "I know." He leaned forward toward his brother.

Armand looked up, still distracted by his own anxious considerations.

"Yeah," Jack continued. "I'm getting married Memorial Day weekend. Nothing elaborate. Just the two of us. That's how we want it. It's at least a second time 'round for both of us..."

"The girl with the Satun...?" Armand smiled.

"Yeah, the girl with the Saturn. Her name's actually Marcia Byrnes. She heads up the Hughesville Health Center Service for the Handicapped."

Armand reached over and shook Jack's hand. "Well, congratulations." He added more thoughtfully, "... but *no* wedding? That'll be hard for Amanda. And Blanche."

"It's a second marriage for me, a third for her. Just a quiet civil ceremony, that's all. Nobody but us. That's what we both want." In a minute, Jack added, "But, I wanted you to know. And, of course, you and Blanche and Amanda and the children are all invited to a five o'clock celebratory dinner at the Logan Inn in Brandywine afterwards. Marcy'll send you a written, formal invitation, of course.

"Thanks, Jack, but I didn't know... and ... and... I've made other plans. Unless you were to change the date, we can't. I've had a long-standing reservation at The Breakers for the whole family. For over a month now. Mother's invited Belle and her granddaughter. And, considering our whole situation, I think it would be best to go with our original plan. I hope you understand."

"Of course," Jack said, instantly guilty that he felt this news lifting more than a small weight off his shoulders. After all, Marcia had never even met his family. Intuitively he knew it would have been a clear case of oil and water. "I understand," he said dismissively.

Armand reseated himself, his focus reshifting to the middle distance, past Jack. "Legally, Jack, you know the distribution of LeClerc assets stands as it has now for many years... as it does... in the Will. None of that's news to you, of course. How you... and Marcia... decide to designate the eventual distribution of your allotted portion is up to you. So there's nothing for me... for us... to do, in that regard. As far as family business goes." Armand sighed. He seemed preoccupied. "Can I mention this to mother and Blanche this evening?"

"Of course. I wish you would." After a few seconds, he added, "I'll be moving out of the Carriage House by the end of July."

"Yeah. I guess." Armand grunted. "I wouldn't mind moving myself. After the condo project is well underway, of course... At least for the winter months... Mother would never consent to giving up Big House... permanently."

"Marcia's ex-mother-in-law was covering the story for the *Record* on Friday. She got knocked down... somehow. Ended up with a couple of broken ribs and a concussion," Jack reported to the room at large.

Armand stood up, carried his tray to the desk, and set it down hard.

"Are you telling me it's *my* fault?" Armand said with unsmiling gravity.

"No. No. I'm just *telling* you. It's something I think you should know."

"Well, I'm sorry, of course. I'm sorry for Friday's whole bloody mess. But it wasn't me who made the mess. It wasn't *my* fault."

"I'd best be getting back to Carriage House. I've got some work to clean up. Are you going back to Wilmington?" Jack asked, standing.

"Eventually..." Armand replied vaguely.

'Give my regrets... sympathy... to mother... to the family... For all the disruption and everything..." Jack murmured lamely and headed out the room.

IT HAD stopped raining, and treading through the wet grass across the front lawn of Big House, he looked down and noticed his loafers were soaked through. He could not stop walking. Not until he reached the promontory at the outer limit of the grounds, the focus of so many juvenile dreams projected from the study window, the bluff declining as it did with its reviving marsh grasses, its smoky dried cattails, poking spearlike through the gorse, its greening mosses and scattered single trees, gnarled but invincible, sloping down to the shallow rock rim of Bay beach beneath.

It *wasn't* Armand's fault. Or only happenstancially. If it had not been Armand, it would have been John, or Brian, or Henry. And if it hadn't been an American Twentieth, or whatever Century, with its proliferating individuals spreading like plankton over the Eastern coast, living their so-called individual lives according to their best lights, reward for their own and there forefather's hard effort and forward vision, but that incidentally, polluted the earth, not expecting the Bay, naturally, choking off fisheries, extinguishing wildlife, paving over wetlands and eradicating forests, then it would have been some other intrepid human Era forcing its will upon the planet and the totality of its creatures, always with comparably ambiguous results. Discounting even the ubiquitousness of rapacity, ignorance, and greed, every step forward, every solution to a present problem created a world anew, with its fresh array of uncertainties. In this impulse for progress, undeniable and inextinguishable as heartbeat, huge blocks of humanity had adjusted, or had not; survived, or had not; moved forward or fell away alongside. Now LeClerc's tiny shard of displaced humanity could only be adjudged expendable, eminently, in this great scheme of warring forces.

He felt so empty, so utterly devoid, suddenly, he could barely turn. Turn back toward his tiny, inconsequential cocoon of a home to lick his wounds. To hide.

ABOVE his mother's wing of the house, the clouds parted, and a shaft of ethereal light as palpable as a column reached down toward Big House, enveloping it in luminous, beneficent nimbus. Over this flaring revelation, through the shadowing dusk, a perceptible, sub-audible music rose, tenuous.

"DAMN," Jack shouted back at the scene. A rough, discordant cackle tore from his throat through his open mouth. "God damn," he imprecated helplessly at this undeniable, unwelcome miracle proffered by that Director of the Biggest Show on Earth.

But only a few steps later, his head bowed, he remembered Marcy and Vivvy; he thought of Alex and Barry; Doran's clenched fist and the flash in McClintock's eye appeared in successive melancholy panorama.

They were part of him, and he of them: he owed them more than some shallow, posturing effort. Perhaps he and they had not prevailed this time, or in their way, but the world was still their home, their only home. They must embrace it and make it their own once more.

Chapter Twenty-five

THROUGH THE days of the first months of summer, derricks and cranes carefully hoisted furnaces, disassembled rolling mills and a variety of container manufacturing machinery and equipment onto flatbed trucks, with only the occasional silent witness of a single grave figure standing far aside of the activity, while during the soft, warm evenings that followed, neighborhood kids resumed their ongoing target practice on all the remaining unbroken windows of the now almost empty buildings of LeClerc Works. By mid-July, in a few short weeks only, the wrecking ball and excavators leveled the rest of the more than half a dozen structures, a motley aggregate of remodeled turn-of-the-century brick factories to '50's low-slung concrete modern rectangular slabs that together constituted the industry and a way of life for more than half of Hughesville's denizens. And now, in mid-August, after the several buildings had been completely demolished, although the surrounding grounds had yet to be cleared and evacuates, the only objects left standing on the formerly LeClerc-owned side of the Bay inlet, were two blackened yellow-brick smokestacks only, raising dual soot-encrusted, accusing, premonitory finger toward the sky

MARCY and Jack delivered Vivvy to Camp Oquaka on schedule and proceeded down the coast to Martha's Vineyard as planned. Perplexing, after their unified, upbeat exhortations and rosy predictions on her upcoming experience at Camp, after the concluding dip into shyly tearful, sentimental good-bye's, both Marcy and Jack, all the way to the Vineyard, fell into an adolescent, awkward shyness with one another. Everything seemed suddenly new, fresh, untried and unpredictable, not only in their immediate environment but between themselves. Their meals became quietly more formal; their walks, marked by long, silent intervals; their lovemaking, enigmatically embarrassed. Each, privately, rejected, then admitted, the disquieting notion that they might have blundered.

Nor was this intimation dislodged throughout the following month of July, when Jack slowly selected the few pieces of furniture and personal effects from Carriage House he had decided to take with him into his new life at Marcy's. Oh, theirs was an admirable lightness and whimsy as they incorporated Amanda's second-best crystal wine glasses into Marcy's already crowded buffet; theirs a credible ribald buffoonery as they quite literally bumped buttocks in the shared master bathroom, scrupulous not to edge into each other's agreed-upon allotted times; and theirs a meticulous decorum in respecting *her* spill-over Center budgetary and clinical business, evenings, and *his* study-incarcerated review of briefs and lengthy, private telephone calls, post-dinner.

Then, toward the end of this month which had already proven so difficult for them, marked by a strangeness that Jack recalled with circumspect honesty was not unprecedented in their life together, as just such a disorienting hiatus had preceded Marcy's ultimate decision that they should be married, they were invited to Big House to meet the family. Grimacing internally, Jack steeled himself to justify the ways of Jack and Marcia to his family. It was, after all, inevitable: it had to be. After a superficial, reflexive annoyance, Marcy had checked through her better outfits, the suggested midweek date on her calendar, and forgot about it. Not so Jack, who in odd, unfilled moments at the office, churned up snippets and bits of encounters between and amongst various family members in ever-changing assortments a kaleidoscopic array of numbing, embarrassing or mortifying LeClerc family scenes.

But through this July evening's cocktail hour, sipping Armand's perfectly blended, perfectly dry martinis, Amanda nonetheless remaining loyal to her glass of Harvey's Bristol Cream, Armand's irrepressible masculinity was undissemblingly overwhelmed by Marcy's petite but undeniable sexuality. Again and again, his brother's not so surreptitious glances swept over her long, black lustrous hair, the cascading fall of which tonight was caught sedately in a silver clasp at the nape of her neck. More often than he was aware of, Armand's eyes lingered about the vicinity of her Prussian blue satin blouse, only to lift again toward those now-made-even deeper azure, enormous provocative eyes. Under the circumstances, Jack was almost moved to forgive Armand.

But, finally, their being called into dinner, Jack could see it was Marcy's turn for a jarring, albeit positive, display. Though hardly agog, she was visibly stunned by Big House's elegant dining room in the grand manner. While they went about the business of sorting themselves out into their assigned places at table, Jack could see Marcy take in a long look at the double-pedestal table and comfortable tufted Queen Anne armchairs; the six-foot cherry sideboard; the tall and magnificent coromandel screen backgrounding the high Sheraton serving cabinet; the blue-and-rose Chinese Oriental underfoot and the triad of ample bow windows presenting a breathtaking view of LeClerc garden, noting that for a full minute she seemed even to have stopped drawing breath. At last, seated to the right of Armand, her expression settled into its usual sangfroid equanimity, but not before Jack had been privy to a full study of her momentary undisguised discomfiture.

While they worked their way through their portions of the regulations standing rib, the regulation static of social amenities was painstakingly, if sluggishly, moved forward. Blanche made a few proudly congratulatory comments about the activities of the LeClerc boys at camp this summer; Armand addressed his dinner without much palaver, as was his usual wont; and Amanda remarked irritably about certain undesirable changes of service at The Breakers that she and Belle had found particularly unacceptable on their last stay. Jack relaxed somewhat, feeling fairly assured they would all arrive at dessert, unscathed.

In an unexpected interval of quietude, Amanda turned toward Marcia.

"What is it you *do* at the Center... as I understand it... my dear?" she inquired of Marcy.

Marcia fielded the blunt question with good-natured common sense. "You do know, Mrs. LeClerc, that it is a facility for the *severely* handicapped?" she explained, by way of introduction. "So, of course our programs... necessarily...are aimed at very *fundamental* improvements... self-care, for example... basic communication. We're very happy sometimes to be able to bring a client to the point of feeding himself."

Before Marcy had finished, Amanda's eyes had glazed over, her fingers unconsciously crumbling a bit of roll onto her bread-and-butter plate.

"Oh. Oh, dear," she murmured finally. "It must be difficult to spend one's whole day amongst... amongst... such... such... *invalids*," she substituted generously, the sighed heavily at the effort. After a moment, she smiled again, rejuvenated, looking about the room. "I guess it is no secret that what *I* most enjoy is beauty. Serving it... having it all... all... around me. Yes, *beauty*. That is a worthy goal, too, my dear," she instructed, smiling approbation at her own more-than-laudable life's ambition.

"Your home... certainly attests to that... It is..." Marcia was interrupted by Armand's brusque excusing of himself upon Ning's having handed him the cell phone at table.

"Now, *what* do you suppose that is?" Amanda remarked to Blanche, oblivious of Marcy's response.

Blanched shrugged, and the table fell silent.

Before he realized he was speaking aloud, Jack heard his own half-murmured rejoinder to his mother's previous remark. "There *is* such a thing as a *tyranny* of beauty..."

"What's that, Jack?" Amanda snapped.

Jack shook his head, hoping her mother would by now have been distracted enough to overlook his incautious, involuntary remark.

"What you were just saying... 'tyranny if beauty?'" she prompted. "Whatever do you *mean* by such an enigmatic statement?" She turned toward Marcy. "As I tell Jack all the time, I do not understand half of what he *ever* says... or means. Oh dear," she confided in Marcy's direction "it isn't that I don't appreciate Jack's intellect or his sensitivity. His teachers were always telling Mr. LeClerc and myself how *absolutely* gifted he was. But," her laugh tingled glassily across the table, "perhaps we ordinary mortals cannot always..."

Armand strode into the dining room and resumed his eat. He picked up his fork. "Cunningham's got the demolition team signed up for the first day after Labor Day weekend. Bad time, I know. Couldn't fit in such a small job except then," he staccadoed, pushing the tines of his fork into a remaining bite of roast beef. He turned toward Amanda. "I'm frankly damned sick of the whole thing, Amanda. So, don't start complaining. Glad it'll be all over, finally. Besides, Mother, it doesn't matter. We're scheduled to pick the boys up at the end of the month; we'll swing down to Uncle Jason's and pick you up afterwards. Maybe we can even take in a show before heading back. God knows I don't want to see those old stacks come down."

Amanda's expression was distraught, near to hysterical tears. "Well, for Heaven's sake, Armand, neither do I. Neither do I." She dabbed at her eyes nervously. "Do you know that I have never, *never* gone down to the Inlet, not once, not ever, to see the... to see *it*. I don't want to see it. Why it's worse than a *death* for Heaven's sake. Worse. Not even when Nels has been driving right by and offered, I've always refused. 'Nels, I can't. I'd be like having grandfather and my late beloved husband exhumed... lying there in the ground,' I've said. Oh, dreadful. Dreadful!"

Blanche had risen and gone over to her mother-in-law's chair. She slipped her arm across the older woman's shoulder.

"Sit down, Blanche," Armand said sternly, his eyebrows raised. "That's enough of that, too, Mother. This is supposed to be a happy occasion, not a wake." He rang for Ning. "Coffee in the living room," he ordered.

But though Amanda ceased her repining immediately, she did not join the rest of the family in the living room for coffee. Neither Armand nor Blanche, Jack nor Marcy, commented on her absence.

DESPITE her infrequent flare-ups of rapidly-spent jealousy or childish, willful resentment, home life freshened when Vivvy came back home from Camp. Her spontaneity and liveliness, even in bad moods, energized them all. Gradually, Vivvy took Jack in, as left to herself, she had everyone else at the Center, scolding him for his smoking habit, as she did her mother, instructing him on how to stack dishes in the dishwasher correctly, and set the table properly, and, in general, assuming a maternal oversight over his many bad and good habits. She liked to snuggle against him during her favorite evening TV programs and didn't even much mind his mussing her hair as he so maddeningly liked to do always, looked forward to his quiet reading and cuddly hug before she must turn out the light and go to sleep. She admitted to Glory-Be that "Jack was a fairly superior person – likely to turn into a pretty good Daddy, after all. Besides, he was *so* handsome." Glory-Be, who had visited Vivy at home a number of times, throughout the late summer, and along with Vivvy, had been escorted to the zoo and been treated to home movies by Jack, had no difficulty in agreeing with her friend. She did not tell Vivvy that she thought he was *wonderful*, only slightly less marvelous than her own Daddy.

So, too towards the end of August, the atmosphere at the Center had notably altered: a perceptible lull, a holding of breath overtook the whole staff. For, not only did many of them have family members who had at one time or another been employed by the LeClerc Works, but the small town's whole future destiny seemed to hang in the balance, and everybody knew it.

Jonesey had recently confided to Marcy that months ago she had gone down to the demolition site one late evening and, responding to their urgent and oft-repeated request, cadged two brick from the piled cadaver of the old factory – one for her grandmother, one for an aunt. It was hard for everyone to see the old walls come down before the wrecking cranes, the interiors of the buildings exposed with tangled wires, gnarled staircases, and plumbing pipes hanging uselessly through the debris. For most people in Hughesville, the LeClerc structures had always outlined this side of their Bay. They were part of it, its shape, and the shape of their own. Now the fields upon which they had stood, lay abandoned, desolate with broken litter, shards of brick, and mud.

All through the Labor Day weekend, the excitement in town mounted unbearably. Not because of the holiday, but what was to follow directly afterward. Hughesvillians reserved picnic spots all along the opposite side of the Inlet, staking their claims with folding chairs, picnic baskets, sweaters and coats, and six-packs of beer and soft drinks. Those who owned smaller boats moored them along this opposite shore, dinghies, and other small craft fanning out in a bright, expectant semicircle along the beach. As zero hour approached, traffic on nearby streets was halted, the downtown area having now been completely deserted. People climbed on the roofs of their vans or trucks as their eyes strained to track a helicopter's slow loops over the demarcated target area.

The end of an era of Hughesville came neither as fiery tongues of flame, nor dark rising clouds of bilious smoke nor even as sprays of bursting sparks. There was little drama and almost no noise. First, one smokestack broke roughly in half, and slowly toppled; moments later, the second followed, it's top half folding, then its lower half falling soundlessly and forever to Earth.

UPON the day set for the collapsing of the stacks, the McClintock, Doran, and Letzger families had agreed to meet in a secluded spot toward one end of the inlet, in former years, a popular locale for Fourth-of-July Union family picnics, but, of recent years, unused and gradually forgotten. Even as each family van drove up, was parked, and cursorily unloaded, the McClintock and Letzger children sensed the ambient atmosphere to be solemn; well nigh oppressive. Intuitively, they stayed back, keeping to themselves, out of their parents' way. None of the families had brought food. Minutes before the repeatedly announced time for the event, the men lined up wordlessly, almost abreast, facing the opposite bank. After IT had happened, the continued standing for several more minutes. Finally, Letzger turned toward his own van, and then, McClintock. After five or more minutes, the Letzger family drove off toward the road. Jamie McClintock lowered the tailgate of his van and lifted in the folding chairs they had brought with them. He looked back. Old Paul still stood mesmerized, staring at the opposite bank, his face frozen into seams and creases of ineffable loss. Before Jamie could allow himself to leave, he walked up to his old friend and put his hand lightly, sympathetically, upon his shoulder. At this cue, Paul Doran's eyes filled with tears, which overflowed down his cheeks, past the troughs aside his nose, a few drops finally hovering precariously on his gray bristly chin before dropping onto his jacket. Jamie stood next to his old friend for as long as he could, but the source of Paul's grief seemed bottomless. Finally, Jamie patted Paul on the back, once, twice, then turned, nodded to Peggy, his wife, who leaned, her eyes wet, against the passenger door of their van, and got into his own car. As Jamie drove off, he saw that Paul had not moved. He was still standing there, a miniature replica of the stacks, waiting for his own turn to be toppled, Jamie reflected.

THAT morning, Mayor Jeb Murray had stopped at Wilken's Liquors and bought the most expensive bottle of champagne in the store. In high spirits, he drove a little distance out of his way, a few short miles out of town, to his Uncle Ed's "farm." He found him in the barn, working on "Old Bessie," his beloved circa 1965 Chevy, which his uncle had adamantly and repeatedly nursed back to barely-performing health each time the Old Lady had succumbed to one of her endless bouts of automotive malaise.

"Good as new," Ed assured, wiping his hands on a piece of old toweling, and letting Bessie's hood drop into place. "What's on your mind, Jeb?"

Jeb held the bottle of champagne aloft and grinned. "I was hoping you'd come out to the Inlet with me this afternoon and help me kill it. Big, b-i-g doin's out there today, you know!"

Jeb followed Ed out the barn, the older man continuing to clean his hands on the towel, half-smiling, looking abstracted. They entered Ed's kitchen. Ed reached down two coffee mugs from the cupboard and slowly filled them from a tall, speckled blue coffee pot he kept on a hot plate on the stove.

He sat down. "You know, I don't think so, Jeb." He took a long swig of coffee. "I don't think so." He looked past his nephew. "You know, Jeb, I just don't quite have the stomach for it."

Jeb chortled, but his eyes questioned his uncle's words, then registered disappointment, even hurt. "Why not, Ed? I thought you were glad to see the old town move ahead... get out of the clutches of that Union bunch at LeClerc's..."

Ed shook his head. His own eyes showed bewilderment. "Well, you know, it just isn't that simple. Sure, I was *against* some of their self-serving, selfish attitudes, their pig-headedness at times... but, but I never thought it would come to this. That it would go so far. This is different. This is *war*." He stood up and refilled their cups. "No. I don't want *no* part of *this*."

"But you've got to know that the Consortium group has a whole redevelopment plan for the area. Luxury condominiums, parks, recreation center, maybe even schools..."

"Yeah, yeah. Sure, I know. I *know*. I read the *Record*, same as you."

They sat in unaccustomed silence, broken only by the liquid sounds of their coffee drinking. Jeb. Stood up. "What are you telling me, Ed?"

"I dunno. I dunno, Jeb. I'm getting on. Too many changes. I can't take it all in."

Jeb walked toward the door. "But I'll tell you this, Jeb," his uncle continued. "If I was you... I wouldn't go *near* the Inlet today. No, sir. You're supposed to be Mayor of *all* the people of Hughesville. *All*. And lots of them are going to be feeling mighty low, come this afternoon. I'd lay low if I was you."

Jeb let himself out of Ed's farmhouse and drove to Hughesville in a mood the exact inverse of what it had been this morning.

THAT evening, when Jeb Murray and his best Alderman friend, Sandy Hickock, met at Jeb's to watch the unspectacular, seconds-long drop of the last remains of the LeClerc Works on a local Wilmington station, they popped open the bottle of champagne, to the sounds of their own laughter and self-congratulations. They reminded each other that ambitious, imaginative plans would be going forward immediately, right away in the very months to come, before the advent of cold weather, and they would be seeing great things happen soon, very soon.

But they didn't manage to kill the bottle. It was already late when Sandy left after midnight, and Jeb carefully corked up the remains of the champagne and set the bottle well back in the refrigerator.

WHEN Jack stopped by Carriage House that afternoon armed with the pretext of having to reclaim a favorite CD he had misplaced and thus forgotten to take along earlier, now only minutes before "the" event, he found Nels seated in a carefully positioned law chair, dolefully staring at the rear garden and west wing of Big House. Jack recognized immediately that this was as close to this afternoon's LeClerc fate their old family retainer meant to get. Instinctively, Jack also knew that what he had been told weeks ago was true: none of the family were there.

After rummaging through the Condo for a decent ten minutes, Jack left with only a nod to Nels. That evening, without any lengthy excuses, Jack remarked to Marcia that he would just as soon omit the eleven o'clock news tonight. Without comment, she agreed.

Chapter Twenty-six

Postscript

ORKING TOGETHER with the University, and interfacing with
federal authorities, as well as state labor and welfare agencies
in several contiguous state of the Delmarva peninsula, by the end of
autumn in these late '90's of the 20th century, Alcon was ready to submit
drafts of more than one well-articulated proposal for state-assisted job
retraining to all those abutting states having responded positively to
the company's contacts and evinced an ongoing interest in such a more
comprehensive approach to their current unemployment dilemmas.
The resources of the University, operating under the supervision of
Dean Crandall, had worked closely with Alcon talent, under John
Blum's oversight, and Barry's continued guidance, to produce final
feasible plans delivered to state agencies for eventual submission to
their legislatures for possible enaction into law.

Concurrently, University Human Resources personnel had
negotiated special arrangements with local unemployment and
welfare agencies to encourage certain basically qualified LeClerc
unemployed to enroll in the retraining pilot program the University
was presently offering. Indeed, the entire University-Alcon team
hoped to encourage Hughesville's former LeClerc employees who
could pass certain basic verbal and mathematical tests to become
part of their unique test-study group and help make this trial an
unrivaled success. Upon Barry's urgent recommendation, it was
additionally arranged that those lacking adequate basic reading and
writing skills should receive counseling and be encouraged to attend

evening or weekend classes until they should receive their high school equivalency diplomas. They would then become eligible to participate in the University's retraining program.

Thus, even as bulldozers marked out the first main streets in the new development, creating fresh travelways upon ancient LeClerc factory land, even as the more elaborate landscaping plan of shrubs, trees, and green areas emerged as parks, tennis courts, and a swimming pool, and simultaneously, a first line of framed Cape Cod type townhouses rose against the Inlet skyline, reviewing the cold figures provided from local unemployment and welfare offices, Barry understood that the University-Alcon plan could hardly be said to be thriving. The win-win situation, so confidently anticipated by University brains and Alcon strategists, was not materializing. Instead, displaced LeClerc employees were showing a mere paltry rate of reemployment through their own independent efforts, while their response to the University proffered retraining course, supposedly beckoning them in a new and challenging direction, was shown to be pitifully negligible. Without being told, sensing immediately, viscerally, Barry knew it would never be right with the LeClerc unemployed until *that* reconciliation could be effected. The reconciliation between themselves and the fate they had just sustained.

Barry brought the matter to Jack's attention, and, after lengthy discussion, together, they decided to take the initiative: they first called upon Harry Warner, who admitted that though the Coalition had been disbanded and the investment money returned, this now-defunct entity still had its account, under its control, original good-ill donations primarily from church governing organization, eleemosynary funds of at least half a million, enough to justify meeting with former Union leadership, McClintock Doran and Letzger, and call upon Reverend Boardman and Father Meara to reopen the matter of what they might do now to ameliorate the present situation of unemployed LeClerc workers.

That is how the Displaced Workers Center came to be and how, by the Spring of the year, Barry and Alex were deeply committed to its efforts.

IT CAME as no surprise to Barry that most of the people who finally showed up at the remodeled basement facility in the old "Y" were angry. Why not? With considerably less justification, he, too, was angry. And had been for years, he finally admitted himself. But their anger was of an entirely different magnitude than his own. Their anger was powerful, erratic, and potentially dangerous. It was a perceptible force, ready to explode at some unsuspected trivial event or chance remark. And as Barry found himself repeating to Alex again and again, unless that bilious anger was somehow purged, until then, and only then, it was useless to send an ex-LeClerc worker out on a job search, because, sooner or later, this feeling would out. It was unavoidable. And both spouse and employer found living with a potential time-bomb unendurable.

As regards Alex, while never having majored in psychology, having been prepared for her present activity only by a few training seminars at the University, but with an experience borne of living, veteran wife of Barry's many threatened jobs, and herself a victim of repeated job loss as a result of Barry's Alcon-mandated moves, she more than "got it." She understood the plight of the LeClercians in the only way it was ever important to understand.

"Yes, but that anger, Barry, it's not all bad!" she had said to him. "It's necessary... even creative. It's a way of getting in touch with yourself, and of making a judgment, too. Yes, and according blame. But that's making a judgment, too. Why last week of my group could easily have debated any college class in sociology, or philosophy. They were honestly struggling with how things really are, how they and people like them fir into this shifting scheme of reality. Basically, what *is* the good life at this end of the twentieth century. What is worth living for..."

From her office, Alex could see the door to the basement lobby being pushed open. Jamie McClintock, looking a decade older than he had last spring, lumbered past her own office door toward the large seminar room at the end of the hall. Alex checked her watch. "He's early," she said to Barry, replacing a folder in a file cabinet behind her. She glanced out the door again as Dora and Liz traipsed by in the same direction. "I'd better getting on..." she murmured toward Barry, who, with a quick nod, bobbed out the room.

"WE'D gotten pretty far along investigating our own feelings... our own thoughts... last week..." Alex began.

Ellie shifted in her seat. "As I've before, what I can't stand, what I positively cannot stand," she said, "is this *attitude* – you get it in the café, at the gas station, from the checker at the grocery store – you know, that somehow we *deserve* what's happening to us. You know you can tell. You can *just* tell."

"Sure, you can. I agree," Dora said, continuing her knitting. "You know, that we're basically lazy, dumb, and have been overpaid for all these years. Now, life has finally caught up with us," she snorted.

No one spoke for several minutes.

Alex was about to introduce another facet of the problem for consideration, when Mrs. Altrop's flutey voice, preceded by her characteristic nervous whinny, chimed in. "My mother and dad, God bless them, they should only see..." she broke off. "Why, Dad, he ran the rolling mill for years. He was *proud* of what he did. He considered himself an expert... a craftsman. He would brag about how he ran the line... his relationship with his men. And, Mom, she was proud of him, too. She thought she was lucky to have such a good, steady provider. Family *mattered* to them... *family matters*," she pronounced categorically, looking complacent and belligerent at the same time. "And, now... even my kids think anybody who'd settle for a life like this that has to have been a 'retard.'"

"They called their grandfather a 'retard?'" Jamie thrust in bitterly.

"Well, no, not in so many words," Mrs. Altrop excused. "But they've called me and Hank 'retards' when they're talking about us. Right there in the kitchen, with us sitting at the table..."

Jamie rose. "Well, I sure the hell would put a stop to *that*, right quick. I sure the hell would!" Alex watched Jamie's right hand, involuntarily clench and unclench into a fist.

Alex pulled at her T-shirt. Everyone was watching Jamie. Some quizzically, some embarrassed, some sadly, their eyes averted.

Don McCarty grinned foolishly. Alex waited another half-minute before speaking.

"What are you feeling, Jamie? Right now."

McClintock whirled on her. "Nothing."

She let it lay there a moment between them.

"Aren't you *furious*, Jamie?"

He sat down. "No... yeah, I guess I am. I guess I am," he said louder. "I'm *damned* mad."

"We all are," Liz murmured.

Jamie did not hear. He spoke to the air. "I'm damned mad, and I'm damned heartbroken. Sue Altrop says she was proud of her Dad. Well, I've always been proud of what *I* did, too. Good hard work, done right, and a leader in the Union. I had a good life, and I tried to make life better for others, too. I'm telling you we ain't heard the end of this yet. 'Knowledge industries,'" he sneered. "We'll see how far that gets us building or rebuilding the country. The infrastructure, they're always yammering about. Bridges and dams, power plants and skyscrapers. Or what use it'll be in another war, why, shoot, you have to have steel-making capacity even to manufacture the robots that are going to fight the next one."

There was a halfhearted ripple of dispirited laughter around the semicircle of participants. Liz, who was sitting next to Jamie, reached over and patted him on the hand.

"Yeah, Jamie's right," Mr.Canby observed after a minute. "Even though our little plan wasn't exactly heavy industry, it was a spin-off, one of the byproducts of our over-all steel-making capacity. We are throwing away or transporting whole sections of our manufacturing capability... iron and steel, for example... and I just hope we don't have to pay for it eventually by having to give up our lead position in the world."

"They think they're *so* smart!" Jamie took up where he had left off. "All those computer wonks and technical gurus. They look down on us. Sure they do. But someone had to work in those plants, didn't they? Someone would have to now if we weren't throwing away our industrial capability with both hands." He shook his head, dejectedly. "I tell you it's a mistake. A big mistake. And we're going to regret it."

We're dinosaurs," Dora said evenly. "Just dinosaurs."

"My grandbaby Davey *loves* dinosaurs," Mrs. Altrop said somewhat irrelevantly. "In fact, he can't get enough of them."

"Everybody does," Don McCarty pronounced. "Look at *Jurassic Park.*"

"They were a *noble* animal," Jamie observed. "Everyone admires a *noble* animal."

IT WAS quiet for several minutes. They felt united, cleansed even, in sharing their grief over dinosaurs. In looking into the gravesites of their own past and declaring their lives had not been in vain. Had been, in fact, not without dignity and purpose. Worthwhile.

THERE were to be still several other sessions, but Alex ventured a new tack.

"Any action on the job front, Mr. Canby?" she gently prodded.

He smiled and shrugged.

"Who wants to sign up for a two-year retraining course to make half as much money as you did before?" Jamie volunteered upon Mr. Canby's remaining non-responsive.

They were all quiet again, having dropped into their own individual worlds once more.

Audibly drawing breath, Ellie finally confided to the group at large, half shamefacedly, half proudly, "I did *real* well on the tests. The reading and arithmetic. I finally got up enough courage to take them!" She giggled. "It was even kind of fun. I'm thinking of signing up for the retraining course. Imagine me, being a... a bookkeeper... or an executive secretary?" She looked around and giggled again. "Hey, why not? You only live once."

"Hey, beats making hamburgers at Burger Heaven..." someone encouraged.

"I've had plenty of experience doin' that, too. Believe me!" Ellie responded good-naturedly.

"I'm going to give it a try," Don said. "I don't really want to be a guard at that new prison downstate, even though they did offer me a job. Pay isn't bad, neither." His face creased into a pattern of anxious seams. "But I hate the idea. It just ain't me."

For the first time that evening, Jamie looked at Don thoughtfully. After a brief pause, he confided, "Me and the wife have talked it over, I may go all the way. Thinking of enrolling at the University for at least an associate degree. She'll stick at her hairdressing business a few more years, and we figure we can make it. Sure, it'll be pretty skimpy for awhile. But if I'm going to get kicked out, this time, I want to have something else going for me. Something those wonks will consider worth having." Grimacing, he looked around. "Besides, who knows, I may even like getting educated!"

"I wouldn't be at all surprised," Alex smiled.

Gayle's voice, unheard all evening, sounded from the next to the last seat on the right side of the semicircle. It sounded suspiciously lachrymose. "I'm glad you're all so... so well on your way," she said, not unkindly. "But I feel lucky to have my job at Burger Heaven. I just wish I had more hours. I don't know how we're going to manage when Rosie has her baby." She twisted her Kleenex into a ball. "I really don't."

"Have you inquired about Medicaid? If she'd be eligible?" Alex questioned. The group had lived through Gayle's daughter Rosie's last trimester, and Gayle was admittedly the most obdurate hard-luck case amongst them. She and her husband had both been employed in low-skill jobs at LeClerc's, and Matt had recently left home in a drunken rage. Fortunately, he had, at least temporarily, curtailed his "visits" home, after one of which Gayle had shown up with an eye swollen into a purple plum, and after another, actually supporting herself on a crutch, having been thrown down her front steps, spraining her ankle and cutting a deep gash in her leg.

"Yes, it'll cover costs, I guess. That part's taken care of, I suppose. But I'm thinking of afterwards. All those expenses."

"Rosie *is* receiving her welfare payments? That's all working as it should?" Alex persisted.

"Yeah..." Gayle acquiesced feebly.

Everyone looked downcast, even embarrassed, at their cumulative helplessness.

"You know, she never even hot her high school diploma," Gayle added hopelessly. "She'll be on welfare for the rest of her life..."

No one said anything. Basically, they knew Gayle was right. If not welfare, something marginal. Something desolate and without reprieve.

FOR another quarter-hour, there were some unenthusiastic, desultory exchanges about the vicissitudes of their individual job hunts, but in the wake of Gayle's entirely innocent plaint, its unmistakable message of misery, a damper had been put on both the anger and the optimism of the whole group. Alex did her best to remain sympathetic and objective, offering factual help or practical suggestions whenever she could. But the meeting, this time, had definitely ended on a blue note. That was just the way it was some time, and she did not allow herself to droop into dejection, as she had early on in these troublous, difficult encounters.

JAMIE looked at his watch. "Hey, I got to go. Muriel and me want to catch the basketball game at the high school tonight. Got to see Eddie do his stuff," he said proudly.

"Hey, good luck to your boy," Mr. Canby said affably. "I hope they wipe 'em out," he added.

"Thanks," Jamie said, smiling.

"I think your plans are very exciting," Alex commented sincerely. "I'm sure you'll make it."

The group began to rise, gather their things, and seek out one another for a final private comment or a good-bye.

"I'm very interested in *all* your plans," Alex broadcast ambiently. "I know I'll be hearing more good news next session."

IT WAS twilight when they took their slow evening walk across their deep back lawn. The daffodils had had their day and stood now with wizened heads, stalwart still. The varietal tulips, ready for their turn, pushed striated vermilion heads from out the ground, gladdening Alex's and Barry's hearts. The indomitable peonies, hard at work, spread multifarious. But the flowering pear, an arresting vision of gossamer purity and flowering luxuriance, stood unabashed and presentationally dazzling before their very living window.

"I'm so glad Madi will be able to make it up for Memorial Day," Alex caught up Barry's hand. "Won't she be surprised to see little Marcy with her pumpkin on a stick lower profile?" Alex laughed.

Barry swung Alex's arm lightly. He was feeling wistful about his younger child, his lovely daughter. Soon after their trip last Labor Day, she and Toda had called off their engagement, although the understanding between them could hardly have been described in such formal terms. They had simply parted. Madi had been – was – adamant about staying with the Lab, in research, and in their circumspect way, she and Toda had both known soon enough that they would inevitably move in different directions. " She dwelt among the untrodden ways,"

...and always would. Madi was that rare individual who could and probably would remain solitary, preferring that state, complete in her own ambience, never becoming brittle or mean-spirited, being alone. Nonetheless, Barry ached for the love of her, a vague sorrow filling his chest.

"Yes, who would have ever thought..." Alex quipped cheerfully, rounding the corner of their modest house. Remembering Vivvy's oft-repeated assertions that "Mommy is pregnant. We are going to have a baby!" Alex smiled, succumbing to her own brand of childish glee. "If Vivvy doesn't take over the entire upbringing of that child..." Alex giggled. "Course she'll have Jack to fight off first! I don't think I've ever seen anyone more incredulous and more delighted," Alex beamed at Barry.

"Glory Be!" Barry proclaimed, while, hand in hand, they entered through the doorway of their century-old home, exultant with spring and further promise of renewal life, happy as persons are ever permitted to be.

CPSIA information can be obtained
at www.ICGtesting.com
Printed in the USA
BVHW030152170520
579803BV00006B/33/J